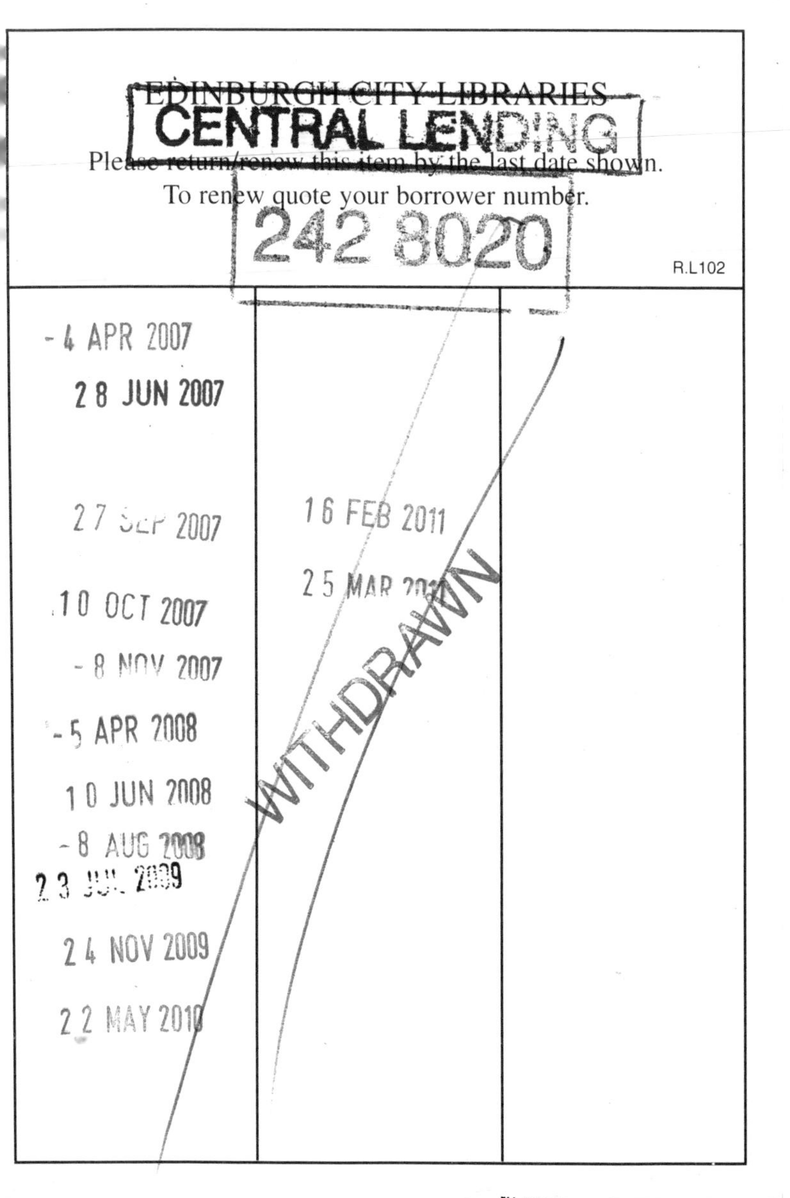

Bound in Shallows

Also by Freda Davies

A Fine and Private Place (2001)

BOUND IN SHALLOWS

Freda Davies

Constable • London

First published in Great Britain 2003
by Constable, an imprint of Constable & Robinson Ltd
3 The Lanchesters, 162 Fulham Palace Road
London W6 9ER
www.constablerobinson.com

ISBN 1–84119–665–7

Printed and bound in Great Britain

A CIP catalogue record for this book
is available from the British Library

For Lora

There is a tide in the affairs of men,
Which, taken at the flood, leads on to fortune;
Omitted, all the voyage of their life
Is bound in shallows and in miseries.

Julius Caesar, Act IV, Scene iii

Chapter One

She was a pretty girl until the floodwaters took her, then tossed her aside.

Early mist laced through the trees and rolled down to meet more rising from the ebbing river. A hawk gliding in search of food was disturbed by a dog barking. Its master trudged the wetness of the Severn's bank. He was freshened by the coldness of the air but annoyed by a pile of rubbish which had been swirled on to mud rising from the river's shallows. The terrier became interested and snuffled in the untidy bundle until a hand with red-tipped nails flopped out and the man was running, running.

The door of the court opened and a relieved police officer, struggling to look tidy in an unaccustomed suit, hurried out in search of hot tea. He was halted by a uniformed sergeant.

'Mickey, just the lad. DI Tyrell's looking for you.'

Eyes which still held the innocence of childhood widened. 'Me? Why? What've I done?'

'DCI Whittaker's orders. You're to go with DI Tyrell. Path lab at the hospital.'

Mickey Walsh groaned and wrenched at his tie, loosening it as he scattered shirt buttons.

'Better get a move on.' The sergeant grinned, revealing teeth aged by too many years of cigarettes and canteen coffee. 'And if you don't watch your back it could be you he does over and has on a slab.'

The young detective made sure he had a cup of what passed for tea before he looked for the inspector. He was not hard to find. Absorbed in the *Telegraph* crossword, Detective Inspector Keith Tyrell could easily have been mistaken for a barrister waiting to be briefed. There was no sign of a policeman in the cut and drape of his dark grey flannel suit, or the strong tanned fingers long enough to be elegant. Even the regular features and thick light brown hair, the way he held his head, had no echoes of cells and muster rooms, riot shields and service cars with their blues and twos.

'Detective Constable Walsh.' Tyrell smiled at Mickey. 'You had a long session in there. Have you had time for refreshment of some kind?'

'Yes, sir. Thank you, sir,' Mickey found himself saying and was surprised by his own deference. He had heard of the effect Tyrell had on others.

'Good.' The DI stood and gathered up a raincoat. 'You did well against Braithwaite. He was out to trip you up and you saw him coming every time. Usually, being patronizing and sarcastic in turn gets him what he wants but you blocked him nicely.'

Keith Tyrell led the way out of the courthouse, Mickey trying to neaten his tie, his jacket, as he followed. From a distance the DI unlocked a dark green Rover and bent to open the door.

'Keith, my dear chap! Good to see you.'

Mickey was surprised to see his recent enemy, Clive Braithwaite QC, grasping the DI's hand and pumping it with every sign of pleasure.

'Clive. Busy day?'

'Not made any easier by your chap, here. Is it you training them to thwart defence counsel? If so, you're doing a bloody good job.'

Tyrell grinned and suddenly looked much younger. 'No credit to me. DC Walsh is his own man.'

'And has a damned good brain. Mind you use him well – and keep him off my witness lists!'

With a wave of his hand Clive Braithwaite headed for his own car as Mickey settled himself into the comfort of the Rover, enjoying a smooth ride through Gloucester.

'Sir, duty sergeant just said post-mortem. Any identity?'

The DI halted the car at a pedestrian crossing. 'Not yet. A girl was found first thing this morning. She matches no one local reported missing.'

'Poor little sod.'

Tyrell heard sympathy in Walsh's voice. 'Yes, you're right there,' he said as he drove on again towards the hospital.

Patients in the wards had views of lawns as well as shrubs of all kinds. Such pleasures were not for the two men who headed for the pathology department, tucked away in a corner of the building furthest from the car park. The labs were protected by an efficient alarm system, and only after being scrutinized by a heavily jowled man with dark, deep-set eyes were they admitted.

'Morning, Inspector Tyrell.'

'Good morning, Pete. I wish I didn't have to be here today but you know how it is. This is DC Walsh. Pete Coombs.'

Pete Coombs was tall and muscular, taking a good look at each man as he helped them with their gowns. DC Walsh, the shorter of the two, dragged hands from pockets as he swaddled himself in green cotton, needing help with the ties. Not one who bothered too much with grooming, Pete decided, and that mop of curls was long overdue contact with a strong pair of scissors. Detective Inspector Tyrell had no difficulty getting ready. He was always well dressed and Pete envied the cut of a suit which hung to casual perfection on a tall, athletic frame.

On the way into the main lab Keith Tyrell sniffed the air. All pathology labs were alike in many ways but he had learned to distinguish those which were well run. This one usually passed muster and today was no different, even if there were trailing wires, workmen's tools and dust sifting over the floors. The noise was unpleasant, annoying the green-clad pathologist.

'Pete, ask the boys if they can cut the drilling for a while – have a tea break or something. I can't hear myself think!'

Anita McBride was petite, trim, red-haired and impatient while she waited for silence.

'Repairs, Dr McBride?' DI Tyrell had a courteous manner and a deep voice free of any accent.

'Rewiring, Inspector Tyrell, and it demands more drilling and hammering than I bargained for –'

The racket ceased suddenly and Anita McBride realized she was shouting. She grinned. 'Sorry about that, folks. Let's get on.'

Reaching for a microphone hanging from the ceiling, she angled it into a position suitable for her height and began her examination. As did everyone present, Keith Tyrell heard the body being described in detail. He made his own assessment. A natural blonde, the girl had the beauty of youth: age had not yet coarsened her strongly moulded features. He could see her clothes were not the most expensive possible but they were still of good quality. The new jeans and leather jacket would not have been cheap.

'. . . right hand, middle finger, gold or gold-type ring with a Celtic design. No sign of scratches or bruising on the hands. Nails recently manicured – not professionally.'

In the quiet room Keith Tyrell could hear a tap dripping as the pathologist examined the under-surface of the nails. She was frowning.

'We'll need samples – if you can get any, Karen. They should tell us where she went in.'

A silent assistant scraped, stored, labelled, then the right hand had the same treatment. Tyrell was surprised the nails and their dark red varnish had remained intact and undamaged. The leather jacket was lifted off the body and searched.

'Nothing in the pockets,' Karen Boyd said. She was taller

than the pathologist and thin, almost boyish, her dark hair drawn back in a ponytail.

DC Walsh might approve Karen's deftness but he was sceptical of her results and did his own searching.

'You'd expect something but there's not even a soggy tissue.'

'Karen does a good job,' Anita McBride snapped at Walsh. 'I trust her implicitly and so can you.'

DI Tyrell thought it time to intervene. 'Jeans pockets?' he asked.

Karen Boyd finished cutting up the sides of the jeans and handed over the relevant pieces. DC Walsh probed thoroughly, his gloved fingers surprisingly nimble.

'Not a thing,' he told the DI.

'Unless we find a handbag, we've no clue who she is.'

'Anyone remotely like her reported missing?' Anita McBride asked.

Tyrell shook his head. 'Nothing current.'

'A girl like her – probably used to going walkies for days at a . . .'

DC Walsh was silenced by the unblinking gaze of his superior. 'Until we know who she is we must not make the mistake of assuming we know how she chose to live her life.' It was pleasantly said but Tyrell's words carried a rebuke.

Anita McBride hid a smile as she turned back to the corpse, revealed to have a solid build with little extra fat. Karen's shears began to slice the tight-fitting top which had once been white.

'Stop!' The pathologist stood back from the table. 'I need photos, please.'

Karen, puzzled, did as she was told and Pete Coombs came forward with a camera.

'What's wrong?' Tyrell asked.

'Have a look yourself.'

'Nothing unusual, I would have thought.' He had noticed that as Karen lifted the top to cut it she had exposed a label on a minute scrap of material. He frowned.

'That's odd. Why would she have her pants on inside out and back to front?'

'Exactly.'

'She could have put them on in a hurry and not noticed.'

'Inspector, believe me, she'd know if pants that shape weren't the right way round – they'd be very uncomfortable.'

Mickey Walsh overcame his nausea to move close and peer at the girl. 'Bet she was used to having help gettin' 'em off.'

This time stares from two pairs of eyes reduced him to silence and a size smaller as he shrank inside his clothes. Dr McBride turned away from him in disgust and continued her study of the torso.

'Bruises've developed, as one would expect from normal river damage.'

'Any pattern to them?' Tyrell asked.

'None that I can see so far.' She gestured to Karen who eased up first one shoulder of the corpse, then the other. 'Yes. There're signs of her being lifted or held from behind. See? A large bruise from a hand and there,' she pointed, 'a thumb mark. Same on the other side.' As the body was laid flat again Dr McBride reached for a magnifying glass. 'I never noticed it before – the change of light angle made it glisten.' She scrutinized an area between the girl's breasts. 'Oil – again.'

'Oil?'

'Yes, Inspector. I also noticed some on her palms.'

'Anywhere else?'

'Not so far – but I'll check again.'

'Samples?'

'If possible. Try, will you, Karen? Both palms and between the breasts.'

While that was being done the pathologist concentrated on the nostrils and used an instrument to open the flaccid mouth. Pete Coombs came forward with a torch and lifted the girl's chin, allowing the doctor a deeper view of the pharynx. Anita McBride looked up at Tyrell. 'There's not enough detritus . . .'

'For someone who lost their balance and fell in?'

Dr McBride was puzzled. 'I would've expected more if she'd struggled to breathe. Still, the trachea and lungs, as well as the blood gases, will be more indicative of how long she was alive in the water.'

'If she was. Surely her nails would've been wrecked as she fought to hang on to anything likely to save her?'

Anita McBride nodded and the DI was thoughtful.

'The initial conclusion must be that she was dead, or nearly so, when she went into the river.'

'I can't say for certain until I've finished. You'll have to wait for my report.'

'I understand,' Tyrell said, 'but at the very least this death is suspicious.'

'Suspicious?' said Mickey Walsh. 'Looks more like bloody murder to me!'

Keith Tyrell drove home on dry roads. For weeks the countryside had been deluged with one rainstorm after another. Across Britain towns and villages had drowned, floodwater destroying homes and livelihoods. Swollen rivers drained away the worst of the excesses, leaving behind farmland and houses reeking with the stench of silt and raw sewage.

Gloucester fared badly but it was used to such inundations, the railway line and roads to the west regularly cut by rising water. For centuries the city had been serviced by the Severn but it could be wilful, its currents treacherous as it claimed lives like a pagan god with a thirst for sacrifice. This winter had been particularly bad, too many people drowning to save dogs caught in a fast flow, or trapped in cars when roadways vanished.

Where had the girl gone into the river, Tyrell wondered? He knew the mudbank where she had been found. It was the first downstream along the course of the Severn as it widened. It might be logical for the girl to be washed up there but where, along the length of the surging river, had she been slipped in the water?

Keith turned the car into the driveway of his home and drove very slowly. He looked across the garden and down the hill to where the Severn meandered between its banks. Moonlight made the broad ribbon of water a silvery beauty but it was not long since he and Jenny had been hard at work filling and stacking sandbags for neighbours living too near the new water-line.

His home had been safe. Two hundred years before, a farmer had built a row of workers' cottages out of sight of a farmstead on the crest of a hill. The farmhouse had long gone, a mass of Victorian gothic replacing it at the whim of an ironmaster from the Welsh valleys. More recently the cottages had been combined, the interior modernized. When the Tyrells bought the result they added a glass-roofed conservatory, efficient windows and modern plumbing. Jenny had done the rest, standing over Keith as he had planted shrubs which welcomed with colour all year round.

It did not take long to garage the car and, once in his home, its light colours and touches of beauty with flowers and paintings stripped Keith of the strains of the day. He breathed in the smell of woodsmoke and an Italian sauce, the garlic subtle. There were quick footsteps and Jenny was in his arms. She was fragrance, comfort, strength.

'Bad day?' she asked.

'Whittaker.'

'Darling, no!'

Jenny pulled him into the warmth of the sitting room, a log fire cheerful in the hearth. Settling Keith in his usual chair she poured a dash of whisky, splashed soda and knelt in front of him to watch him sip and savour. He leaned forward to kiss her gently, thoroughly.

'So, how was your day,' he asked.

'Quiet, for once. Either my patients are over-sedated or

the treatments are working. Either way it was a good breathing space all round. Tomorrow now . . .'

His smile was rueful. 'That's one way our jobs are similar. No knowing what tomorrow will bring.'

Jenny saw the sadness in him and was concerned but she kept her smile in place. 'Today that bad?'

'Not yet.' He saw she was puzzled. 'A body washed up. It could get messy.'

'There've been so many accidents in the last few weeks. That poor couple still with their seat belts in place when the car was pulled –'

Keith was not listening, his mind on the corpse he had seen. 'She hasn't been reported missing. According to Anita McBride the girl had been in the water at least three days.'

'And dead when she went in?'

'Not quite – at least that's how it seems.'

'So, it could be murder?'

'Can't be sure until the post-mortem's completed.'

'Then what kept you so late?'

'Preparing – in case there is a murder enquiry.' Keith lay back in his chair, Jenny seeing tiredness which was more mental than physical.

'Brian Clarke would have been a good help.'

'I didn't have Brian with me.'

He said nothing to Jenny of the ugly whip in DCI Whittaker's voice as he insisted, 'This body, Tyrell, it should be cut and dried – if you don't cock it up. DS Clarke's far too experienced to have his time wasted by you. I'll have him somewhere useful.'

Keith smiled at his wife. Under winged brows her large eyes were filled with her concern for him. With a finger he traced the oval of a face surrounded by a swing of short, dark hair. 'As a treat I have Mickey Walsh.'

'He's new?'

'Very, and has me wondering how he got past all the sergeants he must have encountered. A more untidy mess on two legs I've yet to meet in any force.'

'How did he make CID?'

'I pulled his file. Walsh has topped every exam he's ever taken since enlisting. Brian says the boy's certainly bright but even he thinks CID is only a quick way of getting him out of uniform. There's a story from when he was a cadet. The others training with him filled a bath, emptied a whole bottle of bubbles into it and dumped in Mickey, uniform and all, for the biggest soaking and scrubbing of his life. He got the message and improved – most of the time. There're not many complaints recorded.'

'I suppose he has a strong natural odour?' Jenny asked and grinned.

Keith nodded.

'And DCI Whittaker hands him to you because everyone else steers clear?'

'That's about the size of it.'

'Then tonight all thoughts of DC Walsh are banished and we'll have supper by the fire.'

It was still dark when Keith woke and slid from under the duvet, making sure he did not wake Jenny. His clothes were ready and he padded to the bathroom, closing the door carefully before he shaved, showered, dressed, as quickly as possible. Only when he was half-way down the stairs did he become aware of the smell of fresh coffee and Jenny in the kitchen.

'You're not supposed to be awake!'

'Why not? You need something hot before you go out on a morning like this. Besides, I've a pile of ironing to finish and you know I can only face it when I'm half asleep.'

Keith pulled her to him, the sweetness of her weakening his resolution until toast sprang noisily.

'Scrambled eggs,' Jenny decided. 'They'll be ready as soon as you've buttered the toast.'

'There's no need –'

'Oh, yes there is! It's raining again and you're not only planning a long walk, you've Whittaker to face when you get to the station. I'm not sure scrambled eggs are a fortification against Tricky Dicky. Perhaps I'd better put on some bacon.'

'No, you've done enough and it's too early to argue.'

'I know,' Jenny said and grinned, mischief curling her mouth. 'We'll have to have an early night to make up for it.'

Through the rain the first fingers of light helped Keith Tyrell find his way to the side of the Severn. With the help of the torch he carried he could identify grass that had been flattened by water and then scuffed by many feet, wheels of vehicles. He shone the beam towards the mudbank, cleared by an ebbing tide of any marks left by the girl's body and her silent retrieval.

Sheltering under his umbrella, Keith leaned against the wind and looked upstream, imagining the body he had seen on Anita McBride's table, tossing and swirling in the currents. She must have come from the direction of Gloucester but where on the swollen river had hands lifted, then dropped the weight of the still-breathing girl? He tried to visualize the scene, setting it against what he knew of Gloucester and its river beyond, but no mental images came to help.

Slowly, Keith faced west, seeing a dark mass of cloud overhanging the Forest of Dean. In the cold of the early light he shivered, the chill coming from within. What had attracted him to the secretive hills and trees?

'Hey, you!'

The DI turned and saw a solid figure stumping towards him. It had the shape and colouring of an ancient bull but as the man approached, Tyrell could see the outline was provided by a heavy caped waterproof and a hat with a brim so wide it gave the impression of horns.

'Keith, you dog! What in God's name are you doing here? Of course! You're one of our local bobbies, aren't you?'

Tyrell smiled at the newcomer. 'Morning, Guy. Sorry if I've disturbed your walk.'

'No problem, old chap. Saw a strange car parked and came to investigate. Thought you might be one of those God-awful newshounds – they drove Clo to distraction yesterday. I even caught her swearing at one of them and you know Clo. Sweetest little lady ever to sit a horse.'

Guy Seymour's broad, fair face was earnest with admiration for his wife and Keith repressed a chuckle. Clothilde Seymour was of French birth. Dainty, imperious, she had fingers and nerves of steel as well as a command of English swearwords earning gasps of admiration from builders and sailors alike.

'I'm sorry Clo was disturbed but it should be quiet today. Reporters will be annoying us and our press office.'

'As well as Walter Thomas – the poor devil whose dog found the body. Any idea who she was?'

'Not yet, nor do we have a clue where she went in. Can you help us there?'

'Farm records – I'll have a look. My old dad used to enter any flotsam picked up here and I've kept the tradition going. We've always tried to return anything valuable so there's the odd note as to where things went in. First body in my time, I must say, but you'd be surprised how far stuff travels. We even had a suitcase washed up here from Worcester. Then there was . . .'

Tyrell did not hear the long list of places and items which his friend related. The pull of the Forest was almost tangible and getting stronger by the second. Why?

Refreshed, Keith Tyrell was at his desk in the CID office well before the DCI arrived. He heard his approach. Quick, firm steps. A jovial greeting for some, pleasantries for others. Only when Richard Whittaker saw Tyrell did his manner change and the blue of his eyes become icy.

'When's that autopsy report due?'

Tyrell kept his expression agreeable. 'Dr McBride said ten o'clock, sir.'

'How hard did you have to work to persuade her it wasn't a straightforward death by drowning? I send you out on what should have been a simple job and you turn it into a three ring circus!'

'Isn't that the responsibility of the person who helped the girl into the river when she was dead, or nearly so?'

'A time like this, when we're fully stretched and short of manpower, some idiot half kills his girlfriend and has to land her on my patch. Get it cleared up quickly – and don't expect any extra CID to bail you out. It's bound to be a domestic and shouldn't take even you long to get all the answers.'

'Yes, sir. Thank you, sir.' The tone might have been light, pleasant even, but the left hand in Tyrell's pocket was clenched so hard he felt his signet ring bite into flesh. The pain steadied anger.

Whittaker had made sure his least-favoured colleague had been belittled as publicly as possible. At the same time he was annoyed his DI remained calm, unaware of the effort it took the younger man.

'Who is she, anyway?'

'Not yet known, sir. I'm hoping news reports this morning will carry an item on the girl. It'll bring in the usual spate of phone calls but we may get something useful.'

Whittaker was not a small man. Fair-haired and good-looking, he kept his body fit and well groomed. Investing in the best suits he could afford he had climbed the ladder fast, yet it irked him he felt the need to lift his chin and square his shoulders whenever he talked to Tyrell.

'You can have a couple of uniforms to sort out the calls. What are your intentions if no one comes forward to identify her?'

'If all else fails we'll have to use a photo of the body.'

'Mm. Bit gruesome. It may be better to try a computer version, or an artist's impression.'

'Good idea, sir. I'll get on to it right away. We could need it for house-to-house when we do know who the girl is.'

'Was she raped?'

'Dr McBride didn't think so but when she said that she hadn't finished the PM.'

'Let me know the minute the report's here.'

'Sir.'

'And don't make a meal of it, Tyrell!'

The DI watched him go. There were times when it was hard to control the flare of temper Whittaker kindled in him but Keith was determined not to be needled into a fight.

The first news of the dead girl was broadcast at 8 a.m. and within minutes the phones began to ring. Callers were answered with sympathy, courtesy, but each time Tyrell questioned with a silent lift of an eyebrow he was answered by a shake of the head. Two WPCs busy with the calls had been recording and logging each one. When the flurry of enquiries abated, the DI thanked the girls and asked if any of the calls had been of use.

'Not so far.' Sheila Hipwell was a large, thrusting blonde, anxious to make it to CID as soon as possible. 'There might be later on. Not everyone's up this early.'

Her colleague, Rose Walker, was quiet, thoughtful, with smooth dark hair. She escaped beauty but calm acceptance of an odd-shaped chin and an overhang of teeth gave her an enviable serenity. 'If there is someone who could help they're probably trying to pluck up the courage to ring.'

'We can just hope they do contact us,' Tyrell said.

Rose had no doubts. 'They will. So far we've had the usual ones who call.' She shook her head, saddened by her task. 'It's always heart-breaking to know just how many missing daughters there are, but this one's different.'

'Why do you say that?' Sheila wanted to know and Tyrell, too, waited for an answer.

'They may have heard the first news bulletin and they're scared it's the girl they know.'

'And that's why they haven't reported her missing?' Tyrell asked.

'Possibly. When you love someone and you're afraid they've gone, it's sometimes better to wait in fear and hope than know they're dead – even if you think that's why they never came home one night.'

The DI nodded his agreement. 'What would you say? Boyfriend? Parent?'

'I don't know but I'd guess it's someone who loved her. Does that make sense?'

Sheila Hipwell was sceptical but not Tyrell. 'Perfect sense,' he said. 'Remember, the pathologist thought the girl had been in the water for two, maybe three days. That gives the time scale.' A fleeting memory disturbed him but he smiled at the policewomen. 'Almost time for the news. Good luck.'

Sheila and Rose had a flurry of calls after the 9 a.m. broadcast but they had no news for Tyrell. He was restless, leaving them to their task and returning to his desk. There, he reached for the phone to talk to Anita McBride.

'It's on its way!' she said. 'Stop nagging.'

'This isn't about the PM findings, it's something I remembered. I should have mentioned it when I first saw it but you were busy and on to other things.'

'What on earth are you talking about?'

'A different angle of light – do you remember? You noticed oil on the girl because of it.'

'Yes. Samples have gone to the lab from her palms and breast. It's all in hand.'

'Did you find any on her forehead?'

'No.' The line was quiet. 'Damn you, Tyrell. I'll have to go back and have another look and I'm short-handed today. If there is any oil where you say and I manage to scrape a sample, I'll keep it stored here and only get it to the lab should there be a need to. I can't do more than that.'

* * *

Dr McBride's report had reached DCI Whittaker at 10 a.m. and he read it in his office before sending for Tyrell and Walsh.

'You were right,' he growled at the DI, 'it is murder. "Not enough water in the lungs to account for an accidental drowning and the bruising to the underarms and back suggestive of being lifted. There are no indications of rape, no foetus in uterus or tubes and no semen" – although there is a proviso. Signs of incomplete penetration or premature ejaculation would have been washed away in the flood or by the sluicing off of the mud. Apart from being dead, the unknown female appears to have been in a good state of health.'

'Is there any reason given why she was at least unconscious when she went in?' Tyrell asked.

'None. No heart trauma as would have happened if she had been frightened badly and attacked. No bleeding as in a stroke, not even an aneurysm – whatever that is.'

'Ruptured blood vessel. If it was the aorta the chest or abdominal cavities would be filled with blood, if it was a Berry's then the base of the brain would show it.'

'Thank you for the lecture, Inspector Tyrell. It's nice to know how you and your wife spend your spare time. What's next week's lecture? How to diagnose a nutter?'

Mickey Walsh's curls wobbled as he looked at the DCI and then Tyrell. The antipathy between them was legendary but he had never before realized just how bad it was, or how one-sided. The DI's expression was unreadable, giving no hint of his being affected by his senior officer's remarks. As for Whittaker, his colour was high, except for rings of whitened flesh around nose and mouth.

Whittaker rearranged the papers in front of him. 'Any progress on the ID?'

'Not yet, sir. The two WPCs are doing well but until they get the call they're waiting for –'

'Yes, I know all that. Get that e-fit ready and I'll go on TV tonight if you've not got a result by then. Where she went in, that can be determined before we know who she is.'

'Yes, sir,' Tyrell assured him. 'I've made contact with the nearest farmer, Guy Seymour of Manor Farm.'

'Ah, Sir Guy. One of your friends, I presume.' Whittaker did not even try to keep the sneer from his voice.

The DI took no notice. 'Guy told me what's been found on that mudbank in the past. If anything valuable washes up he tries to trace the owner. I asked him about the girl and, according to him, if the body had been in the water at least forty-eight hours it most likely went in the far side of Gloucester.'

'Off on your local knowledge expedition again, Tyrell? You do have great faith in the yokels who live on my patch. Now me, I prefer to deal with experts. Get on to the river authority people. They deal with facts – and I don't like conducting an investigation on hearsay.'

Mickey Walsh released tense breath when the door of the DCI's office closed behind them. 'Whew! Why didn't you tell him you had me ringing the river authority yesterday?'

'It wouldn't have made any difference to the DCI – anyway, you'd better give them another call. The poor devils are working round the clock just now and have more important jobs to do, keeping the living as alive and dry as possible. They've probably forgotten all about our enquiry.'

Tyrell was thinking of lunch when Rose Walker beckoned. She was listening to a caller, making notes.

'No, Mrs Hackett. If we think it necessary we'll contact you. Thank you for ringing in.'

'Promising?' the DI asked.

'Granddaughter, Julie Parry. Hasn't been seen since she left by car on Friday, about six thirty. Mrs Hackett thought she was meeting up with friends in Gloucester and stayed over. Doesn't know who she was to meet.'

'Parents?'

Rose shook her head. 'Father left years ago. Julie went to live with her grandmother when the mother's new husband wanted the girl out of the way. Grandmother brought her up. School in Lydney and she works there in an estate agent's office. Basic description fits, sir.'

'So does the timing. We'd better go and see her. Where does she live?'

'Murren. Number 5, end of terrace past the railway crossing,' the WPC read from her notes.

'Murren. Do you know it?'

'Never been there, sir. Often passed the turn to it and seen the signpost.'

'Then you'd better come and have a look. Got a coat? We'd better not look too official.'

Rose was surprised. 'Me, sir?'

'She knows your voice. If it is her granddaughter waiting in the morgue, we must be as careful as we can.'

Mickey Walsh was not pleased to be left behind in the station. 'Why's she gone?' he demanded of Sheila Hipwell.

Sheila grudgingly explained, annoyed the quiet Rose had been chosen instead of her. 'Anyway, going to see a granny, the DI probably wanted to take along someone who smelled right. Old ladies can be a bit fussy.'

'What d'you mean?'

'Mickey, how long have you been wearing that shirt? And when was the last time you had your jacket cleaned? As for your trousers – ugh!'

'I've been busy.'

'Busy sleeping late every morning so you never get time for a proper shower?' Able to vent her spleen on the hapless DC, Sheila was beginning to enjoy herself. 'And when did you last wash your hair?'

'Not sure – it takes so long to dry I have to leave it if I'm in a hurry.'

'Then get it cut, for Pete's sake! You do know how to use soap and water, don't you?'

'Come on, Sheel, don't be like that.'

'Someone's got to be. It's about time you listened and cleaned up regular, instead of when it suits – and don't call me Sheel!'

Tyrell knew the way to Murren, a scattering of homes

which was all that remained of a once-thriving community. The Great Western Railway had been a major employer in the past but now, with the station and its master gone, buildings had decayed. Usable houses had become homes for anyone prepared to live there but the yuppie invasion of Gloucestershire had bypassed Murren. There was no school, no village shop, no picturesque church, only the barrenness of old workings and a pub housed in what had once been a railway storage shed.

In its heyday Murren had been prosperous, oak for Drake's warships, then Nelson's, going from the Royal Forest of Dean to be sailed downriver. In the nineteenth century coal began to gleam its way to the main line between Wales and London until the Second World War when Murren became the junction for munitions stored in the Forest. Men and armaments steamed their way east towards vessels sailing on D-Day for the Normandy coast.

Rose leaned forward in her seat. 'She said it was the end house after the crossing.'

Tyrell drove slowly, deciding Mrs Hackett's neighbours in The Terrace were a mixed bunch. Behind each house was a long garden, enough in days gone by to feed a family its basic vegetables. The front gardens were small, the last one with a tiny square of neatened green surrounded by clumps of plants in bud and an absence of weeds. Paintwork was old but not yet the worse for wear and windows shone, as did the brass knocker on the front door. They knocked and waited for an answer, the DI leaving Rose Walker to make the introductions.

'Mrs Hackett, I am WPC Walker and this is Detective Inspector Tyrell. May we come in?'

'You're the one I talked to?'

Rose nodded. Mrs Hackett looked at Tyrell and he sensed fear in her. She was of middle height, possibly in her mid-sixties, and her hair was white. A neat, plain woman, she had a freshness about her which echoed in the air reaching him from her home.

'You all right, Kate?'

Tyrell turned and saw a ferret of a woman with bright

eyes and wild red hair, her rumpled clothing suggesting she had just pulled off an overall. She was already lifting a foot to step up into the garden when Mrs Hackett advanced on her.

'Thank you, Gloria, there's no need for you to come in.'

Mrs Hackett had been firm and Gloria hesitated. 'You sure?'

'Positive.'

Only when Gloria trailed off to her own home did Mrs Hackett sigh. 'My neighbour, Gloria Reilly.' She stepped back, holding the door wide. 'You'd better come in.'

The house was as Tyrell had imagined. It was clean, orderly, and with a sense of calm pervading the rooms. There was no clutter of cheap and unnecessary furniture, no garish vases. What was in place was of good quality and well cared for.

'Do sit down, Mrs Hackett,' he said.

Rose persuaded the woman to sit beside her on a couch which was old but still in good condition. Crochet work covered the cushions and there was further evidence of her skill in mats under prized ornaments. Mrs Hackett began to talk, words tumbling from her as she watched Tyrell walk to the fireplace and lift a photo from the mantelpiece. Rose put her warm hands over the woman's nervous fingers and the words slowed, stopped.

Keith Tyrell looked at the photo he held and saw a girl he recognized, smiling in the sun. She had grown to womanhood in a home where there was warmth and love and comfort, a home to be invaded by police, reporters, unpleasant neighbours. Mrs Hackett was an orderly woman and she would have to endure the disruption of her home. Julie's belongings must be identified, labelled, scrutinized, for any clue they might give. He knew the grandmother's grief would be total yet it would not stop her being polite to the intruders.

He looked at her and she saw in his eyes the realization of her worst fear.

'Mrs Hackett, I am so very sorry.'

Chapter Two

By the time Keith had escorted Mrs Hackett to the mortuary and returned to the CID office, DCI Whittaker's temper had not improved.

'The grandmother, where is she now?' he demanded to know.

'WPC Walker's taken her back home and DC Walsh has gone with them. I've asked Sergeant Willis to put a couple of his men on duty.'

Whittaker could not resist temptation where the young DI was concerned. 'Two? Bit much, even for you.'

Tyrell made himself ignore the slight. 'It's an end-of-terrace house, a long garden at the back. You know yourself, sir, what reporters can be like – let alone so-called friends who insist on going in and reducing clues to zero.'

'So, the girl's been officially identified?'

'Yes, sir.' Tyrell opened his pocketbook. 'Julia Louise Parry, aged twenty and known as Julie. She's lived with her grandmother for seven years. Worked for Deakin and Co., estate agents, Bream Road, Lydney.'

'Parents?'

'Mrs Hackett is contacting the mother – she lives in Swindon with her husband and new family. Father – nothing known of him at present. Was last heard of four years ago, working in an hotel in Llandudno. I tried criminal records and he was a fairly regular offender, petty stuff. Drunk and disorderly, the occasional punch-up, minor theft – all opportunistic. There's been nothing for more than two years.'

'Then he's either found the straight and narrow or he's dead.'

'Llandudno police are looking into it for us, sir.'

'As soon as they let us know and when this Mrs Hackett can tell you she's broken the news to her daughter, we can issue the name of the victim. The press office keeps passing on enquiries.' The DCI frowned. 'You said she worked in Lydney. How did she get there? Bus? Car?'

'Car, sir. Her boyfriend bought her an old banger and did it up well. He's a mechanic.'

Whittaker was visibly cheered. 'Boyfriend? I told you this would be a domestic, Tyrell. Pull him in!'

Keith Tyrell made a supreme effort to hold back a smile. 'Would do, sir, but there's a problem. I talked to the company Pewsey works for and they're flying him home as soon as possible.'

'Flying? Where in God's name is he?'

'Somewhere in the North Sea. He's on an oil rig and has been there for the last three weeks.'

Whittaker's rank allowed him to explode and he thumped the desk with the side of his fist. 'Damn him! Well, this car he bought for the girl. Located it yet?'

'Not yet, sir, but the –'

'Then do something useful for once, Tyrell, and find it!'

Murren had not changed in the few hours since DI Tyrell had left it. The roadway into the old community was as quiet and litter-strewn as before, the cars parked on verges as battered and unable to be moved.

'Not somewhere the council bothers with, by the look of it,' Tyrell said to himself. 'Poor devils.'

He had listened to Martin Draper, the community policeman for the area. 'A right mix living there,' Martin had told him. 'Landlords can't get a good rent so they go on the DSS list. The money's OK but of course, they tell me, "the turnover's so fast there's no time to get repairs done, officer." Then there're the families who've lived there for ever. Mrs Hackett's one of them. Her father was a railwayman and she stayed on when she married. When the company sold up the properties for next to nothing she and her husband bought the house. He died about ten years ago. Nice lady, Mrs Hackett – not like some.'

If Tyrell could do things his way he would go gently, questions inserted here and there to get thoughts buzzing, memories surfacing. Whittaker's method was to fill the place with officers in and out of uniform, question everyone in sight until someone cracked and either grassed or confessed. The DCI would get his result but any community spirit would be shattered. In a place like Murren it would not take long. Afterwards? When neighbour had to go on living with neighbour? Tyrell was already certain the crime did not involve Murren, except as a source of the victim. The answers were elsewhere.

He pulled the car in beside the house, on waste ground. By the time he walked to the garden gate at the front Mrs Reilly was already on her path.

'Dreadful about Julie, in't it? D'you know what 'appened? Nice girl, Julie. Didn' deserve to be battered to death. Was she the one found in the river? Wonder where she went in? Was it off Murren Point? Always a nasty spot for accidents. That's where the ol' man lost 'is footin' an' drowned.'

'Forgive me, Mrs Reilly, I must get on. The sooner we finish here, the sooner Mrs Hackett can have the privacy she needs.'

''Course! Poor soul. Always keeps 'erself to 'erself, Kate. Must be real 'orrible for 'er 'avin' you lot goin' through Julie's things. What the papers might give to 'ave all you get your 'ands on.'

The ferrety features were screwed up in what passed for a smile but the woman's eyes were wide, knowing. Tyrell nodded politely and escaped to knock on the door of number 5. Rose Walker admitted him at once.

'Thank heaven you've come, sir.'

'What's wrong?'

'Mrs Hackett got straight on to her daughter. She's coming as soon as she can get her kids sorted out – two boys and a girl.'

'That's not the problem, is it?'

'No.' She frowned, puzzled. 'You know you got me to look at Julie's room when we were here before?'

'Yes.'

'I think someone's been in. It all seems the same . . .'

'But your instincts tell you otherwise?'

'Yes, they do. For a start, the door was closed and I would have said I left it open, like the others.'

'Then trust your instincts – and your memory.'

Tyrell found Mrs Hackett sitting at the dining table, gazing into space. She was still wearing her coat and he could see misery suffusing her, ageing her as he watched.

'Mrs Hackett, I can't begin to know how you're feeling. Losing a child so close to you must be the worst thing anyone is expected to endure.'

Tired blue eyes swung to him and focused. 'Inspector Tyrell. Would you like some tea?'

'That's very kind of you. May I make it and bring you a cup? I'd like to do something to help.'

'And everyone needs tea at a time like this, don't they?' She managed the faintest of smiles. 'When Eddie died I thought I'd drown in the stuff, then I realized it gave people something to do.'

The kettle in the small kitchen was already filled. As he waited for it to boil, the DI opened cupboards and drawers to find three cups, saucers, spoons. A tray was quickly laid, milk from the fridge added and a sugar bowl. Tyrell carried the tray to her.

'Would you like me to pour?' he asked.

'Please.' She looked at the result of his efforts. 'Your mother taught you well – or is it your wife?'

'Both, I think.'

'Have you any children?'

'No, not yet. We hope to – one day.'

Rose Walker dealt with the cups as he filled them and Tyrell talked of Jenny and her job as a clinical psychologist, the move to Gloucestershire for her new post.

'There's not many men would have done that – given up their way of life for a wife's career.'

'What did I give up? London and an expensive flat for the fresh air between the Forest and the river?' His face darkened as he thought of the countless times he had sat drinking tea with the newly bereaved. 'The work's the same.'

When she had been persuaded to have her cup refilled, DI Tyrell asked permission to search Julie's room. Mrs Hackett paled but forced herself to be brave and agreed with a nod, looking into the depths of her cup as they left her to her tears.

The stairs were steep, narrow, the rooms opening from the tiny landing clean and neat, their colours fresh. With Rose Walker ahead of him, Tyrell stood in the doorway of the pleasant room which had been Julie's and waited. The WPC stared at the mantelpiece, the empty grate, the windowsill with its array of romantic novels, the bed. She shut her eyes.

A minute passed before she opened her eyes. 'I've remembered. After the mortuary, the first thing I thought when I came in here was the smell – it was different. I'd noticed it downstairs but it was much stronger here.'

'Any idea what it was?'

'Smoke. Cigarette smoke. That's why it was odd. It was stale and yet nobody smoked in this house.'

'Was that all?'

'No. Now I remember the smell, other things have come back to me. There were two photos on the mantelpiece. They've gone and so has a book from beside the bed. It was small.' Rose turned and closed her eyes again. 'It was red and had a pen or a pencil attached to it.'

'A diary?'

'Yes, sir. A diary. Where can they have gone? Mrs Hackett didn't come up here before we left for the morgue.'

'Get it all in your notes. I've an idea – but I need you to keep Mrs Hackett busy. I'll ring the station and hurry up the uniformed support. If my hunch is right, we're going to need all the help we can get.'

Seconds later the DI was knocking on the door of number 4, The Terrace. It was opened remarkably quickly.

'Mrs Reilly.' Tyrell produced his card for her to read. 'I am Detective Inspector Tyrell of the Criminal Investigation Department – better known as CID.' Was it his imagination or had she begun to shrink. 'May I come in?'

'Criminal? I 'ad nothin' to do with Julie dyin'. Nothin'.'

'I've no doubt that's true but as a neighbour of Mrs Hackett's you can be of great help to us.'

Air wafting from the house was laden with the stench of unwashed flesh, filthy clothes, rotting food and too many cigarettes smoked in rooms where windows were never opened. The house next door had been built of the same bricks and yet could not be more dissimilar. It was there he had thought his job in Murren was the same as it had been in London. Controlling nausea when entering unpleasant homes was a trick he had learned early and he was glad of the skill now.

Standing in the muddle of scratched and dirty furniture, colours that clashed until they could almost be heard, crockery long past a need to be washed, Gloria Reilly was uneasy. 'What you after?'

'Some items have gone missing from Mrs Hackett's home.'

'Nothin' to do with me.'

'As I said earlier, you might be able to help. Did you see anyone while you were outside?'

'No.'

He smiled. Trap set and sprung. 'There was no one about?'

'No, no one.'

'Pity. You see, if the articles taken are not immediately returned, we're looking at a serious crime.'

Gloria Reilly stiffened, became wary. 'Serious?'

'Very. Theft from a woman while she's identifying a dead body?' He shook his head. 'It won't go down well. Magistrates tend to get a bit heavy-handed over that kind of crime. Then we have to add in interference with a possible crime scene. Now that is a major offence.'

She began to fidget, her eyes flicking round the room to avoid Tyrell's gaze. 'These – articles. What were they?'

'Why do you ask?'

Gloria shrugged skinny shoulders under an overall designed for respectable housewives and reached for a packet of cigarettes. It was empty and she looked hopefully at Tyrell. He was motionless, bulking large in the limited space of the cluttered room as he watched her every move with a level, unblinking stare. He could see she was distinctly uneasy.

'I might be able to 'elp – could put th'word round. Anythin' in it for me?'

'I need what was taken and I need it now. Not in a day or two when "someone" has waited to see if there's a market.'

'You 'aven't said what, yet.'

'To start with, a small red book and pencil. Then there are at least two photographs. Do I need to go on?'

'If Kate 'Ackett said I took 'em she's lyin'.'

'Mrs Hackett does not yet know they're missing. I want to keep it that way.'

'So, 'ow d'you know?'

'CID, Mrs Reilly. It's my job to know.'

She looked despairingly at a whisky bottle lying empty on the sideboard. 'Why shouldn' people make what they can out the papers? They throw cash around when it suits.'

'For stolen goods? Too big a risk. Don't forget, if the aforementioned items appeared in the press, then it would double the original crime, making the paper involved guilty as well. As for the thief . . .' The DI pursed his lips and shook his head. 'Now, if I were to be handed all the things taken – and I mean all – they can be returned before the legal owner's aware they've been stolen. If not, it means a search warrant and a horde of officers tearing someone's home apart. If it was this place, who knows what they might find? Then, when the case comes to court, your past record would have to be read out. That would take a while, wouldn't it?' Martin Draper had given Tyrell an update on Murren's known offenders. 'I understand you've a very impressive list to be read out, most of it under your real name of Winnie Button.'

Gloria glared at him, her mouth tight and angry. She knew men, and this copper might talk soft but he was a tough one. With a sigh of defeat she moved slowly, having hidden her pickings where he guessed she would, under one of the grubby cushions of the couch.

'Did you read the diary?'

'Didn' 'ave time.'

'Just as well for you. Now, if any newspaper prints information that could only have come from you, I'll be back with a search warrant and half a dozen officers. You're sure I have all you took? Remember the consequences if you hold out on me.'

'You got what you come for.'

Tyrell held out a hand. 'The key.'

Her jaw dropped, revealing stained and irregular teeth. ''Ow did you know?'

'Obvious. I suppose you go in and help yourself?'

'Only if I'm out of – milk.'

'And cash?'

Gloria flushed an unpleasant red which did not blend

with the colour of her hair. A key came from her overall pocket and was handed to him.

'Kate 'Ackett can afford a quid 'ere and there. She's not short and she's got Julie's pay comin' in.'

'Had Julie's pay,' the DI reminded her. 'Now, is there anything else?'

The woman stared at the carpet, its pattern long lost in grime. 'You got what you come for.'

'Mrs Reilly, for your sake I hope I have.'

In the fresher air outside Tyrell was thoughtful as the door slammed behind him. He was sure she had held on to something, but what? With a sigh of resignation he looked about him.

Murren.

The DI needed the feel of the place and walked towards the river. The roadway was in a reasonably good state, even if potholed and puddled after the morning's rain. There was a sense of solidity underfoot and Tyrell decided it must be due to the rocky outcrop on which it was first built that had made Murren so useful to shipping.

Signs of previous use still existed, although the wood of former jetties had rotted almost to nothing. It intrigued Tyrell to see the wharf still intact and as solid as it had been when Forest coal was regularly shipped out. Then, rocks and stones had been placed and cemented in with great care, massive steel angle iron edging and protecting from wear. The DI was puzzled, flicking at one of the stones with his toecap as he noted it was granite and not the Forest red sandstone. It must have been part of a consignment of ballast, offloaded and replaced in the ships with hard coal from Forest seams.

Turning his back on the river, Keith Tyrell's gaze took in all he could see of Murren. To his right was what must have been an impressive residence in its heyday. Point House, so he had been told by Martin Draper, had been built by the transport company for its harbourmasters and eventually bought by the daughters of one of the last incumbents.

Between Point House and The Terrace was waste ground, thistles, gorse, brambles, hiding the remains of brick and stone which had once housed countless families. On his left was their modern equivalent, caravans in all stages of decay and almost obscured by the walls of roofless railway sheds, coal stores and a signal box. An embankment was all that was left of the single track that had carried coal to fuel Victorian and Edwardian homes and factories. As he stood there, Tyrell imagined overworked engines in the Second World War tugging freight cars laden with munitions.

It was time to move on and he walked briskly back towards his car. Nearing The Terrace he could see beyond the crossing, although any view to his right was blocked by the high banking. On the left goats grazed and chickens pecked in whatever clear ground there was surrounding an ancient railway coach made bright with paint and gaily coloured curtains. Beyond that small trees edged the field and only the roof of Murren Cottage could be seen. Once it had been home to the man in charge of the railway's links. Keith Tyrell pictured him with a full beard and a curly moustache, strutting along the road to work in a frock-coated uniform, a round cap with a shiny brim set squarely above his eyes.

A car was being driven fast towards him, braking and parking outside Mrs Hackett's house.

'Damn the press!'

The DI broke into a run, determined to keep Mrs Hackett safe from further hurt. Tyrell saw the driver get out of the car and he slowed to a walk, then grinned.

'You're in a hurry. Did you think I was Whittaker?' the newcomer asked.

Almost as tall as the inspector, Detective Sergeant Brian Clarke was thickset, heavy shoulders and massive thighs threatening the seams of his suit. Close-cropped black curls capped a wide head and neck but dark eyes under strong brows were crinkled with laughter.

'Brian! You're a welcome sight. I didn't recognize the car and first thought you were a reporter.'

'Hey! No insults, please. I've come to help you out.'

'Me? Did the DCI send you?'

'None other. He had a phone call from HQ. Reports of a group of anti-blood sports protesters annoying a lady the other side of the county.' Detective Sergeant Brian Clarke tapped the side of his nose. 'It's all very hush-hush.'

'Oh, that lady.'

'Very high-profile for our Mr Whittaker – if he plays his cards right. So, HQ decided in their wisdom you could safely be left in charge of this little lot and Whittaker wants you back in Lydney as soon as you can get there.'

'If not before – and you've been left to see I do the job properly. I mean, I can't be trusted on my own, whatever the top brass may think.'

'You read the DCI like a bloody book, d'you know that? I thought the squash was helping?'

Keith had signed on at a sports centre. If Whittaker riled him badly he would call at the club, hitting squash balls to kingdom come in a game, or on his own, until the demons Whittaker had raised were destroyed.

'Jenny doesn't like me being late home or so knackered because of him. Damn the man!' Tyrell's smile was rueful. 'In spite of Whittaker, I'm glad you've come. I can do with you picking up what you can with those ears of yours.'

Clarke rubbed an ear thickened by many rugby tackles. 'Thank you! Well, is the killer here?'

'No. I'm sure he – or she – is not, but these people knew the girl. Because of that they may know, or have seen, something useful. We need all the information we can get.'

'Any other leads? Boyfriend?'

The DI explained about the North Sea oil rig and the last three weeks. Brian Clarke listened but he had learned much of human nature the hard way.

'Perhaps she's the one with a bit on the side?'

'Not obviously – and that's where you come in. Get

what you can. Martin Draper's the community chap for Murren and he's due back here soon. If I can I'll get him deployed to you full time. Rose Walker's in with the grandmother.'

'Is there a mother?'

'Due any time. When she turns up have Rose with you. She notices things.'

'So do you when you get the chance.'

Tyrell was touched by his friend's comment but he said nothing, becoming brisk. 'I'd like to see the place where Julie worked – talk to the people she spent her days with.'

'Whittaker had someone on that but if you can find an excuse to go and see for yourself, take Mickey Walsh with you. I know he's better at arm's length, now and again, but he's good with computers. Estate agents use them all the time nowadays and he'll be useful.'

The CID offices were quiet, the pile of paperwork waiting for Tyrell on his desk already impressive. He read steadily, absorbing many details, frowning over a few.

'Is there anything I can do?'

Tyrell looked up from the file he was studying. Penny Rogers was a quiet, reserved woman, plain-featured and with light brown hair coiled tidily away from her face.

'Penny! Good to see you. It's kind of you to ask but the DCI left very explicit orders although I've a feeling it's your hand behind these files.'

A flush of pleasure added colour to her cheeks. 'How could you guess that?'

'Everything's arranged so simply and logically. No wonder Whittaker had you drafted in.'

Penny Roger's efficiency as a detective sergeant was legendary. So were the rumours of her devotion to the ambitious Whittaker who had used her abilities to help him rise through the ranks.

Tyrell checked a list. 'I see you've been talking to Julie's friends. Any luck?'

'Two more left to contact. So far, none of them saw her the night she disappeared and not one has any idea where she was going when she left her grandmother's. They're all decent kids and say it would have been unlikely for them to meet in Gloucester. They aren't the clubbing kind. A quiet evening in a country pub somewhere, a decent film – that's more their style.'

Tyrell tapped a file. 'You and Goddard interviewed the manageress of the office where she worked – Bream Road.'

'Not a lot of joy there either. "Julie was a good girl, came on time, did her work and went home," ' she quoted from memory. 'Ms Todd was very anxious to get us out of the place.' A quick smile enlivened her expression. 'We were bad for business, apparently.'

'Was it only the two of them in this office? The Todd woman and Julie?'

'No. There's Kevin Palmer.'

'Of course, you mentioned him in your report but didn't see him.'

'Out delivering keys, Todd said. She wouldn't give us a time we could see him. Do you want me to go back?'

'No, thank you, you're more useful with the girl's friends. It's possible Julie had an interest, a hobby, and I'm sure it's one she kept from her grandmother but there's no mention of anything in her diary. If you can work your magic and get a hint of it from her girlfriends, I'd be grateful. I'm off to check up on any detail, however small, so I'll go and see this Kevin. It'll earn me a break from this damn paper chase.'

Most of Lydney's property dealers were in Newerne Street but Deakin and Co. had been established in Bream Road. The firm had a freshly painted façade between the offices of two solicitors, still the original terraced houses they had once been. The estate agent's premises had been hollowed out by experts and fitted with every modern aid to communication. Walls and partitions were covered with photographs of homes for sale or rent and large red banners adorned properties sold and no longer available.

The woman who rose from behind a wide desk was young and red-headed, wearing a long black jacket with wide shoulders over a minuscule skirt. Her face was a mask of immaculate make-up and professional courtesy. She smiled at the newcomers until she saw the state of DC Walsh in his wrinkled sports coat and unironed shirt. The older man looked a more promising bet, she thought. His clothes were expensive and about him was an aura of success, authority, the heady whiff of money. She could earn herself a good commission.

The DI read her intentions, introducing himself and DC Walsh. 'And you are Miss Todd?'

Annoyance was well hidden behind the perfected skin. 'Debra Todd. I'm the manager. I know all about Julie being the one fished out of the river. We had police here earlier.'

The DI heard a gasp from behind a partition. Ms Todd ignored it. She was busy deciding there would be no sale today and shrugged her shoulders.

'I've said all there is to say to the women who came earlier – I presume you do talk to each other?'

Tyrell stiffened, giving no sign of the irritation caused by her rudeness. 'Very helpful, I was told you'd been, Miss Todd,' he said gravely.

Mickey Walsh remembered hearing it was best to take cover when the DI was extra polite.

'At that time Detective Sergeant Rogers was told of a cleaner who worked here and also a director of the company who checks the workings of this office every week or so. Would Julie have met them? Talked to them?'

'God, no! Julie was a clerk. Just a clerk. She and Kevin had desks and monitors back there.' A manicured hand with a powerful wrist waved at the dividing wall. 'One of them came in here and helped if I was busy with customers. The cleaner doesn't start work until seven at night. Julie was long gone.'

'And the director?'

'Mr Phelps was only ever interested in whether Julie earned her pay.'

The door was opened by a young couple, excited and yet nervous. Tyrell sensed this was their first attempt to buy their own home. Debra Todd fixed her professional smile in place and left her unwelcome visitors in favour of a possible commission. The inspector took advantage of the situation to go behind the partition and meet Kevin Palmer.

Kevin was very young, very thin and very spotty. 'She never said Julie was the girl found in the river.' The hope of a mistake echoed in his voice.

'I'm sorry,' Tyrell told him.

The boy was near to tears. 'Poor Julie. She was always kind to me – never let that old cow get me down.'

Tyrell almost smiled. Debra Todd might resent the bovine comparison but she would hate being considered old.

'You were good friends, you and Julie?'

'Yes, we were. We talked a lot when we were here on our own. Julie was really good with computers and made sure I never got stuck – well, not for long, anyway.'

The DI experienced a familiar tingling at the back of his neck and knew he must tread carefully. There had been no computer in the house in Murren. He nodded to the switched-off monitor and empty chair.

'Did Julie use her machine for personal matters? E-mails to her boyfriend – that sort of thing?'

Kevin listened to Debra Todd's voice. It was loud, persuading, and he could be sure the boss was fully occupied making money. 'Julie did when she could. Mrs Satan kept coming in to see we weren't wasting the firm's time and money but Julie was very good at wiping out records she didn't want checked up on.'

'Was she now?' Mickey Walsh settled himself at the vacant desk and switched on the VDU. 'Any idea what passwords she used?' he asked Kevin and surprised Tyrell with his skill at the keyboard.

'Not here,' the boy said. 'Mrs Satan told us head office had installed a program as could spot when we called up websites and so on. Julie said it was likely and we musn't risk it.'

'Where did she become such an expert?'

'School, at first, like me. Then she went on to college and did computers. I did too, but I never got as far as she did.'

Tyrell sat on the edge of Kevin's desk and smiled reassuringly. 'Julie couldn't use this system as she chose and she had no computer at home so, where did she go? Whose set-up did she use?'

'The cyber caff. It's round the corner and down the hill – just beyond the railway line. Very handy for the kids coming out of school in the lunch hour or in the evenings.'

'Do you know if she used to meet up with anyone there?'

Kevin shook his head. 'Julie liked to be on her own.'

'Could she have been into chat rooms?'

The shaking was more emphatic. 'No way! She knew creeps used them and wouldn't have any truck with that sort of thing.'

'Good for Julie,' Tyrell said, 'and thank you for your help, Kevin. If there's anything you can think of which might help, please call.'

The DI took a card from his pocket and handed it to the boy. Kevin was impressed, then his features crumpled. 'You will find out how she died? Put it right?'

'Yes, we will,' Tyrell promised. He stood, ready to walk away, and then a thought struck him. 'You called a certain lady Mrs Satan. Was it you who named her that?'

Kevin shook his head, the moisture in his eyes needing to be cleared with a sniff. 'It was Julie. She talked about

Satan and the Devil as though they were real people. I think maybe her gran was chapel – something like that.'

Debra Todd had been glad to see the back of non-profitable visitors.

'Mrs Satan,' Mickey Walsh said and nodded. 'The kids got her right. That kind of woman makes you feel sorry for Mr Satan – whoever he might be.'

'It would take some courage to be tied to her,' Tyrell admitted. 'Now, this café. We might as well walk.' He needed fresh air after Ms Todd's heavy, pervasive perfume. 'Anything occur to you in there?' the DI asked as they turned the corner of Bream Road and went down the hill.

'Getting on the Net would be out of the question. There were blocks in place.'

'So, no chat rooms?'

'Not a chance. Any links were all strictly business.'

'You appear to know what you're talking about so I'll leave the technical stuff to you.'

Mickey halted at the door of the cyber café. 'Anything special you want in here?'

'Just follow your instincts. If it's clear she used a particular outlet, I'll try for a warrant and get it removed so it can be checked out. See what you think.'

Mickey was being trusted and became noticeably more cheerful but the owner of the café was not happy to lose one of his machines when students from the comprehensive school could be paying for its use. He did admit Julie had been a regular visitor and the tall inspector did not give the impression of a man willing to be blocked. The owner sighed with resignation, waived the need for a warrant and said DC Walsh could take the machine. That way it might be possible to get back to normal as soon as possible.

* * *

Lydney's police station was quietly busy. Reports were coming in a steady stream to Penny Rogers and such facts as were useful were posted on a massive bulletin board at one end of the CID main office. Downstairs, apart from a duty sergeant, only Rose Walker and Sheila Hipwell were visible. Tyrell ran up the stairs and checked on the progress of enquiries, making sure every possible aspect was being covered well enough to satisfy Whittaker. It was early in the investigation and, as yet, there was not a single lead. The DI was restless and went back to the main entrance.

'Has Mrs Hackett's daughter arrived from Swindon?' he asked as Mickey Walsh began humping computer equipment up the stairs.

Rose nodded. 'Yes, sir. It only took her about three hours from the time her mother phoned.'

'How was she?'

'Upset, naturally, but . . .'

'Not as much as you expected?'

'No. Seemed happy to talk to any of the press who turned up and she wanted to make a TV appeal for the killer to come forward – but I'd guess only after she's made sure her make-up's as good as it gets.'

'Is she like Julie?'

'That's what's so strange. If you could imagine Julie grown old, you've got her mother, though I think Julie would have been a much nicer version – given the chance.'

'That's why we've got to nail whoever stopped her from having that chance.'

'Maybe he's done it before,' Sheila Hipwell said slowly.

'Well, no one in Murren's suspected of a similar crime,' the DI said, 'but it wouldn't hurt to check criminal records again. Murren's population has its floaters.'

Sheila almost smiled. 'It'll be good to have a proper job to do.'

The DI went out into the yard and sat in his car, intending to call Jenny. He switched on the radio and a choir filled the evening air, the music calming and uplifting. It was in a classical style and yet modern. Keith Tyrell lay back in his seat and listened, valuing the singing and the clarity of the diction. At the end a charming voice informed him he had been listening to 'The Lord is my shepherd' from John Rutter's Requiem. The chords might have ceased but one word echoed and re-echoed, crystallizing a half-thought-out idea.

'I wonder . . .' he said aloud and called Jenny. Her voice as she answered had the power to stir him as it always did. 'I'm sorry, darling, I'll be late this evening.'

'Whittaker driven you so daffy you must have at least three games of squash to exorcize him?'

'No, nothing like that.' He explained the protesters and Whittaker's need to be seen busy in the right place. 'I have to keep on this case. No work-out for me this evening – but with Whittaker out of the way, there's minimal stress.'

'Poor you. Anything new on the girl in the river?'

'In a way. There's someone I need to see – ask for their advice.'

'So you do have a lead?'

'A very vague one.'

'Going in the opposite direction to Whittaker as usual?'

'It's not my fault the man's blinkered by his own ambitions and can't see straight. It's a pity because he's damned good when he puts his mind to it.'

'You do what you must,' Jenny said. 'I'll stay on at the clinic for a while. You don't mind, do you?'

He was puzzled by something indefinable in her voice. 'Of course not. Why should I?'

'No reason. You go on and play Devil's advocate for Tricky Dicky. I'll be fine.'

'The Devil. Funny you should say that.'

Chapter Three

Tyrell was glad the light was fading as he drove along the road to Tolland. He wanted his visit to be a quiet one, and should any of the villagers see him privacy was the last thing he could expect.

The village pub, the George, was well lit but not yet noisy. Facing it and across the road the church of St Barnabas loomed dark, its ancient stones forbidding. Keith Tyrell turned into the driveway of the house beside the church and stopped at a front door gleaming with new paint. The evening was still pale enough for him to see pruned shrubs and weed-free borders before his knock was answered.

'Inspector Tyrell! Come along in, my dear chap. It is good to see you again.'

The hall of the vicarage was warm, welcoming, and smelled of polish and flowers. Nicholas Hatton was no longer haggard and in despair and the wife who hurried to join him had a freshness about her which was of the spirit as well as a new skirt and attractive sweater.

'You're both well?'

'Indeed we are – and you are come at a most opportune moment. On Saturday Willoughby is to be married, here, in Tolland,' the vicar said.

Mrs Hatton's smile was ecstatic. 'Such a nice girl – and I don't have to play the organ! The new people at the shop are devoted to the church and Mr Thorpe's a fine organist.'

'You always did very well, my dear,' her husband assured her.

She sighed. 'It was always a dreadful ordeal for me. The relief – I can't begin to tell you!'

Her smile was so happy Keith Tyrell glimpsed the girl who had enchanted a curate. That curate, grown old, touched her hand and they were alone, until Nicholas Hatton remembered their guest.

'This young man looks in need of coffee, my dear. Will you bring it to the study?'

'Of course I will. Such a hard job you have, Inspector. That poor girl from Murren, her family must be devastated.'

'Coffee, my love?'

The study fire was bright, its logs flaring comfort. The DI was ushered to a seat on one side of the hearth and Nicholas Hatton settled in a chair opposite. They chatted of Tolland characters. Tyrell learned of Elsie Slade getting very stiff and cranky with arthritis, her tongue unaffected, her daughter, Agnes, positively a saint.The shop was flourishing again now the Thorpes owned it and how sad it was Major Clawson had fought his last battle but he did have a good funeral.

Coffee came, steaming and fragrant. Mrs Hatton poured, served, then left the two men alone.

'You said you needed my help. A spiritual matter?'

Keith hesitated. 'In a way.'

'And it's to do with this business at Murren?'

'Again, in a way. DCI Whittaker's in overall charge, although he has to spend most of his time elsewhere at the moment.'

'Ah! Mr Whittaker. You are following a train of thought which would not sit well with him?'

Keith Tyrell sipped his coffee and found it excellent.

The vicar understood. 'I will not put you in the invidious position of having to criticize another officer.'

Keith grinned and Reverend Hatton saw a mischievous boy. 'You know us both too well.'

'Now that, Inspector Tyrell, is my job. So, what is it you need from me?'

'To tell me if witches' covens are still functioning in the Forest.'

Pale eyebrows raced towards a fringe of receding hair. 'Oh, dear! I take it you are merely after information and not anxious to join in?'

Tyrell laughed. 'I've many vices but that's not one of them.'

'Glad to hear it, my dear chap. Now, let me think for a moment. All of us in the diocese are aware of the odd rumour from time to time. Old folk in the villages, even in the towns, like to frighten the young ones – there's nothing new in that. Extant covens? There may be a sprinkling of men and women playing arcane games and I could be living in happy ignorance but I would say that is all there is. I know of nothing warranting concern.'

'Is there anyone who might?'

'For the knowledge which has been handed down through the generations – centuries even – you're in the wrong part of the county. Only deep in the Dean Forest itself could you hope to come across those who believe in the ancient gods. They've only survived themselves to keep such beliefs alive by talking to no one – and I mean no one. Certainly not to men and women of the cloth.'

Keith Tyrell's tiredness showed as he lay back in his chair.

'Why did you think of me?'

'When Elsie Slade needed the ghost of the unwanted dead man expelled from her Fred's grave, you knew who to call.'

'Of course! Now, why did I not think of that? Father Andrew! The very man. If anyone can help you, he can.'

Reverend Hatton busied himself at his desk, flicking through a rolling address file and dialling a number he located. Keith relaxed and watched the fire, its flames dying and mesmeric with their slow dance of burning. Across the room the vicar's voice was low, persuading, and it added to Keith's languor.

'Tomorrow evening suit you?' the vicar called out.

Keith roused himself. 'Fine. Not too early, though. DCI Whittaker may decide to find me a long and boring task for my sins.'

Nicholas Hatton cradled the phone and wrote briefly before returning to his seat. 'Here you are. Phone number and address. He'll be in all evening and will expect you when you get there.'

In the canteen next morning Mickey Walsh's hair was wilder than ever and Sheila Hipwell not one to let him escape ridicule.

'I thought you were getting it cut?'

'When I'm ready,' he snapped at her. No way would he tell of the barber's refusal to lift his scissors until the matted curls had been washed and no way was Mickey prepared to let any man wash his hair for him. 'Anyway, I worked late last night – the computer from the cyber caff.'

'Get anything?'

'Not yet. There're one or two interesting connections. Some stupid girl's given her address to a "fun-seeking eighteen-year-old" who wants to meet her.'

'Chat room perv?'

'It's got that feel, so I'll pass it on.'

'Perhaps that's what the DI's after?'

'No, I don't think so. Julie Parry was dead against that sort of risk. It's another angle he's got in mind.'

'Hasn't he told you?'

'Not him. He gets enough stick from the DCI without asking for trouble.'

Rose Walker was curious. 'What is it between those two? Do you know, Sarge?'

Roly Willis had just walked in, searching for hot tea, and Rose had to wait for an answer.

'The old stag, young stag we all have to suffer. What's behind it?' she asked.

'Goes back a bit,' the sergeant said slowly as he sipped

and reflected. 'Whittaker had a DI he liked working with. Pete Simons got results and they made Whittaker look good. Mind you, Pete had his own way of working and it wasn't always kosher. Then there was a complaint. DI Tyrell had witnessed the incident. He was new to division at the time and told the truth at the enquiry. Simons got busted to sergeant – and bloody lucky to get off that lightly. Soon after, there was a bad patch in Tolland – a murder investigation. Whittaker and Tyrell disagreed over who did what and a young lad hanged himself. It turned out Tyrell was right.'

'What happened to – what's his name? Simons?'

'Had a bad car crash which damned near killed him. They got him to Frenchay and he was doing OK until a massive stroke finished him.'

'Tough luck,' Sheila Hipwell decided.

'Luck? Maybe so,' Sergeant Willis said. 'There were some who claimed the old wives in Tolland put a hex on him and that's why he died.'

'Hex? Come on, Sarge!' Mickey Walsh thought the idea a huge joke but Roly Willis was not laughing.

'OK, that explains the aggro with the DI,' Sheila said, 'but what about Rose and me? What's Whittaker got against women?'

Roly Willis's smile was wicked. 'When you meet his wife, you'll know!'

Rain began to fall on Murren. In a heavy, drenching downpour Brian Clarke dashed from his car to Tyrell's passenger seat. Despite the weather the sergeant was cheerful.

'Well, we had a few days' rest from getting soaked. I suppose that's all we could hope for.'

His DI was less optimistic. 'If it keeps up, the flood alert on the Severn will be back to red – and you know what that means.'

'We'll be bogged down in every way.'

'I rang in early and was told your report was on my desk. Thank you for that.'

'Least I could do. There wasn't much to go on – this is three monkeys country.' He nodded towards homes that could be seen through the driving rain. 'It's a wonder any of them survive, never seeing or hearing anything at all.'

'That's why I wanted you here. You'd be able to sniff out what was under the surface.'

Clarke chuckled. 'Sniff? More like hold your nose with some of 'em.'

'For instance? And I've encountered Gloria Reilly.'

The sergeant's broad and powerful finger pointed in the direction of the river. 'Starting at the top, by the river, there's Point House. The two old ducks are very ladylike but they're hiding something – probably not polishing the china cabinet this week. The place is immaculate but I shouldn't think there's much cash. Even if there were they'd still be a very careful couple. Miss Hester and Miss Rhoda are anti every teenager ever born. Said they knew the girl and didn't disapprove of her – which rates young Julie very highly. She visited them, did odd jobs now and again and used to take them out in the car with her gran.'

'What about the caravans?'

'Martin Draper keeps up with the occupants and he filled me in with any previous. Merv Walters lives on his own and a right cranky bastard he is, too. Moves awkwardly and I'd guess it's arthritis. Yes, he knew Julie but not to talk to. "A stuck-up little cow" was how he described her.'

'The others?'

'Don Baldwin and Ricky Holder spend every spare moment in the Bothy. It's a religion with those two but they don't drink much – just like the company. They've both done the odd breaking and entering. It's always off their patch and only when they're short of cash. They were Whittaker's favourites for the burglars he can't suss out. We turned over every square inch of the caravans and the hedges round here, as well as all the derelict buildings. Nothing.'

'Their women?'

'Don's is Leanne Sullivan. She got pulled in once for prostitution but the baby doesn't know that, nor does the one she's carrying. Ricky Holder's girl is just that. She's sixteen now but she wasn't when she got pregnant.'

'And if we pull him in for carnal knowledge of an under-age girl –'

'The CPS will laugh their socks off.'

The two men watched a heavy curtain of rain sweep over them and wash away visibility.

Clarke shook his head. 'God! I bet those goats smell this weather!'

'I noticed a rickety shed by the old railway carriage. Perhaps they shelter in there.'

'Along with chickens and everything else.' The sergeant was resigned to the way some people chose to live. 'Cligwyd.'

'What?'

'That's the name on the door. It's made up from Clianthe and Gwydion, would you believe?'

'You're joking!'

'I wish. Clianthe, as she insists on being known, has her giros delivered here to a Jane Morse.'

'And Gwydion?'

'He is Welsh, or was, somewhere along the line. His giros are for Raymond Jenkins. Raymond's the toyboy, dreadlocks and all, while she sees herself as the original earth mother. That's all either of them see. They're in a world of their own and it's not one we inhabit. Hadn't a clue about Julie – so they said.'

'Anything turn up in the rest of The Terrace? Mrs Hackett I know, and I met Gloria.'

The DS laughed, triggering a bout of coughing. 'Gloria!' He wiped his eyes.

'Originally Winnie Button.'

'That's her. Murren's official working girl. Takes men

back to her place for a few bob – if they've lost their sense of smell and are desperate. It doesn't happen often.' Clarke blew his nose and mopped his face. 'This damned cold won't budge.' He stowed the damp handkerchief in a pocket. 'I could still be listening to Gloria wittering on, fantasizing about her little friend Julie, but we shot next door. Rose Walker's idea. She said Mrs Hackett and Julie had nothing to do with Gloria, if they could help it.'

'Next door?'

'Harry and Betty Gilbert, well in their seventies. Everything done carefully and at a snail's pace. Nice people. Thought Kate Hackett had done a marvellous job with Julie.'

'And the rest?'

'Mandy Stone's a single mum, two boys with the makings of right little tearaways. Martin Draper says they're already in more trouble than they can handle and they're still too young for the comp.'

'Doesn't someone else live there?'

'Kim Studd. She and Mandy are regarded as the local lesbies.'

'Are they?'

'Doubt it. The boys are well used to waking up to new uncles.'

'That just leaves the occupants of number 1.'

'They've been away for over a week but should be back today – and I've still to see Des and Claire Goldsmith at the Bothy, as well as the family in Murren Cottage.'

'Elderly widow, daughter and grandson.'

'That's them.' Brian Clarke grinned. 'Very respectable, except the daughter juggles two full-time boyfriends.'

'Two?'

'That Martin knows of. One's a farmer, the other a lorry driver.'

'I'd better get back to the station and leave you to it. How was Rose yesterday?'

'Great. As you said, she notices things. Between us we'll

have found out more by lunchtime than the DCI and a full team of his bloodhounds could turn up in a week.'

'Do you think the answer's here?'

The DS rubbed an itchy nose. 'Can't be sure until I've seen them all. As of now, I'd say no. Whoever killed that poor kid's not in Murren.'

The Forest was a constant presence on the DI's right as he followed the A48 back to Lydney. Mists which shrouded the greenness were not being swept away by the rain and the daytime darkness of bad weather gave the massed trees added menace.

Had it been so for the ancient inhabitants, he wondered? They could have felt protected, rather than threatened by the woodlands before the entire area was overrun by Celtic Britons, dark-skinned migrants from Asia and then Europe who swept aside all resistance. Bitter fighters, they settled the land under the trees, worshipped their gods and were ruled by priestly druids until the might of Rome marched in. For Caesar's men the prizes were the finest oak, as well as iron, limestone, coal, all at the margins of the great waterway, the River Severn. In spite of success they failed to find the dark corners and caves where men and secrets could be hidden.

Keith Tyrell negotiated traffic on the long hill down into Blakeney and let his memory wander. The Romans had been only one of the forces changing life in the Dean Forest. William the Conqueror and his Normans had set their own pattern in England, huge tracts of prime hunting land reserved for the king and his cronies. His son, William Rufus, extended the boundaries of the Royal Forest of Dean and emptied homes and villages. This gave the king, surrounded by his young men and boys, freedom from treachery and cares of state in the nearby court at Gloucester. Resentment against kings and nobles had been deep and enduring as food from the Forest was denied starving families. That anger had passed down the generations and still erupted against any who hunted.

The DI was reflecting on the length of memories in the Forest when his radio crackled.

'DCI Whittaker's just come in, sir.'

Roly Willis was speaking carefully and Tyrell guessed Whittaker was listening to the conversation.

'He expected you here and wants to know where you are.'

'Just left Blakeney. I went first to Murren to get an update from DS Clarke. He should finish his enquiries as soon as the last householders are available. Not everyone was in last night.'

'No, sir. It's not that sort of place, Murren.'

Tyrell waited for a clear road to overtake a JCB.

'Ten minutes, sir?'

'Less, Sergeant Willis, if I can make it.'

Whittaker waiting for him and in a foul temper was not Keith Tyrell's idea of ideal working conditions. He switched channels on the car radio to find music to suit his mood but none satisfied him. It was going to be one of those days and the DI knew he must be calm when he reached the station. There was no change in his speed or his driving but breaths came more steadily as Jenny had suggested. It helped to keep his mind on matters as far away from Whittaker as possible, yet his thoughts kept returning to the Forest which had fascinated him since his childhood.

The road ahead of him had stretches of beauty, lessening as he neared the outskirts of Lydney. It was a town which had spent two millennia or more straddling the route westward. There were docks at the waterside, natural for a settlement linking the Forest with navigable parts of the river. Once horses had dragged lumber, smelted iron, coal. Then it was trains pulling wagons to the Lydney docks.

The town had not always been dedicated only to commerce. On its western edge were impressive remains in stone and Roman mosaic, reminders that this had been a good place to live.

Keith locked his car, took a deep breath and arranged his features in a semblance of calm as he pushed open the door of the station.

'Glad you could join us.'

DCI Whittaker was pacing the foyer as the DI nodded a 'good morning' to Roly Willis.

'I'm sorry if I kept you waiting, sir.'

'May I remind you this is a murder investigation you're supposed to be running? I come in early to be certain everything's going to plan and where were you? Still in bed?'

'No, sir. In Murren.'

'You should have been here, reporting progress to me.'

'My report of yesterday's work is on your desk. I understand DS Clarke's report is there as well.'

The DCI waved folders at him. 'I have never yet found it possible to question a sheet of paper and receive sensible answers. You should have been here. It's already eight twenty.'

'As you say, sir. I can only apologize for keeping you waiting.'

The calm, deep voice added to Whittaker's annoyance. 'At least it's given me a chance to see what a monumental cock-up you're making.'

They heard the squeak of Roly Willis's shoes.

'Stay there, Sergeant Willis! You must be at the desk at all times.'

Roly cleared his throat, relieving embarrassment as the DCI allowed his temper full rein.

'What do I find when I get here? A properly organized investigation? I should be so lucky! How anyone at HQ can think you competent I fail to see. You've got a WPC out doing CID work and a DC upstairs playing games on a computer you seem to have confiscated.'

Silently, Tyrell counted slowly so as not to snap at the DCI. 'WPC Walker set up a good rapport with the victim's grandmother. She's been with her whenever necessary and, as a result, has learned a great deal about the girl. As for DC Walsh, he has a very good understanding of the Internet and websites and has worked hard on the computer we were loaned from the café. It's the one Julie used.'

'What a waste of manpower on some hare-brained notion of yours! Get rid of that damned machine and send Walsh to Murren. He's to replace the girl you have there and she can be back where she's most useful – behind a desk.'

Tyrell could hardly believe the orders but the DCI was his superior officer.

'Yes, sir. I'll see to it.'

'Now, Inspector Tyrell, have you found the car? No? When do you intend to?'

Roly Willis held up a sheet of paper. 'Excuse me, sir. This came through. The girl's car. Parked in a street in Gloucester. Kingsholme.'

Whittaker's eyes flickered, the storm abating against his will. 'Why was that not in the reports?'

'It came in late last night.' The sergeant read the time of despatch. '23.00 hours.'

'And what's been done about it? Nothing, I suppose.'

Roly Willis's lips tightened. 'Late relief handled it. Inspector Tyrell was contacted at home and he gave the orders for SOCO and the recovery team to deal with it ASAP. That request timed at 23.15. Sir.'

'Liaise with Gloucester and get house-to-house in the area the car was found.'

No soothing technique was going to help, Tyrell decided. He forced himself to be as calm as possible, surprised by how much effort it took, and then he explained that Gloucester's officers were already knocking on doors, hoping to find co-operative members of the public.

'Is there anything else, sir?' he asked and, expressionless, waited for Whittaker's reply.

'Julie Parry's friends. Get on to them.'

'DS Rogers has been covering that, sir. She talked to them all yesterday. The night she went missing Julie never met up with any of the girls she usually spends her time with and there's no hint of her seeing another man while the boyfriend's away.'

'Then that must be your primary objective, Tyrell. Find out where she went – and clear that mass of paperwork. How can you expect the CID office to be run efficiently if you neglect the essentials?'

Whittaker threw folders on to the counter and marched from the building. Behind him silence reverberated as Keith Tyrell stood for a moment, gathering his strength. He made a point of not looking at Roly Willis. The DCI had given orders and they must be seen to be carried out. As he made for the stairs, Tyrell could see the sergeant making a phone call.

'But I've nearly cracked it!' Mickey Walsh was furious at being taken away from the information hidden in the computer from the cyber café. 'Another couple of hours, that's all I need.'

'I'm sorry, Walsh, but you're to go to Murren. DS Clarke must have a DC with him.'

'He's got Rose Walker there and you said yourself she's good.'

'She's not CID,' Tyrell explained patiently. 'Is there anyone else you could suggest having a go at the stored memories? Maybe a civilian on the staff?'

'No. There's no one can break what that bloody server has in place.'

'There's a block on recall?'

Walsh looked up at Keith Tyrell and saw the interest he had sparked. 'It's not unheard of but it would make the website expensive to run.'

'Yes, of course. The server would charge extra?'

'And then some.' Exasperated, Mickey ran fingers through his curls, almost tidying them. 'I'm sure I've met this sort of thing in the past and got round it.'

'Specifically?'

'It could be a password, a code, trips, traps. Once I'd played with it enough I'd have some idea how the programmer thinks. After that . . .'

'I'll find you time, if I can.'

Mickey stared at Tyrell, assessing the value of his words. 'OK. Let me know when.'

'That's a deal. I'd be glad if you'd ask Sergeant Willis for a car. When you get to Murren, hand it over to Rose Walker and she can bring it back here.'

'Rose's not bad with one of those,' Mickey said, nodding at the computer, 'but this joker's beyond most people.'

'Julie Parry?'

The DC thought for a moment, the boy-smooth skin of his forehead wrinkling. 'She may not've come across the block. There's no hold-up getting on to this particular website. The problem is calling up what's on its memory. Makes you wonder what they want to keep hidden.'

'What about times of computer use?'

'That was dead easy and I've printed out a complete list. Not one of those times is when she'd be working at the estate agents.'

'So it probably is Julie making contact?'

'There's no proof but I'd say so. All the other chats I can trace, no problem.'

CID files were opened, dealt with, checked, the office gradually returning to a state of neatness even the DCI would find difficult to fault. A sandwich in the canteen was a solitary affair for Tyrell. He was conscious of stares and whispers, Whittaker's performance providing the day's gossip.

'How's Mrs Hackett?' he asked Rose Walker.

'I think it's just beginning to hit her, sir, and her daughter's no help. She goes on and on, wanting to know why we haven't arrested anyone yet. I'd guess Mrs

Hackett likes her peace and quiet and she's had none of that for the last twenty-four hours.'

'You and Sheila did a good job yesterday.'

'We did try, sir, but all we got was negative.'

Tyrell's smile was rueful. 'You should have had my old chemistry master. "A negative result is as useful as a positive one," he'd bellow at us. No, you covered all the possibles between you. Now we know she was alone when she drove off somewhere. It's still a mystery where she went and who she met. At the moment it's a complete dead end.'

'Gloucester, sir? The car was found there.'

'We need sightings of her in the city. So far, the Gloucester team's turned up nothing. I'm due to look over the vehicle when Forensics've finished with it, though I don't know what it'll tell us. Perhaps we'll find out she did go clubbing after all.'

'Not Julie, sir. Being in that house, you get the feel of the person she was. Clubs weren't her scene at all and even if she'd been persuaded, she'd never have gone on her own.'

Whittaker had soured the day and it continued dark and depressing. However pleasantly officers used phones to request help, none was forthcoming. Every idea, every initiative, seemed blighted and the constant rain added to the misery. Hourly, Tyrell listened to the news bulletins, the list of rivers on flood warnings of all colours growing rapidly. By mid-afternoon it was still an amber alert on the Severn.

'That won't last long.' Roly Willis carried a cup of tea and sat beside the DI in the canteen.

On the table next to them a plate of sausages glistened, chips added a savoury smell and the redness of baked beans was the only cheerful note in the room.

'I've been listening to the Welsh news,' Tyrell said. 'It's rained steadily in the north.'

Roly Willis was equally gloomy. 'Won't stay there long. Trouble is, there's no soakage left. All the fields are standing in water and any extra's got nowhere to go but the river. Shrewsbury, Worcester, Tewkesbury, they'll be getting the boats back out. Then it'll be Gloucester.'

'I'd better have a look at that car of Julie Parry's before it floats away.'

'Nobody saw it dumped?'

'One account of an engine noise in the night. A mother was trying to get a baby to sleep and she was tired herself so she didn't get up to have a look. She did say it sounded as though someone was having difficulty parking. Gears squeaking, that sort of thing.'

'A driver not used to the car?'

'Probably. The fact that he parked where he did does suggest knowledge of the area.'

'Not necessarily.' Roly Willis's lined face with its shrewd eyes glared at his cold tea and he pushed the cup aside. 'Kingsholme?'

'You mean rugby?'

'Why not? Regular invasion when there's a match. Bet you there're blokes all over England could walk you through Gloucester to the ground at Kingsholme – and back again. Know it like the back of their hands.'

Keith Tyrell's grin was a welcome sight in the canteen's gloom. 'Thank you, Sergeant Willis, you've made my day.'

'There'll be a break soon, lad. You've left nothing to chance.'

Tyrell was not so hopeful. 'I must have or we'd know more.'

The DI was lifting the last folder to be read when his phone rang.

'Just talked to the lorry driver boyfriend of the woman at Murren Cottage,' Brian Clarke said.

Tyrell sensed the man's elation. 'And?'

'That Friday night he was returning from Ireland. A48 back to Murren. He saw Julie.'

'He's sure?'

'Certain. He knows the car and said it was definitely the girl from the end house of The Terrace who was driving it. She was on her own and he had a clear sight of her while she waited for him to pass before she could turn right.'

'Where was this?'

'Far side of Blakeney. Julie was taking the Soudley road.'

'Not Gloucester, then?'

'Opposite direction altogether.'

'So, where was she going?'

'Apart from heading up into the Forest, you tell me.'

'At least we now know where to start asking questions.'

'It's too late to start tonight. Surely all you can do is set up the organization for the morning?'

'You're right. Call me if you get anything useful – but I must go. There's someone I've got to see.'

Chapter Four

There was no easing of the rain and night came early. Tyrell mentally reviewed all that had been set in place and had swished through Aylburton and Woolaston before he satisfied himself nothing had been neglected. Roly Willis had been left in charge, the sergeant's heavy features tightening almost into a mask of pleasure when the DI asked for his help.

'There's no one knows the area better,' Tyrell had said, 'nor the people going out to ask the questions.'

'You may be right, sir, but what about DCI Whittaker?'

'All that matters is getting results. Just make sure everything's on paper and on his desk. I know how well you get things done, Sergeant. There'll be no faults to find.'

Roly Willis was on the point of speaking but Tyrell had smiled gently. 'Putting the right man on the job – he can't complain about that, can he?'

'No, sir. Where will you be?'

'Following up an idea – at the end of my mobile.'

'If you're going Gloucester way, sir, watch it. The road could be flooded again by tonight.'

Father Andrew lived not far from Thornbury and it was why Tyrell aimed for Chepstow and the first Severn crossing. Taking that route there and back would ensure travelling on drained roads.

* * *

'Come in, Inspector Tyrell. We have met before, of course, but you were very busy that day.'

Father Andrew was not as Keith remembered him. Then, he had been a tall, ascetic figure, white hair flowing as freely as the lace-edged surplice under a long black cloak. The man welcoming him was jovial, the face still lean but relaxed, beaming, white hair tight to his head. A huge butcher's apron covered most of his length and when he turned, Keith could see a rubber band holding a ponytail of froth that gleamed in the hall light.

'You're surprised, Inspector? Not the man you thought I was?' His chuckle was a warm, mischievous sound. 'You saw me performing. Oh, it was all genuine, I assure you, but when you deal with the public you must dress the part. Take that very nice suit you're wearing. Anything less and Joe Public would lose a little of his regard for you – not bother to answer your questions in a way you would like. You, too, have learned to get what you want by costuming yourself for the part.'

The kitchen into which the DI was ushered was well lit, an Aga dominating one wall. A large table was strewn with vegetables and on a chopping board were the remains of a cooked chicken.

'Forgive me carrying on, will you? My wife is out and I promised to have dinner ready. We can talk as I work.' Father Andrew began peeling carrots. 'Nicholas Hatton said you had a query about the Black Arts – as people like to call them.'

'It seems ridiculous but it was something I noticed. It didn't mean much at the time and then I was listening to Rutter's Requiem. A word jumped out at me, crystallizing an idea.'

The cleric stopped peeling and looked keenly at Tyrell. 'The word?'

'Anointed.'

'Ah! Describe what you saw – I assume it was on a body?'

'Yes. Oil on her palms, between her breasts and on her forehead.'

'A young girl?'

'Twenty.'

A potato was picked up and lost its skin. 'Sounds highly likely.'

'You don't seem surprised.'

'At the thought of witchcraft? Do the evil things one human does to another astonish you? It's one of the tools of your job and mine, I would say. Facing the enemy without flinching.'

Coffee was poured, milk and sugar offered. As Keith Tyrell sipped, his host sliced vegetables into a large dish, added diced onion, chicken and the thickness from a tin of condensed soup. 'I cheat,' he said and turned to stow the dish in an oven of the Aga. In seconds the table had been swept clear, his striped apron consigned to the back of a chair.

'You're ready to tell me?'

Keith realized he was. Watching Father Andrew's preparation had been soothing and he had been released from the cares of the day.

'Could the girl have been involved in a Black Magic circle?'

The cleric took time to shape his answer. 'It's possible, Inspector. It would be very foolish of me to assume there are no worshippers of the Anti-Christ in this locality. Having said that, it would also be wise to admit there are those who may choose to indulge in some of the practices – secret meetings, dressing up, the odd orgy, that sort of thing. This poor child of whom you speak may have been caught up in an amateurish group dabbling in some of the pagan ceremonies – part of the DIY culture.'

'Pagans?'

'Quite normal people, most of them.' Father Andrew nodded to himself. 'Do remember there are two schools of thought – and belief. Christians, as well as those of the Jewish and Islamic faiths, regard as pagan any who refuse to believe in the one, true God – heathens, to you and me. Then there are those throughout history who have seen divinity and spirituality in nature. They see gods in the sun and stars, wind and rain, trees and rivers.'

'As well as people?'

'Of course – and in other animals. It's a form of paganism which existed long before Akhenaton in Egypt and Abraham in Jerusalem worshipped the one and only God. In the earliest civilizations the divinity of nature was revered and the belief migrated, as did those early pagans when they were driven from their lands.'

'From Asia to Europe and then to Britain?'

'You're thinking of the Celts, are you not? Of course you're right to do so – which is why I keep an open mind while I live here.'

'Because of the Forest?'

The lines in Father Andrew's face were deeply graven. 'I believe it's wise to do so. Remember, the original Indian pagans had a priestly caste, organizing worship, carrying out rituals to honour gods and the spirits of the dead.'

'Just like the druids who ruled here, across the river?'

Father Andrew nodded. 'The offering of the most precious gifts to appease gods or ask favours of them – even, it is said, the gift of life. The priests – druids – they made such gifts sacred.'

'Sacrifice.'

The Christian priest was pleased. 'You were well taught. Yes, that's what the word sacrifice means, to make sacred. Then there was the way the druids worked on their people with mind-controlling herbs and chantings – explained away as magic.'

Tyrell grinned. 'Now you've invoked Merlin. I can see your train of thought but how does it relate to Julie Parry?'

'Is that her name? Poor child. She may have been caught up in a more modern movement. Recognized religions are seen to be old hat and definitely not for the trendy. To the young, paganism has much more to commend it –

worshipping and preserving Mother Nature. After all, it's as old as time and we Christians, when we came along, merely took over some of the holidays, didn't we? Tell me, Inspector, do you watch much tea-time TV?'

'No,' Tyrell said and laughed.

'Too busy working, I've no doubt, but if you're a girl in early teens and suffering from bullies at school, have unpleasant parents, spots – or zits as we must learn to call them – you sit and become enthralled by beautiful, positive young women who pat their black cats and conjure up useful spells. Bullies are reduced to babies in wet nappies, hectoring teachers become frogs you can squash with your foot and parents are suddenly wizened old crones unable to move. These successful TV witches never have a dreaded zit, their features are always perfect, hair always shining. If that's what magic does for you, then you want some. It's not uncommon and partly accounts for paganism being the fastest growing religion.'

'Julie had a rather dreadful boss she nicknamed Mrs Satan.'

'And if she was computer literate – as so many young people are today – she may have surfed the Internet for an antidote to her woes.'

'She wasn't searching for Black Magic?'

'I think not. TV images of devil-worship and its ceremonies are frightening to the young as well as to the old – it's an essential part of those practices. When you frighten the life out of people they become subservient and do as they're told. It's a field in which politicians are experts.'

'Put like that . . .'

'I think what Julie may have encountered is Wicca.' Father Andrew spelled the word for Keith.

'Wicca?'

'It's the religious cult of modern witchcraft and legal for fifty years or thereabouts. The Forest of Dean is one region you might expect to find it. Hardly surprising really. Centuries of kings forbade churches in the Forest. If you were a peasant, poorly fed, no strength to walk to the churches which were eventually allowed to be built outside Forest boundaries, you stayed close to home and carried on as you'd always done. Wicca is really the natural progression.'

A phone bell interrupted and Father Andrew lifted a handset from the wall beside the cooker. Keith Tyrell drank his coffee and stretched long legs into comfort under the broad table. It was not easy to ignore the strong, powerful voice in the room as it argued, then cajoled and finally persuaded. With a grin Father Andrew replaced the phone and refilled their cups.

'Sorry about that – an archdeacon with his knickers in a twist. Gets very high-pitched when that happens. My wife would dose him on large quantities of vitamin B given half a chance. Your wife a vitamin freak?'

'Only when I've a cold, or she thinks I'm too tired.'

'Let her get on with it, my dear chap. A little TLC and vitamins hurt no one – and can do a lot of good. Now, this poor dead girl, any of her friends like-minded? With Wicca, I mean?'

'I don't think so. The night she disappeared she was on her own and none of her friends have any idea where she went.'

'You do?'

'She was last seen turning off the A48 towards Soudley.'

'Tell me, did she own a computer or have access to one outside working hours?'

'Yes.'

'Then the chances are that's how she made contact, or was contacted. Ah, I see by your expression I've hit a nail on its head.'

Tyrell explained the elusive website and Father Andrew's eyes gleamed. 'Really! That sort of protection comes very expensive. Hardly the set-up one would expect of a teenage nerd – I believe that is the modern terminology?'

The DI agreed. 'Nor, I'd imagine, a Forester brought up in the old ways.'

'You're looking for an incomer, Inspector Tyrell. Someone with money, computer expertise – probably someone who's bored. When did she go missing?'

'Friday evening.'

'Then he's either a weekender or he's moved to live in the Forest and works there, probably from home. Look for somewhere isolated – land around a building well out of sight and access not easily overlooked.'

'You're very sure.'

'Above all, these people need privacy.'

'Why, if what they're doing isn't illegal?'

'Secrecy is part of the attraction, Inspector, and secrets are very hard to keep in the Forest. It's one place where your neighbours could even tell you what you had for breakfast and yet you've seen no one.'

'The original nosy neighbours?'

'How do you think they've survived? They need to know what's happening around them. They need to know who is their friend and who their enemy. A website now – a means of communication without your neighbours knowing anything at all? Perfect.'

Tyrell's mental processes were sluggish and he knew he needed sleep to function efficiently again. One thought persisted. 'Why did the girl have to die?'

'It was murder?'

'She was unconscious when she went into the river and drowned.'

'I see. He may have thought she was already dead and was merely disposing of the body but if he was aware she was alive then his actions led to murder. Tricky.'

'Not when I find him.'

Father Andrew considered his guest with shrewd eyes. He liked the younger man and approved of his integrity.

'You have a hard task ahead of you. May God go with you.'

* * *

Father Andrew's advice and his blessing, aided by the strong coffee, sustained Keith Tyrell through the ordeal of a long journey in unremitting rain. Visibility was limited but the motorway presented few problems. Back on the narrower A48 approaching cars loomed frighteningly close as their drivers struggled to see the roadway.

Radio news bulletins held no hope, the list of flooded towns followed the meanderings of too many rivers. So far the waters had not yet reached the levels of two weeks ago. Total misery in the Severn Valley was in check, dependent on the volume of rain pitching down on Welsh hills.

The note was brief and bleak. 'Soup ready in the micro-wave. See you in the morning. J.'

Keith switched on the machine and watched his supper rotate on the lighted turntable. He was not hungry but after arriving home so late the least he could do was eat Jenny's soup.

She had always been so patient, so supportive of his odd hours but lately there had been subtle changes in her. Jenny's own work still satisfied her as it had always done and Keith was morose as he sat at the kitchen table eating soup. With an ongoing murder investigation and a bad-tempered Whittaker driving him to seek relief in the squash court or swimming pool each night, how could he take time off? Or even leave work early? Yet Jenny needed him, needed his time.

Time. The one thing he could not have while Whittaker and a murderer controlled his life. Keith pushed away the soup bowl with a sudden spurt of anger and creamy leeks spilled out. Moving like a robot he cleared up the mess, rinsed the bowl clean and stacked it in the dishwasher, switching it on before going upstairs to bed.

Jenny was already asleep, curled away from the emptiness which was Keith's. He undressed quickly and slid in beside her, trying to hold her. She moaned, a quiet sound, and curled more tightly, almost defensively. She did not wake and Keith had to lie apart from her, worrying himself into oblivion.

Jenny had breakfast almost ready next morning when Keith, heavy-eyed and still tired, went into the kitchen.

'I suppose I needn't ask why you went back to the station last night?' she asked as she stowed a dish in the oven.

'Just checking.'

'And making sure every scrap of paper was ready on Richard Whittaker's desk?'

'When the Devil's your master . . .'

Words trailed into silence and Jenny stopped for a moment, really looking at Keith and seeing tiredness of the spirit as well as the body.

'Can you tell me?'

The gentleness of her words undid him and he wanted to talk, to release his fears. Instead Keith could only tell her all he had learned from Father Andrew.

'Fastest growing religion,' he said slowly, 'modern paganism. Then there's witchcraft – but that's a different issue.'

'Isn't witchcraft illegal?'

'Not since 1951, apparently. The modern religious cult incorporating it is Wicca, it's what the witches believe in. It became official as soon as it was legal. Books, the Internet – anyone can be a witch.'

Jenny poured cereal into bowls and watched as Keith began to eat, slowly at first, then more normally.

'Can I put a spell on Whittaker?' she asked.

'If you think it would work, be my guest. I don't know about Wicca and witches but pagans believe all of nature is sacred – even DCI Whittaker.'

'And there's me thinking you'd found a way to turn him into a human being.'

'He's that all right but what's interesting is that pagans

believe whatever you do will be returned to you three-fold.'

Jenny was intrigued. 'So, if I do good –'

'It comes back times three.'

'And Whittaker?' she wanted to know.

'Well, when he gets his just deserts, it should be very satisfying.'

Jenny stood and cleared the bowls, then reached for the pan of eggs she had ready.

'What about you?' Keith asked. 'You had to work late too. When did you get home?'

Bending to the oven, Jenny's face became flushed by the heat as she reached in for the sausages and mushrooms. She laid the dish carefully on the table, making sure Keith had a serving spoon to hand.

'Not too late.'

There it was again, he thought, the change in her voice. Perhaps he was imagining it. Tiredness could play tricks on the mind. He had heard Jenny and her friends say that often enough.

'This girl,' Jenny said, 'you think she dabbled in witch-craft somehow and ended up murdered? Will Whittaker agree?'

'Not if I suggest it.'

'And you being you will have to tell him.'

Keith buttered toast. 'I've no choice. You can imagine his reaction to anyone spending time and effort on an idea of mine.'

'It's all circumstantial?'

' 'Fraid so. If only there was something – anything – that tied her into it but I've no hard evidence.'

'Nothing in her room?'

'No, damn it! Nor in her diary. If there had been I might have persuaded Whittaker my theory's viable. I'm sure I'm on the right track and she must have left some trace of her interest in Wicca. Why can't I find it?'

* * *

The buzz in the station quietened as DI Tyrell walked in. He was puzzled, collecting a copy of an updated report and taking it to a quiet corner to read. He could hear footsteps on the stairs and was conscious of men and women coming and going.

'Rose! Guess what?' It was Sheila Hipwell's voice. 'I saw Steve Archer last night.'

Tyrell realized the two girls had met and stopped to talk above his head.

Rose's giggle was gentle. 'Hobnobbing with the movers and shakers at HQ again?'

'Why not? Get some interesting goss that way. Especially on Whittaker.'

'What's he done now?' Rose asked.

'Nothing, that's the point. He's been sidelined.'

'Whew! He won't like that. What happened?'

'His lordship thought he'd landed on his feet when he got allocated to that security job.'

'But?'

'A very hot lady from the Protection Unit came down and said our Mr W. was surplus to requirements.'

'So he lands back here? Aren't we lucky? It'll be non-stop filling up records and cross-referencing for you and me.' Rose sounded glum.

'And with the mood I've heard Whittaker's in, DI Tyrell had better climb into some decent body armour,' Sheila added before the girls parted.

Tyrell eased himself away from the angle of the stairs where he had sought a little privacy. The conversation had been enlightening and he was glad of the warning. What he had heard still did not explain the DCI's stress levels before he crossed the county full of hope and ambition. Keith Tyrell was used to bouts of jealousy aimed in his direction, they had plagued him from his first weeks at Hendon, then on the beat in the Met. In recent weeks Whittaker's attitude had changed, become unpredictable, but his actions and the tongue-lashing dealt out to a mere

DI had a more serious root cause than envy of a younger man.

Taking a deep breath and squaring his shoulders, Keith Tyrell was ready for the day and preparing to run up the stairs when the main door was thrust open. Whittaker strode in and was as unpleasant as expected. Barking out an order that he wanted everyone mustered immediately, the DCI was impatient until he was in the room and its swing door was closing on the last entrant.

Whittaker opened his onslaught by railing at the waste of half a Canadian forest in data which told him that absolutely nothing had been achieved in his absence. DI Tyrell was held personally responsible and was in the middle of receiving a tongue-lashing when Mickey Walsh burst in, waving a sheet of paper.

'No luck yet with these, sir,' he said to Tyrell. 'I wondered if I should try anagrams?'

There was an uneasy silence and the young DC blushed and shuffled his feet. The DCI held out his hand. Mickey looked at Tyrell who nodded and, reluctantly, the paper was handed over. Battered by the atmosphere, Mickey began to retreat.

'I'll get back and –'

'You will not, DC Walsh!' Whittaker was livid, rings of white around his eyes and mouth. 'There's been enough time – and resources – thrown away already.'

'But, sir, this was what Julie was keying into when she used the computer at the cyber caff.'

'Can it be proved – without a shadow of a doubt?'

'Well – no, sir. Not yet.'

'I thought not. Get the computer back where it belongs. There's already a claim for loss of its earnings while we have it here.' Whittaker glanced at the list Mickey had carried. 'What's this? Wicca, pagan, Samain?' He read quickly. 'And Walpurgis?' The DI had Whittaker's full-throated displeasure. 'You've encouraged use of police time so Walsh can indulge himself?'

It was early in the day and Keith Tyrell was ready to

defend his actions. 'You said yourself, sir, every possible lead was followed to no effect. We – I – concentrated on what Julie's interests might have been when she was away from Murren. The cyber café appeared to be a major draw and DC Walsh has done excellent work getting the website she used.'

'You think she used.' The sarcasm was heavy. 'It's all vague in the extreme.'

'But it is a lead, sir,' Tyrell persisted. 'Remember, that last night, Julie didn't spend it with known friends and she was seen turning up into the Forest. I think it's most likely she was going to a meet connected to the website.'

'Fortunately for you, Inspector Tyrell, I read and interpret what's put in front of me. This lorry driver who says he saw her?'

'Kevin Doyle, sir.'

'Lives in Murren, shares some woman with a farmer and everything he says is gospel?'

'There's been no reason to doubt it.'

'Then find one! Julie was young, blonde and up for it. This Doyle's probably lying when he said he saw her going towards Soudley – hoping to put the gullible off the scent.' Whittaker's smile encompassed all his listeners. 'It would seem he's succeeded.' The smile was gone. 'I've told you before and I'll tell you again. The answer's in Murren. I'll have a full team back there as of now and this time, no kid gloves! Tyrell, you and Walsh can take over those robberies that've been causing problems. It's just possible there's a link to Murren and Julie got herself caught in the middle. Even you can't do much harm checking back on those cases.'

'Surely we should be helping search the Soudley route?'

'Because you've got it all organized?' Whittaker hesitated. He would have enjoyed cancelling the hunt along the Forest road but he was a good detective and knew it was a trail which must be followed. 'Sergeant Willis, carry on – but cut the manpower used. A third of the officers you suggest should be enough and we'll have the rest in Murren.'

'Sir.' Roly Willis was not pleased but he had learned, during his many years in the force, to keep his feelings well hidden.

'As for you, Tyrell, get that computer back where it belongs and grovel to the owner. You personally might have cash to throw around but our budget's a different matter. I want you full time on the burglaries – no sneaking off and using the force's time and equipment playing "hunt-the-witch". If you want to play around with that, it's in your own time and with your own computer – not ours.'

Such officers as were sent to the Soudley road worked hard talking to householders, passers-by, drivers of cars and vans. Armed as they were with photos of Julie, her car and its number plate, there was hope of a sighting.

'Nothing!' Roly Willis was as disappointed as his DI.

'Perhaps it was the wrong time to do it.'

'You mean leave it till Friday evening and catch anyone normally around at that time?'

'Why not? People with regular habits often notice something out of the ordinary.'

'It's worth a try – if you can swing it past DCI Whittaker.' Sergeant Willis was tired but he brightened at the idea.

'First opportunity I get I'll check out the route myself and see where best to concentrate what eyes and ears are allowed.'

The sergeant pulled gloomily at his chin. 'Can't see us getting many deployed next time.'

'The DCI's right. Our men and women must be used where it's most likely an answer can be found,' Tyrell said and decided a long, hard swim would be necessary that evening before he was in a fit state to go home to Jenny.

* * *

It had been a fruitless morning, driving round the area, seeing what could be seen and asking questions already answered by burglary victims. The DI was not surprised. Whittaker's team had scoured the Forest haunts of known offenders, determined to put an end to the spate of break-ins causing such misery. Men and women on the county's list of fences had been raided and turned over until they were calling lawyers and bellowing 'harassment'. The same thing happened to any man, woman or child with a record for theft. Not a single item had been recovered, even when the list of stolen goods was posted in police stations across mainland Britain.

It had been natural for DCI Whittaker to hand over a failed investigation to a man he enjoyed humiliating. With awkward questions being fired from above at regular intervals, DI Tyrell was the man he wanted to see in the firing line.

'Weeks ago you people were here and now you tell me you've not yet caught who did it?' was the reception the DI and Mickey Walsh received. Even householders prepared to admit them and talk were not enthusiastic. 'I've been through all this before – and I had to clean up the mess your fingerprint woman left,' was a chorus they began to expect each time a bell was rung and they waited for an answer.

Tyrell was courteous to each victim, learning again what he had read in the reports. No one had been home at the time of the robbery. Nothing had been broken and only easily carried valuables had disappeared. Silver had been the most usual target but the thief or thieves had been interested in any collections of ivory chessmen, jade figures, rare clocks.

Most householders had recovered from their first shock and vented their spleen on insurers taking too long to pay up what was due. Two of the more recently burgled, Arthur and Maureen Baker, were the exception. Both big and bulky in matching new leather jackets that rippled like silk, gold gleaming at neck and wrist, they were impatient to get into a waiting taxi and leave for an extended cruise. Enough time was spared to berate Tyrell and Walsh for lack of effort before the Bakers slammed out of the house and on with their holiday.

One woman stayed in Tyrell's mind and haunted him. The house burgled was in Flaxley, not far from the ancient abbey, and on a quiet road beside Westbury Brook. As he approached it with DC Walsh, the DI had seen the house was double-fronted, its paintwork and surrounding garden immaculate. He knew from the notes made on the first visit that the owner was a Mrs Flegg. She had lived there for many years with her husband, their money from a factory in Gloucester. The business had sold well and retirement began full of travelling and hopes. When he died the travelling had stopped and Mrs Flegg busied herself with voluntary work, leaving committee importance to others.

DC Walsh had been overawed by the quiet luxury of his surroundings but Keith Tyrell was puzzled. Mrs Flegg was perhaps only in her late fifties and still attractive, vibrant. It echoed in the styling of the grey hair, discreet make-up on features that still had beauty. There was no concession to age in the swirling magentas and royal blues of her skirt, the exact match of strong pink in her sweater and the contrast in the knotted elegance of a blue scarf. While the policemen sat and watched she moved slowly about the room, laying her fingers on spaces amongst the ornaments on a small table.

Mickey Walsh was restless and raised an eyebrow at the DI, wanting haste. Tyrell shook his head. He was prepared to wait until Mrs Flegg was ready to talk. The house and its mistress had a silence, a sadness, which he guessed was quite recent but there had been no mention of bereavement in the meticulous notes made by DS Penny Rogers. Tyrell sensed Mrs Flegg's need to unburden herself but it did take time.

'It was the photographs, d'you see?' she said at last. Her back was towards the two men but Tyrell knew from her voice she was crying. 'The frames were silver, which was probably why they were taken, but they don't matter. The photographs, three of them, were all I have . . .'

Still Tyrell waited. A tissue was drawn from a pocket and used. At last Mrs Flegg turned to her visitors.

'We had – have – a daughter, Verity. She met this man we thought charming. Griff had him checked out and all seemed well, no police record, good income, no existing wife – that sort of thing. They married and were very happy, especially when Verity became pregnant. That's when it all changed. Hamish took her to New Zealand but would never let Verity tell us where they were living. Christopher was born there and we never knew, not for months. Then Celia, and after her, Torquil.'

'You've not seen your daughter? Or your grandchildren?' The sympathy in Tyrell's deep voice brought a flood of tears as Mrs Flegg shook her head.

'Griff put an agency to work but Hamish had money and kept moving them. There were times I'd get an address and write.' A tissue was used discreetly. 'I never knew if Verity received my letters.'

'The photographs?' Tyrell asked gently.

'One of Verity with the three children when Torquil was born. The other two were snapshots, taken from a distance, of the children playing.'

'The agent's work?'

'Yes.' She looked down at her hands and he saw a redness flare in her cheeks. 'I'm ashamed to say that he stole the one with Verity in. I didn't mind. I just needed to be assured she was well and happy. You do see that, don't you?'

Tyrell did. A husband's extreme possessiveness featured in too many crimes he had dealt with. It was a disease which caused great suffering.

DC Walsh could be patient no longer. 'Why didn't you get copies made?'

Mrs Flegg's hand tugged at the ends of her scarf.

'I couldn't. Not even for a day would I let them out of my sight.'

Even Mickey was silenced by her anguish. Tyrell rose and went to the distraught woman. 'Believe me, Mrs Flegg, we'll do all we can.'

She looked up at him and saw not good looks and fine tailoring, official rank, only his very real concern.

'Please.'

The office was quiet and Tyrell was restless. Across the empty room Mickey Walsh concentrated on updating computer files. Until he had finished there was nothing more for the DI to do on the burglaries so he pulled a book from a drawer and began to read of laws governing witchcraft. Gradually, he became absorbed, cross-checking with the current legal boundaries and realizing what now constituted a witch, as well as the statutes governing their behaviour.

'Good book?' Brian Clarke stood in the doorway, then leaned against the frame. 'It's certainly more peaceful here if there's time to read.'

Tyrell's smile was warm, quietly welcoming, but he was concerned. The sergeant was a first-rate detective and clearly not happy.

'Something on your mind?'

'General tactics,' Clarke said. 'Everything's being pushed too hard.'

'It is a murder enquiry,' the DI reminded him and pushed a chair towards him with his foot.

DS Clarke was big and sat carefully, easing massive thighs to a modicum of comfort. ' 'Course it is – but it was a slow killing, maybe even an accident. Whoever was responsible took time to think about disposal.'

'What's your point?'

'Going into Murren like a herd of bulls in must and at the wrong gate's no bloody use!'

Tyrell waited as the fingers of two great hands were pushed through a cap of crisp curls.

'Did I ever tell you my old man was a copper?'

'No. This force?'

The DS nodded. 'Never made it past sergeant but he didn't mind. He liked people – even some of the bad ones.'

'Was he keen for you to follow him?'

'No way! He kept telling me there were too many smart alecks flooding in,' Clarke said and grinned at Tyrell. 'Didn't make any difference. This is all I ever wanted to do.'

'Today's different?'

'Not really, just typical. I mean, Murren? The place is in the DCI's mind to start with because it was handy for the burglaries, then poor little Julie lived there before she got herself killed and he's off like a ferret after a rabbit, convinced there must be a link.'

'I've tried to tell him the girl died out of the area because of her interest in witchcraft –'

'And in doing so you've given him the best laugh in weeks. You two! He's always picking on you and yet you smile back sweetly and make him madder than ever.'

'Clash of personalities?' The DI kept his features and his tone of voice pleasant. Not even to Brian Clarke would he reveal the damage Whittaker could cause to his peace of mind.

'You clash? You won't bloody fight him!'

'Of course not, he's my superior officer.' Tyrell made a supreme effort and smiled. 'I'll overtake him.'

'You've got a long wait,' Brian Clarke said morosely then leaned back in his chair. 'Yet – I don't know. The way things are moving these days.' He became more cheerful. 'I'd like to be there when he gets his come-uppance.'

'Meanwhile, I want to pick your brains on the subject of these burglaries. You interviewed Mrs Flegg.'

'Margaret Joyce Flegg. Nice lady. Very composed, very stiff upper lip. Only small stuff taken – all easily sold on.'

He frowned. 'That's the oddest thing about the whole run of these crimes. Nothing's ever floated into the market.'

'Several of you followed up the reports, I know that.'

'Apart from Mrs Flegg in Flaxley, I did the one in Littledean.'

'Out past Orchard Farm?'

'And the two in Soudley. By then Whittaker had decided Murren was a possible base but he still got permission for us to look over the shoulders of teams in other areas.'

'We keep coming back to Murren. Why does it figure so much in his thinking?'

'He sees it as a sink of iniquity. No church, chapel or shop – only a pub.'

'Ergo, all the inhabitants must be working the wrong side of the law. Does he really see it as his duty to clean it up?'

'Must do. There's not a shred of hard evidence to link in the burglaries or the murder but we had to go in mob-handed today because that's the way the experts tell us gets results – and they probably read it in some bloody book. Let's face it, all we've got in Murren is the oddest group of people you'll meet in a month of Sundays and the only help they can be is to give us the background on Julie Parry who probably died a long way from home.'

'Maximum knowledge of the victim is vital,' the DI reminded him.

'Of course it is, but pressurizing everyone being questioned isn't going to get us anywhere. The wily ones have all watched *The Bill* and know just the answers to annoy. The rest are so terrified and confused they no longer know what day of the week it is.'

'Has nothing useful emerged?'

Clarke shook his head. 'Not so far. The only inhabitants of Murren enjoying it all are those two young rips from The Terrace. Might as well lock 'em up now and be done with it – save a lot of time and trouble. Neither of 'em eleven years old and they've an answer for everything.'

'Nothing else?'

'Not worth a spit.'

Tyrell's eyes narrowed as he looked at his friend. 'Julie growing up. What's the general opinion?'

'Nice girl. Quiet, shy, didn't mix.'

'Murren – it's an odd place, odd people. You mentioned two old ladies once.'

Brian Clarke's gloom lifted. 'Miss Hester and Miss Rhoda. Nice old ducks. Penny's the one should have been interviewing them, she'd have been good. No, our Pen, poor cow, has been setting up and running an incident room in the Bothy – another of the DCI's bright ideas. Damned shame! Whittaker thinks that's all she's fit for, organizing and paperwork.'

'What about the new DC?'

'Bryony Goddard. She spent most of the day helping Penny. Her only run out was to talk to the boys – after a couple of the men drew blanks with them and their mother. It's a tragedy. Like Penny, she'd make a good fist of it – given half a chance. The DCI and women! It can't just be down to his wife.'

Tyrell grinned. 'Jenny explained it. He's afraid of being subservient to women and " 'e ain't the boss at 'ome," ' he said, assuming a very effective south London accent. 'This is how he compensates, by ensuring the women he's able to command are kept under his thumb and frustrated.'

DS Clarke swore quietly and fervently. 'Why does he have to bring his hang-ups to work with him?'

'He's got more?'

'Well, there's you, for a start.'

Across the room Mickey Walsh heaved a loud sigh and reached for another file. It attracted Clarke's attention.

'God in heaven! He's had his hair cut!'

Tyrell looked up and smiled. 'Used some of his lunch break. Whoever it was did a good job.'

'Did you tell him to smarten up?'

The DI was shocked. 'Me? Never! As far as I know it was all his own idea.'

'Get away! Everyone in the nick's been trying to change

Mickey then he starts working with you. Hey presto! He showers almost daily and gets his hair cut. Coincidence?'

'Absolutely. We've been too busy to talk personal details, in fact he was so upset Whittaker wouldn't let him finish the computer hunt for Julie's secret meeting, I've said he can use our set-up at home. It should be powerful enough.'

'Is that wise?'

A smile flickered across the DI's face. 'Probably not but it stops him using a buddy who hacks into files she's not supposed to know about. This way I can keep control and make sure everything he does is logged and filed legally – even if it is on a privately owned machine.'

'You're taking a helluva risk, aren't you?'

'I've witnesses the DCI insisted I was only to continue working on the witchcraft theory in my own time and with my own equipment. If I'd let Walsh carry on as he wanted to, all evidence he got hold of would have been banned by any self-respecting judge.'

The sergeant was puzzled. 'Why?'

'A computer user who finds "holes" in a server's set-up?' Tyrell shook his head. 'Evidence supplied by an illegal hacker doesn't stand much chance in court. A defence counsel would think he'd won the lottery. My way it can be legal.'

Brian Clarke shook his head slowly, admiringly. 'You know, you're devious enough to outsmart Tricky Dicky – God help him!'

'All I'm after is the man who slid Julie into the Severn and hoped she'd be washed out of his life for good.'

They were disturbed by quick footsteps.

'Clarke!' Whittaker was at the door, glaring at the aura of friendship he sensed and envied. 'Welsh Bicknor. Body of a young blonde washed up there. He's done it again!'

'Not strictly our patch, is it, sir?'

'The chief super's given us permission to liaise as it's obviously the same man behind it.'

Tyrell began to rise from his chair. 'Sir.'

'I don't need you, Tyrell. Carry on with the burglaries – you'll be of more use to me getting those cleared away.'

Whittaker was gone and Clarke looked at the DI.

'Go on, Brian,' Tyrell said softly. 'Keep your eyes and ears open. In particular, find out who's doing the post-mortem. That's when we'll find out if it's the same killer.'

There was little time for the DI to settle back to his book before Roly Willis came into the CID room.

'Something for you, Inspector. A call from Murren.'

'DCI Whittaker –'

'Has left the building and said you were to handle whatever came up. Funny. It could've been meant for you.'

'Go on, Sergeant Willis. Don't keep me in suspense.'

'Those two delinquents living there, they're young enough still to enjoy the odd game. With all this rain about they were digging near a stream to make a dam, then freeing the water to rush across the road when a car came.' Sergeant Willis paused, letting Tyrell imagine the scene. 'The second time they did it, bones were uncovered. Human bones.'

Chapter Five

It was a tiny skeleton and incomplete.

'Nothing changes,' Chris Collier growled at Tyrell. 'All through history unwanted babies have been tucked away where they couldn't be found.'

'And that's what happened here?'

'Your guess is as good as mine. It was obviously an irregular burial, quite shallow, I'd say, so done in a hurry.'

'Any idea how long?'

The doctor stood and was as tall as Keith Tyrell, his lean body angular with tiredness. He stripped off plastic gloves, ran long fingers through thinning fair hair and sighed.

'Sorry, Keith. Not a hope on that one. It could be any time in the last hundred years – or more. Your forensic crew will have to decide how long the poor little soul's been there. All I can do is confirm death at –' He looked at his watch, frowning, until a helpful PC aimed a torch beam. 'Thank you. 5.15 p.m. What next?'

'There's not enough light to do much more. We'll get the immediate area cordoned off. After that it's a matter of guarding it through the night.'

'I don't envy them that job.' Dr Collier looked up at the darkening sky. 'These showers are getting heavier. I'd say we're in for another soaking.' He smiled wryly at the DI. 'With all your experience with bones why don't you go for a career change?'

'To what?'

'Forensic archaeologist. You could get a posting somewhere hot.'

'You're early tonight, Matty.' In the Bothy Des Goldsmith pulled a half of bitter for the old man and placed it carefully on the counter in front of him. 'Hoping to pick up more gossip now we've got a new mystery?'

Matty Jukes counted out his coins as usual, checking each pile to make sure no extra penny reached the till. 'No,' he said at last. 'Finished me supper.'

Des chuckled. 'Did you cook it or go out for it?'

'None yer business.' Matty sipped slowly, relishing each dark brown drop. 'Were rainin' so I stayed in.'

Mervyn Walters lumbered to the bar. 'Best not go out while the coppers're around, Matty. They'd catch you comin' home wi' your meat for the week.'

'Wass it t'you?' Matty was becoming annoyed and carried his beer to a table by the door.

Stiffly, awkwardly, Mervyn followed him. 'An't you yeard? Bobbies foun' nuther body.'

Matty was distressed. 'Nuther gurl? Where?'

'They two wild young 'uns from The Terrace was diggin' and foun' bones. Babby, I yeard.'

The old man was silent as he stared at his beer.

'Not a noo one – been ther' donkeys' yers,' Mervyn said and wiggled his empty glass hopefully.

'Coupla hundred perhaps,' Gloria Reilly called to the two men. 'Old enough to be one of yours, Matty?'

The little figure stood and swayed, red rushing to his face and mottling his skin. 'Don' you talk like that! It's not like it was. Any gurl 'ad a babby then as didn' ought, 'twas the end of 'er life – and why? Cos a fools like you wi' yer mucky minds!'

Mervyn persuaded Matty to sit and finish his drink but the old man only held the glass between crabbed fingers. He said nothing as he stared into the brown depths and relived memories.

'What's got into 'im?' Gloria demanded of Des Goldsmith.

'Well, he was right, wasn't he? Whoever gave birth to that poor little bastard, it was a tragedy for some poor kid that'd last her the rest of her life.'

Des busied himself wiping the bar and collecting what empty glasses there were that early in the evening. A group of strangers in a corner had ignored what was going on but Des guessed it would all be reported and recorded in police files. He had seen the men and women going in and out of his function room since it had been commandeered by the police.

With the incident room in Murren fully staffed the CID office in Lydney was quiet, echoing.

'Do you still want me to come?' Mickey Walsh asked.

'Of course,' his DI told him. 'There's not much we can do until the path lab dates the bones. Everything else has been set in place and reports from the interviews with the boys and their responsible adults are ready for DCI Whittaker in the morning.' He smiled at Mickey. 'No need for road blocks and house-to-house on this unexplained death and as for the burglaries, that map of the area you called up and worked on saved a lot of time.'

'It was you mentioned the building work going on.'

'That was the easy part,' Tyrell said and laughed. 'Getting all the data in place was the real grind. You really do know your computers, don't you? Now, we'd better take both cars in case I get called out in the night.'

Before he drove home the DI visited Murren and spent time in the incident room, talking to each officer still on duty there and making sure there were supplies of food for the night shift. He also insisted heaters were switched on and clothing dried when the men and women guarding the tented area had their breaks.

'It's not too bad,' he was assured by one PC. 'Mrs Goldsmith's lent us a microwave and brought in some soup. She says it's home-made but I doubt it's like my mum's.'

Tyrell's laugh was a warm sound in the desolation of draughts and fading decorations. 'Home-made from a packet, I expect, but it was still very kind of her.'

Mickey liked the look of the Tyrells' home. From the gate it appeared small, simple. Only as he tailed the DI along the drive did the house seem to grow. By the time he walked in through the front door he was wide-eyed and speechless.

Keith touched his wife's hand and laid his lips in her hair, gentle gestures to keep their guest at ease. Neither had any idea how moved Mickey was by such minimal expressions of affection.

'DC Walsh, I'm Jenny. May I call you Mickey?'

She held out her hand and smiled. Mickey shook hands, mumbled something and stared at her, his eyes round, unblinking like a young owl's as it learns its world. Keith said nothing, used as he was to the effect Jenny had on susceptible strangers.

'Are we eating in the kitchen?' he asked his wife.

'Yes, and you can start the instant you've washed.'

Mickey was shown the cloakroom tucked under the stairs, the gleaming basin and toilet offset by towels as thick and fluffy as he had ever seen. Locked in privacy he smelled the soap and decided it was lavender, inspected framed cartoons dotting the wall, the subjects all strangers to him. Refreshed, he took a deep breath and opened the door.

'In here,' Keith called.

Mickey followed the sound and was in a bright, airy kitchen. Surfaces were clear of any clutter and in the centre of the room the bare wooden table had three place settings and one yellow candle in a pewter holder. He watched the

DI and his wife laughing as they lifted dishes from the stove and turned to include him in their merriment.

'You must be hungry,' Jenny said. 'I know what those canteen meals are like. All thick bread as a base and stewed baked beans to moisten it.'

Keith did not agree. 'Watch what you're saying! So far it's out and out slander – we've got very decent cooks in the canteen.'

Jenny surrendered and began serving. 'Who cooks for you at home?' she asked Mickey.

'Me?' He found it hard to answer. 'Well, me.'

'You live on your own? Then take your time and eat up before this husband of mine gets the whip out to you at that wretched computer.'

It might have been chicken he ate, and the mashed potatoes had a fluffiness and a tang never before experienced. Vegetables were like jewels on his plate and the sauce blending the meal together had Mickey and his taste buds deciding they were being spoiled rotten.

'Would you like ice cream with your tart?' Jenny asked when the first course was cleared away and Keith stacked the dishwasher.

'Please,' was all Mickey could manage.

'I'm cheating with the tart. A friend of mine gets them from the village WI market for me. Mrs Goodman makes them and she's the best pastrycook in the county.'

Jenny was right and Mickey succumbed to a second helping, allowing her to pack the remainder of the fruit and pastry for him to take home. With the kitchen clear Keith decided it was time for work.

'It's already been a long day for us all so we'd better get you started before you fall asleep,' he told Mickey. 'This way.'

In the sitting room a log fire burned and Keith switched on lamps which gave perfect illumination for anyone working at the computer keyboard. Mickey inspected the assembled parts in silence then looked up at his DI.

'This is a great set-up.' He grinned and Keith saw the

mischief of a small boy. 'Just as well you're in the force, sir. With this lot you could be a real wicked hacker.'

'Then don't show me how. Remember, what you do can be traced back to me and I don't fancy doing time because you've ordered hair dye for the Queen.'

Mickey settled himself, breathed a sigh of utter content and was instantly lost in his search. Behind him Jenny curled up in a corner of the couch with a book and Keith stretched his length towards the fire. Newspapers held his interest enough to allow the occasional doze. He stirred once to answer the phone and a message from the station. Jenny had a call on her mobile and left the room for a while, returning with flushed cheeks and three mugs of coffee.

'Anything wrong?' Keith asked, concerned by her heightened colour and restlessness.

'No, nothing,' she said and turned a bright smile towards Mickey as she put his mug near him. 'Work.'

'A problem?'

She shook her head. 'I brought some files home. Someone – was just making sure I took them back, ready for a case conference in the morning.'

It all sounded possible and Keith forced himself to let his questioning drop. Jenny never hounded him about his work and the way it intruded. Whatever was going on in the clinic, he had every confidence in her ability to cope. He began a crossword. The room was quiet now but for logs settling. The phone rang again and Keith lifted the handset. He listened, then sat up, casting aside the broadsheet and scattering its pages. Jenny looked up with an unspoken question.

'Hang on to him. I'll be there as soon as I can.' He stood and went to Jenny, leaning over to kiss her swiftly. 'It's Brian. He's in the station and has Julie Parry's boyfriend in the cells – drunk and raging. Apparently, he'll only talk to me.'

'Then you'd better go – and don't be too long.'

Keith breathed the perfume of her. 'What about Wonderboy?'

'Leave him to me.'

He chuckled. 'That's what scares me.'

Brian Clarke was surprised. 'That was quick! I thought the rain would slow you down.'

'So did I. I think it meant all other traffic was off the road while their drivers slept in front of the TV. Mind you, there were one or two unpleasant downpours.'

'All rivers around us are still on amber alert but only just. How the farmers are coping, God only knows. Livestock must be swimming around and any crops planted have been flushed out long ago – unless they've some sense and taken to growing rice.'

'That'll be the day! Now, this boyfriend.'

'He says he's her fiancé but they didn't want to tell the grandmother just yet. Chris Pewsey. Built to be a rigger, not had any alcohol while he was working, nor when he first got here.'

'What changed him?'

'A row with Julie's mum. He went out and tied one on, then started fighting anyone who mentioned Julie's name. Dr Collier's been wrapping up a few who were rash enough to tease the poor devil. They're waiting to make statements. No charges as yet and there's nothing serious – which is a small miracle considering Pewsey's size and temper.'

'You said he asked to talk to me?'

'By name. If you're in luck he's started to calm down.'

'Then I'd better see him before he gets to the next stage and falls asleep.'

The interview room had dark corners and lights directed at any individual being interrogated. Chris Pewsey blinked up at the DI as he walked in and sat down facing him.

'Good evening, Mr Pewsey. I'm Detective Inspector

Tyrell. Detective Sergeant Clarke you've already met, I believe.'

Brian Clarke carried in a tray of coffee, not in plastic cups but in solid beakers, the freshness of the brew spiralling in the still, dank air. He placed a mug in front of Pewsey and pushed a bowl of sugar towards him.

'Do help yourself,' the DI invited. 'It's a rotten night out and you've had a rough time recently. Understanding that is one thing. Tolerating you beating hell out of the male population I'm paid to protect is quite another.'

It was said in an even tone but there was no mistaking the underlying toughness in the man who spoke. Chris Pewsey straightened in his chair and glowered at the DI. In his turn Tyrell assessed the man he was to interview. They would have made a fine couple, he and Julie, Keith Tyrell decided. Pewsey was big but not puffy. Like Brian Clarke his size was a matter of bone and muscle. The difference lay in control. Brian was in full charge of his power, while this man, his head close-cropped and shining, his large features bloated with the night's activities, was a mental mess.

The DI leaned towards him. 'I'm sorry about Julie. Very sorry. It must have been a terrible shock for you.'

Startled, Pewsey blinked, unsure of the inspector's approach.

'I don't suppose you've had much time to grieve since you first heard the news. I was told you were air-lifted out immediately.'

Pewsey nodded and gazed at his hands, surprised to see he was twisting the huge fingers into knots. 'It was the flight and then the reporters. Wherever I went they were there.' He looked up at Tyrell. 'Only with Julie's gran, Mrs Hackett, could I even breathe.'

'She's a special lady,' Tyrell said. 'How is she?'

'Holding up pretty well. I suppose she's more used to it, Julie's brother dying like he did. That was before I met Julie,' he said softly and Clarke would swear afterwards he saw the glint of tears.

'Her brother, when was that?' Tyrell asked, his voice gentle.

'Just before Julie went to live with her gran. That bitch of a mother of hers said she had to get away and start a new life.'

'The father had already left home?'

'Years before. He used to send the kids presents, so Julie said. Not very often – and then they stopped coming.'

'Any idea when?'

'Julie had the last one for her fifteenth birthday. She didn't miss him. She had her gran.'

'Did Julie talk much about her brother?'

'Peter? No, but she used to get cranky if she had to visit someone in hospital.'

'That's where he died?'

Pewsey nodded. 'Tonsils. Died while they were doing it.'

A frisson of excitement sped through Tyrell but he gave no sign. 'And you were engaged? From all I've heard of Julie she was a delightful girl.'

'The best,' was all Chris Pewsey could whisper. 'I wanted us to get married straight away and have our own home but she didn't want to leave her gran – said there was no hurry.'

This time there was no doubting the tears which flowed. Tyrell pushed over a box of tissues and Pewsey took a handful, mopping his face and blowing his nose hard enough to startle Brian Clarke. At a gesture from the DI he collected the mugs and went in search of fresh coffee. It did not take long and by the time he returned with his tray Pewsey was calm.

'This evening you went drinking,' Tyrell began. 'It's not something you usually do. Why tonight?'

'That bitch, Julie's mum!' Fingers clenched into fists. 'She's selling her story to a bloody reporter and wanted me to tell 'em about me and Julie, what it was like with her. The stupid cow even said she was going to tell the papers Julie had it off with men while I was on the rig. No way would Julie do that – and her mum knew it. All she can see is how to screw more cash out the papers!'

'Did your argument get physical in any way?' Tyrell asked.

'I swear I never touched her.' Pewsey made a supreme effort to slow his breathing. 'Mind you, it's the nearest I've ever come in my life to hitting a woman. I knew if I started I'd never stop so I got in the car, the one Julie used, and just drove. I finished up here and went in the first pub I could see.'

'I gather that after a few drinks everything went pear-shaped?'

Clarke bent towards a man clearly still in a state of torment. 'What triggered the fight?'

'A little man, he followed me in. I didn't know he was a reporter. He started smiling, nudging me and asking if Julie had another man and did I know who he was. So I hit him.' Pewsey leaned back in his chair and was almost asleep.

Tyrell knew he had little time left for questions. 'Why did you ask to see me?'

'Mrs Hackett. Said if I needed to talk, make sure it was to you – you'd understand.' Massive shoulders sagged and a huge yawn almost split Pewsey's face in two. 'She was right.'

Tyrell stood. 'Goodnight, Mr Pewsey. I'll be available if you need to talk again – but there's no need to thump anyone to get here. Just ask for me.'

Between them, Clarke and the night duty sergeant helped Chris Pewsey to his feet. Tyrell had given very specific orders. The other participants in the pub brawl were to be persuaded to drop any charges as they had deliberately goaded a grieving man. If the reporter wanted to press a charge of assault he was to be reminded it was illegal to incite violence. A charge of offensive behaviour likely to cause a breach of the peace could follow.

'Something got to you in there,' Clarke said when Chris Pewsey had been bedded down for the night.

'He'll be OK?'

'Andy Nicholls has got him in the recovery position and will do regular checks through the night. As soon as Pewsey's fit to drive he'll be discharged out of sight of any newshounds and scooted off home – wherever that is.'

'Drybrook.'

'Come on, what was it sent your antennae off?'

'The brother's death. I must get it checked out in the morning as well as finding out if the Parry father is dead – and how.'

'Julie's could have been natural causes?'

'No. Whoever put her in the river made sure she died. What made life appear extinct, that's what's beginning to glimmer.'

'And I have to wait until you're sure. Well, I've got some news for you. It came through as I was getting the last lot of coffee. The new super.'

'Mortimore's successor? Whoever it is will have a job filling his shoes.'

'After all those stand-ins we've got a permanent one at last.'

Tyrell was resigned to the idea of bad news. 'Whittaker, of course. He's expecting it and he is next in line.'

Brian Clarke could not conceal his pleasure. 'Nope. Rodney Copeland.'

Tyrell was surprised, savouring the taste of it and realizing it was not unpleasant. 'He's been based in Cheltenham.'

'Tell me about it. He's on his way up and has overtaken Tricky Dicky. It won't go down well. He's five years younger than our would-be god.'

'Have you worked with him – Copeland?'

'Once. He's OK as long as you're getting results that'll stand up in court. That means helping him get his promotion. He doesn't look favourably on anyone he sees as holding him back from all that silver on a chief constable's uniform.'

'So, our DCI Whittaker must wait even longer for his next step up?'

Brian Clarke's grin was wide and merry. 'Couldn't happen to a nicer chap.'

Jenny was dozing in front of dying embers when Keith reached his home.

'Walsh's car –'

'I know,' she said. 'He wanted to wait for you and we sat talking but he was so tired. He's asleep in the guest room.'

'Did he get what he was looking for?'

'About an hour after you left. There's a pile of papers waiting for your signature.'

He riffled through the printouts. 'Great! He's done a marvellous job.'

'I'm glad. He's so anxious to please you.'

Keith was surprised. 'Is he really?'

Jenny nodded and patted the cushion next to hers. In the late evening's peace they sat companionably. She remembered Mickey Walsh at the dinner table, watching Keith's every move and copying him.

'What did you talk about?' he asked her.

'Himself. I don't think it's something he's done very often.'

Keith pulled Jenny to him. He felt no resistance and knew relief. 'Whereas you, madam, are so well trained in getting him to open up you could lecture MI5, 6 and 7 on interview techniques.'

'You're not so bad yourself and he's very interesting when you get to know him. Mother died when he was three and since then it's just been him and his father. A neighbour minded him until he was old enough for school and it must have been a bleak existence. Dad was a car mechanic, working out of hours as well as at his job.'

'Hobbling?'

'Cash in hand, Mickey prefers. Dad saved enough for his

own garage and bought Mickey his first computer when he was eleven. He repaid Dad by doing housework and keeping the books. I think he was better at the book-work.'

'Not much life for a teenager, no chance to make friends.'

'I doubt Mickey's ever had any real friends. Children who smell because they and their clothes need washing are often the loneliest on earth.'

'Then they grow up.'

'And are still lonely – until they find a reason to change.'

Next morning Jenny worked her magic and Mickey came down to breakfast showered and shaved, his teeth gleaming. Keith recognised one of his old shirts making his DC smarter than usual.

'That was good work you did last night. Well done.'

'I expect you could've done it yourself, sir. That gear's a pleasure to work on.'

'Maybe I could but it would have taken me hours – days – longer than you. You've a real talent, Walsh. I see the word was ANTEPLEC.'

Mickey grinned. 'Anagram of pentacle. It still only opens links to the website and not from it.'

'Never mind, it's a big step forward. This person signing themselves as Eostre was definitely on line at times when Julie could have been in the cyber café?'

A mouth full of cereal had Mickey nodding a reply.

'Eostre?' Jenny queried. 'Surely that's –'

'The goddess of spring? That's her,' Keith said. 'Damn it! We've still no proof it was Julie.'

Mickey watched what the DI chose to eat, the way he handled his knife and fork. Jenny was aware of the silent pantomime, Keith seeing only the adoration of his wife that shone from the younger man. Talented – and with excellent taste, he decided silently as he poured a second cup of coffee.

Rain clouds were being driven by strong winds and an umbrella was a useless defence in the early morning darkness. The incident room in Murren smelled its worst, a mixture of very stale beer and tobacco almost overladen with the must of wet clothes and decay. Discreet lighting in the Bothy's function room did not help, designed as it was to hide so many imperfections. Around the room glowing monitor screens punctuated the gloom and heightened the murk of the day.

'I appreciate it's early but I'd be very grateful for any help you can give me.'

Tyrell tried to hide a yawn as the voice at the other end of the phone line argued.

'Yes, it is part of a murder enquiry,' he confirmed. 'If you're not convinced of that please do contact the county police headquarters and check that I – and my request for information – are genuine. Do you want the number?'

He was told it would only mean extra work and what was it he wanted to know.

The DI listed the dates of admission and surgery. 'Idris Parry, aged forty-eight, died during the operation.' Tyrell paused until the splutters ceased. 'The case is not being reopened, I am merely seeking the cause of death.'

He held the phone away from his ear as the sound coming from it became too high-pitched for comfort.

'I know about patient confidentiality. Not only are we talking about a dead patient, there was an inquest. All the facts surrounding his demise are part of public record. You have those facts. I don't and I need them. Now.'

Keith Tyrell waited, unaware of movement at the door. DCI Whittaker's temper had not improved overnight. By the time he entered the incident room that morning he had been drenched by the rain and was furious so many members of his team were safely under cover. He glimpsed

Tyrell, busy at the back of the room, and marched towards him, ready to vent spleen. Intent on his conversation, the DI did not see or hear Whittaker's approach.

'I'm extremely grateful for your help, Miss Hutchinson. We've a tricky situation here and you've helped clarify it. Thank you again.'

Whittaker had no more patience. 'Who was that?'

Surprised by the interruption, Tyrell turned to see his DCI glaring at him. 'An executive of a hospital in Wrexham, sir. North Wales police were very good and got me through to the right person.'

There was an attempt to steady breathing and the flare of red in Whittaker's cheeks lessened. 'Did I assign you to investigate the baby's skeleton found yesterday?'

The DI stood and faced his inquisitor, realizing it would not help to add to the fury. 'You did, sir.'

'And you were also supposed to be working on the robberies?'

'Yes, sir.'

'Tell me, which of those cases involve the North Wales police and the NHS?'

'Neither, sir. I was following up an interview I had last night with Julie Parry's fiancé.'

Whittaker was livid with fury. 'You had no right! I specifically ordered you to leave well alone!'

'Pewsey was taken to the station in Lydney after a fight. He asked to see me and I was the senior officer on call last night.' The DI knew he had done only what was his duty and he was prepared to stand his ground.

'Morning, Richard.'

In the dimly lit arena of their battle neither man had seen the newcomer arrive. Whittaker made a visible effort to be calm and pleasant.

'Good morning, sir – if we can call it that.'

Rodney Copeland, the new detective superintendent, was tall and slender, his dark hair precisely cut and brushed above deep-set eyes which missed nothing. His glance went from Whittaker to Tyrell, while the rest of the room's occupants held breaths and watched.

Whittaker drew on reserves of civility. 'DI Tyrell, sir –'

'Keith and I met earlier.' Copeland acknowledged the younger man's presence with a nod.

This puzzled the DCI. 'Earlier?'

'Yes, Richard. I wanted to see the new crime scene for myself before all those damned TV crews and their equipment blocked the way and their reporters asked unnecessary questions. Keith was here ahead of me, seeing that the officers who had been on duty all night were relieved and had something hot in them before they drove home.' He smiled at Tyrell. 'I hope you've managed to dry out yourself. This weather's a damned nuisance and it won't be helping you get up all the skeleton.'

'No, sir. I'm afraid some of it may have been lost when the boys first started playing.'

'So that's why you extended the taped area? Well done. We don't want half the fourth estate trampling evidence in the mud, do we, Richard?' DS Copeland turned to Keith Tyrell and gave him his full attention. 'Now, this chap Pewsey. Useful?'

Whittaker would have spoken but Copeland held up a hand.

'It's all right, Richard. I had a quick look at the files while I was here.' Again, he turned to Tyrell. 'Was your suspicion confirmed?'

'Yes, it was, sir. The hospital admin had no idea Parry had any living children so there was no way to warn Julie.'

The DCI was feeling excluded. 'What's all this?'

'Malignant hyperthermia, Richard, a genetic condition. Keith spotted the possibility and it could account for the death of the first girl.'

'And the second?'

'Hardly likely,' Copeland said. 'It does add weight to the idea the second murder was a copycat killing. I think it would be best to put Keith back on the investigation, don't you, Richard? It's good to have these young people and their enthusiasm working for us, don't you agree?'

Fortunately for the DCI the dim light allowed him to recover his wits in relative privacy. 'As you say, sir, although I'm a little concerned about the cases Tyrell is already handling.'

'The skeleton? A forensic team's taking over as soon as the light permits so there's nothing for CID to do until it's decided when the child died and was buried. As for the robberies . . .?' Copeland looked enquiringly at Tyrell.

'Actually, sir, DC Walsh has devised a program which could be of enormous help. It does mean he needs time to complete entering of the data we already have as well as visiting the burgled houses to fill in any gaps.'

'This Walsh is good?'

Tyrell grinned. 'Let's just say, sir, it's as well he's on our side.'

'Then that's all taken care of. You'd better liaise with the division investigating the second drowned girl's death. Who would you choose to take with you?'

'Detective Sergeant Clarke, sir. He's a Forester.'

Copeland's eyebrows rose. 'That's important?'

'I believe it is. When Julie Parry was last seen she was driving up into the Forest. I'm certain the answers are there.'

Chapter Six

'What's your plan of campaign?'

Tyrell looked over the roof of his car at the solidity of Brian Clarke and smiled wryly. 'Get out of the rain and get out of here.'

They drove west along the A48 in silence, Clarke puzzled by the DI's frown. 'What's eating you? I thought you'd be pleased the new DS overruled Whittaker.'

'It's not that, it's why he did it I find disturbing.'

'You mean, did he do it to annoy Tricky Dicky or because he wanted to keep in with your old man?'

Tyrell was rueful. 'You see too much.'

'More than you, anyway. All Copeland did was put you in the right place to do a proper job and that's good man management. If Whittaker doesn't like it – tough. As for your father, he carries clout, I admit it, and Rod Copeland's not the one who'll offend him. He's a nice chap, your dad, although I've only met him the once and that was at your place.'

The DI almost grinned. 'I know. You've never had an appeal allowed against one of your convictions.'

Sir John Tyrell was an influential voice in the Bar Society and a regular occupant of a seat on the Appeal Court bench.

'Not yet,' Clarke said. 'No, it's not your dad but there is an old boy involved and one Copeland believes, chapter and verse. Roly Willis.'

'You're joking!'

'Didn't you have a minder when you came out of

Hendon as green as they come? I thought the Met looked after their probationers.'

'Sergeant Willis was Copeland's minder?'

'Trudged the back streets of Gloucester, they did. Roly says he knew from day one Copeland would make it to the top. As for the new DS, Roly's word is gospel. I'd guess he's given you a favourable reference.'

'But I never . . .'

'Looked for it? If you had, Roly'd have cut you down to size in seconds. Now that's out the way, where're we going?'

'I want us to follow Julie's route from the A48.'

'Where no one remembers seeing her.'

'Her car was never spotted parked there but she could have turned off somewhere.'

Clarke sighed. 'OK. You're the boss.'

'But you know these roads better than I do.'

They had travelled through Blakeney and were held by a set of lights guarding roadworks.

'Brian, see if you can get through to the path lab in Gloucester. I need to talk to Dr McBride.'

The DS was deft and his requests for Dr McBride soon met with success. Keith Tyrell pulled into a lay-by, parked, and was handed the car phone. He made his apologies for disturbing a busy pathologist but explained that he needed her advice.

'If it was Frank Broughton doing the PM you haven't a hope! Even your chief constable would have a job getting the time of day out of him. What is it you need to know?'

'The girl at Welsh Bicknor – she'd been in the Wye. There's a school of thought insists she's number two by Julie Parry's killer.'

'And you don't?' Anita McBride asked.

'No. Two deaths by the same person suggests planning and I'm sure Julie's death doesn't fit in.'

'Except she drowned when chucked in the river.'

'Granted – but I've a hunch whoever did that thought she was already dead. Her brother and her father both died during surgery, long before it was completed.'

The two men could almost hear Anita McBride thinking. 'You're suggesting malignant hyperthermia? Feasible, I suppose. Usually it's halothane causes it in theatre.'

'Could it be any other form of anaesthetic?' Tyrell wanted to know.

'I'd have to get back to references for that. Possible, I suppose.'

'What about a mixture of chemicals – gases, drugs?'

'Someone trying to get her woozy and it went wrong because she was a sitting target for MH? Could be. Enough of a fat solvent in the blood can knock out the body's temperature control.'

'Like a one-off glue sniffer?' Clarke said softly.

Anita McBride had sharp ears. 'What was that?'

Tyrell repeated the comment.

'Tell DS Clarke he could be right.' She paused. 'It might have been an accident.'

'Most likely,' Tyrell agreed. 'Will this Dr Broughton talk to you?'

'Half a ton of butter and I might get somewhere. Specifics?'

'Was oil used, if so where and what kind? Tell him as little as possible and see if his blood screening threw up any odd results.'

'Particularly volatile organics?'

'Yes – and you could try for atropine, hyoscyamine, coniine and digitalin.'

Dr McBride was startled. 'You've been busy.'

'A bit of reading up on the Internet.'

'Give me the list again so I can jot it down.'

Tyrell repeated the names of the alkaloids.

'OK, got that,' she said. 'I suppose you also want a full screening of the oil on Julie as well?'

'I'd be grateful if you can manage it.'

'And see if any bruising was similar?'

'Clothing, too,' he added.

'Pants, you mean. You know, Tyrell, if I've to go out to dinner with Broughton to get all this, you owe me!'

* * *

Matty Jukes was grumpy. 'A pint – and quick,' he demanded of Des Goldsmith.

With the beer pump working smoothly, Des glanced up at his customer, tidier than usual. 'Had a busy morning, Matty?'

The old man watched the beer rise up the glass. He kept staring until Des let the foaming head settle and filled the glass to the top, transferring it carefully to the shining wood on which Matty leaned. A careful sip, tongue rolled round lip, then a long, long swallow. With half the beer gone Matty regarded what was left and sighed.

'Bin on th'bus to Noonam.'

'Of course,' Des said, 'pension day. Was Newnham busy?'

'Like 'ell it were. They shopkeepers, by God they can whack up prices. Says it's cos so many on us use they bloody supermarkets. In't my faul' so why should I pay through me nose? Dayligh' robbery!'

Two more customers were served. Don Baldwin lounged against the bar, his lean youthful good looks hidden by years of stodgy food and long nights in bars. He wiped grease from his hands as he waited and Ricky Holder whistled through his teeth. Ricky still had a young man's clean bones, heavy in jaw and forehead, only the dullness of his expression suggesting his level of intelligence.

'God's sake! Bloody din!' Matty pointed to his beer. 'Keep a eye on it, Des. Don' wan' nobody drinkin' it – or spittin' in it. Can't trust these young fellers,' he muttered as he traipsed slowly towards the toilets.

The landlord smiled, was resigned, but Don's grease was a bit much in a respectable house. 'You don't usually end up here like that. How come?'

'Oh, I been doin' a bit to help that trucker as stays in Murren Cottage. Engine's OK but he was havin' trouble with the door release.' Don grinned. 'A bit of force and a lot of oil – sweet as a nut.' He was not making much headway, the rag he was using as a flannel merely spreading grease.

'There's soap and water in the Gents,' Des said, pleasant

but firm. 'Use 'em and you'll enjoy your sandwiches better.'

Don looked down at his hands, almost surprised. 'Good idea,' he said and began to walk away from the bar.

'And don't annoy Matty,' Des called after him.

Ricky Holder stopped whistling to raise his eyebrows. 'Why? What's wrong wi' the old bugger?'

Des shrugged his shoulders. 'Don't really know but he's been like it since the baby's skeleton surfaced.'

'Is it his?'

'No way. I heard Matty and his wife would have given anything for kids but no luck. There was no IVF in those days – not even for the rich. At least you and Don don't have that problem – a couple of walking stud farms the pair of you.'

Ricky smirked. 'If you've got it . . .'

'Where are the girls?' Des asked. 'We don't usually see you in here at lunchtime.'

'Gloucester, shoppin'. By tonight Don and me, we'll be broke.'

Claire Goldsmith pushed through the swing door from the kitchen. She carried two plates of sandwiches. 'Who're these for?' she asked her husband.

He nodded towards Ricky. 'Him, and he'd better pay for 'em while he's got cash in his pocket.'

Matty Jukes stumped back to his glass and inspected the level of beer in it with great care.

'No need to worry,' Des assured him, 'not with our friends over there.' He nodded towards a group of customers in a corner, busy eating very late breakfasts.

Matty barely gave them a glance. 'Coppers? 'Ow d'they 'ope to fin' oo killed young Julie? 'Alf the time they miss they bloody mouths!'

'What do we look for?' Brian Clarke asked when they reached the road Julie had used to go up into the Forest.

Keith Tyrell shook his head. 'I wish I knew. As of now, all I can think of is to drive where the mood takes us.'

'What're you trying to do? See if you can find inspiration?'

'Possibly.' Tyrell drove slowly, giving his passenger time to scan their changing surroundings.

'What was all that about with Dr McBride?' Clarke wanted to know as they travelled through an avenue of trees. 'Atropine – and what have you?'

'Witches used to be anointed with flying oil. I suppose it was old world aromatherapy. Foxglove, belladonna, hemlock, they were all ground up in what should be baby's fat or bat's blood.'

'God almighty!'

'I don't know if it actually worked. The poor devils probably only flew in their imaginations. Apart from suffering paralysis and delirium the witches are said to have hallucinated.'

'Keep it to yourself,' his friend advised the DI, 'or some free-thinking chemist'll be marketing it to teenagers.'

They were passing lights for roadworks, the highway already narrowed by walled banks. Above them small houses climbed the hillside.

'If she got out of her car here someone would've spotted her.'

'You're right, Brian, they would and no one's come forward.' Tyrell slowed the car. 'Tell me if you think there's anywhere she could have turned off without being noticed.'

'OK. You're the boss,' Clarke said and Tyrell increased his speed, easing up on the accelerator if there was a possible feature to investigate.

It was an attractive route, the natural scenery of the Forest enhanced by tiny gardens sculpted between rocky outcrops and colourful even in the rain. Neither man spoke as they thought of Julie and her last journey. Had she been calm or excited, apprehensive or thrilled, by the meeting ahead of her?

Only after the number of cottages had dwindled did Brian Clarke wriggle in his seat and lean forward, his gaze sweeping from one side of the road to the other. Once more Keith reduced the car's speed, sensing they were near. To what?

'There's one!' Brian said and pointed to a track leading past a modern, timbered house built by the side of the road.

The DI reversed the car and parked it on the grass verge. 'Call Sergeant Willis and see if the occupants had a visit.'

Clarke used the car phone to good effect. 'Roly's checked the reports. No sound of a car passing that evening. They were in and having a quiet supper at the time in question and would have heard any noise.'

The Forest of Dean engulfed them, rain and hanging mist a continuous curtain hiding full beauty. Centuries of royal privilege had kept the magnificence intact before navies were huge and needed three thousand oaks per ship. Then came industrialists cutting away the trees for fuel and buildings until laws ensured greedy men were stopped from denuding great stretches of woodland. Preserved at last with the trees was the undergrowth which in summer would be spiked with foxgloves and made mystical with massed elderflower and wild roses.

The DI saw a road diverging and glimpsed water. 'There?'

'Mallard Pike Lake. Don't know of any buildings,' Clarke said and marked the slip road on the map he held.

Tyrell drove on, pulling into a picnic area and switching off the engine. Clarke looked up from his map and was puzzled. 'What's the matter?'

'It's odd. I just have a feeling we've come too far.'

Clarke slowly nodded. 'Snap.'

The men looked at each other, aware of a tenuous and unseen force dictating their actions.

'Instinct's only a response to inherited memory and a mass of stimuli we've already absorbed and organized,' Tyrell said quietly.

'Of course it is. Tell me why it doesn't feel very logical?'

Clarke wanted to know as he repressed a shiver. 'Let's get on.'

With Brian Clarke using the map to give directions, Keith Tyrell aimed the car along wide highways, narrow lanes, twisting roads, turning back when one of them sensed they were travelling away from their quarry.

'Well, we've some idea where it happened or where he's holed up but one thing puzzles me,' Clarke said at last. 'How the hell do we write this up?'

'You mean, who'll believe we've been isolating an area to investigate on pure instinct alone?'

'That's easy. No one in their right mind.'

'Then let's get off the patch,' Tyrell decided and headed for Speech House, its comfortable hotel and hot soup.

It was noisier in the Bothy. A lunch break had just begun for some of the workers in the incident room and hungry police officers rushed in to feed, not knowing rumours of new developments and a press release which had just begun to circulate. They were jostled and questioned at the bar by reporters who had been waiting to pounce but each member of the county force was intent on hot food and as much peace and quiet as possible.

Baffled newsmen and women turned to the locals present but most had disappeared like mist in a wind. Only Matty remained, still disgruntled by his shopping trip and staring at an almost empty glass.

'Any idea whose baby's been found?' he was asked by a tough young woman in a trouser suit, her strangely red hair spiky.

Matty's milk-edged eyes surveyed her from the tip of her boots to her unlikely coiffure. 'Nun yer bus'ness.'

He was a tight-lipped old crosspatch, she decided, having dealt with his kind before. Like a Cairo youth responding to a tourist she began to harass Matty, trying to get him unsettled enough to let slip a useful comment or two which would keep her editor happy.

'Get out a yur, ya bitch. Leave decent folk be – an' that

babby. D'serves respec' it does – even from the likes of a 'arlot like you do be.'

It was time to get back to Murren and the incident room, both Tyrell and Clarke loath to leave the peace of the Forest and drive south. When they were back on the road Brian Clarke lifted a questioning eyebrow at his friend.

'You're more keyed into the Forest than you let on. How come?'

Keith Tyrell's smile was rueful. 'Only as an outsider.'

Clarke persisted. 'That doesn't explain this morning.'

'No, you're right. When we were little my mother had a woman in to help her. Imogen, my sister, was a baby and Jeremy and I must have been something of a handful. Lily arrived in our home and Lily was as Forest as they come.'

'Foresters don't like being away from home. What was she doing your side of the county?'

'Married a plumber. She was a stranger in the village and bored – we were light relief.'

'This Lily certainly made an impression on you.'

'She certainly did,' Tyrell said softly and smiled, remembering. ' "Call me Lil!" she used to say but my mother would have none of it. "No, Lily. They must learn to be courteous." '

Brian Clarke rumbled a laugh. 'And your mum won.'

'Always.'

The DI saw the road ahead clearly but it was haunted by a sturdy figure with a wide neck and broad shoulders, thick black hair bushing about features that might scare children if it were not for the humour and the kindness in the eyes.

'Lily was a character, no doubt of it. For hours she'd tell Jeremy and me stories of the Forest and the people who lived there. Miners cutting out land for themselves and building their homes overnight. "Squatters, they were," she'd say, "and why not? The Forest's theirs." She told us of Clearwell, its castle and its caves, the water there the purest on earth. Then there was the legend of Wintour's

Leap as well as the old stones above Staunton where people worshipped long before Stonehenge was built. She made it a magic place for us, a land where strange things happened, things that couldn't be explained.'

'She got that right.'

'When we were old enough, our parents let Jeremy and me go cycling and camping round here. Lily's brothers kept an eye on us and made us ring home regularly. Apart from that we were free to go where we pleased.'

There was silence in the car as Keith Tyrell negotiated his way past yet more roadworks.

'Lily was right,' he said softly when they were on the move again. 'It is a magic place.'

Brian Clarke gazed out of the window at the passing scenery, seeing nothing. 'Did she tell you to be careful?' he said at last. 'The old Foresters – and I don't mean the elderly, but those whose bloodline here is old – they live as they've always done.' He turned back to look out of the window as though he had said too much.

'When you say the old ways, you mean the old gods?'

There was a shrug of the massive shoulders. 'Sometimes it's not a good idea to try and ferret 'em out – whatever you want to call them.'

Tyrell turned off the main road and in seconds was parking beside the Murren incident room. He shivered and told himself it was the cold, damp air striking him as he left the warmth of the car.

'Inspector Tyrell!'

The DI turned and saw a white-clad figure approaching. Only as it drew near could he see clearly through the drifts of rain and mist. 'Have you completed your search?' he asked the forensic officer in charge of the site.

'I have. The team is just packing up.'

Eric Livermore had a moustache. Darker and more lustrous than his thin, coffee-coloured hair, it was large and neatly trimmed. Tyrell had met him often and only now realized that without the extra facial hair the man's features would be without any discernible character. He listened to Livermore's account of the hunt for the missing bones.

'The weather's made it extremely difficult for you,' Tyrell said. 'You're to be congratulated on finding so much evidence. Not much left of the wrappings, you say?'

'No, a few strands only and no colour we could detect under these conditions. A towel of some sort, I thought – tea towel rather than fluffy bath type. Probably the baby's mother didn't want to waste anything on a child she intended to discard.'

Tyrell stiffened. 'Perhaps it wasn't the mother. Whoever buried the baby, it was possibly a death after childbirth and that's always a tragedy.'

Eric Livermore smoothed his moustache, caressing it with a gentle fingertip. 'If you say so. Now, the dating of the skeleton, its age at death, all that will take time. As for DNA, I don't hold out much hope, but I do insist on taking the greatest care to be accurate and I will not be hurried.'

'Of course not,' the DI agreed. 'I would expect nothing less of you. We depend on you completely in this case and our own investigations must wait on your conclusions.'

The indistinct blob of a face twitched in a smirk. 'Nice to hear CID admit it for once,' Livermore said and strutted off to hector his underlings.

Inside the hall Penny Rogers looked up from her paperwork and smiled a welcome. 'You two have had a busy morning.'

'We've been going over the territory, getting the feel of it,' Tyrell said. He looked round the room. Most desks were empty. 'Walsh?'

'Mickey finished entering available data. He said you were right about the builders and went off to get more information. Was that OK?'

Tyrell smiled at her. 'Great. I was going to ask him to do that but the pair of you have beaten me to it. Now, the skeleton. I've just seen Livermore and he's on his way out of here. There's nothing more we can do until their lab results start to arrive.'

'Perhaps there is.' Penny handed the DI a sheet of paper she had taken from a file and he read it quickly. 'Gerry

Cross said the old man was really upset. If he didn't know the baby, it sounded as though he had a damned good idea who did.'

'What old man?' Brian Clarke wanted to know.

'Matty Jukes. Murren resident and way too old to be a suspect for Julie's death. Has no car and can't even drive,' Penny added.

'I'll go and see him when we're up to speed,' Tyrell promised. 'Bear with me while I go through what we already have on Julie.'

Penny began placing files in front of him, checking they were in a logical order. Satisfied, she returned to her own desk.

'Hey! Where're you off to?' Tyrell called to her. 'Come and join us.'

'You don't need me.'

'Brian and I insist on it. There's no one with a better grasp of detail, nor with a clearer mind to see what's useful and what's not.'

Penny did little to enhance her looks. A becoming flush warmed her cheeks and she almost smiled. 'Are you sure?'

'Yes,' Tyrell said and Clarke nodded agreement as he pulled up a chair for her.

They worked hard, file by file, until Tyrell leaned back with a sigh. 'As far as I can see, every possible contact of the girl's been checked out and double-checked. Everyone's done a good job.' He turned to Penny. 'Would you say a possible suspect's already been interviewed?'

'I don't think so. A few candidates have form and they've been put through the wringer but not even one man smells suspicious. Mr Whittaker's even been talking of mass DNA screening,' she said.

Tyrell was surprised. 'Why? There was no sign of semen or any other body fluid.'

Penny looked down at the file open in front of her. 'I think he hoped news of a compulsory survey might get someone running for cover.'

Clarke raised eyebrows. 'A bit desperate, isn't it?'

'Of course it is.' Tyrell rubbed his forehead and realized how little sleep he had had recently. 'All this time and effort and we've got nowhere.'

'What about this morning's search?' Penny asked. 'You followed Julie's last known route, didn't you?'

'Up the Dean road, yes. We drove around, looking for possibilities.'

Penny stared at the DI. 'You're still convinced she went off to meet a stranger she contacted on the Internet?'

'Too much points that way – in my opinion.'

She sighed. 'I think you may be right. How do we find out who it was?'

'Thanks to Mickey Walsh we have a trail.' Tyrell reached for a folder and handed it to her. 'I brought this in this morning.'

Penny was a fast reader. Her eyes were wide with excitement when she finished and looked up at Tyrell. 'Do you want me to get on to the server and use county clout, or would you rather wait for Mickey?'

'My guess is we'll need a warrant. It'll take time to persuade any magistrate our search for Wicca worshippers is worthwhile.'

Brian Clarke chuckled. 'Knowing you, Plan B's ready.'

'Find where he lives.'

The big man scoffed. 'That's easy. Needles and haystacks mean anything to you?'

'Hang on. This morning gave me the idea. We know roughly the area he lives in – Brian will tell you how we reached that conclusion,' Tyrell explained to Penny. 'All we need is the address of a house sold recently – the last year or so.'

'Is that all?' It was Penny's turn to be derisive.

'Leave that with me,' Clarke said. 'There's a retired builder I know who keeps an eye on all property movements in case he can put work his son's way. He doesn't miss a trick.'

'Make sure he understands we're looking for a house near water,' the DI said.

'Water? Why's that so important?' Penny wanted to know.

'Because there's so much of it in the Forest,' Tyrell said. 'Wherever our joker lives a stretch of water isn't far away. He could have wrapped and weighted the body, dropping it in any of the lakes, flooded quarries, old mine workings, and the remains might not have been found for months – years, maybe.'

'But he took her to the Severn – water a long way from any near him. Then he parked her car in Gloucester, implying she could have been taken there from anywhere, the Midlands even,' Penny said. 'I see what you mean. He was in a panic and doing all he could to lead us away from his home and water was uppermost in his mind.'

'Perhaps that's not the only reason for the river,' Tyrell said slowly.

Clarke's eyes narrowed. 'What else d'you think it could be?'

'An ancient belief – putting a dead body into water, especially moving water, helped return the spirit of the person to the underworld from which it came.'

Tyrell broke the stillness his words had caused by reaching for another file. 'That leads us to the second girl,' he said and there was busyness and rustling paper.

'Tina Halliwell,' Penny began. 'Aged seventeen. Lived in the Milkwall area of Coleford with her parents and younger brother. Reported missing on the 23rd –'

'The day after Julie was found.' Clarke's comment was almost a groan.

They looked at the photos Penny handed round. Tyrell saw she was more slightly built than Julie, her features and figure those of a child although there was, at first glance, a superficial resemblance.

'I see DCI Taverner's in charge of the investigation,' Tyrell said. 'I've worked with him, he's good.'

Clarke tapped the close-packed facts. 'Everything's been covered.'

'I agree,' the DI said. 'There's nothing I'd have done

differently. Penny, you know this data inside out. What's your opinion? Same killer or a copycat?'

She gazed steadily at Tyrell. 'You believe Julie's killing was a one-off and, knowing you, it's with good reason.'

'But?' he prompted.

'So many details from this post-mortem are similar to what happened to Julie and none of it was released to the press. The only way Tina's murderer could have known all that was if he had done the same to Julie and was following a pattern.'

'That makes sense,' Clarke said but he had seen the DI shake his head. 'You're not convinced, are you?'

'Not yet. If both girls were killed by the same man his method of killing would have been exactly the same in each case. Were they?'

Penny spread out the data, comparing the ways in which the two girls had been treated and consigned to rivers. 'Nearly dead when they went in. Julie has no injuries that can't be explained by prolonged immersion in currents. Tina had bruising around the mouth and nose, as well as on arms and wrists, but the undertow was running strongly in the Wye.' She held up photos of partially undressed girls. 'Pants on back to front and inside out. No means of identification. Then there was the oil. Like Julie, Tina had it smeared on her breast and palms.'

'As you say, Penny, many similarities.'

'Enough for you?'

Tyrell gathered up the papers referring to Tina Halliwell and tidied them away in a folder. 'Let's keep an open mind for now. After all, Tina's death is Taverner's business, not ours. The best thing we can do is find a realistic suspect for Julie's killing. Who knows? If we do, it may just as easily solve the riddle of why Tina was killed. First, we need to find a possible home for our mystery man. Maybe we can also tie the website to him – when we can slap a warrant on the server.'

Penny was glad to have something to do. 'Which of you gets the warrant on these Internet whizz-kids?'

'Brian,' Tyrell said. 'I have to go and see this – Matty Jukes.'

It was not worth taking the car. The wind had dropped and rain irritated in a steady drizzle. The DI collected an umbrella and walked along the A48 until he glimpsed Matty's cottage, almost hidden behind overgrown elders and blackthorn. Two-storeyed, it might have been built for midgets. Downstairs, small squares of windows hid the interior with ancient net while the bedroom panes were overhung by eaves. Walls had been whitewashed so long ago any caustic effect was history. Lichens, moulds, mosses, covered them in a patina of grey and green. The DI knocked but was not surprised when a shrill voice called to him from the far end of the house.

'Wha' d'ya wan'?'

At the side of the cottage was a lean-to, its door open. Matty Jukes stood half in, half out, ready to rush for cover and lock himself in. Tyrell held out his warrant card and began to explain.

'I know 'oo you are – seen you down the Bothy. An't you supposed to be in twos when you does yur nickin'?'

He was given a reassuring smile but Matty continued to glower, incongruous in such a small man barely five feet in height and with few teeth left in his jaws. A well-worn shirt and waistcoat hung around his ribs and old tweed trousers could have been wrapped twice around skinny shanks. On his feet were carpet slippers, the colours bright with their newness, while around his neck a fresh red and white kerchief hid most of the scrawniness.

'Mr Jukes, I only want to talk to you. I'm hoping you can help me.'

Matty was perplexed and a scaly hand crabbed with arthritis rubbed at the nearly bald whiteness of his scalp. 'In't that wha' they do say to get folks in the nick – then they charge 'em an' don' let 'em goo?'

Tyrell shook his head. 'Not my style at all. If you need arresting I'll do it straight, no nonsense. As I said, I'm here to talk. Nothing more.'

The DI was surveyed by eyes peering under brows bushed by age, then thinned with even more years.

'Can I come in?'

The old man turned away but he left the door open. It was as near an invitation as Tyrell was likely to get. He followed, past a row of wellingtons and shoes crusted with mud and wear, into the dimness of a scullery and its cluttered sink. An oil stove was almost a museum piece, its surface thick with dust yet still with the pinkness of paraffin in the glass reservoir.

Another step or two and Tyrell was in the tiny living room It was a warm cave, walls dark with woodsmoke and old-fashioned pictures hidden behind years of neglect. A fire burned steadily in a grate raised between two hobs, a kettle warming on one, a pot on the other.

'That smells good,' Tyrell said as Matty Jukes lifted the lid and stirred. 'Rabbit stew?'

His attempt at pleasantry was rewarded with a scowl. 'Wha's it t'you?'

'My mother makes it. She says there's nothing to beat the gaminess you get from a wild rabbit.'

The old man stared at him and Tyrell waited, savouring the smell of the room. Seldom cleaned, he guessed, if ever, but not unpleasant. There was the tang of earth, the outdoors, and the fragrance of burning logs allied to the richness from the pot.

Matty Jukes sat in the only comfortable chair, cracks and wear in the ancient leatherette covered by an old army blanket. He pointed and the DI followed the finger, moving a pile of local papers from a wooden chair which stood against the wall. Looking for somewhere to put his load he saw a treadle sewing machine under the window and stacked the papers on the top before pulling out the chair and swinging it to face his host.

'Well?' Matty was in his own home and in challenging mood.

'Have you lived here long, Mr Jukes?'

'All me life. Born yer.'

'Then you're just the man I'm looking for.' Tyrell smiled

at the suspicion he faced. 'Nothing criminal, I assure you. I just want to find out what I can about Murren in days gone by – when it was a flourishing community and trains from the Forest kept the coal coming through. You'll remember it well, I expect.'

'An' if I do?'

'Tell me about it. Your home, for instance. Wasn't it a lodge for a big house?'

' 'Til it burned. The Karchers, they ha' it then. Pulled down wha' was lef'. Drive got overgrown and it's jus' like it never was.'

'You're still here.'

'Aye. Ren' free fur life, they said. Saved 'em spendin' a penny on it – an' I weren' gonna use me savin's puttin' in th'lectric. All y'do is pay bills an' 'ave fussy folk comin' roun' meddlin'.'

'Your wife didn't mind – the electricity, I mean?'

Matty's gaze shifted to the fire. 'She were gone by then, bless 'er soul.'

'I'm sorry.' Tyrell waited again. He needed the old man relaxed if he was to garner facts from the past. Gradually, they came. Of dances in the Bothy, cider made there in wartime from apples bought from farmers or 'scrumped' from the acres of cider apples grown nearby.

'God, the Yanks as used to come then! Farm boys, they were, all togged up in they fancy ooniforms but they'd pay Josh Sawyer anythin' 'e ast for a drop o' good cider. Said it made 'em feel at 'ome . Kep' talkin' 'bout Johnny Appleseed – ooever 'e were. Mus' a bin importan' to 'em. Let 'em talk an' they'd buy cider all roun'.' His mind was back in the long ago when he was young and his wife waited for him.

'What about the girls in those days?'

'Gurls? In the Bothy? No decen' gurl'd be seen dead in a pub then! Don' you coppers know nothin'?'

'Wartime, Mr Jukes. A shortage of men round here and Murren gets flooded with fit young Americans. Are you going to tell me the local girls didn't notice?'

Matty was shocked, the sinews of his neck strained and

tense as he wriggled in his chair. 'You'm after the babby! Min' me now, you leave well 'lone. Some things're bes' lef' be.'

There it was, the unease mentioned in the report. The DI knew he must be careful. He sighed, as though regretting what he must do.

'I wish I could, Mr Jukes. If the mother's still alive and knows where the baby was buried, she must be in a state of torment. Perhaps you're right. It might have been better if the baby had never been found but it has. It's my job to try and identify it before it can have a decent burial. In this country we're all entitled to that, no matter how small and insignificant we are.'

The fire creaked and Matty leaned forward to poke it and add extra fuel. 'Decen' burial. Poor liddle mite never 'ad that fus' time roun'.'

'Did you have a family?' Tyrell asked gently.

'No such luck. Me an' my Sybil, we wan'd young 'uns. Not to be. Tried 'ard enough, tho',' he said and the DI could have sworn there was an extra twinkle in the bright little eyes.

'You and your wife would have guessed when a local girl was having a baby, especially if there was no husband around.'

'Aye, Sybil allus knew. She'd a bin good wi' babbies.'

'What about the unmarried mothers?'

'Old Doc Prichard, 'e allus knew good 'omes fur adoptin'. Nun they social workers then, muckin' 'bout.'

'No, things have changed. It's no disgrace now for a girl to bring up her baby alone but in the old days I expect there was always someone ready to get rid of an unwanted baby – at a price.'

Matty nodded, his eyes fixed on the fire as memories surfaced. 'Maggie Phillips, Blakeney way. Nice 'ouse she 'ad an' we all knew 'ow she earned it – bobbies an' all.'

'Everyone?'

'Well, decen' families, they might not 'a yeard.' He shook his head. 'You 'ad t'be in the know to get to Maggie. Sharp, she were. Like a knife.'

'I bet the gossips thought a girl in that situation was anything but decent.'

The old man's temper flared, the violence of his sudden colouring concerning the DI.

'You'm no call talkin' that way! Takes two makin' a babby an' if one of 'em's a good gurl . . .'

'Then she'd been raped,' Tyrell said softly.

A gnarled fist was shaken at the DI. 'You'm usin' dirty words! Some gurls're clean, God-fearin'.'

'I'm quite sure she was, but her rapist? That's another matter.'

'Should 'a knowed better! Right disgrace 'e were but my Sybil said 'ush up. Say owt, do owt, only makes worse.'

'Is the girl still alive?'

'Nun yer busness – comin' in 'ere wi' yer smarmy questions.'

Tyrell waited. 'Her rapist. Dead?'

'Dead an' gone t'the Devil – an' the bastard deserved it!' The old man trembled with righteous indignation.

'Was he a local boy killed in the war?'

'Tcha!' A gobbet of spittle reached the fire and sizzled.

'One of the American boys coming to Murren for cider? It's powerful stuff when it's home-made.'

'You know sod all!'

'Can't you help me, Mr Jukes? When I've written my report the baby can be buried and I can go away. If the mother's dead too, no one is left to be hurt.'

'An't there? You coppers allus bring trouble an' misery.' Matty was tired and leaned back against the grey wool and leatherette. 'Goo away an' leave me be!'

Chapter Seven

'Sir?'

'Come in, Keith.' Superintendent Rod Copeland waved him to a chair.

'There're are a couple of things I needed Mr Whittaker to see but I've been unable to find him.'

'Yes, I know. I'm afraid Richard's out of action for a few days.'

There was something in the older man's voice which puzzled Tyrell. 'I'm sorry to hear that. Nothing serious, I hope?'

Rod Copeland looked hard at his DI and saw only a genuine interest. 'Not as far as I know. I'm sure he'll be back on duty as soon as he's able. Now, what's bothering you?'

'The skeleton at Murren.'

'It's causing problems? Surely you've to wait for actual dating to be finalized before you can proceed?'

'Yes, sir. It's just that I know the baby's parentage and the mother's still alive. Putting my report through the usual channels might result in a leak to the press. I don't think she deserves that – she's suffered enough.'

'How old is she?'

'Seventy-plus, sir – or thereabouts.'

'How did you get on to her?'

'DS Clarke mentioned something he sensed in an interview at the start of the Julie Parry enquiry. Then there was a report of a minor incident in the Bothy – the bar, not the incident room. Neither was important.'

'But together they gave you a lead?'

'Yes sir. I talked to Matty Jukes first and began to have a glimmer of an idea about the mother. I tried to be unobtrusive, visiting every inhabitant of Murren over the age of seventy.'

As Copeland reached for and began to read the file Tyrell handed him, the DI had time to reflect on his visits. The first was to Murren Cottage, home to widow Dorothy Downing, her daughter, Vicky Pierce and grandson, Alex. The two women refused to be separated and faced him, identical moons of heavily powdered marshmallow, the only significant features their mouths which were matching arcs in downward curves of constant disapproval. Mention of an unmarried mother added an acid spite to the pudgy faces and this, he realized, in a home kept comfortable by Vicky's servicing of two men.

There was no hypocrisy from Harry and Betty Gilbert. They had come to live in Murren after the war and had strong views on 'all this sleeping around nowadays'. Tyrell listened patiently but they had no useful information, although some sympathy for any poor girl forced to endure an unwanted pregnancy and a dead baby.

Mervyn Walters was as cranky as ever. He had come to Murren when his caravan was emptied by a police raid and the arrest of its former owner occupant. 'Did me a favour of a sort, your lot.' As for the buried baby, 'Gals can't wait to get up the duff these day. New baby, more benefits.'

Only then had the DI knocked at the door of Point House. As he trailed round Murren he had seen a face at an upstairs window. It was some time before the door opened and the Misses Hester and Rhoda Avery invited him in.

The house had an eerie stillness. It was one in which daily habits and cleanliness mummified the air, a home where there was never a party and few visitors to disturb the habits of a lifetime. The sisters were almost mannequins in a museum of life in the fifties, grey hair and the finely wrinkled suede of their skins showing age and the passing of time. They were dignified, gracious, yet Tyrell sensed his arrival at their door had been expected and feared. Both seemed relieved he was alone.

Words had not come easily to the old ladies. Miss Hester first, telling of the birth of her child, the slow tears of old age giving ease of a kind. Miss Rhoda added, so quietly it was hard to hear her, that the baby cried when their father wrapped it in a towel from the kitchen and hurried out into the night.

Rustling paper brought the DI back to the present as Copeland pointed to a section of Copeland's report.

'You say here conception was the result of child abuse – incest, in fact.'

Tyrell nodded. 'Yes, sir. Miss Hester confirmed it, so did Miss Rhoda.'

'With both daughters?'

'Yes. It was after the birth and burial, when the father started on the younger girl, that Miss Hester hit him. Josiah Avery had come back from the Bothy reeling drunk – it was a cider night. When she heard her little sister cry out, Miss Hester picked up a heavy skillet and went for her father. He tried to run down the stairs and fell. She hit him again, then opened the front door and pushed him out. That was the last the two girls saw of him.'

Copeland found the relevant entry in the file. 'Josiah Avery, found in the river, you say here. Clothing caught on submerged metal and the tide battered him against the quay wall. Coroner recorded a verdict of accidental death.'

'Appropriate, sir. It was wartime and there was still a death penalty,' Tyrell said slowly.

'For killing the baby. Presumably by smothering it and burying it possibly still alive?'

'Yes, sir.'

The superintendent returned to the file and gave Tyrell time to remember Miss Hester and her faltering words as she told him how she had followed her father, hitting him at every opportunity until he disappeared from her sight into the Severn.

Copeland's chair creaked as he leaned forward. 'I see your problem. The CPS won't be interested, only the press in search of a lurid story. As you say, the Avery women have suffered enough.' He sat back and closed his eyes.

There was no evidence left to be recovered and used. Even the skillet had been handed over to a metal collection in aid of the war effort.

The superintendent stirred. 'I agree with you, Keith. By the time Livermore's conclusions reach us, our friends in the media will have lost interest. I'll keep this copy of your findings so nothing can leak out.' He smiled wryly. 'One good thing has come out of all of this.'

'Sir?'

'That damned incident room in Murren – a waste of time and money. The admin people are due there first thing tomorrow to clear it away. Now, what was the other matter you wished to raise?'

'Warrants, sir. Julie Parry's murder. It was while I was at the Averys' I got the link I needed.'

'Really? You surprise me.'

'It was pure chance. I was admiring their books – an excellent collection. Some are very old and deal with Forest topics. They told me Julie had been a frequent caller, taking the two of them shopping or just sitting with them. She read many of their books and they showed me her favourite – one she had borrowed on several occasions. Just riffling through the pages I could see it was on ancient rites in the Forest, including some of the more common spells and their results.'

'So, Julie really was interested in witchcraft after all?'

'I believe so. DC Walsh has an e-mail connection between Julie and someone who lives in the Forest. DS Clarke has identified the house and DC Walsh has confirmed the address from the computer link, via the server. We need a search warrant and it would be advisable if we had an arrest warrant when we go in.'

Copeland's eyebrows rose.

'Miles Kennedy, sir. Mill Cottage. There's a great deal of money been spent on the building. The owner's a single man who brought in a specialist firm from Bristol – same job at twice the price of local men. Kennedy's father is –'

The senior man was on the alert in an instant. 'Don't tell me it's Frank Kennedy?'

Financial sections of newspapers were filled with Frank Kennedy's exploits in the world's money markets. Major glossies carried photos of him socializing with the rich and politically useful, his shock of white hair contrasting dramatically with perma-tanned skin and strong black brows.

'I'm afraid it is him, sir. He'll have the highest priced lawyers on the run as soon as we walk in.'

At that time of the evening the road to Parkend was quiet, few cars to be seen. The cavalcade travelled north, then west and followed the DI's turn into a narrow lane which dipped towards a bridged stream. Only when he could see the glint of water did Tyrell pull on to the grass verge and cut the engine. Out of the car he found it was wet underfoot but at least the rain had stopped. Standing in the roadway he watched each vehicle come to rest and empty of officers, some changing shoes for rubber boots.

'A final check. I want everyone clear as to their own and each other's objectives.' Tyrell spoke quietly but his voice carried well in the damp air. A few hands were raised in salute, most of the team nodding agreement.

'DS Clarke?'

Brian Clarke patted his coat pocket. 'I've got the warrants. Keep him reading them, talking – and away from phones and computers.'

'DC Walsh?'

'Computers, sir. Make sure nothing's wiped and any memory made safe for transport.'

'Good. DS Rogers?'

'Paperwork. Every possible scrap.'
'WDC Goddard?'
Bryony's eyes shone in the headlights. 'Anything female to be logged and bagged.'
Two uniform WPCs were standing to one side, Sheila Hipwell bursting with excitement and Rose Walker calm but with a hint of anxiety.
'Remember,' Tyrell said, 'I want anything odd or out of place that catches your attention. Make a note of it. If there's time, refer to the officer responsible. That just leaves security. Sergeant Willis, the front door, if you please. DCs Cross and Baxter round the back – and watch nothing gets thrown out of the windows.'
The sound of a motorbike engine was growing louder and the DI walked towards the sound. The rider pulled on to the verge and cut the noise, parking the bike and striding to the inspector.
'Hope I'm not late.' He pulled off his helmet and silver hair gleamed.
Tyrell shook the man's hand. 'Just in time, Father Andrew.' He introduced the newcomer to his colleagues and explained that the cleric would stay out of sight unless called. 'And that will be your job,' he told Sheila Hipwell.
The DI faced the waiting officers. 'When we go into Mill Cottage I want it done as quietly as possible. There could be hidden alarms and I don't want our task hindered by half the Law Society. Right, let's move in.'
He beckoned to Roly Willis and Brian Clarke. The three of them headed the team, walking along the slippery turf edge of the lane, then the driveway to make sure no gravel heralded their approach.
It was easy to guess there had once been a much smaller building on the site. The mass of a restored mill wheel loomed wetly at the side of the architecture that went by the name of Mill Cottage. Of local stone, the walls were formidable and a soaring window marked the stairway. The front door was of solid oak studded with iron and

when the DI walked towards it powerful security lights switched on.

'Thank God they didn't put in a moat and drawbridge as well,' Clarke muttered as Tyrell reached for the door bell.

They waited for footsteps but heard none. The DI was about to ring again when the door was opened by their quarry. The sight of Miles Kennedy was an anticlimax. His file recorded him to be in his early thirties but as he stood blinking at his visitors, a thin, timid man with a weak face and floppy blond hair, he looked little more than a scared boy. He tried to speak but nothing came from between paralysed lips.

The DI introduced himself, indicating which of the solid bodies flanking him was Detective Sergeant Clarke and which was Sergeant Willis. Brian Clarke drew out the search warrant, explained its use, and Kennedy shrank back against the doorframe.

Tyrell led the way into the house and Roly Willis called in the search team. As men and women followed the agreed plan to leave nothing unnoticed, Clarke urged Miles Kennedy to help them.

'Now then, sir, you're on your own,' Clarke said. 'Do you often have visitors?'

Kennedy nodded. 'Sometimes,' he whispered.

'Men and women?'

Another nod.

'Do they stay overnight? I mean, you've got plenty of room here.' The DS looked around him, appreciating the care taken with design as well as the money spent to produce a tasteful home. 'It's a nice place. Has it been finished long?'

'Six months.'

'Who designed it?'

'I did – you can get plenty of help from the Internet.'

'So, you're a computer buff?'

Head and hair flopped a 'Yes.'

'And is that your line of work too, sir? Computers?'

'I check out things for my father.'

'That's interesting.' Clarke could be very smooth. 'I bet he has a lot of people getting paid good salaries. He needs to know they're pulling their weight – and are on the up-and-up.'

'Something like that. I keep a watch on bank accounts, money transfers – that sort of thing.'

'Very useful too, I should think. In business these days you can't be too careful and I'd guess your father's a very careful man.'

Thoughts of his father's reaction to what was happening made Miles's blood pound and he began to panic. 'I must phone him!'

It was painful to watch the man-child's terror. 'There's no need for that, is there, sir?' DS Clarke's bulk and his deep voice with its Forest echoes could be very reassuring. 'I mean, all we're doing is looking to see what's here – to help us with our enquiries. You've surely no objection to that?'

'No, of course not.'

Brian Clarke had learned to recognize people who telegraphed lies and Kennedy was one of them.

'As you can see, Mr Kennedy, no one's messing your things around. A few items will have to be taken to the station for further investigation but there'll be a receipt for everything. Inspector Tyrell's a stickler for that sort of thing.'

Miles Kennedy sat on the edge of his chair and watched the comings and goings of plain-clothed and uniformed officers. Clarke found it hard to believe this lump of human jelly was a murderer. The DI was right. Forensic evidence was vital if a jury was to be convinced such a wimp bore full responsibility for Julie's death.

Across the wide room furnished with pale-coloured sofas brightened with cushions, Rose Walker was talking to the DI. Tyrell straightened and walked to confront Kennedy.

'Some items have been found in what appears to be a

spare bedroom. I'd be grateful if you would accompany me.'

Clarke knew what it must be costing Tyrell to remain civil. It was part of the job to be polite to a suspect, aware all the time that he, or she, had been the one to cause immeasurable grief in a family. Breaking bad news was only part of the agony. Suffering with those left behind after a sudden death was never mentioned in reports but it was what put iron in the soul of all whose task was to exercise justice as well as the law.

In a bedroom at the back of the house an open drawer held lining paper, loosely covering what lay beneath. With a gloved hand Bryony Goddard lifted the paper and the contents of a girl's handbag were exposed. Tyrell was saddened by the simplicity and obvious use of objects Julie had thought essential.

'Julie's?' he asked.

'Yes. Her driving licence is there and so is an engagement ring.' Bryony Goddard spoke quietly.

'Charge him, Sergeant Clarke,' was all Tyrell could manage.

Footsteps raced up the stairs. 'Something you should see, Guv – sir.'

'Baxter! I thought you were supposed to be on watch outside?'

'I am – well – I was until Sheila spotted something and called me over. The garage. It's longer than it looks. Part of the inside's been cut off.'

In seconds the DI had men and women reassigned and by the time he was outside the house a four-wheel-drive vehicle and a sleek sports car had been manhandled out of the way. All that could be seen was an ordinary garage with its complement of skis, tools, lawnmower and pots of paint.

'I looked through the window over there,' Sheila Hipwell explained. 'The back wall seemed much too close to me for the length I still had to go before I turned the corner. That's when I called Ed Baxter.'

'Ask DS Clarke to come here with the suspect – and then fetch Father Andrew. I think we may need him.'

Tyrell waited until Kennedy arrived, handcuffed to the DS, a pathetic figure in the harsh neon light. Father Andrew stood at the door. He was a solid black mass, the flash of white at his neck and the sternness of his expression triggering a deep shuddering in a wealthy boy who had played a fatal game of magic.

'Look at the marks on the floor. I think the door may be behind that set of shelves and they pull out,' Sheila suggested.

'Photographs first,' Tyrell ordered and flashing bulbs added extra light from many angles before gloved hands began tugging at the shelves.

'That must've cost a bit,' was Clarke's comment as part of the wall swung silently towards him.

'It certainly did,' Tyrell said, 'and it was why he had to have builders from Bristol. If he'd used Foresters his neighbours would have known too much about this and he needed his privacy, didn't he?'

Torches were aimed at the darkness beyond until DC Baxter found a switch. Diffuse lights arced up black walls, creating a cave effect. It was enhanced by shimmering draperies and swathes of velvet in purple, magenta, the blue of an ocean and the green of waves edged by surf.

'Whew!' Clarke was impressed but not by the lingering aromas of incense, candles, exotic perfumes that reached him. 'We could do with more light in there.'

'I saw a portable light on the way in,' DC Baxter said. 'Won't take a minute.'

With stronger illumination shadows disappeared, taking with them an aura of the occult. Even through the narrowness of the doorway they could see five-pointed shapes in paint, metal, wood. A huge silver one marked the floor, others hung on the walls.

Father Andrew was impatient. 'Can't we go in?'

'Not yet.' The DI had a strange sense of panic but it was an emotion coming from outside him. He faced Miles

Kennedy, the smaller man twisting away, avoiding the sternness of Tyrell's gaze. 'Was it here she died?' he asked softly.

White-faced and panicking, Kennedy was pathetic. 'I never killed her! I didn't!'

'There's a pile of robes, or something similar, in there. Were you all naked?'

Almost in tears, Kennedy was holding on to the shreds of his dignity. 'It wasn't like that.'

'Like what?'

'An orgy. We just wanted to be clean – pure. Julie used a bathroom upstairs and robed there. When we met . . .'

The DI waited but the weak man was lost for words. 'You burned incense. How many types?'

It took time for understanding to penetrate Kennedy's misery. When it did he opened his eyes wide with surprise. 'How did you –'

'Tell me,' Tyrell said, his firmness an order.

'Three.'

'The anointing?'

Miles Kennedy had been so proud of his cleverness, his ability to conceal all facets of his existence from ignorant neighbours, yet his home was filled with strangers who knew every detail of his life. 'Who told you?'

Tyrell's face was an expressionless mask. 'Where're the oils?'

The finger pointing to a corner cabinet carved in a church style was almost steady. 'I don't know why but it was soon after that Julie collapsed. No one touched her – she just sighed and went down in a heap.'

Tyrell acted swiftly. 'Penny, get Forensics here. No one is to go in until they've cleared it. Brian, you and Sergeant Willis get Kennedy to the station. I'll interview him as soon as I can – and he'd better have that lawyer.'

Before anyone could move, car wheels screeched in the driveway and doors banged. Gerry Cross could be heard challenging a newcomer and there was a brisk exchange before DCI Taverner and his DI, Bob Vidler, marched into the garage. Taverner was grim-faced, his manner urgent. A widower in his late forties, he was stocky and fit, the grey in his hair not reflected in the speed with which he worked.

'I hear you've arrested someone for the first murder. I need to talk to him – now!'

Tyrell was not to be hurried. 'I'm sorry, sir. I have to clear this case before I can hand him over to you.'

'You don't understand, man. I'm in overall charge in DCI Whittaker's absence and it's not just about Tina Halliwell I want to question him. Another girl's turned up – this time in the Severn. She was seen floating just below Gloucester and this Kennedy could have done it.'

The interview room in the Lydney station was clammy, corners dark, with Miles Kennedy slumped in a chair, his choice of solicitor at his side. Ray Sumner was more used to conveyancing and contracts in the city of Bristol. His knowledge of criminal law was rusty and he knew mistakes would never be forgiven by the client's father.

Two hours passed in a steady stream of questions. There were times when Tyrell had difficulty extracting an answer, then DS Clarke would become avuncular, coaxing Kennedy to help himself as well as the police.

'Best you do,' he would say. 'Tell us what you know – everything – and we can begin to get things sorted out for you. Don't you agree, Mr Sumner?'

Between them Tyrell and Clarke had all they needed by the time Kennedy was exhausted and tears not far away. The recorder was switched off, Kennedy and Sumner given their choice of tapes.

'Is that all?' Sumner asked. His bald head shone with sweat and he was longing for a stiff whisky.

'As far as I'm concerned,' Tyrell said, 'but DCI Taverner is ready to talk to your client.'

When Miles Kennedy heard that he laid a tired head on folded arms and heaved as he sobbed.

Tyrell hoped the lawyer was functioning more normally. 'You must understand, Mr Sumner, two more girls have been found in remarkably similar circumstances to Julie Parry. It's possible your client was responsible for those deaths –'

'No! I never!' Kennedy said, startled out of his despair. 'Julie collapsed – I never meant to kill her!'

DS Clarke leaned over the young man, the planes of his face grave. 'But you did put her in the water while she was still alive.'

The DI was equally stern. 'The friends who helped you may have told someone who copied what you did – they may even have done it themselves.'

'No! They'd never! And we made a pact not to tell anyone what happened. I've given you their names, isn't that enough?'

'Whatever you agreed to then is no longer relevant,' Tyrell continued. 'DCI Taverner's in charge of investigations into all the murders and he must have all the information you can give him. I'd advise you to hold nothing back. Nothing at all.'

The two officers left the room while Ray Sumner bent over his client. In the corridor outside DCI Taverner was impatient.

'Finished? About time! I thought you'd gone soft on him, all those cups of tea you kept sending out for.'

'We've cleared up all the outstanding points on Julie's death. It wasn't planned but almost immediately someone became aware of details which meant he could appear to kill in the same way.'

'Copycat? Surely not! First choice must be Kennedy.'

Tyrell shook his head. 'Not necessarily. One of his little helpers – or anyone they told.'

Clarke held out a sheet of paper. 'Names and addresses of all those present that night – and you could do with taking in some tissues, sir.'

DCI Taverner was not amused. 'This is serious, Sergeant.'

'I agree, sir, but he does cry a lot, Kennedy, and Mr Sumner's run out of dry hankies.'

As Taverner thrust his way into the interview room, followed by his DI, Tyrell and Clarke heard Miles Kennedy start to wail. They had little sympathy for him as they made their way to the CID office. Penny was waiting for them, the smell of freshly brewed coffee welcoming.

'Any developments?' Tyrell asked.

'Forensics have been busy. They've done all they can tonight and your Father Andrew will be over in the morning to give you his findings.'

'Pity. I'd have liked to see him tonight.'

'We had a little chat,' Penny said. 'He has a pretty good idea how you work.'

Tyrell raised his eyebrows. 'So?'

'We guessed you'd want to call on Mrs Hackett tonight.'

She was calm, resigned, sitting by her fire in a faded blue woollen dressing gown, the frill of a brushed cotton nightdress below her chin and her hair combed ready for bed. Mrs Hackett waited for Keith to speak.

'We have a man in custody,' he said at last, tiredness biting into him.

Breath was released slowly, tension ebbing from Julie's grandmother. 'You've worked hard, lad,' she said gently. 'I knew you'd never give up on my girl. Tell me, there's one thing I have to know. Did he say how she died?'

'She just crumpled. He thought she'd fainted. That was all.'

'She didn't suffer?' Her eyes were intent on him, demanding the truth.

'No,' he said and she believed him. 'Julie would have known nothing.'

Mrs Hackett lay back in her chair and closed her eyes, difficult tears edging the lids. The room was quiet as the DI waited.

'Has he got a name?' Her voice was shaky.

'Miles Kennedy.'

Mrs Hackett blew her nose and discreetly wiped her eyes. 'A family?'

'Only his father. He's a very wealthy man.'

'Was,' she said and her mouth was grim. 'Wait till that daughter of mine hears about him. She'll sue him for every penny he's got.'

Next morning Mickey Walsh was exhausted and Tyrell concerned for the young DC still sitting in front of a computer.

'Did you get any sleep?'

'Not a lot but it was worth it.' Mickey grinned, a weary effort. 'I remembered what happened last time with DCI Whittaker, so I copied every disk and CD we brought from Mill Cottage as well as what I could get out of the hard drive. Yes, I remembered what you said and logged everything properly.'

'Anything of interest?'

This time Mickey was fully awake when he smiled. 'That Kennedy's like a squirrel with its nuts – hides the best in the oddest places. Look at this.' He handed Tyrell sheets of paper from the printer. 'Just done it. All the correspondence about the robes they dressed up in. Best washable velvet, apparently, and that file was in the middle of dealings an office of his father's in Bristol had with one in the Cayman Islands. There're even bank statements.'

It took a few seconds for Tyrell to realize all the implications. 'Mickey! Do you know what you've got there?'

'Legal access to Dad's monkey business? Little Miles has stitched him up good and proper. I think Junior accessed transactions and bank accounts he wasn't supposed to know about.'

'You're saying young Miles was hacking into his father's private dealings?'

'On a regular basis, judging by the dates. It seemed to be

his hobby – that and chasing up every Wicca reference on the Internet. There're e-mails to and from everyone in sight on that subject.'

'Julie?'

'She's there but she wasn't the only one. You know, sir, Miles was real canny when it came to who he invited to Mill Cottage. For Julie it was her first visit but the others there that night, they'd been before. It's all recorded.'

'Thank you, Mickey. You've worked wonders. Now, go home and get a good sleep.'

'I'll be OK, sir. I'll get a shower downstairs and I've a clean shirt in my locker.'

Someone in a corner gasped and Bryony hid her face behind the buff cardboard of a file.

'If you're sure.' Tyrell was not happy but he knew better than to curb a genuine enthusiasm.

'You see, sir, there's something odd about those Cayman Island transactions.'

'Odd?'

'I do my dad's books for him – have done for years – but that's tiddler stuff compared to what's in these accounts. They don't feel right.'

'Anything specific?'

'I'm not that good an accountant but I know what figures should look like when they balance. Some of these . . .' He shrugged his shoulders. 'It's just a hunch and probably useless.'

'Not at all.' Tyrell had heard rumours Kennedy Senior sailed close to the wind and a fraud squad from the City of London force had been investigating him until budget demands pulled them off the case. 'Keep a record of everything you do – and I mean everything. Get my signature, or DCI Taverner's, on your reports and remember, you're officially checking all computer data found at a crime scene as part of an ongoing murder enquiry. Anything you notice must be logged properly. By the book, Mickey, or we'll get one thrown at us.'

* * *

It was the same smell, astringent, antiseptic, its undertones bearable. Missing was any sign of workmen, not even hammering and drilling in the distance.

'You're early.' Anita McBride was trim and fresh, green working clothes crisp and red hair glinting in the bright lighting.

'Mr Copeland would've been unhappy if we'd been late,' Tyrell said and smiled. 'As it was Brian driving, there was no chance of us dawdling. You know Sergeant Clarke, of course.'

'Old friends,' the pathologist said, 'especially when the floods keep us busy.' She looked down at the girl on the table. 'Is this part of a pattern – or is the Severn having the last laugh again?'

'We need your conclusions to answer that one,' the DI said. 'I understand she's been identified.'

'And confirmed. Stepmother came in this morning with DCI Taverner. A hard bitch, I gather – the stepmother – but she had reported the girl missing.'

'Which is why, when a body surfaced, Superintendent Copeland asked us to be here for the post-mortem.'

'To see if there's any connection with the Parry girl or if what we find today is more like the findings Broughton made on his cadaver from the Wye. Right, let's get on. Karen?'

Quietly, efficiently, Dr McBride's assistant wheeled instruments in place and adjusted the height of the microphone hanging from the ceiling. Pete Coombs lifted his camera and took the first shots of the dead girl as the pathologist prepared to itemize the body's outward appearance.

Clarke was intrigued as Tyrell bent and scrutinized the girl's face from different angles. The DI shook his head at Dr McBride's unspoken question, then he stood back and watched Karen remove a tight-fitting plastic jacket. It looked the worse for wear, although its bright cyclamen colour was unaltered by immersion in a swollen and muddy river. The flimsy cloth of a short black skirt was torn and the silver top she wore was minus many of its sequins.

'Michelle Mary Watts, liked to be known as Shelley. She lived in Bream,' Clarke read out quietly from the file Taverner had left for them. 'Aged twenty-three.'

Tyrell was surprised. In the limpness of death which defied age the girl looked older than twenty-three, harder. She was a blonde but not as Julie had been. The roots of this girl's hair were dark and her features were sharper. Lines in the skin revealed she frowned a lot, perhaps smoked often and might have had, while alive, a restless, angry expression when she was on her own.

Clarke continued to read. 'Mother cleared off when Shelley was thirteen. Father did what he could. Married again five years ago and his new wife has a daughter of her own.'

'I don't suppose that pleased her,' Tyrell said quietly, making sure their comments did not disturb the doctor and her work.

'Shelley can't have been interested in school,' Clarke read on, 'she left as soon as she could. Had odd jobs at first then worked in bars as soon as she turned eighteen.'

Tyrell was thoughtful. 'She'd have been in contact with a lot of men.'

DS Clarke's frown deepened. 'And we'll have to check 'em all out.'

Karen had finished removing the clothes and was parcelling them in evidence bags, taking care with the labels. Anita McBride continued her commentary, noting slight bruising around nose and mouth, as well as under the arms and on the wrists. Fingernails had been long and enamelled a dark purple but several were broken and the pathologist carefully excised any material that remained underneath. Oil on the girl's breast and on her palms was noted and samples for lab analysis were sealed and labelled.

'Any sign of sexual interference?' the DI wanted to know.

'Outwardly, not recently – no bruising caused by rape, if that's what you're after.'

'Then there's no sexual reason for her death.' Tyrell knew that had not been the motive for Julie dying, nor in the killing of Tina Halliwell.

'For that conclusion you'll have to wait until I've finished,' Anita McBride snapped at him.

Except for a phone call from the pathologist it was a silent journey back to the station and to Copeland.

'Well?' The superintendent was not waiting for the courtesies.

'Again, similarities to Julie's death but there're stronger links to Tina Halliwell's,' Tyrell said.

'Such as?'

'Bruising round nose and mouth and on wrists, finger-nail damage – all these were absent in Julie's case. Then there's the patch of oil on the forehead. So far it's only been found on Julie, not on Tina or Shelley. The oil on the last girl is probably different to the one Kennedy used. It was so for Tina.'

Copeland leaned back in his chair and studied Tyrell. 'More evidence for your idea that Julie's death was the trigger and the other two girls died in copycat killings?'

'Yes, sir.'

The superintendent noted Clarke standing beside the DI. 'What about you, Brian? Do you agree with Keith's theory?'

'It makes sense of some very odd facts, sir.'

'So, who's carried out the last two murders? Have we got some poor inadequate roaming at night or a freak who bays at the moon?'

'Neither, sir,' said Tyrell. 'Whoever he is, he's clever.'

'Not Kennedy?'

'No, sir. Way too spontaneous and yet practical to be him.'

'Is the motive sex?'

'I would say not, sir.' The DI hesitated. 'But this new girl, Shelley Watts. She was pregnant.'

'Oh, my God! The press'll have a field day!' Copeland's mouth tightened but he gave no other sign of his annoyance. 'They've already labelled the deaths the River Murders. Now they've an unborn baby to salivate over.'

'Apart from the baby angle, they're right – for once,' Clarke said. 'Each of the girls, including Julie Parry, was finally killed by river water.'

Tyrell was thoughtful. 'And each one from a local family. Julie from Murren, Tina Halliwell from Coleford and now Shelley Watts from Bream.'

'The link between the girls is the Forest, is that what you're saying, Keith?'

Both Tyrell and Clarke were nodding agreement when there was a knock at the door and Penny came in carrying a sheet of paper.

'Sorry to interrupt you, sir,' she said to Copeland, 'but I thought you'd want to see this.'

'A missing person report?' He glanced through it and then began to read aloud. 'Fay Ryder. Last seen 9.30 p.m. yesterday evening when she left friends in Lydney early to get a bus back to Whitecroft.' Copeland reached for the phone. 'We'd better have a river watch – catch him in the act.'

Tyrell shook his head. 'Too late, sir. My guess is she's already in the water.'

Chapter Eight

Two days passed and Fay Ryder's body had not surfaced.

The incident room which had been set up in the Lydney station for the investigation into the deaths of Julie, Tina and now Shelley was a hive of activity day and night. Extra men and women, CID and uniformed, had been drafted in to help as every possible contact of Shelley Watts, however trivial, was listed, interviewed and added to the growing mass of stored files. Alibis were constantly checked for the time Shelley went missing and rechecked for the dates Julie and Tina had last been seen.

Superintendent Copeland and DCI Taverner became familiar faces on TV as they explained, calmed and promised what they could. Reporters and TV journalists were irritants as were the constant phone calls, faxes and e-mails flooding in. Most offered sympathy, help even, but too many were messages from cranks and wasted the time of fully stretched men and women.

A sense of grim urgency pervaded the workrooms, the canteen, the locker rooms. Every officer was aware that when Fay Ryder's body was finally located, not even a whiff of a lead in the earlier murders must be left unnoticed or unchecked. Co-ordinating the mass of data that poured in made computer use vital. Burglary enquiries had been put on hold and Mickey Walsh commandeered to help find patterns in the results of such hard work. The information amassed had been fed into a database, along with the hope that electronic wizardry would isolate one individual to be targeted if Fay Ryder was found and proved to be another of the 'River Killer's' victims.

'Nothing!'

Superintendent Copeland was as tired as everyone else working on the cases who had gathered in the incident room. The county had lost too many young women and he was determined the River Killer would be caught before the casualty list in the Forest grew. DCI Taverner had spent every possible hour in the hunt for the abductor and murderer of Tina Halliwell. He was a good detective and added the Lydney team to his own, working from their station, to locate the killer of Tina, Shelley, and possibly now Fay Ryder.

'We do have a list of sorts, sir,' DCI Taverner said. 'It's long, I grant you, but everyone on it's worth another visit.'

Copeland agreed. 'Can we make sure that before anyone knocks on a door this time round, they've read reports on the previous visit?'

'Good idea, sir,' Taverner said, nodding. 'We could send one officer who's been before plus a new face – fresh pair of eyes and ears, as it were.'

'Good thinking, Nick.' Copeland smiled at him and then turned to the large team at his disposal. 'Now, has anyone got an idea we can use?'

DI Bob Vidler was a young redhead, quick and determined. 'Isn't it about time we had a really fresh approach?' His voice carried well and heads turned. 'We've a list a mile long and maybe our man's not even on it. What about using a profiler?'

'To tell us we're looking for a nutter?' someone at the back of the room scoffed.

Tyrell was ready to speak when the door opened on DCI Whittaker. Copeland waved him to a seat.

'Good to have you back, Richard. We can do with your input. You were about to say, Keith?'

'Just to agree with the idea of a profiler – but one who has some experience of the Forest. What works in a city isn't necessarily useful here.'

Whittaker did not look well but he began to enjoy himself. 'Back on the old hobby-horse, Tyrell? This time it's the Forest of Dean and only you understand it?'

The DI felt himself flush. 'Not at all, sir. I don't know the Forest that well – few people do. All I was asking for was a profiler who was one of them.'

Whittaker's smile was the kind given to small children who mean well. 'The old obsession, Tyrell? Getting to know the locals? In my experience a serial killer is the same wherever he operates. This one'll be no different.'

The DI's head went up and his eyes were angry. 'Perhaps not, sir, but the territory in which he's operating is unique. If we're to catch him –'

'You're both quite right, of course,' DS Copeland said, his smoothness an attempt to defuse the situation. 'Let's keep in mind the fact that when Fay Ryder disappeared, Miles Kennedy was in full view of many of the officers here today. It adds weight to the argument for two killers – one for Julie and one for the other girls.' He turned to Whittaker. 'We must remember, Richard, it was Keith who persevered with Julie Parry's interest in witchcraft and that's what gave us Miles Kennedy. Perhaps we should allow him a little leeway?'

Whittaker gave no hint of inner fury. 'Of course, sir.'

'As to a profiler,' Copeland continued, 'what we personally want is irrelevant. HQ will decide which of these great minds they will employ – as they undoubtedly keep a weather eye on the cost.'

'Time for a quick one?' Clarke asked Tyrell.

'Yes, I have, as it happens. Jenny's working late again tonight.'

'They keep her pretty busy at that clinic but I suppose,

if you're off your head, day and night don't mean much and the staff have to work accordingly.'

'Something like that.' Keith Tyrell smiled pleasantly, hiding his own disquiet. At first Jenny had been happy to be so involved with her patients and the running of the institution able to help most of them back to a normal life. Lately, she had begun to look drawn and tired, doing little more when she arrived home in the evening than slide into bed and fall asleep in an instant.

The DI did not often stay on for a drink after work but he was learning to relax and enjoy the company of his colleagues. Clarke roped in Mickey Walsh who protested there was one more thing he must chase up.

Tyrell would have none of it. 'You need a break. Come and join us. The first one's on me.'

'You'll be sorry you offered,' Brian Clarke said with a grin as the group in the station's local grew.

Penny Rogers and Bryony Goddard were slumped in their chairs and looked exhausted. Mickey had persuaded Rose Walker to join them and Sheila Hipwell was determined not to be left out.

Pleased with his impromptu party, Clarke leaned on the bar, and watched Joe, the barman, cover a tray with bottles and glasses, lifting it effortlessly as Tyrell sorted out the notes to settle the bill and leave a respectable tip.

It was a pleasant half-hour or so, everyone's stress easing with the effect of alcohol and good companionship. Bryony eyed her DI.

'Bet you wish you were back in the Met and getting some real excitement.'

Tyrell chuckled. 'Don't you think we've got enough here to be going on with?'

He was persuaded to talk of cases reaching London's courts and entertained them with wry accounts of small-time criminals longing to be seen as feared gangsters.

'None of the real sort, then?' Mickey asked.

'Plenty, but the top brass like to be seen up against those

– can't have a lowly PC – or a DC – getting one of the big boys sent down.'

Brian Clarke gazed at what was left of his ration of beer. 'So, nothing different up there, then?'

'Nothing.' Tyrell looked at his watch. 'I'd better be gone or I'll be in trouble at home.'

'Me, too,' Clarke said and drained the one glass he had allowed himself. 'Brenda will be ready to get my guts in a state to hold up my socks.'

The car park outside the pub was dark, wet, quiet. Brian Clarke faced his friend. 'You've something on your mind. To do with the job?'

'I don't think so.'

'Jenny? A workaholic like you and a wife as gorgeous as Jenny, best not take her for granted. There's always some bastard ready to move in on the gap you leave.'

'No, it's nothing like that,' Tyrell assured him, almost too quickly. 'I think I'm being followed.'

'Think? If it's got to that state, you're damn sure. Any ideas?'

Tyrell shook his head. 'It's being very well done – expertly, in fact.'

'Reporter? You must have had them dogging you before this. They can sniff out which member of a team is likely to get results and they keep him, or her, in their sights – ready to be on hand for a scoop.'

'Yes, I've met them.'

'And this isn't the same?'

'No. It feels – personal.'

'When's it happening?'

'Finishing a shift.' Tyrell paused. 'A couple of times when I've left the station the hairs on the back of my neck start waving.'

'When does he disappear?'

'I don't know he does but I'm sure it's a he – the driver's outline in headlights when another car overtakes the pair of us. Once I turn off the main road to go home, the tension disappears and so does he.'

'That could be because Jenny's waiting for you.'

'Or that he knows where I live and doesn't need to track me any further.'

'Look, don't take this the wrong way. Could he be working for Jenny?'

Keith waited a moment before answering. 'I don't think so. If Jenny was worried about anything she'd have asked me straight out.'

'I'm sorry, but in the job you get to see and hear too much at times. Coppers' wives sometimes wonder if husbands really are working late. Even if that's why they're not at home, the girls're considered fair game by chancers after a bit of a challenge. See a woman left alone too often – it's very tempting to some men.'

It was what he feared and Tyrell had started to wonder about the extra phone calls Jenny had been getting on her mobile at home. Always, it was confidential clinic matters and must be dealt with out of his hearing, she told him.

'Who's got it in for you?' Clarke asked. 'Apart from Tricky Dicky?'

'No one I can think of.'

'Could someone have followed you down here from the Smoke?'

'Why? I was small fry. Who'd bother?'

'Well, you know what you've got to do. Get everything logged and recorded. I'm off home.'

Both men ducked into their cars as the falling rain increased in severity. Clarke was the first away, Tyrell following more slowly. He was deep in thought and did not see his sergeant's car tucked away in a side turning. A small two-door runabout edged its way into the traffic behind the DI and Brian Clarke tailed it, keeping his headlights dimmed. Only once did he allow himself to be directly behind the suspect car and then for as long as it took to get the registration number.

'Gotcha!' he said out loud before swinging away to Brenda and his supper.

Jenny was tired. Her day had drained her of energies of every kind but she saw Keith's distracted air and greeted him with a smile.

'Pooh! You smell of a pub. Hope you haven't drunk too much or your meal's wasted.'

He explained the customary 'quick one' after work and his orange juice, Jenny laughing as she scooped dishes from the oven.

'And you feel you must stand your round now and again so they don't think you a stingy old miser?'

'You're right. I'd rather be on the squash court or on my way home but it's got to be done. I have to get to know them outside working hours.' He helped set out plates and glasses. 'They're a good crowd so it's no hardship.'

Jenny mounded casserole, rice, vegetables on his plate and Keith saw the swirl of colours which appetized almost as much as the aromas being released. Automatically, he forked and ate the food in front of him, the warmth and flavours unloosening knots. Gradually, Jenny's words, her smile, added their healing and he was happy. She was as she had always been.

Jenny waited. Something was wrong but she knew he would tell her what worried him when he was ready. The normality of clearing away dishes and preparing for the next day helped and they settled in front of the fire, the dishwasher humming and thumping in the distance. Keith read the day's papers, began the *Telegraph* crossword and threw it aside. For once his mind was not geared to cryptic clues. He reached for the remote control and switched on a news programme but Jenny protested.

'Not tonight, darling, please! It's enough getting doom and gloom all day at work without having bright-eyed presenters getting excited about the latest set of horrors.'

Keith was contrite. She spent so long listening to the

worst of things one human being did to another, draining ghastliness as a surgeon drains an abscess, until the patient was free to talk about a dreadful life often enough to expunge fears and experience healing.

'Was it that bad a day?' he asked.

'No worse than usual.'

He watched the flames of the fire until his eyes ached. 'Tell me,' he said at last, 'do you get any patients who become possessive about the person treating them?'

'Not often. The director's very hot on that – which is why we're all monitored regularly. The first sign and she switches therapists.'

'So they don't get a hang-up on one of you and start haunting you as soon as they're released?'

'It has happened in the past – years ago. That's why we follow the new regulations.'

Keith sank back against cushions and felt stress ease a little. If he was being followed it had nothing to do with Jenny. She, in turn, now knew the reason for Keith's tension.

He was being stalked.

By 10 a.m. next morning the news reached all corners of the station. Fay Ryder's body had been found in the Severn. Sighted downstream from Gloucester, the girl had been pulled from the water by a police launch, the men and women on duty sickened by the damage.

In the pathology lab CID officers gathered and were silent.

'This won't be an easy one,' Anita McBride said as Pete Coombs' camera clicked and whirred.

'Did chummy do all of this?' DCI Taverner wanted to know.

'I doubt it,' she said and bent to look at the wreckage of an arm. 'I'd say the body was trapped in massive debris of some kind and then wrenched free by the extra-strong currents of floodwater coming downriver last night. It's amazing the face has so little trauma.' Dr McBride stepped back and viewed the body. 'Perhaps the Severn's angry at being used this way.'

As well as DCI Taverner and his DI, Bob Vidler, Tyrell and Clarke were there as witnesses. Anita McBride had no objection, providing they all kept out of her way. Tyrell bent close to the head of the girl, inspecting it from one side and then walking round to view it from the other. Only Anita McBride knew why he did it and she waited until he had finished. He shook his head and the pathologist continued her task.

The post-mortem followed the pattern of the others the DI had witnessed recently. No identification in the clothes, pants on inside out and back to front, Anita McBride's silent nod towards him as she scraped palms and between breasts, the scrapings carefully labelled and put aside for further investigation.

Clarke's anger exploded as soon as they left the lab. 'I don't know about the river being angry. I'm bloody furious! This bastard picks up some poor kid, half kills her and then dumps her in a river to finish the job and let him get clean away. Who the hell does he think he is? He's not even got the twisted morals of a Jack the Ripper – wiping out fallen women. These are young kids, pretty girls with their whole lives ahead of them.'

Tyrell understood. Brian and Brenda Clarke had daughters and what was happening in the Forest was every parent's nightmare.

'Two things we know for certain,' Tyrell said slowly when they were back in the car. 'Kennedy was only responsible for the first death – Julie's – and the others aren't as a result of a leak from the station.'

Surprise lifted Clarke upright and slewed him round in his seat to stare at the DI. 'What did you say?'

'Only Julie had oil on her forehead and it was sweet almond oil. On the other girls that patch was missing.

Forensics identified what was used on Tina and Shelley – cooking oil. It was light but it could fry chips. I'm betting what was on Fay's from the same batch.'

'OK, you've explained three of the murders are by a copycat – with details not released to the press. Then you say reliefs in the station might have been involved?'

'Possibly. In the last three cases what was missing was that third area of oil – on the forehead.'

'And the type of oil used. That means . . .'

'Whoever passed on the information could only have done so on day one of the Julie investigation. It was the next day I remembered seeing the gleam of oil on Julie's forehead and asked Dr McBride to check. By then Tina was already missing.'

'How can you be sure someone in the job wasn't in on it?'

'At first, I couldn't. Then we got ready to pick up Kennedy. A lot of people were involved in that sortie and the whole thing was complex and long-winded. It's possible someone was talking out of turn –'

'Or was even the murderer.'

'Agreed – but then the mystery man or woman would also have known when Kennedy was in custody, or under surveillance at the very least.'

Clarke frowned at the logic of the situation. 'You're right. Whoever abducted and murdered Fay didn't know. He's been trying to get all his murders landed on Kennedy. By killing Fay when we could all give Kennedy an alibi, he gave himself away.'

There was silence in the car as they drove along the A48 towards Lydney.

'Whoever it is must have had access to the first PM report,' Clarke said at last.

'Any one of us could have read it and talked – or it could have been leaked from the path lab. Don't forget there were workmen there doing a big rewiring job at the time,' Tyrell reminded him.

'Shouldn't they be chased up?'

'All in hand. They're from a Gloucester firm, so that CID has the checking out to do. So far, no luck.'

'You kept that quiet.'

'I went to Copeland about it. He set it up, with Taverner's approval. No one else was told in case the mole was "in house", as it were.'

'You couldn't trust me?' Clarke kept his voice deliberately calm.

'Of course I could but it's how Copeland wanted it. We were trying to protect you, you know.'

Clarke was stung, hurt. 'Gee, thanks!'

Only when they were on the steep descent into Lydney did Brian Clarke clear his throat. 'Sorry for that. Who else is left?'

'Karen Boyd.'

'McBride's assistant? But she's as professional as they come! Why her?'

'The day I phoned Dr McBride to check for the extra patch of oil she said she was short-handed. Later, when I wondered how the copycat got his details, she looked up the records for me and explained why. Karen lives at home with her father and he's riddled with arthritis as well as incapacitated by emphysema and minus both his feet. She had the day off to take him for a scan.'

'Who did she tell?'

'That's what we don't know. Karen has a boyfriend, a charge nurse in the hospital. He's married, has children, and was definitely at home or on shift in his ward on all relevant dates for the disappearances of the victims.'

'So what happens now?'

'That's up to Copeland. Gloucester's had a whisper a Yardie gang's planning to move in so any more work there, it's up to us.'

'Whew! If there's a turf war –'

'Dr McBride'll need to take a sleeping bag to the lab. She'll have no time to breathe,' Tyrell said.

* * *

No one did. Every man considered a possible for the killing of Fay Ryder was systematically interviewed and a fresh crop of names, addresses, alibis, added to the mass of data on the computers.

'If your theory's right, Keith, whoever this bastard is he won't kill again.' Copeland prowled his office, stopping only to look out of the window at yet more rain. 'I want him so badly I can taste him! He's out there, on my patch, laughing at me like some damned hyena.'

Tyrell refrained from telling the superintendent hyenas did not as a rule kill their prey, they merely disposed of them. He rolled the idea round in his mind. They might kill when strongly motivated by hunger but was there a human hyena killing because it was driven by another urge? Not sex, that had been proved at all the post-mortems. He closed his eyes and remembered Jenny talking of human emotions. Love, hate, fear. Fear?

'Was he afraid of one of the girls?' The DI was surprised when Copeland, Taverner and Whittaker turned to him. He had not realized he was speaking aloud.

Copeland was interested. 'Go on, Keith.'

Tyrell was tired and it seemed to take a great effort to express his idea logically. 'He could have been scared of one of the girls, maybe for some time. Then, when he heard how Julie died, he copied the method of disposal.'

'Different river,' Whittaker pointed out, annoyed his DI was getting so much attention.

'It might not matter to him,' Tyrell said, 'not if one river was much like another to him.'

Taverner was interested. 'Are you saying Tina Halliwell was one of those scaring him?'

'It's possible. Or she could simply have been a trial run after he heard about Julie.'

'We went through her entire life with a fine-tooth comb,' Taverner said. 'There was nothing – nobody.'

Whittaker was restless. 'And yet an innocent girl like her can pose a real threat. Suppose she'd been sexually assaulted in some way, maybe years ago, then promises to reveal all to us. She's a girl who'd have been believed. By him and by us.'

'Good point, Richard.' Copeland nodded. 'If it is possible some of the girls could be – window dressing – as it were, we must still tackle each murder as though the girl in question was the intended victim and not one picked at random.'

'What about Kennedy's money?' Whittaker asked. 'Could the father have bought similar murders to confuse the issue? From what I've heard of Frank Kennedy's less attractive habits, I'd guess he's quite capable of doing something like that.'

'Then he must be researched too,' Copeland decided, 'although I gather he was incandescent after his son was arrested. One would have to assume it was the first he'd heard of it and he's never struck me as the kind of father who'd do what he could to protect the boy. Himself – yes.'

Tyrell leaned forward and caught Copeland's eye. 'Excuse me, sir. Kennedy Senior could have been upset knowing we had access to his financial dealings. He'd pay well for a smokescreen to cover those.'

Copeland stood. 'It's time we had outside help. I'll get on to HQ. Budgets apart, it's time we had the best profiler available – one who understands the world of mass money. Perhaps he – or she – can get us out of this morass.'

'Where're we going?'

Clarke was curious, having seen Tyrell laughing and smiling as he used his mobile, making notes, then clipping the phone shut as he marched back to the car.

'Yorkley Slade. That's why I needed you with me. Your directions will get me there quickly.'

'Why are we going there?'

'HQ will send us a well-qualified idiot – as far as the Forest's concerned. They may know all there is to know about men driven by greed for cash but it's not enough. After all, what is a profiler?'

'The ultimate expert who teaches us all to suck eggs?' Clarke said with a grin.

The DI chuckled. 'You're not far wrong on occasion. No, it's not only someone who has knowledge and experience, they must have instinct as well – and that doesn't come from books and seminars.'

'The last one we had was a psychologist – most of 'em are. What about your Jenny having a go?'

'No way! She can take her job to heart too much. I wouldn't like to turn her loose amongst some of the evil minds we have to deal with.'

'Don't you believe it! Jenny's a tough one.'

'Not in this case.'

He swung the car round a steep bend. Jenny had been preoccupied before he left home. There had been another call to her mobile and she had left the kitchen to talk in private, coming back to the breakfast table flushed and pensive. He could not ask the question burning on his tongue, even if it tore him in pieces.

'I want someone with a thorough knowledge and understanding of Forest ways,' Tyrell said when the road straightened out.

'The old ways?'

Tyrell nodded, his eyes on a sharp curve ahead.

'Then watch yourself. You don't know what you're getting into.'

'That's why we're off to see my original guide to the Forest – Lily. I rang my mother for the address. Which way now?'

'Turn left at Nibley Green.'

Tyrell concentrated on the twisting highway, with only an occasional glance at homes and gardens climbing steep hillsides.

'It always puzzled me why people chose to live on such sites but Lily explained it was the only way they could ever get a home of their own in the old days. If they could find a piece of land and get a house built, furnished, and a fire in the hearth, all between sunset and sunrise –'

' "Raisin' the smoke", they called it,' Clarke said, lapsing into the distinctive Forest idiom. 'Didn't matter what your job, who you married. Enough friends and family and you'd got a home for life.'

'There'd certainly be plenty of stone around for the walls and chimney.'

The DS grinned. 'Especially if you were a quarry worker and took a few home in your bag every night from the waste tip.'

'Wood from the trees –'

'Lying there just asking to be picked up.'

'Furniture?' Tyrell asked.

'A bed, a table, stools, pots and pans, some blankets. Made or gathered over weeks and months, it was enough.'

'A couple would have found it hard to do on their own.'

Clarke nodded sagely. 'Round these parts your friends and family are what mattered. Still do.'

The house was almost in Yorkley Slade. On the edge of the village, it was one of a handful of homes built on flat land with sizeable gardens at the back. Once a small, low-roofed home, it had recently been enlarged, an extra storey added and a garage built on the side. Local stone had been used and the solidity of real slate defied the weather. Whoever had planned the alterations had kept the spirit of the old homesteaders but a gentler hand had shaped the garden.

'Someone's spent a few bob,' Clarke decided as they waited for the ring of a door bell to be answered.

When it was, they were regarded with great suspicion. 'Yes?'

Tyrell smiled at the woman. He knew her to be almost seventy but she looked younger, her hair thinned and whitened by age not framing her face as harshly as it used to. Her body was more frail than he remembered, yet she had an air of youthfulness and Keith could see that her pale green shirt and slacks were expensive.

'Good morning, Lily. I need your help.'

She stared at him, puzzlement succeeded by dawning pleasure. 'By damn! It's young Keith. Come in, boy. Come in! Haven't seen you since your wedding.'

He kissed her cheek and was hugged fiercely in return, smelling her perfume.

She ushered them into her home. 'God, I've missed you boys – and that whippet of a sister of yours. What's young Imogen up to these days? Your mam said she was in London – and who's this you've brought with you? I thought a copper's big as you could manage without a keeper.'

Brian Clarke was introduced, calm under Lily's intense scrutiny of him. Finally, she nodded.

'Sit down, the pair of you.'

They did as ordered, Tyrell wondering why the room was so familiar. Eventually, he realized it had been decorated and furnished much as his own mother had done at Dakers. He was begged for all his family news and only when Lily was satisfied that she had extracted all she could, did she remember her duties as a hostess.

'Big lads like you must be parched. Tea do you?'

She refused help and the two men were alone. Tyrell was restless and wandered round, inspecting framed photographs covering a small table.

'Good God, it's us! I remember that photo being taken.'

Clarke went to peer over Tyrell's shoulder. Mr Justice Tyrell still had hair in those days and was sitting cross-legged on the ground, his daughter's arms round his neck. A younger version of the judge was pulling a face at the photographer and the DI, aged about ten, was busy making sure his mother's wrap was in place.

'Mum and Dad had given Lily a camera for her birthday. This was the first shot.'

'Best I ever took,' Lily declared from the doorway. The tray she carried was laden with tea, cakes, biscuits. 'Come on now. Get this lot down you and tell me what it is you want.'

They were grateful for the refreshments but Keith Tyrell did not waste time. 'It's these murders, Lily,' he said as she passed cups of tea and urged food.

'I guessed it would be, they've affected us all. Young Tina's gran and me, we were in school together.'

'Double View?' Tyrell asked, his voice gentle.

'You remembered! Aye, she was a nice enough girl, Betty Pedley. Fair, she was – like Tina. Bit simple but kind. Married a 'lectrician from the mines so their kids were a bit brighter. Then there's that new one.'

'Fay Ryder.' Clarke gazed at his plate, still seeing the mangled body on the pathologist's table.

'Ryder,' Lily said slowly. 'It was when I was away with you lot a Jack Ryder come here from Bristol. I only know that 'cause he married Phyllis Bromley from Whitecroft. She's auntie to my Bernard's wife – you remember? Bunny, we used to call him. He's got his own business now, very respectable.'

Tyrell remembered. He was fascinated by Lily's ramblings but he was there with a purpose. 'We've got to get him, Lily, this killer. That's why I'm here. He lives in the Forest, moves around as though he knows it well – and yet . . .'

'You don't think he's one of us?'

'No, but he's using the Forest for his own ends. Tell me, is there someone I can go to who knows as much as there is to know about this area? Not just the roads and the waterways, the mines and the quarries, but the ways of the Forest.'

Lily's right hand crept along her left arm, stroking it, soothing, reassuring. 'The old ways?'

'Yes, Lily. Will you help us? Please?'

'I warned you about this years ago.'

'I know, but this killer must be caught. If I've got to take risks, then I will.'

She turned to Clarke. 'You're from round here, can't you make him see sense?'

'I wish I could.' The sergeant's voice was rich with Forest warmth. 'It was only two days ago we saw Fay Ryder's body. Not long before that it was Shelley Watts, and earlier Tina Halliwell was hauled out of the Wye. We'll both do anything to get the man responsible. Can you help us?'

'I can't.' Lily's anguish was almost tangible.

'But there's someone who can?' Tyrell asked.

Fingers twisting together revealed the state of her mind. 'I knew him when we were growing up.' There was a wan smile for her 'young Keith'. 'Not Double View. He was cleverer than me and went to the grammar school at Cinderford. East Dean. He didn't want to go away from the Forest like the others.'

Keith Tyrell crouched in front of the woman who was fighting tears. 'Take me to him, Lily. If not for my sake, then for the families of those dead girls. We all owe them.'

A silence in the room grew, was almost a movement, became calm.

'I'll give him a ring,' she said.

Tyrell held his breath while Lily made contact and began to talk. He turned to speak to Clarke and saw his friend was staring out of the window, then realized he was intent on the half of the conversation that could be heard. Lily had lapsed into a strong version of the Forest dialect and, for Keith, it was a language he had difficulty in understanding. By concentrating, Brian Clarke could follow what she was saying and there came a time when he relaxed against the cushions of his chair.

Lily came back to them. 'He'll see you now – and I'm to come with you.'

* * *

They would never have found the house without her help. The DI had envisaged an old cottage deep in the Forest so the modern bungalow beside a main road came as something of a surprise, as did the man who opened the door as the three of them walked up the path. A retired headmaster lived in Tyrell's home village and this could be the man's double. There was the same spare figure thickened with age, neatly trimmed grey hair and shrewd eyes which missed nothing.

'Lily! Good to see you again. God, it was dull when you were over the other side of the county. What made you marry a man from there? Weren't any of our boys good enough for you?'

'I came back when my man died, didn't I? That should be enough – even for you, Lawrie Grundy.'

They were gestured into the house. It was comfortably furnished and there were books in every possible nook and cranny. The man held out his hand to the DI. 'You must be the "young Keith" she's told me about.' He looked enquiringly at the sergeant and Tyrell introduced him. 'Clarke? You've the look of Bob Clarke.'

'My father.'

'Ah! He was a good bobby. You lived near here as a youngster.'

'When my father was stationed at Bream.'

'So your school would have been Lydney. Rugby player by the look of you.'

Brian Clarke grinned.

'Always good at sports, Lydney boys – and girls,' Lawrie Grundy conceded, 'specially hockey. Rugby too, when Ted Parfitt was coaching you – or was that before your time?'

Talk of old matches, old players continued and the DI knew, as did his sergeant, that the old man was using questions and answers to allow him to judge Brian Clarke. At last he glanced at Tyrell, then back at the man whose father had been a respected member of the police force in the Forest. What signal passed between them Tyrell could not see but he sensed he had been accepted.

The DI had to be sure there would be no misunderstandings. 'You realize there're some things I can't talk about – part of police confidentiality?'

Lawrie Grundy nodded. 'Let's see what we can do,' he said and gently, insistently, he questioned Tyrell and Clarke, much as an official profiler would have done. When he was quiet again the old man sat at his ease, elbows on the arms of his chair and his fingers steepled in front of him. He gazed at their tips, then slowly began to tap them together.

'Of course I've read the papers and followed the cases as well as I could. What you've told me today makes clear many things. You want me to tell you about this man?'

Tyrell nodded.

'You agree?' he asked Clarke.

The sergeant was less sure and stared at Grundy for what seemed an eon. At last there was a sigh of surrender. 'I agree.'

'Firstly, it is a man. A strong woman could have carried out the acts but the recurring pattern was wrong for that. The man you seek is not one of us.'

'You mean he's not a Forester?' Tyrell asked.

The grey head nodded. 'He knows the roads and the byways well, he's used to driving along them. I would say he has a powerful car and he likes it to be recognized – to show how powerful he is – but that's not the car he uses when he gets rid of the bodies.'

'How do you know?'

Grundy smiled. 'Like him, you don't see the eyes around you as you go about your business. Foresters want this man caught. If he'd used his expensive car to get rid of the girls, he would have been seen and never known he was being watched. No, for that job he must have the use of a car so nondescript it passes without notice, perhaps at night when the number plate is difficult to read and remember.'

'Hardly the kind of car to inspire confidence in a young girl on her way home.'

'Quite right, young Clarke. You tell me the girls have all been picked up when going home from an evening out, so he knows the night life of the Forest. It could have seemed perfectly innocent, a generous man at a bus stop, outside a bar or a disco, offering a lift away from the incessant rain.' The angles of Grundy's facial bones sharpened. 'Innocence? It's like a magnet to a man such as him. He's like a stoat, rustling in the dark, waiting to hypnotize his victims.'

The words were soft, sibilant, and a coldness crawled over the patch of skin between Tyrell's shoulder blades.

'You need to look for a man who can charm easily and has the appearance of being a nice, cheerful, responsible individual with a good make of car. That's the only kind of man these girls would have trusted. They may even have known him or, at least, known of him,' Grundy explained. 'Even when he first made contact he must have had ready a vehicle no one would bother to notice and a way of moving the girls from one to the other in private. Yes, he's interesting. I'd say he has money and he's made it since coming to live here. Almost certainly he's married but he doesn't like women – thinks them objects he can use and discard.'

Tyrell was curious. 'Why does he kill?'

'To protect himself. He would think quickly, act quickly to deal with what he saw as a threat to his own safety, maybe even the safety of his money. Whatever his motive, the girls had to die.'

Tyrell was frowning, puzzled. 'Are you saying all three threatened him?'

'I doubt it. Most likely one did and the others were to make it difficult for you to catch him. He took their lives to save himself. He's wrong, of course.'

'Why do you say that?' Tyrell wanted to know.

'Because you and Bob Clarke's son are clever men and you'll find out who he is.'

Clarke had been a silent witness to the conversation but now he stirred. 'That's not all, is it?'

Grundy's smile was a rictus that chilled his guests. 'No. He lives in the Forest, he's made his money here, yet he despises us – all of us. Many have done that, laughing at us behind our backs and to our faces. He's one of them but it was he who took our girls and ended their lives.' Grundy aged as he sat there, then became ageless. His face was a stern mask and his eyes hardened, glinting like granite. 'For that he must answer to us as well as to you.'

The DI was uneasy. 'Vigilantes, Mr Grundy?'

'We do have our own methods but they've nothing to do with the half-baked ideas outsiders have as to what goes on in the Forest. I've heard fools talking about inadequate idiots prancing round in horned masks and damn all else.' His smile chilled. 'Yes, and I've heard the other stories. Naked virgins and chicken innards tossed artistically to reveal omens. Or perhaps you prefer the version in which half-witted females chant spells and get so high on drugs they drive round on broomsticks?'

Tyrell hid his reaction and Grundy became serious.

'I'd guess, Inspector, you go to church?' Grundy saw the DI's nod and almost smiled. 'When you walk into a cathedral do you feel the full force of all the hopes and prayers built up through the centuries in the air and the walls?'

Again, there was a nod.

'Then see the Forest as we do. It's a city filled with cathedrals, a hundred or more, and each one created not from walls but from living, breathing entities – the trees. So, Inspector Tyrell, you pray in your cathedral and we'll pray in ours. After all, we're praying to the same God and we want the same thing.'

'Do we, Mr Grundy?'

'Oh yes,' the older man said softly. 'We both must have justice but you rely on the courts and fickle juries.'

'And you, sir? What do you rely on?'

Grundy's smile did not reach his eyes. 'Evil, Inspector. The evil in a person's heart. When any man desecrates the Forest and its people, the evil in him earns its own reward.'

Chapter Nine

Lily was a silent passenger. Tyrell drew up at the door of her home and she stayed in her seat.

'When you were a nipper I used to tell you to leave things be. You and Jeremy – no more sense than you were born with. Both of you, you had to know. Still, no more'n to be expected, the dad you had – and your mum. Sticklers for the truth, no matter what. It's the right way but it can be dangerous. Your friend knows.'

Nibley Cross was negotiated and the DI settled to a steady speed. 'Was she right about the danger?' He had to wait for an answer.

'My dad told me about a case he was on once,' Brian Clarke said at last. 'A bad one. A girl of twelve was raped so savagely she was badly damaged. Never have children.'

'Oh no!' Tyrell groaned. 'Did they get him?'

'Not really.'

The sergeant stared through the side window seeing nothing as Tyrell turned on to the A48.

'He was born here – the rapist,' Clarke said as rain started and wipers swished. 'He knew the Forest like the back of his hand, knew how to hide. Dad said they had police, tracker dogs, miners off shift. Every man who could turned out to hunt him, women too. Days went by, then he was found face down in a stream but nobody would touch him. Dad was called and only when he got there was the bastard pulled out. It was Dad who had to turn him over.'

There was a drench of heavy rain but they were soon through it.

'It was the look on his face. Dad said he'd never seen anything like it – nor wanted to again. Sheer terror. It turned out at the PM he hadn't drowned, as they thought. He'd been frightened to death.'

'Who? How? There must've been evidence. Tracks? Footprints?'

'Not a thing.'

They had reached Lydney and the traffic was noisy.

'Are you trying to tell me Lawrie Grundy, or someone like him, did that to the rapist?'

'Dad said it was best not to ask.'

'There you are, Tyrell. Wondering where you were. Job for you.' DCI Whittaker was pleased with himself. He looked better but there were still signs of strain in his eyes. 'A name's cropped up in Murren – of course it means travelling now instead of having the convenience of an incident room on site.'

'Yes, sir. Who is it?'

'Leanne Sullivan.'

Tyrell remembered her. 'She lives in a caravan with Don Baldwin.'

'Thank you, that much I know.' The DCI was not a patient man. 'We turned it over months ago when the burglaries first started – Baldwin's got a history of thieving. As I recall, Leanne's housekeeping skills weren't up to much but she's been listed as a former colleague of Shelley Watts. They worked together in a pub just outside Cinderford. We need background and we need it fast.'

'Yes, sir. Any links to the baby's DNA turned up yet?'

'No, damn it, and no likely candidate's run shy at the idea. Go and see what names Leanne can add to the list. You'd better take DC Walsh with you. He needs to get out from behind a computer and see what proper investigating involves. All that software's no good without viable facts to be fed into it.'

DS Clarke waited until Whittaker began to move away. 'I'll get on to that flash car – start with Bentleys and work down.'

'What's that?' Whittaker had sharp ears and swung back.

'Just a thought, sir. Each of the girls was picked up after a night out. A decent car and plausible driver would have persuaded them it was safe.'

'Excellent thinking, Sergeant. Get on to it at once and use any help you need. You may find DCI Taverner's team has a file of sorts. It'll be a start.'

As he marched away Brian Clarke grinned at Tyrell. 'And you've got Mickey. I could've done with him clicking his mouse for me – we'd have been finished in half the time.'

Murren was wet and unwelcoming. The DI parked as near as he could to the caravan and hurried to knock on its door. Mickey Walsh ambled over to where Don Baldwin had his head under the bonnet of a car, its rust patches painted with anti-corrosive.

'God! Not you lot back again?' Leanne Sullivan stood in the doorway, masking a gust full of nappy odours overlain with cigarette smoke and the stench of stale lager.

Tyrell had had worse greetings in his career and smiled pleasantly. 'May I come in? I need to talk to you about Shelley.'

'That poor cow. I s'pose so.'

Leanne led the way into the cramped space of her home. It was tidy enough and not obviously dirty; Tyrell guessed that ventilation was difficult in cold, damp weather when you lived in a metal can. Leanne herself was clean in a red sweatshirt and blue jeans, her fair hair shining and held back by a rubber band. A makeshift playpen was against one end of a built-in couch. In it and above a large dummy a baby stared at him, its dark eyes hardly moving.

The girl eased the bulk of her pregnancy round a table covered with a brightly patterned cloth. 'D'you want a cuppa?'

'No, thank you. I don't want to disturb your day for long but we do want to get whoever it was killed Shelley.'

'Wasn't it this River Killer? I thought you got him?'

'No. The person responsible for Julie Parry dying is waiting to be tried but Tina, Shelley, and now Fay Ryder, we believe, were abducted by another man and finished up in the water.'

'So he is a copycat? The paper said so.' She pointed to a discarded red-top news sheet on the couch.

'It seems so. It's essential we find out if the girls he chose were picked at random or whether he could have had a motive. That means finding out all we can about them.'

'Like you did with Julie?'

'Yes. It was by studying her life we managed to find the man who put her in the river.'

'I liked Julie and Mrs Hackett's always been good to me and Peter.'

Peter, his fingers curled around a rail of his pen, stared at the DI.

'Shelley?'

'She was all right but she looked out for herself first. Her stepmum came into the pub with her dad now and then. She weren't too keen on Shelley. Always called her Michelle when they were there – knew it annoyed her.'

'What about her father?'

'Big, quiet. Always looked tired. He worked in a sawmill so p'raps the dust got to him.'

'Was she a good worker – Shelley?'

'Very. Always earned her pay and was good with the customers. She liked to dress well and if some chap wanted to pay to be – with her – if you know what I mean?'

Tyrell nodded.

'Well, then. No harm done.' Leanne gazed at the condensation on the window, watching a droplet trickle down. 'She used to say when she found a man who could keep her she'd hang on to him. I got knocked up with Peter and Shelley was on at me to go to a clinic she knew – even offered to help with the cash.'

'Shelley had had an abortion?'

Leanne shrugged her shoulders and her fingers massaged the swell of her belly. 'Whenever she needed.'

'How many?'

'Two, that I knew.'

Tyrell had to be careful. 'Did she ever say she wanted to have children some day?'

'Only when she found a man with enough money in the bank.'

'Did you have any luck with Baldwin?' Tyrell asked as he sat with DC Walsh against a wall of the Bothy's bar.

'He's a good mechanic.' Mickey was hungry and watched for the food they had ordered to start its journey from the kitchen. 'His own car's a real rust bucket but there was another one waiting to be repaired.'

'I gather from his file our Mr Baldwin earns a bit on the side. No cash charged – or seen to change hands – so the DSS and Inland Revenue haven't been able to get to him. Much as they'd like to.'

Mickey Walsh heaved a sigh of relief. His mound of burgers, chips, peas, was being carried towards him, Tyrell's soup and roll balanced in Claire Goldsmith's other hand.

'Quiet here, now you've gone, Inspector,' she said as their plates were positioned, cutlery and napkins deftly dealt.

'Should I say sorry or are you glad we're no longer next door?' Tyrell said.

Her grooming was as precise as ever but he noticed tightened muscles around her eyes and mouth.

'Swings and roundabouts. The bank manager was happy for a while, then that bitch turned up and wanted half of all she saw.'

'Another Mrs Goldsmith?'

'The only one. Mine's a courtesy title, shall we say.'

'You're still here and the food's as good so I'm guessing you saw her off,' Tyrell said.

'Solicitors are chewing it over but everything's in my name so she won't get what she's screaming for. Enjoy your lunch.'

Generous hips swayed as Claire returned to the peace of the kitchen. Mickey lost interest, his attention devoted to spearing chips. Tyrell's soup required less effort once he detected some pasta and decided it was minestrone. He watched the main door swing open.

'Baldwin's just come in for his half-pint,' he told Mickey. 'No, don't look.'

Tyrell chatted to his companion, ate his meal and watched Mickey Walsh clean his plate. Anyone interested in the two men would have said they paid no attention as the door opened again on Matty Jukes.

'Matty in brand new boots,' the DI said under his breath.

Mickey stretched, replete, then crumpled up his napkin. 'They're good ones. I thought he was always broke.'

'Not necessarily. Granted he might not have much more than his pension but he's got no rent to pay, no electricity bills, grows and catches much of his own food and, unless I miss my guess, he makes a few bob with his ferrets, catching and selling any game going.'

'Do people eat that sort of stuff now?'

'Would you know the difference between rabbit and chicken in a pie or a stew? Most don't. Claire Goldsmith will.'

'Are we supposed to do anything about his poaching?'

Tyrell did not answer immediately. He was watching Matty head for the bar. The old man appeared ready to talk to Don Baldwin but the younger man turned away. Matty veered off to one side and stood against the wall at the end of the bar as he waited to be served.

'Now, why would they do that?' Tyrell wanted to know, not expecting an answer.

Even the air of the room in which they all gathered was tired. All day the men and women waiting for Superintendent Copeland had questioned and recorded, checked, double-checked and looked again.

'Any joy?' the DI asked Brian Clarke.

'Cars? Taverner's crew did a good job. There were no expensive machines seen outside the homes of any on the list of suspects for Tina's killer. Shelley? There're so many men to go through it'll be a while before we get makes of car for each of them. As for Fay Ryder, it's just the beginning. I told you I could have done with Mickey.'

'Can't Swansea help?'

'The DVLA's used to being given the number of the car, not just the name of the owner. I'll have another go in the morning.'

Talking ceased as Copeland came into the crowded room and stood in front of the information boards. He was flanked by his two DCIs, Taverner and Whittaker. They were as exhausted as everyone else present.

Copeland held up his hand for silence. 'Thank you. You've all had a hard day and I'll not keep you longer than I must. I have your preliminary reports. Has anything new or unexpected cropped up?'

Few had anything to add to the day's results. A woman held up her hand and Copeland nodded.

'What about the DNA testing to match the baby's, sir?' she asked.

'You've been handling that, Nick. Progress?'

Taverner stood away from the wall. 'All I can say is swabs have been taken from every man whose name's surfaced. Credit must go to DS Rogers. Her idea of overlapping circles has proved very helpful in drawing up lists of contacts.'

'Would you explain it to us, Penny?' Copeland asked.

'It's very simple,' she said. 'The first circle is the immediate family and friends of the deceased. Then, you take each individual and collect their circle – and so on. The basic idea is that when you're dealing with two or more crimes, at some point names will be repeated.'

Whittaker did not like to be silent for long. 'DI Tyrell's been interviewing one such contact of Shelley's today. Perhaps he can enlighten us.' There was a sting in the words, an expectation of failure.

All eyes swung round as Tyrell stood. 'I talked to Leanne Sullivan. She worked with Shelley for over a year and got to know her quite well – as well as any woman could.' There were murmurs of assent from others who had investigated Shelley's past. 'Of one thing she was certain. If Shelley was pregnant it was deliberate and then only because she had found a man with money.' He thought of Claire Goldsmith and the official wife turning up for her share of the Bothy's profits. 'Shelley may have picked a man already married. It's not unusual for an ambitious girl to see a lifestyle she envies and decide to do whatever it takes to push her way in. The man in question may have been unwilling to pay off a wife and family and replace them with Shelley and a new baby. If one had to go, he could have decided it must be Shelley.'

'If that's so,' said Nick Taverner, 'we're looking at a man who'll kill not only his mistress but his own child.'

'With that scenario and Shelley as the target, we have to keep in mind the fact that two innocent girls died as a smokescreen,' Copeland added. 'Let's face it, without two unnecessary murders – if that's what they were – we could well have been on his doorstep by now. Still, with luck, a DNA match'll give us our man.'

Tyrell was not so sure that was all that was needed. 'There's the matter of how he knew the details of Julie Parry's death so quickly.'

'You're right, Keith. It's got to be tied down or the CPS will throw the case straight back at us. Conclusive DNA convinces juries so tomorrow we'll get a swab from every man in the Forest, if necessary, starting with the high income brigade. One way or another, I want this bastard.'

'I don't know about you but I could do with a drink,' Brian Clarke said as the room cleared. 'Time for a quick one?'

'Why not – even if it's only orange juice.' Tyrell was tired but restless. He felt the need to unwind before going home to Jenny. Half an hour would make little difference.

When they reached the pub it was quiet, few from the station amongst its customers. Tyrell recognized no reporters as he stood at the bar to order drinks.

'A half of bitter and an orange juice? Certainly, sir. Take a seat and I'll bring them over.'

The DI paid, automatically registering the barman's appearance. He was new, pleasant, efficient. Tyrell shed his mac and draped it over an empty chair.

'Service tonight? Old Manny must be trying to upgrade the place.' Brian Clarke stretched his legs under the table and yawned. 'God, I'm tired.'

'A good night's sleep'll –' Tyrell began but was interrupted by the barman with their drinks.

'Orange juice?'

'That'll be mine,' Tyrell said, annoyed to see the man had topped up the glass with ice cubes.

'You must be the driver, sir.' The comment was accompanied by a professional smile. Carefully, a glass of bitter was placed in front of DS Clarke. The barman flicked his tray and was gone, the DI frowning a little as he watched him go.

Brian Clarke stared at the head on his bitter as it oozed over the rim of his glass and began its descent. Before it reached the beer mat he lifted the glass and drank slowly, steadily, quenching his first thirst. When he put the glass down he pulled a face.

'Hell, I must be tired. Even my taste buds aren't appreciating a good brew.'

Tyrell lifted his own glass and sipped, savouring the cool freshness.

'Don't drink any more, Brian. I think we're being got at. I'd guess vodka – and it's why I've got so much ice. The colder it is, the harder for the tongue to detect.'

The DI beamed at his friend, two men enjoying a quiet drink together.

'Are you sure?'

Tyrell risked another sip. 'Positive,' he said after a few more drops of liquid had rolled round his mouth.

Clarke moved, ready to take action.

'Sit still and look as though we're having fun.'

'Fun! If that bastard's trying to get us kicked off the force I'll have him!'

'First, I want to find out who's behind it.'

The sergeant uncurled his fists. 'Makes sense. So, what do we do?'

'Announce you'd better ring your wife and tell her you'll be late. Instead, ring the station. If you can, get hold of Penny Rogers and ask her to bring over – very discreetly – a stack of evidence bags that won't leak. If we're to prove anything, we'll need samples.'

There were an entertaining few minutes as Clarke talked loudly to his 'wife', then covered his mouth and his mobile as he apparently whispered sweet nothings. 'As quick as possible, darling,' he said, beaming fatuously as he pocketed his mobile phone and took a long time sipping his beer. Only the DI saw he never swallowed any.

They did not have long to wait. Penny arrived and joined them, soon followed by Mickey Walsh and Rose Walker. They stood at the bar until they were served, carrying drinks for the three newcomers.

'How do you want to play this?' Penny asked the DI.

'We need a sizeable bag to carry out the samples, once we've got them.'

Rose Walker grinned, excitement giving her an attractive colour. 'Mickey thought of that.' She swung a small ruck-sack into view and stowed it under the table.

Tyrell approved. He handed Mickey a couple of notes. 'Five minutes more then get another round in. The same for DS Clarke and myself and whatever you want. It's essential to find out if it's anyone in the job being targeted or just DS Clarke and myself.'

Penny Rogers began filling and labelling evidence bags, protected by the bulk of Brian Clarke as he leaned close to her.

'You do realize that if Brenda walks in now, I'm dead?'

'She'll know it's all in a good cause,' his DI reassured him, accepting his empty glass from Penny and giving the impression of draining it for anyone who might be watching.

Mickey and Rose returned from the bar.

'He's bringing the drinks?' Tyrell asked.

Mickey was anxious. 'Is that OK, sir?'

'Exactly what we wanted,' the DI assured her. 'I just wish we'd got more cover.'

Penny completed packing away the first set of labelled bags. 'No problem. Bryony Goddard and Sheila Hipwell are parked outside where they won't be noticed and Roly Willis is at the back door. DS Copeland's in command but said to follow your orders.'

'Then we appear to play along until Penny's got all the samples she needs.'

The barman's tray was heavier this time and it took longer for him to serve them all. Tyrell and his colleagues had time to study the man and commit his description to memory. The DI beamed his thanks, apparently a customer well on his way to happy inebriation.

'Who d'you think's behind it?' Penny asked.

Tyrell laughed immoderately. 'At this point, no idea. It could be a reporter after a story.'

They were a merry party, one or another leaning forward to tell a joke and block the barman's view as the DI tried each drink in turn.

'Only Brian's and mine. The rest seem OK but will all have to go for testing – just in case. Sorry about that.'

Mickey was puzzled. 'How did you know your OJ was spiked?'

Tyrell grinned. 'I was about nine or ten when my father caught my brother and me at the drinks cupboard. He sat us down and mixed every possible concoction, making us taste each one again and again until we could recognize exactly what was in it.'

'Did it take long?' Penny asked.

'Hours. I know Jeremy was sick four or five times afterwards. Me? I lost count.'

It was a pleasant sound, Tyrell decided, the laughter of these friends. 'Tell you what. If we can get to the bottom of all this, I suggest you come to our home one evening. Jenny will cook and I'll see you have something really drinkable.'

'You're on!' Mickey could not wait to enjoy more of Jenny Tyrell's cooking.

'Right, here's how I suggest we play this. Mickey, I want you and Rose to go to the bar and stay there when we leave. My guess is the barman'll make a phone call. If it's on a mobile make sure you get it when you arrest him.'

'What charge, sir?'

'Let's start with conspiracy to pervert the course of justice. It always sounds impressive.'

'If he uses the pub phone?' Rose queried.

'Make sure no one else touches it until you can get the number he called.'

Penny Rogers had been a silent listener. 'You know what's going to happen, don't you?'

'I've an idea, that's all. My guess is he'll phone an accomplice or the police, reporting that the driver of my car is behaving oddly and is probably under the influence. One way or another the information will get to our colleagues and I would have to be stopped and breathalysed. Whoever's set this up expects me to be well over the limit.'

'And sacked immediately,' Penny added.

The DI was under no illusions. 'You do realize that if we have blood tests to prove we're sober, whoever's behind this can always accuse us of a cover-up. You'd all be blackened with that charge.'

'No problem,' Penny assured him. 'That's why DS Copeland has the Gwent force on standby. They'll take over any testing that's necessary.'

Tyrell was silenced, overwhelmed by the massive support which had swung into place so quickly.

'Let's get on with it then,' Clarke said, scattering glasses and chairs as he attempted to stand. 'I didn't get the full whack – thanks to my buddy here – but I've enough vodka swilling round to make acting out this bit too bloody easy!'

'I'd better get him home,' the DI announced loudly as he gathered up coats.

The two friends made their irregular way to the door, Mickey and Rose already stationed at the bar and Penny using her mobile. The barman they had all come to know so well hurried to help Tyrell with the sergeant's weight. Clarke breathed his thanks over the man, hoping there was enough alcohol in the air to be convincing.

'Just as well you stuck to orange juice, sir,' Tyrell was told and he strengthened his hold on his sergeant to ensure no 'accidental' punches found their mark.

'I'll soon have him safe,' Tyrell assured the barman. 'Thanks for your help. You're new here. What's your name? For when we come again?'

'Dan, sir.'

'Just Dan?'

'It's enough.'

The DI and his sergeant wove their way to Tyrell's car. With Brian Clarke folded into the passenger seat, Tyrell stumbled as he reached for the driver's door.

'D'you think someone's watching?' Clarke asked.

'Who knows? We'll soon find out.' Tyrell deliberately

made a hash of starting the car but when the engine purred they were on the move quickly. 'Two cars following us,' he said, 'one from the car park and one from the lane outside.'

'Sheila and Bryony were to be in the lane. Can you get a good sighting of the other one? If not, drive badly enough and you can stop him in his tracks.'

Tyrell did what he could while Clarke used his mobile phone to contact the station and then Bryony Goddard. The girls were instructed to detain and identify the driver of the mystery car. The chase did not last long. They were hardly out of Lydney when a flashing blue light in the rear view mirror alerted them.

'Here comes the cavalry.'

'That was a bit hectic.' DS Copeland was tired and yawned behind his hand.

Almost numb with exhaustion, Tyrell was still anxious that all loose ends were tidily knotted. Clarke rubbed fingers across his eyes and drank more coffee.

'We'll have to wait for all the test results before we can rule a line under this episode,' Copeland continued, 'but I was most impressed by the teamwork. You two had some good people on your side – thank heavens!'

Tyrell agreed. 'The strangest being the chap following us.'

'Freelance reporter from Bristol, he claimed – and it checked out.' Copeland smiled. 'Said he was tipped off to a hot story involving you and police corruption generally. Rather gratifying he ended up being the star witness to how wonderful we all are. It makes you believe there is such a thing as natural justice.'

Clarke was like a bear with a sore head. 'I'd like to know which SOB set us up.'

'We may – in time,' Tyrell said. 'Dan, if that's his name, isn't talking but his prints have been fed into the system and we might get something on him by morning.'

Copeland was hopeful. 'Daniel Nichols was the name on

the first report. Last entry in records – suspected theft from previous employer. Owner of the bar in Cheltenham dropped charges.'

'I heard his phone call was to a local number. Any joy?' the DI asked the superintendent.

'Home address of a certain Raymond Sumner, solicitor of some unlucky parish in Bristol. It's becoming clear there was an attempt to discredit the two of you before Miles Kennedy came to trial.'

'Miles?' Brian Clarke swore quietly, fluently. 'He's no more than a spent squib.'

'His father isn't,' Tyrell reminded him.

'They don't come much more devious than Frank Kennedy,' Copeland agreed. 'My betting is he was the one behind the other attempts on you, Keith. I heard about the luscious lady chatting you up at the bar the other evening.'

The DI chuckled. 'She was a beauty but I did a stint in the Met on Vice. However expensive she was, however good she smelled, she was still a hooker – and not the rugby kind.'

'You saw her off most politely, I gather, but Brian had a word with Sergeant Willis and he had the lady quietly investigated. We know who she is.'

Tyrell was surprised. 'Her real name or her working alias?'

'Both,' said Copeland with a smile. 'She lives in some style in Clifton, Bristol, entertaining the very best of clients. Then the chap who was tailing you – Roly got his details from the DMV in Swansea. A private investigator, no less, and at the pricey end of the market. He's also based in Bristol and not likely to keep his licence unless he co-operates.'

Keith Tyrell rubbed his forehead, trying to ease tiredness. 'You know the worst part?'

Copeland and Clarke waited.

'All the effort and resources used up because someone wants to play dirty. Yes, Brian and I have a good result, thanks to so many of you, but that energy should have gone into the murder enquiries. If another girl goes missing because of this . . .'

'Once all the information's in I'll set the legal eagles on to Frank Kennedy.' Copeland had no doubts. 'He's the one behind all this.'

'How can it be proved?' Tyrell wanted to know.

'As yet I don't know,' the super admitted. 'A great deal of data's churning round in a mass of software. Let's see what happens.'

Keith Tyrell had been told to get a good night's sleep and not report until 10 a.m. When he did he was refreshed but still not as alert as he would have liked when he learned he had a visitor. The reporter insisting on speaking to DI Tyrell was a stranger. He was checked for tape recorders and one sat on the desk between the two men, its reels not moving. It annoyed the newsman but he watched intently as the DI opened the small package he had been handed.

Keith looked at the glittering pentacle. It was small enough to sit in the palm of his hand, its enamelled colours glittering as he turned it this way and that. 'Did you have to pay much for this?' he asked.

'Not too much.' The man tried to sound sure of himself but he did not like DI Tyrell's grim expression.

'Paying for stolen goods is always a waste.'

Part of this journalist's job had been to develop the ability to look innocent. 'I had no idea –'

'Of course you did! You're here hoping I'll give you a story for your paper in exchange.'

A smile came easily. 'Well, you scratch my back and I'll –'

'Scratching backs is not a habit of mine. I'm more likely to arrest you for receiving. How do you fancy sitting in the dock with Gloria Reilly? The two of you charged with stealing from a dead girl? Now, that's a story.'

The man scuttled away and Keith Tyrell propped the

pentacle against a stack of files. He was still looking at it when Clarke came into the room.

'Where'd that come from?'

'Gloria. I was sure she'd held on to something. I guess Julie must have had this hidden in a drawer and she poked around the girl's things often enough to know where it was kept. When she lifted the photos and the diary, this must have gone too but I'd got no proof. She only gave me back what I knew was missing. If only I'd been able to –'

'Stop torturing yourself. OK, you might have got to Miles Kennedy earlier but there's no guarantee you'd have saved any of the girls.'

'Fay Ryder might still be alive.'

Clarke had no doubts. 'Then blame her death on Gloria Reilly for being the greedy, cunning bitch she is.'

'Sorry, Brian. I wish I could.'

'Have you heard the news?'

It was nearing lunchtime and Tyrell was in the canteen, trying to drink enough coffee to keep himself awake. He looked up at a jubilant Brian Clarke waving a sheet of paper.

'Miles Kennedy's defence team have lodged a complaint against us – you and me. Remember Copeland wanted Ray Sumner left alone last night? Well, it paid off. He must have contacted his high-powered buddies as soon as Danny phoned him and they went into action first thing.' He cleared his throat, ready to read. ' "Since the two senior detectives who entered Mill Cottage with warrants to search, seize and arrest are both facing disciplinary charges and possible expulsion from the police force, it is requested that all evidence acquired by those two men on that occasion be declared illegally obtained." ' He lowered the paper and beamed at Tyrell. 'How's that for starters?'

'They've jumped the gun!'

'Aye, they have – and the silly sods've shot themselves in the foot.' The sergeant settled himself across the table from Tyrell. 'It's funny. I could never imagine Frank Kennedy going to these sort of lengths for his son.'

Tyrell looked down at the dark dregs he was swirling in his cup. 'It's the ongoing tragedy in that family. I don't think he ever did – or would.'

'How come?'

'You said "all evidence"?'

'The complaint was specific. If it was upheld the prosecution couldn't use anything of Julie's we found there which places her at the scene, nor any of those oils it's cost an arm and a leg to get analysed –'

'No, nor any of the computer data Mickey Walsh just happened to uncover from Kennedy Junior's disks. A hard-working team up the line in the Serious Fraud Office were delighted to get their hands on it. They think they've enough to nail Frank Kennedy to the floor.'

Clarke bowed his head and cursed the crumbs on the table. 'We were to get the sack to keep that bastard out of jail?'

Tyrell nodded. 'Are you surprised? He's a man who'd jeopardize his only son's defence against a murder charge if it would clear his own name. Give me an honest criminal any day.'

'Is that really what last night was all about?'

'I was awake a long time when I eventually got to bed – time to think.'

Jenny had not returned from work by the time Keith had stumbled in. When she did arrive home she was prepared to listen to what had happened but seemed distracted, almost embarrassed by the lateness of the hour. Keith had stayed awake long after she slept, his mind far away from Frank Kennedy.

Clarke rocked back on his chair as he considered all that had happened. 'I suppose what you say makes sense. By the way, Copeland wants to see us.'

'Thank God it's not Whittaker. He was in a foul mood this morning and nobody seems to know why.'

Intent on the patterns in the plastic of the table, Clarke began tracing them with his finger.

'You know.'

'Not really. A whisper. It's something to do with his wife.'

'Is she ill?'

'Maybe. Whatever it is, everyone's clammed up.'

'Poor devil,' Tyrell said softly.

'Forget about that. We'd better get to Copeland.'

Released early from duty, Keith drove home slowly. He was not sure what to expect but Jenny had not stayed on at the clinic and they had a pleasant evening, each being careful what was said, what was done.

Keith soaked in a hot bath and Jenny was already in bed when he went downstairs to turn out the lights and make sure all locks were fast and the alarm set. She did not welcome him as she used to but neither did she turn away as he lay beside her. He was relieved, almost happy, but before he could plan what he should do, he was asleep.

Next morning he woke heavy-eyed and to the smells of bacon, toast. Jenny was already at the breakfast table, engrossed in a newspaper.

She looked up at him, delighted. 'I know it's you but you've all been disguised so well.'

'That was Copeland's promise.'

Sheets of their regular daily broadsheet were spread across the table, an account of a foiled attempt to get two police officers compromised given pride of place. The reporter tipped off by Frank Kennedy's underlings had got his story but it was not the one planned and would be added to the elder Kennedy's list of crimes when he eventually stood trial.

'So, what now?' Jenny asked.

Keith pushed aside the remains of his scrambled eggs and bacon, beginning to butter toast and spread marmalade thickly. 'After I've indulged myself with this, it's back to work. The Kennedys have wasted too much of our time already and we've got to get our hands on the real killer – it's imperative. Now he can't shift the blame on to Miles Kennedy he should call a halt to these murders. Even if he does, the mood right across the Forest is distinctly volatile and the smallest incident would be like putting a match to gunpowder.'

'If he doesn't stop? This River Killer?'

'He must. We've got to get him – whoever he is – and soon.'

Keith finished his breakfast and dropped a kiss on the top of Jenny's head. She did not draw away and he wished he could stay and make more of the day. Silently damning the unknown murderer, he smiled at his wife. Everything had its price. What must he pay for doing his job?

Chapter Ten

'Another girl's gone missing!'

The news swept through the station faster than sound and every available officer raced to a briefing, determined not to waste a second of the precious early hours while clues and memories were fresh.

Rumour was even faster. As a grim-faced Nick Taverner read through a report sheet and prepared to speak, a rumbling grew in volume outside the building.

'God! The press got on to it quickly,' a DC near Tyrell said.

'It's not just them,' Bryony Goddard added. 'Joe Public's here and as mad as hell.'

'I'm not surprised. I live in Ruspidge and the mood there's growing. This'll tip it over the edge.' Gerry Cross nodded towards Taverner. 'If the Guv doesn't get a move on he'll have lynch mobs to cope with as well.'

'That's if we ever find the bastard for them to hang from the nearest tree,' Bryony whispered as Taverner held up his hand for silence.

'This one's even younger,' the DCI began. 'Alison Mary Gear had her fifteenth birthday only last week. She lives at home with her parents in Whitecroft and goes by bus to school in Lydney. Yesterday, she left home as usual but never returned. After school, Alison was in the habit of staying in Lydney for an hour or so with a friend who lived just off Bream Road but she always caught a bus back or was given a lift home by her friend's parents. Her own parents both work and when it got to seven o'clock and no Alison they began searching for her, the Lydney friend the first call they made.' Taverner paused, the lines on his face deepening. 'Not only had she not been there, she never arrived at school yesterday morning. As of now, Alison's already been missing twenty-four hours.'

Two DCs began handing out sheets of paper, copies of a photograph of Alison and such details as were available of the girl and her way of life.

'We'll use DS Rogers' system of listing contacts,' Taverner said when the room was quiet again. 'It's proved very useful with our other cases and until we know otherwise, this girl must be regarded as a victim of –'

'Surely this is a different pattern, Guv?' Gerry Cross's voice cut across Taverner's. 'For a start she's much younger and she's not blonde.'

'That's right,' Bryony agreed. 'And she disappeared in the morning, not after a night out.'

'Those are the only reasons I have for any hope,' Taverner said. 'It might mean someone other than our killer has Alison and she could turn up alive and well.'

Even as he spoke Taverner knew hope was a very fragile thread. He became brisk, allocating teams to the school, the bus company, Alison's family in all its ramifications, her own and her parents' friends.

'The rest of you house-to-house, radiating outwards from the school. At least you won't have to worry where to park your cars – you can all walk,' he added with an attempt at levity.

'No sign of Tricky Dicky,' Clarke said as he and Tyrell collected their clipboards.

'He was in first thing but a call from HQ had him hurrying.'

'Either he's in favour there or he's deep in the you-know-what.'

'Could be the latter,' Tyrell said. 'He didn't look very happy.'

Brian Clarke looked at Alison's photograph. 'If this lass is already in the river, no one'll be laughing.'

'Gone missing from our own doorstep!' DS Clarke slammed his clipboard down on the canteen table. 'Talk about thin air! She got on the bus, rode it all the way to Lydney and then nothing.'

Tyrell was weary, despondent, his sandwich and coffee untouched. 'Getting back in through that crowd at the door was bad enough. I could almost imagine what it's like being on the receiving end of a pack of hounds baying for blood.'

Clarke pushed away a half-eaten pie. 'By their reckoning she's the fifth local girl to be taken.' He looked up at the person lifting a tray over their heads. 'Any joy, Mickey?'

'Nothing. Alison got off the school bus and vanished. Masses of parents were dropping off kids and no one saw her go.'

'Come and join us,' Tyrell said as Mickey searched in vain for an empty space.

Mickey hesitated but he was hungry and put down his tray, settling to a mound of chips, beans and something brown topped with an egg.

Watching Mickey eat fascinated Brian Clarke, used to seeing the younger man shovel in food like a stoker behind schedule. Today, knife and fork were wielded carefully, almost daintily, the fork no longer overloaded. The young DC chewed carefully, lips closed firmly as his sergeant marvelled at the transformation. It was generally agreed that working with DI Tyrell had improved Mickey's manners but Brian Clarke was prepared to bet a woman had helped with the polishing. Rose Walker?

Tyrell had been silent a long time. 'I've been thinking,' he said at last. 'Something you said, Mickey.'

The DC laid his cutlery neatly on his plate. 'Me?'

'You mentioned parents driving children to school. In that early morning rush, especially with the rain we had yesterday, who'd notice if a child got into a car instead of out of it?'

A clerk came into the canteen, her arms full of paper. More information was passed round, the minutiae of Alison's life to be spattered with coffee, butter, sauce.

Brian Clarke scanned the words he had been handed then looked up. 'You're saying it was planned? Yes, damn it, it was, wasn't it? By both of them. She knew whoever it was spirited her away.'

Tyrell tapped the paper he held. 'What puzzles me is why Alison? Dark-haired, hazel-eyed. Loves reading, listening to S Club 7, Charlotte Church recordings and looking after her pet rabbits. Why her?'

'Say that again!' Mickey demanded. He had been too busy eating to read the latest data.

Tyrell repeated the list and Mickey thumped the table.

'It's her! There can't be many girls with the same description and hobbies. Cyber café – remember?' he asked the DI. 'You had me checking websites, chat rooms, Julie Parry might have used. I told you about the one I thought was iffy and you said you'd pass it on to the special unit. Did you?'

'Of course. The information was fed in that day. It should have gone through regular channels.'

'Then we can get the name and address of whoever made contact with Alison.'

Brian Clarke was still not reassured. 'Let's pray we get to her in time.'

'Mind you,' Mickey said, 'I think the girl gave her age as sixteen.'

With every possible effort being made inside the station tensions fractionally eased. There was no such let-up amongst the mass of people gathered at the entrance. Press briefings were promised but with no girl arriving safely in a police car, no blanket-draped man being hurried towards an interview room, the temper of the crowd darkened.

At the end of the shift tired officers struggled to reach the comparative haven of busy corridors and offices, DI Tyrell amongst them, until he was called to a hushed room and a waiting DS Copeland and DCI Taverner.

'We've called you in, Keith, because there's a problem.'

'Sir?'

Tyrell was wary as he faced his superiors. Both men were seated, their expressions forbidding.

'This information you said you sent up the line regarding possible misuse of a computer – the chat room business which might involve the missing girl.'

The DI eased one foot sideways an inch or two. Instinct told him he needed to be ready to withstand unpleasantness.

Copeland was stern, frowning as he gazed at Tyrell. 'DCI Taverner's been on to the chap in charge of the special unit with the powers to expose Internet users in unique categories. He insists no communication has been received from you.'

'I don't understand, sir. By now the abductor should have been identified.'

'He should indeed but the information's not available and I'd like to know why. DC Walsh was prompt enough in spotting the situation and you took it upon yourself, as his senior officer, to pass the data to the appropriate collator. Have you any proof it was sent?'

'An entry in my pocketbook.'

'Get it, if you will.'

In spite of the smooth words it was an order and Tyrell wasted no time going to his desk and unlocking a drawer. Brian Clarke was puzzled.

'What's up?'

There was only time for the briefest of explanations then Tyrell was back in Copeland's office and the opened notebook was being scrutinized by Copeland, then Taverner.

'At least you've enough here to locate whoever it was in contact with the girl.' Copeland passed the book to

Taverner. 'See to it, Nick. Too much time's been wasted already.'

DCI Taverner opened the door, revealing Brian Clarke ready to knock, Mickey Walsh in his shadow.

'A word, sir?'

Copeland waved him away. 'Later, Sergeant Clarke.'

DS Clarke was not to be moved. 'Now, sir – if you don't mind. I think DC Walsh can be of help.'

Mickey wasted no words as he described Tyrell sending off the information and logging its transmission. 'I've checked, sir,' he said, 'and that despatch isn't in the working memory.'

The superintendent's brows met in a frown. 'Even if that were so, the intelligence would still have reached the unit.'

'What if it was immediately followed by a request to cancel?' Clarke asked.

Copeland was surprised. 'Why would that happen?'

Mickey Walsh was nervous, moving his weight from one foot to another. 'Straight afterwards the computer from the cyber café had to be returned. It was because – someone might have thought DI Tyrell had taken it away from the owner without proper authority – so we were told.'

'And any evidence you found in its memory could be argued as illegally obtained and therefore inadmissible?' Copeland asked.

'Something like that, sir, but Larry – the chap as owns the caff – he said we could have it as long as it was back by the time the kids came out of school.'

'Walsh, I'm told you're a bloody good hacker. Does that mean you stand a chance of finding that which may have been "accidentally" deleted?'

Mickey was delighted. 'I can try, sir. When?'

'Now.'

The door slammed behind Mickey before Copeland had finished speaking.

'DC Walsh can move fast when he chooses. Thank you,

Brian. I'd heard you were a good man to have behind one in a crisis.'

'No, Paul,' Jenny whispered.

The voice in her ear went on and on, urging, persuading, and she became agitated.

'No! I don't want Keith to be told! You don't know him – he'd go straight to the director and before Cooper realized what was happening, she'd have told Keith everything.'

Misery swamped her as Paul reasoned with her but Jenny fought for control. It took some time and cascades of syllables bombarded her.

'I've made up my mind,' she told him. 'I'll explain it all to Keith later – when the time's right. To do it now would have him finding out all the gossip as well as the facts and that could mean the end of our marriage – and for what? A few drinks, a meal now and then?'

The sound of him became louder, the words more compelling, and anger began to seethe in Jenny.

'How dare you say that of us! Keith and I had – have – a good relationship, in spite of what you've been trying to do.'

Paul was an expert in his field and she had heard him work on patients exactly as he was trying to manipulate her responses.

'You knew what would happen when Sonia was transferred to you from my list,' she accused him. 'It was obvious she'd centre her life on you but Cooper thought you were experienced enough to cope – and maybe you were. Maybe this mess is just what you planned.'

Had she been more calm Jenny would have heard in him the beginnings of desperation.

'That day she caught you trying to kiss me, Sonia insisted she had an appointment with you and that was why she barged in and got upset. I didn't believe her at the time but I do now.'

Paul talked quickly, his phrases alternately soft and forceful, but he could not see Jenny shaking her head.

'Sonia had no reason to lie to me. I can see now it was just one of your tricks to help split me from Keith. It wouldn't be so bad if you'd cared. It's taken me far too long to accept you were playing some twisted game with me.'

Whatever he said in rebuttal she no longer heard.

'And Sonia? You've set her treatment back months – making sure she has an assault on her record. She didn't deserve any of it – and neither did I.'

Jenny's head lifted proudly. She was sure of herself at last and ignored Paul's pleading.

'I mean it!' she shouted, drowning out his pleas.

Switching off the phone Jenny began to shake. She had tried to be calm but reaction was beginning to spiral out of control. Before she became a complete mess she stumbled to the kitchen, boiled a kettle and filled a hot water bottle. It took enormous concentration. Cradling it to her she felt warmth reaching a frozen core and was able to breathe deeply enough to pour milk steadily, heat it in the microwave and stir in chocolate.

Steps were halting, shaky, until she curled in a corner of the couch. Jenny sipped her drink and let time reduce the waves of panic until the peaks were slow enough and low enough for her to push at them. When she felt able, Jenny rolled back her cuffs and inspected angry weals around each wrist. There would be bruises but the weather was cold enough to allow long sleeves and high collars. She touched her throat and tears started, draining stress from her.

When she heard Keith's key in the door Jenny straightened, pushed the hot water bottle under the couch and greeted him with a smile.

'You're later than you said you'd be. Hard day?'

'It's had its moments,' he admitted. 'Cocoa?'

'Want some? It's very soothing when it's cold and damp outside.'

'What is it you say? Chocolate's the best natural anti-depressant. I'd better have some.'

Jenny began to get up but Keith leaned over and kissed her, pushing her back against the cushions.

'You sound a bit hoarse.'

'Beginnings of a cold, I expect.'

'Then stay there.'

She did not have the heart to tell Keith moving would have presented a problem, joints and muscles no longer co-ordinating.

'Tell me about it,' she said later as Keith settled beside her on the couch and curved his free arm round her.

She listened as he talked of Alison Gear, the efforts to find her, his apparent negligence.

'Was Mickey able to help?'

'He was, thank God, and Brian was a tower of strength. You should have seen him being tough with the super. Then Mickey worked on the main computer for what felt like hours and dug up the original message I'd sent, as well as the order cancelling it.'

'I don't understand.'

'Whittaker will tomorrow. He'll argue it was because of protocol I'd ignored. My mishandling of the original situation will be to blame for any action he might have deemed necessary to clear up the mess.'

'But?'

'If he'd let Mickey's original discovery go where it should have done, the squad chasing paedos might have rounded up whoever has Alison Gear and she'd have been able to live her normal life, undisturbed.'

'Will she be found in time?'

'Who knows? If she is, what state of mind – and body – will she be in? Actually, if we'd been able to find her quickly it might have cooled off the press rats and disbanded the so-called vigilantes pouring in from all over the Forest. They're really getting themselves organized and worked up.'

Jenny said nothing but she could see how disturbed

Keith was by the current situation. He needed no more worries that evening.

'Is there likely to be trouble?' she asked.

'I don't know – it's too early to say. All I can be sure of is that we've got a very hostile army at our gates.'

Neither Jenny nor Keith wanted supper. There was more hot chocolate, this time laced with brandy. Keith was persuaded to have a warm bath and by the time he was ready for bed Jenny was already snuggled deep under the duvet, only the silky cap of her hair showing.

'I didn't ask what sort of a day you'd had?'

'Oh, not bad.'

'It still needed your anti-depressant,' he reminded her.

'I had a difficult patient but she'd been transferred to someone else and was playing up a bit. The director's seen to everything, so it's settled.'

'Had she been getting obsessive, this patient?'

'Something like that.'

Jenny was showered and dressed when she carried Keith his first cup of coffee of the day.

'What's the rush?' he asked.

He pulled her to him and buried his face in her neck, nuzzling down the high collar of her sweater.

Jenny pulled away. 'I've bacon grilling and you don't want smoke alarms going off – not to mention the stench from burned fat filling the house.'

'Bacon? I could've managed with toast and cereal.'

'You had a rotten day yesterday, and no supper. Come on.' She pulled the duvet from him. 'Eggs poached or scrambled?'.

'Why not fried, with fried bread?'

'Not good for you. I know you men when you're in the canteen. If it wasn't for the women working with you the cooks wouldn't be allowed to buy in a single lettuce or tomato – not to mention yoghurt.' She stood, her smile lighting the dark morning. 'Five minutes.'

The time with Jenny was pushed to the back of Tyrell's mind when DCI Whittaker strode into the CID room for the first briefing.

'DCI Taverner's on his way to Reading,' he announced to the waiting detectives. 'He's driving the Gears to meet with their daughter. She's in hospital for a check-up and Thames Valley police have the man in custody.'

The relief was enormous and there were cries, spontaneous clapping, smiles all round. Every other girl had surfaced to lie on a mortuary slab. Alison Gear had survived.

'Is she OK, Guv?' a voice called out and there was an instant hush.

'She's frightened but physically intact,' Whittaker said. 'Of course, it would have been better for her not to have been picked up in the first place. A salutary lesson for us all – to make sure we follow proper procedures when gathering evidence. Had that been done, who knows? It's people like you and I who have to clear up the mess left behind sloppy policing.'

'I don't believe it!' Brian Clarke was furious. 'That little sod painted himself into a corner and now he's climbing across the ceiling to get out of it! They must have believed him at HQ.'

Tyrell had been watching Whittaker, his high colour, extravagant gestures, curling lip. 'I don't think they did. He's still in a corner and very unsure of himself.'

'Him? That cocky bastard? If you're right, then watch your back,' Clarke warned.

'We all need to. If he's the one meeting the press with this news his manner with them – and with the public – could screw up tensions in the Forest a few more notches.'

Whittaker was assigning the men and women in the

room, aiming to intensify the search for the killer of three girls.

'Inspector Tyrell. Get back to the burglaries and for God's sake get them cleared up! Slipshod work is not acceptable, do you understand?'

Tyrell faced him squarely and inclined his head slowly. 'Perfectly, sir.'

The DCI's colour darkened. 'You can have Walsh but Brian's with me. I must have efficiency.'

In the past Whittaker's sniping at Tyrell had raised smiles in a briefing but things were changing. Too many people listening to him today knew Mickey Walsh could make a computer sing to him if he was so minded. As for Tyrell, he was invariably courteous to everyone in the station, whatever their rank. His handling of the malodorous Mickey had been approved, the pleasant young man emerging from the scruffy clothes and hair was turning into a first-rate detective. Then rumours from the previous day had woven themselves into the legends of the station, the DI and Mickey doing their damnedest but being foiled. No one had named DCI Whittaker as the culprit but neither was anyone in doubt who had pulled the plug on them.

Whittaker marched out and the room gradually cleared. Tyrell watched his colleagues go, many of them stopping to ask about the burglaries and offer their help. There was no need for such gestures but he was heartened by them.

'Well, Mickey, it's you and I again and I'm relying on that computer program of yours. What's the state of play?'

Mickey went to his desk tucked away in a far corner and returned with a folder. 'Print-outs. The summary's the top sheet.'

The DI was a swift reader. 'You've worked wonders,' he said and in Mickey there was a flush of pleasure reddening cheeks, shyness returning at the praise.

Brian Clarke came back into the CID room and sat on a

nearby desk, kicking it with a swinging heel. 'You two getting anywhere?'

Tyrell nodded. 'Mickey's found a pattern.'

'Two or three days after there's been a delivery from Westley's in the area, there's a burglary.'

'Westley's?' Clarke queried. 'The building suppliers?'

'I've checked the drivers' rosters,' Mickey said. 'One name kept coming up – Ricky Holder. He lives in a caravan in Murren.'

'Murren again,' said Clarke. 'Everything keeps coming back to that damned place.'

'Yes,' Tyrell agreed, 'and it's an impossible area for effective surveillance. Old Matty Jukes, for instance –'

Clarke shook his head and laughed. 'You're not saying he's involved? Good God, there'd be wellie prints all over the shop if he had.'

'No,' Tyrell said slowly, 'but if anyone in Murren's involved, Matty would know about it.'

New slippers, new rubber boots, new neckerchiefs. It was hardly splashing money about, yet in Tyrell's memory the fresh colours of Matty's purchases stood out in the khaki and grey of the old man's existence.

'One odd thing,' Mickey added, rubbing his forehead. 'No single car's been spotted near the burgled houses.'

Brian Clarke turned his head sharply. 'Always a different car? Is there any link with a pattern of stolen vehicles?'

'No, I looked,' Mickey said.

Different cars, Tyrell mused as he tilted his chair on to its back legs and stared at the ceiling. The others watched the still figure until the DI rocked forward and grinned at them.

'Who do we know lives in Murren and often has strange, unstolen cars next to his caravan?'

The young DC grinned. 'Don Baldwin.'

'And who's his neighbour and drinking buddy?' Tyrell asked.

'Ricky Holder!'

Brian Clarke was not convinced. 'Whittaker hounded

those two and their alibis. Every minute was checked out – I know that because he had me working on it. Wendy backed up Ricky's stories and Leanne covered Don's. She insisted the only time he was out of sight was when he was test driving cars he'd been working on.'

Again, Tyrell grinned. 'And he couldn't remember where he'd been because he was just driving at random?'

'You've got it.'

'Evenings?' Mickey asked.

'If Leanne and Wendy were in the Bothy for a couple of hours, the men were left to baby-sit.'

'What's to stop Don and Ricky taking the baby with them in his car seat?'

Mickey gazed at Tyrell, horrified. 'Take a kid on a job? Never!'

Brian Clarke saw the reasoning and it made sense. 'Why not? There and back before Leanne and Wendy get home from the pub. Who's to talk? Baby Peter?'

'Then where's the stuff they take?' Mickey asked him. 'I've been through the original files again and again. Straight after the earlier robberies've been reported those caravans were searched. Nothing.'

Tyrell leaned his elbows on the desk. 'I've an idea about that. If I'm right, we'll get the job-lot.'

Mickey was not so sure. 'It still doesn't explain where all the stolen goods go. Nothing's ever surfaced.'

'Not in this country,' Tyrell agreed. 'Try the Garda.'

His idea startled Mickey. 'Ireland?'

'Why not?' the DI asked him. 'Whittaker's got good instincts when he puts his mind to it. He sensed these thefts and the selling on were to do with Murren –'

'The driver living with the moon-faced woman! I wondered why he spent time with such a misery.' Mickey was learning about life. 'It meant he was on the spot to transport the goods to Ireland. I'll get on to Dublin –'

'Try Wexford,' Tyrell advised. 'It's where the lorry's based and there're plenty of tourists haunting antique shops for small items. Not too expensive and easily packed for a flight home to LA or New York.'

'Murren as a centre of international crime?' Clarke shook his head. 'Nobody'll believe it.'

'Believe what?' An irate Whittaker stood in the doorway.

'Mickey, go and make that phone call.' Tyrell sensed the DCI was spoiling for a fight and he wanted to reduce the number of listening ears.

'Sir!' Mickey swished through the door. He hated rows.

'He's certainly smartened up,' Whittaker commented. 'I suppose you sneered at the poor fool long enough for him to take the hint?'

'Sneered?' Tyrell was icily polite. 'I don't think it's a habit of mine – but I have noticed that when anyone uses it as a technique the results are distinctly counterproductive.'

The DCI glared at his adversary and his lips tightened. 'Clarke, with me!' he barked and turned to leave.

Brian Clarke followed with a deceptive meekness, one hand in a fist behind Whittaker's back, its thumb raised in a salute. Tyrell allowed himself a smile although he was ashamed of himself. What he had said was petty, childish, even if he had known a moment of exhilaration. Perhaps Whittaker would hesitate in future before using him as a verbal punch-bag.

Once DI Tyrell's identity had been verified, Garda officers became polite, interested and very efficient.

'They're on standby and have the lorry's depot in Wexford under surveillance,' Tyrell told DS Copeland.

'Murren? Run the details by me again.'

'Setting up any kind of observation there is tricky. Anyone remotely like a copper sticks out. Fortunately, the food in the Bothy's not bad and DC Walsh has agreed to make regular visits.'

'He's not a sore thumb?'

'Not when he's with WPC Walker, sir. The cover story's that they need somewhere to get away from all of us.'

'Will it work?'

'There's enough truth in the arrangement to make it very credible indeed,' Tyrell said and smiled.

'Then they can have any meals on expenses – within reason.'

'The Bothy's not expensive, sir.'

'Just as well if there's to be a long wait for any action.'

Tyrell had to be patient, watching his colleagues use every means at their disposal in the hunt for a killer. Rumours seeped through that a team from the National Crime Squad was ready to move in and take over but Copeland was a county man, born, bred and trained. He had come to agree with Tyrell and Clarke. This was Forest business.

Meanwhile, Mickey had escorted Rose for an evening out on two occasions before he was able to report the date Kevin Doyle was due back from Ireland with his lorry.

'That means any stolen goods are still in storage. Make sure you're not spotted,' Tyrell warned the small team he had been allocated. 'There's no doubt the gang'll want to add to the goods for transport. Remember, Baldwin and Holder are fit enough. As for Matty Jukes, he might be ancient but he's got all his faculties. DS Clarke and I will be close by and I want to know when anyone moves.'

Patience dwindled. When the timing was right the DI and his sergeant parked in a field gateway on the A48, a mile east of Murren, and shared a flask of hot coffee. The radio crackled. Brian Clarke reached for it and listened to the transmission.

'Mickey made contact when the two girls reached the Bothy. That was twenty minutes ago. A car's just left Murren. Two men and a baby.'

'Cross and Baxter have been warned not to get spotted.' Tyrell was anxious. 'Following someone at night in the Forest isn't easy.'

'Those two are good at it,' his friend assured him. 'The best.'

Tyrell would have been happier in the fresh air and able to pace about. 'Where're those biscuits?'

The packet was finished, the thermos flask drained and the car's occupants decidedly stiff by the time the message came.

'They're running east of Underdean on the A48.'

It took very little time for the suspects' car to reach its destination, and Tyrell and Clarke were on site seconds later.

'Everyone in place?' the DI asked Martin Draper.

'And getting a bit damp since the rain started but we thought brollies might be a bit conspicuous. DCs Cross and Baxter have just arrived and are waiting in their car as back-up. There's been some shouting inside but it's suddenly gone quiet.'

'Get everyone moving in,' Tyrell said.

There was a sense of urgency. Camouflaged in dark clothes for a night watch, a ring of men and women moved forward, tightening the net around the house. The DI went past the old shoes, boots, slippers. He pushed open the door ahead of him. The smell gushing towards him was the same, the fire as bright as he remembered, but it was Don Baldwin who sat slumped in Matty's chair, hiding his face in his hands. Matty was a pathetically small heap on the floor, Ricky Holder standing over him.

Tyrell knelt beside the old man and felt for a pulse in his neck. Nothing. He touched the hand furthest from the fire. In spite of the stifling room Matty was already cooling. The DI glanced up at Martin Draper. 'When did the shouting stop?'

Draper looked at his watch, bending towards the fire-light to read the dial. 'Three, four minutes ago.'

Tyrell sighed and looked up as Clarke came into the room. 'Get Chris Collier.'

'Paramedics?'

'It's too late.'

Ricky Holder was shivering. 'I didn't do anything!'

His words shook Don Baldwin from his stupor. 'Didn't you? When he wanted more cash it was you argued and grabbed him.' Baldwin's head swung towards the DI. 'He just dropped like a stone. Never moved.'

Ricky was cautioned, handcuffed, led away. Already Matty's skin was blue, his mouth a purple slash.

Tyrell was motionless, gazing at the body. 'You stupid, greedy old man,' he said so softly no one heard him.

As the words took shape he was angry with himself. Matty Jukes had been a real person, getting old in the most primitive of homes. What had there been ahead of him? No wife, no good pension, no family at hand to see he did not suffer. Tyrell had no fear of age except for failing health and strength. Matty had merely found a way to get hold of extra money with which to lighten the darkness creeping in around him.

Don Baldwin pulled at Tyrell's sleeve. 'Peter?'

The sleeping baby had been Tyrell's first priority. 'He's safe.'

'Leanne'll kill me!'

'I'm sure she will,' the DI said. 'Taking the baby with you wasn't the best idea you've ever had.'

'What could I do? Ricky needed the cash, what with the baby coming and Wendy keeping on about a house. He couldn't afford any of it on what Westley's pay.'

'How did Matty come into it?'

'He heard us talking to –' Baldwin's lips snapped shut.

'To Kevin Doyle. We know he's been taking stolen property to Ireland. How did Matty manage to hear you?'

Baldwin was startled but too sunk in his own despair to react. 'The Bothy – in the bog. He came in, heard a few words and guessed the rest. Offered us storage.'

'That was when you were being turned over regularly?'

'More'n six months ago. It was Whittaker. He even had people going through the rubbish and opening up Peter's nappies. It wasn't safe to go on leaving valuable stuff in hedges,' Don Baldwin said with a strong sense of grievance.

Clarke tried to keep a straight face. ' 'Fraid it might get nicked?'

'Matty knew everything that moved in Murren,' Tyrell reminded Baldwin. 'Did it never occur to you he was on to you from the start?'

Brows met in a frown as Baldwin puzzled out the situation. 'He did say, way back, he couldn't understand Kevin with Vicky Pierce. There must be another reason for him to get into bed with a puddin' like her.'

After Don Baldwin had been dealt with and taken to a police car, Tyrell and Clarke were left alone in a firelit room with the body of Matty Jukes.

The DI stretched his neck muscles. 'We can't do much more tonight. Once Chris Collier's certified death and given an estimate we can do a preliminary search in here. I doubt Matty used much more of the house.'

Minutes later the police surgeon was with them, his examination of Matty brief but thorough. 'Heart attack – and I'd guess it wasn't his first. Pathology will give you chapter and verse. As to time? Within the last hour.' With a tired wave of the hand, he was gone.

Gloved officers went through the house as best they could with limited light. It was Mickey Walsh who turned over a pile of papers in a dark corner.

'Look, sir!'

Tyrell recognized the photographs from a grandmother's description. 'Mrs Flegg's.' He turned to the photographer. 'When they've been tested for prints get some good copies done as soon as you can.'

'Any sign of the frames?' Tyrell asked Mickey, busy bagging the photos in clean plastic.

'Not so far. The only gear we've found was in that holdall and most likely from tonight's raid.'

The DI stopped the photographer leaving. 'Can you make a complete record of the ferrets? And keep going while Cross and Baxter take them apart. You'll need sacks of some kind to hold the animals,' he told the two young DCs, 'and take care. You're strangers to them.'

'Under the ferrets?' Clarke asked.

'Let's wait and see.'

It was quiet in the room and Matty, decently covered, waited for an ambulance. Keith Tyrell stopped looking at the minutiae of an old man's home before it was cleared away. Life and work must go on.

'The only loose end now is Doyle,' he said as the fire rustled and settled.

'How's the Irish connection doing?'

'Last position given was on the ferry. He'll be picked up when he lands at Pembroke Dock.'

Brian Clarke frowned. 'Don't we need the lorry too?'

'We'll get it. The Garda have been very helpful. They want Doyle when we've finished with him.'

'So that's that?'

'Is it?' Tyrell looked round the tiny room and imagined it peopled with a young Matty and his Sybil. 'If I'd concentrated on the burglaries properly Matty Jukes might still be alive.'

'Get real! You heard Chris Collier, the old man's time had come, that's all. If you'd arrested him weeks ago the poor old devil would've popped it in a cell at the nick and with you standing in the doorway.'

There was a distant bellow of pain and Tyrell grinned. 'Town boy?'

Clarke nodded and sighed. 'Probably Gerry Cross – he thinks he knows it all. I'd better go and get him free. Trust him to give a ferret a chance with a finger. Thank God he didn't try storing it in his trousers as Matty probably did when he went poaching.'

Tyrell followed, in time to see a ferret's mouth clamped

between Clarke's tightening finger and thumb until the widening jawbones drew needle-like teeth from Cross's flesh.

'Get him to Casualty,' the DI advised, 'and make sure he gets all his shots – especially tetanus.'

Clarke watched the injured DC go. 'You know, Whittaker had Murren taken apart but he never thought of looking under those ferrets. He must be a town boy too. He's certainly happier on a patch where all the streets are close together and connect nicely.'

Tyrell was thoughtful. 'I think he sees the Forest as a great undisciplined rural sprawl, but he was right. He knew the answer was here, in Murren, all the time.' Puzzled, the DI shook his head. 'I'll never understand why I bring out the worst in him.'

'You don't know, do you?'

'No, I damned well don't! Not really.'

Clarke shook his head. 'He trusts you.'

Tyrell was stunned into silence.

'I'm not kidding,' his friend assured him. 'Tricky Dicky trusts you.'

'I'd rather he didn't.'

'Come on, face it. The man's always got a full head of steam. Something's wrong with his private life at the moment and it doesn't take much for him to blow his top. Who else can he blast at round here and be sure he won't get his teeth knocked down his throat?'

Keith Tyrell mulled over the idea for some time. 'I had a great aunt like that,' he said at last. 'She made her daughter's life hell because anyone else would've cut and run.'

'There you are, then. Two of a kind, her and Tricky Dicky.'

It was a tired smile the DI managed. 'In the end the daughter married secretly and cleared off to Canada.'

'No problem,' Brian Clarke said and grinned. 'You can always join the Mounties.'

Chapter Eleven

Mrs Flegg was so pleased to see the inspector and his sergeant. 'I will get them back, won't I? The originals?' she said as she held copies of her photographs.

Tyrell nodded. 'Of course. Once the court case is over I'll see they're returned to you. I must warn you, we may never be able to trace the frames.'

'They don't matter.' She smiled at the two men. 'You've been so kind through it all. No one really understands what it's like to be burgled – the sense of violation as well as the loss.' She stopped and gazed at them. 'How silly of me!' she scolded herself. 'You must see so many like me. I understand you've arrested the men involved?'

'We have. The evidence against them is very strong.'

'And one died?'

'I'm afraid so. He had a very bad heart condition and there was an argument before we got to them.'

Mrs Flegg stroked the faces of her grandchildren. 'What a price to pay for a few pieces of silver.'

'She's right about the price,' Clarke said as the two men drove away. 'Children being born and growing up without fathers. The driver, Doyle, has a wife and four children in Wexford. They're going to have some travelling to do if they want to visit him – wherever he's banged up.'

'Think about it, Brian. How many of the ones we put away have the ability to look ahead and see what will really happen? If they could, crime rates would nose-dive.'

'Hey! Don't go all philosophical on me. At least you'll be able to have a good laugh at the Bakers.'

Tyrell's chuckle was infectious. 'They'll be furious when their property's returned. Over-valuing for the insurance means they'll have to pay back more than the original goods were worth. Good news for them when they get back from that very expensive cruise.'

'Serves them right,' Clarke said as he steered the car into the station yard. 'Hope there's something decent left in the canteen.'

Sergeant Willis joined them as they ate, ready to enjoy a large slice of a Bakewell tart generously smothered in custard. 'Pity the old boy died but there's no doubt it was natural causes,' he said between mouthfuls.

'In the course of a crime or crimes being committed?' Tyrell queried. 'It's up to the CPS to decide what charges they'll take to court. I can't see them going for murder, even if Holder does admit to shaking Matty.'

Roly Willis pushed aside his empty plate. 'It's rough it had to happen. There was already a lot of tension before the news of yet another death with police involved – and this damned rain doesn't help. It's playing pop with my lawn.' He stood and stretched. 'I'd better get back to the front desk. We're getting a helluva lot of visitors these day – and you wouldn't believe some of them! I'll be glad when all this is over. There're too many experts chasing us with theories and not one of them's getting us anywhere.'

Tyrell and Clarke watched him go.

'He's right,' Clarke said. 'Every possible scrap of information has been collected, checked, double-checked, collated, analysed – and that damned profiler called in is as much use as a bad dose of flu.'

'Perhaps we need Mickey to devise another of his whizz-kid programs.'

'I think we need something simpler than that. If anything, we've got too much data. It's like looking for a needle in a dozen haystacks.'

'No,' Tyrell said slowly, 'a stone in a carpet. Jenny lost one from ear-rings her parents had given her. She was frantic, searching every square inch.'

'Then you walked across in bare feet –'

'I got a torch and so did Jenny. We lay on the floor, aiming the beams from different angles.'

'You found it?'

'In seconds.'

Brian Clarke's brows drew together in a frown. 'I see what you're getting at. We've got to look at the basics from a completely different direction – or directions. Where do we start? Julie Parry's death?'

'No, the post-mortem. All the copycat deaths were based on information from that first day.' He rubbed tired eyes. 'Let's get out of here. We need fresh air and clear heads.'

The DI drove steadily, appearing to follow no recognizable route.

'Where're we going?' Clarke asked.

Tyrell grinned at him. 'No idea.'

There was a rare burst of sunshine and it sparkled raindrops on trees, shrubs, grasses. The DI saw a picnic site ahead and pulled into its parking area. Both men were glad to get out of the car, stretch tense muscles and breathe in air washed clean. Trees around them stirred in a freshening breeze. Above, clouds scudded across the sky, flickering sunlight as they passed. It was easy to relax in the beauty of the surroundings, blood enriched with oxygen fresh from greenery.

'I've been thinking,' Tyrell said. 'Pete Coombs and Karen. Who would they chat to about their work?'

'Pete? Chat? He's not a matey bloke.'

' "Plays bowls, has one drink after a game and goes

home. Wife can't stand him talking about the corpses." '
Tyrell quoted softly from a remembered report.

'That leaves Karen. Lives with an invalid father and has a married boyfriend who also works in the hospital. I suppose she'd talk to him.'

'Is it known where they meet?'

'Yes. Bryony Goddard was on to that. She followed her to Willy's. All Karen and lover-boy do is sit in a corner and talk. Then she goes back to Dad and him to his wife and kids. There's never any more than that.'

Tyrell's spirits lifted. 'Now we're getting somewhere. They've a common interest in what goes on in the hospital and they chat in public. Someone could have overheard them. I think we ought to take a look.'

Clarke was doubtful. 'Not easy in Willy's. It's small and strangers are watched every second they're in there.'

'So we can't go in with our size twelves?'

'Speak for yourself! We need a couple who'd blend in at a nearby table – see if they can pick up details of conversation. What about Mickey and Rose?'

'Not on. Karen Boyd knows Mickey.'

A hawk swept across the clearing and perched high in a tree. They watched it inspect them, then turn its head smoothly until it caught a minuscule movement in the grass. Seconds later the predator pounced and lifted a squirming mass of fur and flesh, carrying it out of sight to be devoured.

'Jenny might do it,' Tyrell said. 'It would do her good to get out for an evening.'

'What about Brenda? She'd be up for it if her mother's free to look after the girls.'

'We'd be outside,' Tyrell assured him.

'Then let's ask them.'

Tourists seldom found the pub, King William of Orange. It had once been a terrace of three small cottages where two tracks crossed. The tracks matured into roads but the cottages changed little on the outside. Ben Cook, the owner, had the blue-marked skin and cough of a man who had spent years in a mine. With compensation from an accident he had taken possession of Willy's, the quiet, out-of-the-way licensed premises no brewery was interested in modernizing.

Karen Boyd was known there but not because she was a major drinker, that had been her father's occupation. Alcohol combined with heavy smoking had ruined his health and shortened his legs as gangrenous sections were amputated. Neighbours felt pity for a girl who was condemned by duty to live with the unpleasant wreck who was her father. If she met up with a friend now and then, who could blame her? Certainly none of Ben Cook's customers, delighted the misery that was Ted Boyd lost his daughter's servitude for an hour or two.

'You're sure they'll be there tonight?' Clarke asked the DI.

'I had Mickey checking the hospital rosters. Karen isn't working late and the boyfriend was on early shift.'

The two men were on watch, their car well hidden behind some trees but with a good view of the road leading to Willy's and the cleared space at the side where cars could be parked. Clarke read out the registration numbers of any approaching vehicles for Tyrell to check.

'That's the boyfriend,' he said of a well-worn blue estate wagon, child seats visible in the back.

'So where's Karen?'

Not much patience was needed, Karen's small red Vauxhall arriving a few minutes later.

'You can tell the girls they're on.'

Tyrell spoke softly into a microphone and was answered by Jenny, sounding more cheerful than she had been for weeks.

'Just going in now,' they heard her say. 'Brenda's leading and I'm switching you off in case one of you sneezes and blows everything.'

'How did you get hold of this equipment?' Clarke wanted to know.

'Roly Willis. He OK'd it with Copeland.'

'You really are playing it by the book.'

There was little to do but listen to the muted chatter from Willy's bar and record the few cars bringing customers to the pub.

'A Merc!' Clarke was surprised. 'Don't often see one of those here.'

'Local or passing trade, d'you think?'

'Not local. That number's only two years old and there's no expensive houses for miles.'

A couple of motorbikes roared in, their riders taking time to dismount, take off helmets and amble towards Willy's open door.

'I'm tempted to radio through those bike numbers,' Tyrell said. 'They're a likely looking pair but I don't want anyone to guess Willy's is under surveillance.'

'Log 'em here and leave it at that. Who knows, we might be giving them an alibi.'

The DI was about to reply but was interrupted by Jenny's voice. She was not speaking to them directly and they heard background noise, a murmur from Brenda, a man.

'He's chatting her up!' Tyrell was annoyed and his companion grinned at him.

'If she didn't want you to know she'd have whispered. Listen!'

They heard a man's smooth tone, words indistinct as he urged and persuaded. Jenny's replies were clear. She was polite, firm. Brenda joined in, insisting they were there for a quiet evening away from men and children.

Brian Clarke leaned close to the radio's speaker. 'Can you hear them? In the background?'

'I can just make out a pair of voices, a man's and a woman's, but I can't hear what they're saying.'

'Thank you, no. I do not want another drink. In fact I'm ready to go home,' Jenny said.

Her husband chuckled. Jenny could enunciate with remarkable precision when she was angry.

Brenda joined in. 'Let's go,' they heard her say. 'We'll get more peace at home – and that's with the kids screaming.'

Noise of movements, voices surging and fading, a door banging. Footsteps crunched on small gravel, car doors opened and shut, an engine started.

'Did you get that?' Jenny asked. 'We were doing fine until he turned up.'

'Nothing much to him but he thought he was God's gift to women,' Brenda added and a switch was flicked.

'What about Karen Boyd?' Keith Tyrell asked.

'You were right,' Jenny said. 'She can be overheard. They talked about ordinary things – her father's health and temper, the boyfriend's children. They also compared notes about their days' work.'

Keith stirred the fire and used small logs to feed it into flames. Brian eased stiff legs and sank back in a large armchair. Followed by Brenda with a large plate of succulent sandwiches, Jenny carried in a tray of steaming mugs.

'Brenda's put in your brandy ration,' she told Brian.

He pulled a face. 'That means she's not driving home.'

'No, I'm not! It was my night out, remember? We'd still be sitting there if it hadn't been for that waste of space bothering us.'

'Forget him,' Jenny said. 'I have.'

Time flew as the four of them relaxed and talked, small things causing laughter. There was a sense of achievement in the gathering, Brenda and Jenny serious for a moment as coats were gathered, farewells said. The visitors were waved away, Jenny returning to the fire and crouching in front of the warmth welling from its dark red heart. Keith locked the doors and set the alarm. When he saw Jenny and the arc of pain that was her head and neck he was on his knees beside her.

'My darling, I'd never have asked you to help if I'd known it would have affected you like this.'

'It's not that,' she murmured as she leaned against him. 'Tonight I reached for something and Brenda noticed. If I don't tell you about it, she will.'

Keith waited until Jenny pushed back the cuffs of her sweater. The weals on her wrist were paler than they had been but he had seen too much damage of this kind. Only grooves deep in the skin could leave such marks.

'God, no!' Keith reached for her but she held herself aloof. 'Why have you hidden these – and why didn't you tell me before now?'

'You were busy.'

'Too busy for this? What kind of man do you think I am?'

'Those poor girls. You were so determined to catch their killer. Then, when I'd decided to tell you, it was the day the old man died. You blamed yourself and I couldn't add to your worries.' She lifted her hands, turning the palms uppermost. 'This was over and I was all right. There was no need for you to know – besides, it was all my fault. I thought I was in a situation I could handle. I was wrong – so wrong.' She bowed her head and Keith could almost touch her despair.

'How long were you going to hide it from me?'

'The marks would soon be gone – then there'd be no need.'

'How –?' Keith began, then he remembered. 'Was this the patient who had to be transferred?'

Jenny nodded. 'She'd become obsessed with me and when I was no longer to see her it affected her badly. She waited until she got hold of some flex –'

'What idiot left it lying around?'

'No one. She'd torn it from a light fitting. Don't forget, some of our inmates can become abnormally strong on occasion. I got tied up.'

'Were there no alarms?'

'That came later – when I could get to it.' She giggled, sounding tired. 'I sat on it.'

Keith was finding it very hard to be calm. 'Was that all that happened?'

Slowly, Jenny pulled down the high collar of her sweater. The moving shadows of the fire added an extra dimension of horror as Keith gazed at his wife's throat. Bruises might be fading but he could see the yellowish residue where fingers and thumbs had dug into soft flesh.

Jenny raised her collar again and would have curled as a foetus but Keith had to hold her. He was careful to be gentle, crooning as he soothed her until she straightened and relaxed against him. Tiny muscular twitches revealed the depths of Jenny's misery and Keith rocked her, hoping he was hiding the blinding, searing rage which engulfed him.

An eternity passed and, for the first time in his life, Keith knew he had it in him to kill another human being.

'Guess whose Merc it was?' DS Clarke waved a folder at Tyrell next morning. 'Malcolm Henry Foster.'

'He's on the shortlist, isn't he?'

'Was. Alibis for all the murders. Wife said he was home with her on two occasions. He was in his warehouse at the relevant time Shelley went missing.'

'Have you ever interviewed him?' Tyrell wanted to know.

'When I was with Whittaker. Foster seemed harmless enough – no edginess or hesitation. Your regular Mr Nice Guy.'

'Just as Brenda and Jenny described him,' Tyrell said. 'They thought there wasn't much to him – except for the size of his ego – yet there must have been a reason for Whittaker to deal with him personally.'

'Malcolm Henry had a fling with Shelley. Then we found out his DNA didn't match the baby's.'

'Up until then he was a possible father?'

'And then some, judging by all his activity in that field. Insisted he'd gone off her months ago.'

Tyrell began to look pleased. 'We now know he visits Willy's often enough to be taken for granted by the usual drinkers there.'

'So he could have heard Karen talking about the PM on Julie,' Clarke decided.

Tyrell grinned. 'Let's go and find Penny Rogers.'

Once Penny accepted they had not come to laugh at her circle theory she found the summary of the file she had made on Shelley Watts.

'The first circle is family, the second one those known to have had more than a one-night stand with her,' Penny explained. It was a long list. 'These are the ones we know about – there could be more.'

'Some girl, our Shelley,' Clarke murmured as he read Penny's notes. 'You've discarded quite a number as suspects. Why?'

'Alibis rock solid for at least one of the murders. Limited intelligence – whoever planned these killing was sharp.'

'Malcolm Henry Foster?'

'As a razor,' Penny said. 'He came here from Birmingham with only a vanload of cheap foreign imports. When he'd sold those off at a profit he rented an empty shop and hauled in a lorryload of tat. Prices were low, profit margin healthy and the turnover gave him money in the bank. He hasn't looked back.'

Tyrell stirred and leaned forward. 'I suppose in the pre-war Forest he'd have been called a pedlar?'

Penny smiled. 'Always an attraction for the ladies.'

'He certainly fits our own profile of the killer,' Tyrell said, 'but if the baby wasn't his there's no obvious reason for him to kill Shelley.'

'Do we pay him a visit?' Brian Clarke asked.

'Not yet. I'd like to get a few things clear before that.'

'Such as?'

'Leanne Sullivan. She might have been working with Shelley at the time Malcolm Foster was sniffing round. Then there's the chap who did father the baby. Leanne said Shelley never did anything without a reason.'

Mass DNA screening had matched the baby with a nineteen-year-old, Steve Bayliss.

'Bayliss has perfect alibis for two of the murders,' Penny reminded them. 'Hospital records are specific – a burst appendix. It's not easy to do much when you've got peritonitis and connected to a drip for two or three weeks.'

Tyrell was unusually gloomy. 'Let's hope it hasn't affected his memory.'

Leanne was not willing to talk to them. Mrs Hackett hovered with tea and scones, determined the girl should not be harassed by her visitors as Peter played with a Thomas tank engine at their feet.

'Come and join us, Mrs Hackett,' the DI said. 'We need all the help we can get.'

'Still no nearer catching the killer?' she asked him.

'Every day we work all hours but none of us can rest until we've got him.'

Mrs Hackett understood. 'Peter could do with a nap, Leanne. I'll take him up and leave you free to talk. They're right. This man's got to be stopped from taking any more girls away from their families.'

An uneasy silence followed Mrs Hackett's departure with a sleepy child.

'Mrs Hackett's world ended when Julie died,' Tyrell said. 'You're helping her just by being here. Can you stay?'

'We've nowhere else to go. Even when Don gets out I can't trust him again. I mean – taking Peter? He ruined our lives – or he would have done if it hadn't been for Mrs Hackett.'

'That's the hardest part of the job for us – the victims. They don't just lie on mortuary slabs, they sit in homes which have lost someone who brought light, or in houses wrecked by vandals. They're all victims, just as you are. Then there are those who get frustrated, angry, because of what's happened. Believe me, the mood of people in the Forest is getting uglier by the day. Everyone between the Severn and the Wye feels personally involved and you know Foresters. They don't sit idly by.'

Leanne stared out of the window. She was resisting Tyrell's words as hard as she could.

'The longer we take to find and nail this killer the more violence there'll be. One man's already been beaten up and landed in hospital with broken ribs and a punctured lung. We know he couldn't have killed Shelley, or any of the others, but the mob that's growing in number and ferocity doesn't listen to us. We've got to get the right man – and soon.'

The girl stopped twisting a strand of hair and closed her eyes, resigned to what must follow. 'OK. What d'you want to know?'

Steve Bayliss was convalescing, his skin pallid, mousey-brown hair limp. 'I told all the others, I never killed Shelley. I never even knew I'd started a baby. It was only the once she invited me back.'

Clarke was impressed. 'They should bottle what you've got, Steve, and sell it to fertility clinics.'

Bayliss was little more than a boy and blushed. 'Why d'you have to keep coming?'

'She died, Steve,' Tyrell said. 'Shelley was murdered. So were two other girls. We have to get the killer.'

'I thought you had him already?'

'The man awaiting trial was responsible only for Julie Parry dying and we can prove it. Someone was quick off the mark and copied what happened to Julie. This one's not only clever, he's ruthless. He picked up and killed three girls in a matter of weeks.'

The boy was miserable, almost crying. 'What about my baby? Every day they go on in the papers about the girls but my baby died too.'

'You're right, Steve. If this man knew Shelley was pregnant, he deliberately murdered your child and we must get to him. Help us.'

Gently, the two policemen questioned Steve and, wearily, he told them all he could. He had met Shelley in the pub where she worked. She had talked to him, flattered him, got him drinking tequila. He remembered stumbling into a taxi and falling up the front step of Shelley's home. His clothes came off and he was on fire, Shelley rubbing him until it hurt and there was only one way to get relief.

'I don't remember any more – must've passed out. Next thing I knew I was walking down a road, away from Shelley's. Never saw her again.'

'I think he was telling the truth,' Tyrell said as they drove towards Lydney and paperwork.

Clarke agreed. 'No reason not to. Shelley wanted a father for her child and decided he was to be the one.'

'But why Bayliss? He's hardly a rampant stud – you could pass without seeing him in a crowd of two people.'

'I wondered about that,' Clarke said. 'Does Bayliss look like the man she intended to blackmail? Remember the abortions? Shelley wanted this baby and expected it to give her what she planned. Money?'

'No,' Tyrell shook his head 'not just money. She'd seen some chap with a comfortable lifestyle and she wanted in. Bayliss must have been necessary when she thought the other chap was cooling off.'

'But Shelley wasn't thick. She'd know DNA would prove the baby's parentage.'

'After it was born,' Tyrell added. 'Then, if it started to

grow up looking like the target, it wouldn't take much to convince people the tests had been rigged.'

'That's a helluva long wait for a cash return!'

'Not if the profit made it worthwhile.'

Clarke had his doubts. 'Can't be Steve Bayliss. No cash, no car, no home of his own – he lives with his mother, for Pete's sake.'

'I grant you he's not father material but just imagine him fit and well. You've seen far more of the likely suspects than I have. Which one of them would he resemble?'

Clarke whistled quietly for a few minutes as he reflected on possible matches. 'The nearest look-alike I've seen is Malcolm Henry Foster.'

'Malcolm Henry Foster has money and a good car,' Tyrell said softly. 'He knows the Forest roads well and he's the same man who can be found in Willy's where Karen Boyd meets her boyfriend – the only person with whom she discusses her day's work.'

Clarke wriggled himself upright in his seat and his eyes sparkled. 'We'd have to pin down Foster as being in Willy's the night of the first post-mortem.'

'Agreed.'

'His alibis – they'd need serious vetting.'

'Very serious. The way the girls were killed there's little or no forensics to go on.'

'Malcolm Henry Foster.' Clarke relaxed against leather, a smile hovering around his lips. 'When do we go after him?'

'As soon as I've seen Copeland. He's due in the station after lunch.'

Tyrell halted at a red light near roadworks.

'Are you OK?' his friend asked. 'You don't look as though you got much sleep last night.'

'Didn't Brenda tell you?'

'Brenda? Tell me what?'

The DI swung the car into a stream of traffic. 'Jenny.'

'No, but then she wouldn't. It was Brenda and her like got thumbscrews invented. What's wrong?'

Tyrell did not answer immediately. 'Shortly before Matty Jukes died Jenny was assaulted by a patient and almost killed. She didn't tell me when she planned to because I was upset an old man had had a heart attack.'

Bitterness ran deep but Tyrell still drove with care, negotiating past a group of reporters and protesters.

'Jenny seemed OK last night.'

'You know Jenny,' her husband said. 'She'll sort out what's wrong in her own way.'

'The patient?'

'Locked away where I can't get at her.' A huddle of grieving women caught the DI's attention. 'I understand them now. I know how they feel – the helplessness, the frustration.'

'And the anger,' Clarke said quietly. 'Don't forget the anger. It's out there and it won't go away.'

Superintendent Copeland listened to them, called in DCI Taverner and both senior men agreed Tyrell and Clarke should pay Foster a preliminary visit. By the time they had managed to get their car through the crowd outside the station neither man was in any doubt as to the strength of public emotion. It was a silent drive north to the luxury of Foster's home.

'Mr Foster?'

DI Tyrell was being most polite as he and Sergeant Clarke displayed their warrant cards.

'You can't come back, can you? I've a load coming in from Folkestone and I need to check it when it arrives. Y'know how it is. If you're not seeing to everything personally, some bastard tries to rip you off.'

As Clarke persuaded Foster his assistance was invaluable, Tyrell took only seconds to commit the man's appearance to memory. A slight, muscular figure in a beige cashmere sweater and dark brown slacks which had been flawlessly tailored. Short, expertly trimmed hair was the same colour as Steve Bayliss's would be when healthy. It was easy for the DI to register Foster as a few inches shorter than himself but the face was difficult, the skin clear and tanned with no feature significant enough to make identification easy.

Foster twisted a wrist and frowned at his watch. 'I can give you five minutes – but I need to make a phone call first.' A very small mobile was lifted from a pouch on his belt. 'Joey! Hang on to that driver until I've seen those invoices for myself. You know what happened last time.' With the phone back in place Foster was smiling, relaxed. 'You'd better come in.'

The grounds had been impressive and prepared the two policemen for the house. No expense had been spared to create a stylish interior for the modern version of an Edwardian villa. Antiques from Greece, Italy, Spain, were displayed to advantage in hallway and rooms painted identically in anonymous cream. The chairs in which they were invited to sit were upholstered for extreme comfort in a thick fabric which matched the walls, few touches of colour to add highlights to the décor. The only prominent items in the living room were photographs of two children as they grew from babyhood to their teenage years.

'Now, your time's as precious as mine,' Foster said. 'What do you want from me?'

'Your help, sir.' Tyrell smiled, putting Foster at his ease.

Clarke prepared to enjoy himself. He knew the DI in this mood. Briefly, Tyrell outlined Penny Rogers' circle theory, any one of its members being a suspect. Neither of the detectives missed the almost invisible signs of relief.

'I'd better warn you I know hundreds of people.'

'Of course you do, sir. Your business, for a start. Benjy's? The name's a puzzle.'

Foster pointed to a basket almost hidden in a corner. In it was sleeping a large, long-haired golden Labrador. 'My wife's dog. Benjy!'

Reluctantly, a big head lifted and swung to Foster.

'Can't stand dogs myself. Hairs all over the place and they always need walking when it's most inconvenient.'

Patiently, Tyrell led Foster through a list of his friends and acquaintances. Clarke made notes of the conversation and studied Foster's body language as the DI probed. The man was restless, small movements he made were quick, verging on jerky.

'I don't know how all this can help. You got a DNA match for the baby – it was in the papers. What about that man's alibis?'

'Even better than any of yours, Mr Foster,' Tyrell said and smiled urbanely.

Clarke explained the peritonitis and noticed a stiffening in Foster's expression.

'You had no problem giving a DNA sample?' the DI asked.

'No. Why should I?'

'You did admit to a full sexual relationship with Shelley Watts and we all know accidents can happen.'

Foster began to fidget, disturbed by the calm solidity of the men waiting for his answer. 'I had the snip – six years ago.'

'Did you, sir?' Clarke asked. 'Judging by all these photos you love your children. Was it your wife who didn't want any more?'

Foster hesitated. 'It was my decision. She doesn't have to know, does she?'

Clarke could be smooth too. 'Of course not, sir. All this is confidential. We can't have wives knowing everything, can we?'

It was Tyrell who was curious. 'What made you decide?'

Eyes flicked round the room as Foster sought comfort, assurance. 'I was away all day and half the night getting the business established. She had time on her own . . .'

'And you were afraid she might look for company elsewhere?' Tyrell's words were deceptively soft.

'Yes.' Foster was distinctly edgy. 'There's no way I was

taking the risk of paying to bring up someone else's brat.'

'Naturally.' Tyrell understood the man. He turned the conversation to clubs and pubs Foster frequented and more names were added to Clarke's list. 'There're some really interesting old places in the Forest. Willy's, for instance. Have you ever been there?'

More notes were made, recording Foster calling in at Willy's if he happened to be in the neighbourhood. They took him through his alibis for the three murders and he insisted on adding his movements at the time Julie Parry went missing.

'Just in case you need the information, Inspector. I was in Ireland on a golfing holiday. Witnesses were mostly sober.'

The sergeant duly entered the data, making it clear, under instruction from Foster, that he had only returned the day before Julie's body had been found.

'Is that all? I really feel I've helped you as much as I can but the business doesn't run itself, you know.'

Foster stood and waited for them to rise. As they did, Benjy was out of his basket in one lithe movement. His master put out a hand to the dog but it was avoided, the animal sniffing Tyrell's legs and receiving a caress behind an ear. Then it was on to Clarke and a similar gesture.

As they returned to their car they could hear Foster shouting down the phone at the luckless Joey.

'He's our man,' Clarke said.

'Yes, and the dog knows it too. Problem is, how the hell do we prove it?'

Chapter Twelve

The conference had begun and Superintendent Copeland was open to suggestions.

'We have to keep up surveillance on Willy's,' Penny Rogers told him. 'If Foster's the only suspect on our list to be found there it strengthens the evidence.'

Copeland was pleased. 'Good point, Penny. I'll leave the organization to you.'

Tyrell noticed Penny was taking much more care of her appearance. DCI Taverner was spending increasing time with her and she was softening, blossoming. The DI was mentally approving her new hairstyle when Clarke cleared his throat.

'One thing,' he said. 'Anything that moves round there soon gets back to Ben Cook. If he puts the word out we're interested in his customers, they'll disappear.'

'Any chance of getting him on side?' Copeland asked.

'It's possible – but he's cagey about us. Very cagey.'

The superintendent smiled. 'Like to try, Brian? We could still keep an eye on the comings and goings, but discreetly.'

'Alibis, sir.' It was Bryony Goddard who spoke. 'They've always been assumed to be cast iron. If Foster is guilty they can't be. It'll mean checking his times and places on the ground to see if what we believe happened could have been done in the time scales.'

Copeland was pleased a DC could see all the implications. He had a good team under him.

'One thing to be wary about,' Tyrell said. 'When the

murders are even hinted at, Foster invariably brings in Julie Parry's death. He was in Ireland for that one and derives a very good aura of innocence for all the killings because of it. He's a very wily customer – used to wriggling off the hook.'

'Do we have an early record?' The super waited until he was handed a file, and skipped through the entries. 'Birmingham police were kept busy. Plenty of mentions, few convictions when young. Handling stolen goods, receiving. Ah! I see Customs disapproved of all the visits made to France and Belgium and his return with vanloads of liquor.' Copeland frowned. 'That sort of activity attracts the interest of serious gangs. Presumably that was when Foster high-tailed down here. Anything known since then?'

Sheila Hipwell raised a hand. 'Nothing in the records, sir. He was married with a couple of small kids. Rented a terraced house in Drybrook and sold from the back of a van whenever he could. Wife helped him with the first shop and she's been behind him all the way. It's Mrs Foster does the books and VAT.'

The door was thrust open and Whittaker was in the room. 'Am I interrupting something?'

'Not at all, Richard. Glad you could join us.'

The super outlined the investigation which had begun after Tyrell and Clarke had set up the evening at Willy's. Few could miss the DCI's growing ill humour.

'I knew nothing of this! Why was I not told? If Clarke and Tyrell had any information it should have been brought to my attention! Yet again correct procedures have been ignored.'

No one moved.

Copeland's body language was hard to read. 'You were not available, Richard, when DI Tyrell tried to find you. Since that was not possible, he came to me.' The super's expression was still pleasant but there was a whip of steel in his words. 'I think it best we continue. Your input would be most welcome – if you have the time.'

Whittaker stalked to a corner from which he could watch every face in the gathering.

'The major problem we have,' Copeland continued, 'is that all evidence so far is circumstantial. Even if you manage to crack the alibis there's not a shred of forensic data which could help the prosecution. I'd hazard a guess the CPS would rather leave these murders on the books than risk a trial with what we've got.'

'Sir,' Mickey Walsh called out. 'I'll have a go at putting what information we do have into a system. It won't give us anything new but we'll be ready in case some forensics do turn up.'

Copeland saw nods of approval. Walsh had been accepted by very picky colleagues.

'Thank you. The rest of us will have to get back to the scientists and the pathologists and persuade them to go hunting for anything at all – even if it seems ludicrous to them.'

'Dog hairs,' Tyrell said. 'Golden Labrador.'

Raised eyebrows were turned in his direction.

'Benjy, the dog. It leaks hairs like mad.'

'Then there's Joey, sir,' Clarke added. 'He works for Foster and the way he's spoken to, I don't know why he stays. Carefully handled he might give an angle or two.'

Copeland agreed. 'Penny, may I leave you to select the officers for those assignments? You'll know the right people to detail.'

Men and women began to disperse and Whittaker, ignored in his corner, was rigid with fury. When he was able to move again he headed for his desk. It was quiet in his office and he opened his laptop, gazing at a screensaver of swimming fish. The beginnings of a smile hovered around his lips.

'I'll have the last laugh,' was a whispered promise.

There was a sense of progress.

From a large photograph of Malcolm Henry Foster pinned to a data board in the incident room radiated a growing mass of facts. Each one linked him to three murders. There was constant updating as officers returned to Lydney and added anything useful they had been able to glean, and late in the evening Tyrell gave Penny his findings for the day.

'Any luck?' Clarke asked him.

'Not yet. Persuading Eric Livermore to go over material already investigated was a nightmare. Apparently, by doing so, I'd called his professionalism into question and that debate took some time.'

'Not an easy bird. Feathers still ruffled?'

'He still looks like a crow in a huff but he sees the reasoning behind what he's been asked to do. I don't hold out much hope of anything new. To be fair, he's very thorough and wouldn't have missed a lot first time round.'

'Dog hairs?'

'That cheered him up a bit. I don't know who works with him but they'll have every seam to check.'

'Poor sods.'

'How about you? Any joy with mine host of Willy's?'

'He's willing to co-operate but very agitated by the idea of us setting up surveillance. "Everyone'll know you're there, Sergeant Clarke, then where'll I be? No customers – and that's no use to your lot." ' Brian Clarke had mimicked Ben Cook well, Forest sounds roughened by a harsh throat and a miner's wheeze.

'He's got a point.'

'Also,' said the sergeant, 'he's got a CCTV camera.'

The DI was surprised. 'Has he indeed? It should be able to tell us how often Foster's called there.'

'I managed to get that out of old Ben. Two or three times a week. Occasionally lunchtime, usually in the evening. No set pattern.'

'Can we have the tapes for evidence?'

'Yup – and he's agreed to putting in a mini-camera behind the optics, aiming it at the corner where Karen Boyd sits.'

'Very amenable, your Mr Cook. Not the time to ask what he's trying to hide from us. What does Penny say?'

'She's delighted and so are Copeland and Taverner. It saves on CID overtime.'

They watched Penny questioning Bryony Goddard. The girl kept shaking her head.

'Anything we can do to help?' Tyrell asked.

'It's these alibis,' Penny said. 'Bryony's worked hard but Foster's car has never been spotted near any of the locations where and when any of the girls went into the rivers. Without sightings we've no way of tying him to the scenes.'

'Then we need to find the second car Foster used – one that's anonymous and therefore invisible to Joe Public,' Tyrell explained. 'It was probably ready and tucked away somewhere out of sight.'

Penny added to her list of priorities.

'Could Foster have already decided to get rid of Shelley when he overheard Karen Boyd?' Bryony asked.

'Highly likely,' Tyrell said. 'I'd guess she was after a slice of his money and if his wife got to hear what was going on he could have lost half of everything in a divorce.'

'Especially when he knew the baby wasn't his,' Clarke added. 'We heard him. "Not prepared to spend a penny on someone else's brat" – or words to that effect.'

'Then he overheard the details of how Julie died and saw a way out,' Penny said slowly. 'If Shelley went the same way, whoever killed Julie got the blame. Foster tried it out on Tina the same night.'

'It's when she went missing,' Clarke added and there was a moment of mourning.

'Wasn't he taking an enormous risk?' Penny asked. 'He must have had so few facts to go on yet he was going to make sure Kennedy was framed for that death too.'

'A gambler? Do we need to take a swing round the local bookies?' Clarke wanted to know.

'I doubt it. This is a different sort of gambling. It reminds me of . . .'

'Something from your murky past, sir?' Bryony asked the DI.

'Not really. A description of loggers riding the logs floating on lakes and in rivers. Too long on a tree trunk and they'd sink, so they have to keep on running – keep on taking chances. It's the only way to cross a waterway thick with timber.'

Clarke could see what his friend was getting at. 'He has to take a gamble at every turn – to stay afloat and ahead of the game. If there're enough bodies, the kind of oil he used is less important?'

Tyrell nodded. 'Something like that. He's used to taking big risks – and he's used to getting away with them.'

'Unless we can stop him,' Clarke said quietly. 'We have to, or there could be more bodies in the rivers.'

'And it all began with Tina.' Tyrell's expression was grim, determined.

'To take a girl because she's young and blonde, then kill her – just to see if it works! What sort of man is he, for God's sake?' Bryony demanded to know.

Tyrell had no doubts. 'Very rare.'

'OK.' The girl was still uncertain. 'Shelley I can understand, Tina at a pinch, but Fay?'

'Cover,' said the DI. 'If we hadn't pulled in Miles Kennedy when we did there could have been more girls missing. It's stopped him – for the moment. Who knows what he'll try if he feels threatened. If only –'

Clarke became brisk. 'No good going down that road. You got to Kennedy faster than the rest of us would have done. Anyway, you weren't idle. The burglaries were cleared up.'

'And Mattty Jukes died.'

'But not before you got the answer to the baby mystery.'

'Baby?' Penny's eyes were bright with interest. 'The skeleton?'

Tyrell prepared to lie in a good cause. 'Mattty had an idea about a family – long gone from Murren. He'd been suspicious and the dates tallied.'

'You were lucky to get a result from Livermore on that one,' Clarke said. 'Our Eric must have been a busy boy.'

Tyrell tried hard not to grin. 'It's apparently an achievement to narrow the dating of the bones to "somewhere between 1900 and 1950".'

'So, that case is closed?' Penny gazed at the DI and he was puzzled. Why did he feel she was apologizing? Surely not because she had once idolized Whittaker?

'Yes,' he said gently. 'No one to take to trial. Just a baby to be buried.'

Brian Clarke switched on a fresh batch of coffee. 'Let's be thankful Malcolm Henry Foster's only responsible for three corpses.'

'Four. Don't forget Shelley's baby. He really wanted that one dead.'

'OK. To be able to charge him we've got to break the creep's alibis. How do we do it?'

The DI had no doubts. 'Go back to Tina's murder. It's the one he carried out as an experiment and might have a few loose ends trailing. After all, killing's easy for a murderer. What's difficult –'

'Is disposing of the body in a way which means you don't get caught and someone else gets to carry the can,' Clarke finished for him.

'Is it certain where Tina went into the Wye?' the DI asked.

'Not exactly,' Penny admitted. 'First time round DCI Taverner had help from the rangers. Both banks were searched but there were no odd tyre marks, no footprints, no signs of a body being dragged.'

'She still went in.' Tyrell was quiet, reflective. 'Someone must have seen or heard something and probably doesn't understand the significance.'

'Taverner's crew went over it all and we have too,' Bryony groaned. 'Foster was home that evening and his wife backs him up.'

'Corroboration?'

'Neighbour walking his dog. Saw Foster drive the

Mercedes back through the gates and heading for the garage by nine thirty. It stayed there.'

'He could have had Tina unconscious in the boot. If the Merc didn't get Tina to the Wye, what car did?'

Bryony shook her head. 'Wife's car was checked. Nothing.'

Tyrell frowned. 'Is hers the only car in the Forest?'

There was a brooding silence broken by Clarke. 'Time for those torches of yours?'

'You could be right. Get up there and nose around?'

'Worth a try.'

Penny became businesslike. 'It's Taverner's patch. You'd need to clear it with him – and DCI Whittaker.'

'Going over old ground – again?'

Whittaker was not impressed but DCI Taverner was prepared to listen to reason.

'I know it couldn't have been done more systematically first time,' Tyrell admitted, 'but there was no face to the killer then. Now we have a good idea who was there.'

'Fresh eyes?' Taverner asked.

'Yes, sir.'

'Right. Go for it.'

Taverner might be in overall charge but Whittaker was not pleased.

'I can't have Clarke and Tyrell going off on a wild goose chase. Niblett's being brought in for questioning and I want Clarke on it – he's good with yokels.'

Tyrell raised an eyebrow in a silent question.

'Joey,' Clarke explained.

'Funny, I never thought of him having a surname.'

As Tyrell drove north he remembered Lawrie Grundy and his strictures on those who despised Foresters. In the past, governments had ceded to the power of the men and women between the Wye and the Severn but would Whittaker? He was uneasy in the Forest and despised its inhabitants. What was he risking?

Thoughts of Whittaker were banished as Tyrell watched the Forest scenery flip past until he could see the River Wye rushing between its banks, a rippling muddy ribbon under the trees. He met up with the other members of his team.

'Why did he pick the Wye?' Bryony Goddard asked yet again. She was a tall girl, narrow-boned in body and face, her fine pale hair with a hint of redness held back in a ponytail. She frowned. 'It doesn't make sense.'

'It must have done to Foster,' Tyrell said. 'Perhaps he thought he'd be spotted getting a body into the Severn – felt safer here.'

Bryony was not so sure. 'If he wanted to copy Kennedy, it should have been the Severn.'

'And if we're right,' Tyrell said, 'Tina's murder really was an experiment.'

'After which he polished up his technique?' Bryony asked bitterly.

The DI stamped his feet to warm them, the mud of the river bank seeping through the grass on which he stood. He looked down, seeing the tussocks mangled and distorted by the activity of the three of them.

'Penny, remind me what the weather was like that night.'

She knew her notes off by heart. 'It wasn't raining then but it had been torrential. The river was full and running fast.'

'Was rain likely the next day?'

'No, I don't think it was.'

'Then Foster could have believed footprints and tyre tracks would last. He'd have stuck to the roads, damn him! Why the Wye? He'd have been safer with the Severn and bridges. There's no crossing hereabouts to help him.'

'There's the chain ferry near Symonds Yat,' Bryony said and was startled by the DI's surprise.

'I'd forgotten that! Is it still working?'

'Some friends of mine used it a few months ago,' Bryony told him. 'They were staying this side and wanted a short cut to the pub across the river.'

'Is there a hard approach – enough so a car could get there?'

'I think so.'

'Let's see for ourselves.'

It was a short drive, few signs of life, before they stood and looked at the old ferry.

'Foster could have driven here, no problem,' the DI decided. 'He wouldn't even have to move the ferry and make a noise. Just climb on board and slip Tina into the water on the far side.'

Penny agreed, her expression grim. 'Quick, easy, no muddy prints and no questions. He knew about this.'

'As well as the currents in the Wye,' Tyrell added. 'Fast and lethal, especially with a head of water behind them. He must have been sorely tempted to use the same route for Shelley and Fay, but Bryony's right. If he'd done that he couldn't go on adding his bodies to Kennedy's bill, it would have been too glaring. The Severn must have seemed riskier – more chance of being spotted – but it had to be done.'

'Shall I call a SOCO team up here?' Penny asked.

'Foster's canny and I doubt he's left any traces but we'd better go through the motions. If he gets to hear what we're doing here, it just might help to unnerve him a little.'

He answered the ringing of his mobile phone with a curt, 'Tyrell.'

'Finished there?' Brian Clarke asked him.

'Just about. Why? Has something come up?'

'Joey Niblett. Whittaker's stormed out, calling the man half-witted. I don't think he is an idiot or being awkward. We've got minor stuff out of him so far but we need a different approach.'

Tyrell understood. 'Penny's more than capable of taking over here. Give me half an hour.'

*   *   *

'That was quick!' Clarke said as he came down the stairs from the canteen.

Tyrell grinned. 'I remembered side roads I used to cycle with my brother.' He looked at the tray the sergeant carried. 'Mugs of tea and chocolate biscuits? It used to be a chunk of orange at half-time.'

'Joey's hard going and I needed a break.'

It was unusual for the DI to see his friend so tired. 'What do you want me for? Good cop, bad cop?'

'No, that'd dry him up. I've a hunch he's holding something back and talking non-stop to cover it.'

'Is he that loyal to Foster?'

'Loyal? Scared, more like.'

Tyrell pushed open the door of the interview room and saw Joey Niblett chatting amiably to the PC who had been left in charge. Joey took his mug and cradled it in his hands before sipping noisily until his thirst was quenched, then he beamed at the heap of chocolate biscuits, nibbling one much as a squirrel deals with a nut. By the time he had started on the second, the DI had had a chance to study him.

Small, lithe, Niblett was pale, the bulges of his bony forehead suggesting intelligence. Tyrell looked at the man's hands, surprised by their size and strength. He decided the over-large rugby shirt was not for effect. Joey was brawny, powerful, and with so many crates of cheap goods to be heaved round, a distinct asset for Foster.

After introducing himself, the DI sat down and was subjected to a barrage of ideas from Joey, each designed to be helpful. Clarke drank his tea and waited for a lull.

'Do you do much of the driving, Mr Niblett?' he asked.

Joey launched into a recital of his week's work, day by day, hour by hour.

'The Mercedes?' Tyrell inserted as Joey drew breath between Wednesday's and Thursday's routes.

'Mercedes?'

'Yes. Do you ever drive Mr Foster's Mercedes?'

'Me? Never – well, only when it has to go to the garage.'

A long explanation began but Tyrell raised a hand and Joey was silent.

'Do you have a car, Mr Niblett?'

'Yes – well, no. There's one I can use if it's there.' He drew breath but Clarke was ready for him.

'Where, Joey?'

Between them, Tyrell and Clarke had Joey answering questions. They were asked pleasantly, logically, inexorably, with no time for the man's mind and tongue to wander. It made him uncomfortable and the DI noticed the shining bulges of Joey's face becoming speckled with sweat.

'Mr Foster likes his car spotless – I clean it for him at least once a week. He gets good and mad if he finds a scrap of dirt or one of Benjy's hairs. Grease now – he nearly explodes.'

'And you, Joey?'

The car he used was a Nissan. Foster drove it when he had something too dirty for transport by the Mercedes. It had been filthy recently because of the rain.

'The outside mostly,' Joey said. 'Very muddy it's been – so bad I have to hose off the number plate first, to make sure it's the right car.'

He beamed at the two policemen filling him up with tea and expensive biscuits. Few people listened to Joey and he was enjoying the attention. Tyrell pushed the last biscuit towards him.

'How many times has the car been that muddy – so the plate's been obscured?'

'Not that often, really. Two, three times.'

'Bet you can't remember when that was,' Clarke teased.

The challenge was too great to resist. Weather information, nearness to weekends, deliveries from Birmingham, Folkestone, Bristol, poured from Joey. The detectives had enough information to be able to calculate the exact dates.

* * *

Penny looked up, a finger marking the page of a file she had been reading. 'You'd best get to your beds, you both look done in. Was he that much hard work?'

They nodded. Joey had talked them to a standstill.

'Where's Niblett now?'

'With Mickey and a computer. He's helping put on the area map all the short cuts he's ever shown Foster,' Tyrell said and yawned. 'If Bryony tries those routes against Foster's alibis, who knows what she'll find.'

Clarke rubbed a hand over tired eyes. 'It could take hours.'

'Did you get what you wanted from him?'

Penny was answered by two satisfied smiles and Clarke handed over his pocketbook. She read the details of the days Joey had to clean the badly muddied car and the importance of a bottle of cleaning fluid, used to remove the slightest trace of oil from the upholstery of the Mercedes.

Tyrell poured coffee for Brian and himself. They did not wait for milk and sugar, feeling energy return as they sipped hot liquid.

'Industrial cleaning fluid?' Penny queried.

'Foster likes his status symbol spotless – literally. He brought this stuff back from Brum and it's such a fire hazard he has Joey scared rigid,' Clarke said.

'The chemical's so volatile it must be kept locked up at all times. If spilled it can render people unconscious,' Tyrell added.

'I'll be damned! Who do we wake up and ask for a search warrant?' Penny wanted to know.

Next morning Whittaker insisted on being in charge.

'You went off duty too late last night to be of any use to me now,' he told Tyrell and Clarke. 'Walsh is as bad. He can stay here as well.'

The DI was furious they should be reduced to the rank of naughty schoolboys. All the three of them had done was persist with the questioning of a difficult witness, and in the long hours enough had been learned to make possible the search warrant Whittaker was preparing to execute. Tyrell knew he was in danger of speaking his mind in front of the full shift so he picked up a file and stalked to a corner, concentrating on the first page until he could breathe steadily and his pulses stopped racing. Only then did he realize he had been reading again and again a report of a woman reporting a neighbour behaving strangely and the follow-up comments of officers sent to investigate. 'This happens every time a crime is made public,' Bryony Goddard had written. 'Have checked station files. She dislikes the man and wants him jailed.'

I know just how she feels, Tyrell thought, knowing he had no recourse to justice.

The incident room emptied while Tyrell regained control of himself. 'Right, our turn for a break,' he said and sent Mickey to the canteen with a crisp note and a request for bacon sandwiches.

Clarke was concerned for his friend. He had seen the flare of blood and temper, the fight for control. 'You should have gone to Foster's, Keith.'

Tyrell yawned and stretched. 'Maybe. Whittaker'll be thorough and he'll certainly see the rest are.'

His sergeant got the message, a familiar one in such a situation. Business as usual. 'As long as he gets that damned cleaning fluid.'

'It'd be hard to miss. Joey was very specific.'

Food was long gone when the phone rang. Clarke stopped pacing like a restless bear and scooped up the handset, barking into it before listening with interest.

'Livermore for you,' he said to Tyrell.

'Eric, any news for me?'

Clarke left his friend to talk, listen, make sympathetic noises.

'You'll start with what you've got and need a sample from me ASAP? I understand,' the DI said. 'It'll be couriered to you with my thanks for a brilliant job.'

'Well?' Clarke said as Tyrell dialled a fresh number.

'So far, two hairs – blond but not human. Probably a dog. A long-haired dog.'

'As in golden Labrador?'

Clarke had to be content with a nod as Tyrell began to speak and then was halted in mid-sentence, his expression one of growing disbelief. The sergeant picked up an adjacent phone, flicked the appropriate switch and listened in, shaking his head to clear it of anger. The conversation ended abruptly and there was a moment of silence.

'Whittaker'll get round to it if he's got time?' Clarke's disgust was monumental. 'We've at last got the chance of forensic to nail the bastard and all it takes is a few dog hairs. The house, as well as the dog, is plastered with them. For God's sake, all the man's got to do is sit on a bloody chair! Come on, Mickey.'

'Where're you going?' Tyrell wanted to know.

'To get the damned sample myself and deliver it to Livermore personally. I want Mickey as a witness.'

Mickey ran to start the car as Brian Clarke turned at the door, not seeing Roly Willis about to come in.

'If Whittaker's spoiling for a fight – he can have it!'

Paperwork cooled the DI's mood and by the time he had updated computer files he was tired, needing a break. Brian Clarke's return to the incident room was a good excuse for deserting data.

'Are they bringing Foster in?' he asked after being assured Benjy's hairs had reached the forensic science lab.

'Nope. It was bad enough when Bob Vidler collected samples of oils in the kitchen, then went after the cleaning fluid. Foster got on his high horse and made his wife call a lawyer, insisting Whittaker's people had no right to take any more than a small amount for testing. He needed the stuff for his business, he said.'

Tyrell was surprised. 'How?'

'Foster said the Mercedes was his trademark and had to be kept immaculate at all times. He told Tricky Dicky he might be content to slide his backside on a dirty seat –'

'And the balloon went up?'

'You kidding? For some reason Dicky boy's fuse is shorter than ever. DI Vidler tried to intervene and got shouted at for his pains. Only Penny could calm things. She took over and Mickey and I scarpered.'

They were not left in peace for long, a disgruntled search team returning without the prime suspect.

'Foster's right, his bloody car is as clean as a whistle. How long did we spend going over it?' a furious detective from Taverner's squad asked.

Gerry Cross was as mad. 'His wife's car's the same and they kept on about how it was always like that. "Nothing slipshod here, Constable." '

Whittaker was in no mood for conversation when he stormed into the incident room. He needed an outlet for his fury and the sight of Tyrell working at a computer was just the release he longed for. Words tumbled from him, some making no sense at all. The tone of the DCI's voice was rising higher when Copeland appeared. He did not look surprised and Clarke guessed the super had been warned what was happening.

Copeland held Whittaker's elbow and spoke of an urgent situation which had risen in Gloucester. 'You're just the man, Richard. Can you leave everything here? I'm sure DCI Taverner can manage now you've been to Foster's. His solicitor's been on the blower, by the way. Does want things by the book. I don't know which one he's referring to – the man has a very dodgy reputation around the courts. Still, we must get on.'

The super led Whittaker away and a combined sigh of relief whooshed normality back into the room. Tyrell returned to the report he was entering into the system and appeared to be ignoring the susurrus around him.

'What do we do now, sir?' Mickey asked him.

Tyrell tried a smile and it almost worked. 'Wait. We can't hurry the scientists so we're really back to breaking Foster's alibis – and anything else we can drum up on him to get him to admit what he's done. You could try working out possible routes he could have taken with the three girls, based on the entries Joey helped you make last night.'

'Good idea, sir,' Mickey said and sought solace from his computer and the reliability of a mouse. He was not the only one in the immediate vicinity to be amazed at Tyrell's cool appraisal of the situation so soon after Whittaker's outburst.

Clarke leaned on the DI's monitor. 'How much longer can that go on? You shouldn't have to take any of it!'

Tyrell leaned back and stretched. 'It's funny, but that's the first time it didn't feel personal. Perhaps you're right after all, Brian.'

'It's still not on and he shouldn't be getting away with it.'

'What's a mystery is why the top brass let him go on working in the state he's in. Something's up. They know about it and they're sympathetic. If we knew perhaps we could help.'

'Is there a St Keith?' Clarke asked with a grin. 'Your emblem could be a back with a dozen knives sticking out of it.'

'I can feel every one,' the DI said, trying to keep his tone of voice calm, pleasant, in spite of the vengeful attack he had endured. 'Yet even as he is now, I bet Whittaker didn't miss a thing in that house.'

Roly Willis put his head round the door. 'Mr Copeland wants you two. Now.'

Tyrell was puzzled and the answer to his questioning look at Clarke was a shrug of massive shoulders. The DI picked up his jacket and tidied himself as they walked towards the super's office. Brian Clarke, hands deep in his trouser pockets, was in no mood to button his collar and straighten his tie.

Copeland was watching movement in the car park below, turning as they entered. 'I'd like you both to take some time off – get a breather. When we can move forward and have Foster in for questioning I'd like DCI Taverner to take first crack at him. I gather our Mr Foster'll be a very wily animal. I heard how you two coped with Niblett and the pattern could well be repeated so, if you don't mind, get the hell out of here and get some rest. I'll call you back when there's something to go on.'

Clarke had no doubts as they walked away from the super. 'That's the nearest you're going to get as an apology but time off with pay? Now, that's talking!'

There was time to sleep, to read and sleep again. In the hours before Jenny's return in the evening Keith could continue a game of chess on the Internet with his friend in the Met, Stephen Childs, or surf cyberspace at random, amused and horrified in turn by the websites he found.

Sanity returned, and reason. There was even a whole day driving around the Forest with Jenny, revisiting favourite haunts and calling at Lily's home for tea. Lawrie Grundy was there, not asking questions of Keith.

'Always remember, boy, when an evil man or woman is finally brought down our way, it comes harder than the justice you and your courts deal out.'

Those words echoed and re-echoed as Keith drove back to the station from Lily's after a call from Copeland. DNA results had sped from Eric Livermore. Benjy's hairs matched the few found in Tina's and Fay's clothing and Malcolm Henry Foster was furious he had been arrested.

He maintained an air of injured innocence, abetted by a solicitor who came running from Gloucester and screeched objections. The pair of them exhausted questioners, Taverner and his DI, Bob Vidler, needing a break. Brian Clarke was already in Lydney and Copeland was waiting.

'Right, Keith. You and Brian – see what you can do.'

Only Roly Willis saw Whittaker become rigid, a circle of white around his mouth revealing the extent of his control. When the friends walked towards the interview room and hours of hard work, Whittaker went to his office to add to the report growing in his laptop.

* * *

Foster's self-satisfied smirk pleased Ronald Kellock, his solicitor. The client was doing well and there was no real evidence against him, if DNA from a dog could be discounted as well as some iffy chemical. He watched two tall men come into the interview room. Neither had the swagger of a confident adversary and he dismissed their threat to his client.

The detectives had a list of questions to which they wanted answers. The first had Foster and Kellock rebutting it with sustained noise but the policemen were patient, waiting for the suspect and his lawyer to tire. Almost imperceptibly Foster realized there was to be no escape from the men facing him. This would be a fight like no other but Foster was used to winning and they were only a couple of coppers.

Whenever he could Foster dragged in Julie Parry's death. 'I can't be the killer of all those girls. I wasn't here when she went missing and you didn't find any dog hairs on her, did you? If I didn't kill her I didn't kill the rest of them.'

Slowly, inexorably, the DI and his sergeant built their case against the man they held. Girls had been picked up, made unconscious by being forced to inhale an industrial cleaner, their underwear changed round before their hands and breasts were daubed with oil.

'From your kitchen, Mr Foster,' DS Clarke said. 'Unfortunately for you it was from a bottle of cooking oil in which your wife had soaked rosemary. The forensic team got a perfect match.'

There was shouting, bluster, and Kellock insisted his client had a rest. It gave Tyrell and Clarke a chance to report to Copeland.

'So far, so good,' the DI said. 'He's at last talking sensibly but this interruption and some hot food will probably get him going again.'

'Has he accepted we've got plenty of circumstantial evidence and a growing list of forensic data to throw at him in the dock?' Copeland asked.

'It's heading that way, sir,' Clarke acknowledged, 'but

we're not there yet. He still thinks he can slip out from under.'

'I've watched you play rugby, Brian. Not many fly-halves got away in a hurry. Is this any different?'

'Yes, sir. Then we were playing to a known set of rules. Foster's got his own.'

'And you don't like him?'

'No, sir. If you want the truth, I think he's a right little shit.'

There was no hint of DS Clarke's animosity as the questioning continued. Alibis were examined.

'Isn't my wife's word good enough?'

'For us, of course, Mr Foster,' Tyrell assured him, 'but a jury? Each member with a mind of their own?'

'They can't overlook the fact I was in Ireland!'

Clarke sighed. 'We have explained, you know. You're not involved with that killing.'

'Then I shouldn't be here because of the other girls. They were all killed the same way.'

Tyrell was at his most courteous. 'How can you be so sure, Mr Foster? Was it because Tina, Shelley, Fay, were all alive when you tipped their bodies into flooded rivers?'

Kellock woke up to his responsibilities and argued as best he could but Tyrell knew the psychological moment had arrived.

'Strange how you've never realized it was what you did with the girls that differed from what happened to Julie which told us there were two killers. That's why we came looking for you.'

'Differed?' The old Foster was there, alert, wary.

'Oh, yes. Detective Inspector Tyrell spotted it straight away. Took a bit of stick for it at the time but he was right.' Clarke was enjoying himself. 'The oil, Mr Foster. You cocked up there.'

Foster's gaze swung from Clarke to Tyrell and his breathing quickened.

'You used a different oil on Tina,' the DI said, 'then

Shelley, then Fay, and we can prove it. Why? Because you didn't know what kind of oil had been used on Julie. That one was full of a very strange collection of alkaloids.' Not only the ones Tyrell had asked to be looked for but a whole host of others, a few still causing the lab people headaches as they tried to identify them. 'Quite unique you might say, unlike what you used. Another thing you didn't know. Julie not only had oil on her breast and palms, she was also anointed on her forehead.'

'But I –' Foster began, then bit his lip to keep silent.

'Oh yes, Mr Foster. You "overheard" all the details from a girl in Willy's – or so you thought. There was something of which that girl was never aware. It was later, the next day in fact, that the pathologist confirmed oil on Julie's forehead. Too late for you, wasn't it? Tina was already in the water. So, when she had no oil on her brow, nor Shelley, nor Fay . . .'

Foster was silent, breathed deeply and began to argue but his body language and his words marked his despair. Kellock barracked for a break and even Clarke thought regulations must prevail.

Only when they stood in the corridor and watched Foster led away, Kellock scuttling behind him like a tug late for duty, did Tyrell realize how exhausted he was.

Brian Clarke struggled into his jacket. 'Time you were home,' he said. 'Me, too.'

'We're so close to getting him!'

'And if we push harder tonight, Kellock'll be right. You'd have to watch Foster walk on a technicality. We'll finish him tomorrow.'

Keith was almost too tired to drive home. He sank into a chair as soon as he had had a shower to ease the ache of exhaustion. 'When did you get back from Lily's?' he asked Jenny.

She chuckled and he was cheered by the sound. 'It was after ten when they got me home. They were great company, she and Lawrie. I had a long talk with him. You know, he sees more than you want him to.'

Keith stiffened. 'Why? What did he do to upset you?'

'I wasn't upset. I found myself telling him about the time we were deep in the Forest near Speech House – the effect of the trees around me.'

He knew it was hard for Jenny to reveal her feelings. 'Grundy's certainly left an impression on you.'

'He made such sense. How primitive people needed to believe the old gods existed to explain the seasons, what happened to them living as they did amongst the trees. Clever ones who used plants for healing, they had magic in their hands.'

'Your considered opinion, madam. Is Lawrie a witch or a warlock?'

'Neither, the opposite in fact. He talked of the majesty of a tree, its life spent in one spot. Water coursing up its veins, sap seeping and being carried to all vital cells. He insisted these movements result in a force, an aura around each tree and when you're in a wood, a forest . . .'

'Sensitive people can be affected?'

'Something like that. I was happy that day at Speech House because you were with me and I felt joy rise, almost burst.'

'I must go back and thank those trees!'

'Don't tease! Lawrie also made me see that because trees are living entities, it's also possible they can absorb forces from us. Over the years they could have imprinted unbelievable quantities of emotions.'

'And you? Do you go along with all this?'

'I don't know. What's odd in one century can probably be explained by a scientist in the next.' She sat up and turned to frown at him. 'By the way, you'll need a fresh suit tomorrow. I first thought, when you got in, you'd come from one of those brown cafés in Amsterdam.'

'Blame Foster. Judging by his house and his car I'd have sworn he was a non-smoker but an hour into the interview he bummed a cigarette from his solicitor. Brian loved it, making Foster squirm because we didn't smoke and there were no freebies. We knew then we'd got him.'

'Because he smoked?'

'Come on, you're the psychologist! An old habit suddenly readopted? The time between each cigarette becoming shorter until he's almost chain smoking? What does that tell you?'

'An addict severely stressed.'

'Bingo!'

Jenny leaned against him and stared into the fire. 'Lawrie ...' she began.

Her husband condemned Grundy to hell.

'If he's right and if Foster's ever loose in the Forest, the trees could have an effect on him, don't you think?'

'Who says Foster will ever be free again? When Brian and I have finished with him tomorrow, the Prison Service can have him for life.'

DCI Whittaker was an early arrival at the station and he found few in the incident room.

'Get Foster ready for questioning.'

Gerry Cross was wide awake enough to be astonished. 'Sorry, sir. He's already being interviewed.'

The DCI erupted. 'Who's with him? Don't tell me it's Batman Tyrell and his Robin!'

'No, sir. It's DS Rogers and DC Goddard. They're taking him through the details of his alibis and comparing them with times and routes they've worked out themselves which prove he could have done 'em – the murders, sir.'

The senior man tried to calm himself, his breathing noisy. 'Two lower ranks – and women? They should be making tea, not taking my place in the interview room. Who allowed them in there?'

'The super, sir, he's organizing it. When Penny and Bryony have finished, that's when DI Tyrell and Sergeant Clarke take over.'

'Do they really? We'll see about that!'

Whittaker stormed into Copeland's office, forcing him to

listen to a cascade of sputtering fury. Only when his DCI slowed, then stopped, was Copeland able to speak.

'The two officers have all the data at their fingertips. As a pair they've proved invaluable in dealing with Foster – and you know only too well, Richard, how annoying he can be. I intend to let them carry on when the women have done their job and afterwards we'll see which aspects still need to be covered. Maybe then you –' but the super was talking to Whittaker's back.

Neither he, nor anyone else, saw the DCI sit at his desk and open his laptop. Impatient to begin he did not bother with the security ritual. Instead, he called up a document, read it through, amended the odd word and connected his computer to the main system. This not only linked him with every other machine in the station, it also put him on line to the county control centre. Whittaker typed in the name and rank of the person due to receive his report, added a missing 'e' in the chief constable's name and pressed the 'send' key.

Once assured his complaints would reach the highest authority, Whittaker left his desk. He did not see the message telling him transmission was complete, nor did he see the small flag begin to flash in the bottom right-hand corner of his screen.

It was still early in the morning and not all computers were switched on. A sleepy constable entered his password on a monitor, began to open the file he needed and almost shot out of his seat with shock when he noticed the pulsing flag.

'Sarge!' he bellowed at his supervisor. 'Hackers!'

Chapter Thirteen

With limited time in which to hold the suspect, Foster was allowed no leeway and the hours of interrogation began to tell on him. Floods of words to hide or evade answers were replaced by the 'No comment' learned from TV programmes. Occasionally Foster regained his panache and loftily informed the officers, 'I have no intention of discussing that with you.'

Time wore on. The list of questions Tyrell had in front of him was being worked through steadily when DCI Taverner came in. He was frowning, his manner brisk. With a hand on Clarke's shoulder to keep him seated, he leaned close to Tyrell.

'Mr Copeland needs to see you – now.'

The atmosphere in the station puzzled the DI as soon as he reached the corridor. Shut away in the interview room and engrossed in their task, neither he nor Clarke had any idea of the hectic activity which followed a phone call from HQ. Every computer had been checked, not one giving any sign of a fault in its security which could have allowed a hacker access to the system.

'Most likely a rogue laptop,' the expert from HQ had relayed to all stations.

As had been done everywhere else in the county, the building was searched and any laptop found processed to make sure all data protection schemes were in place. One was missed. It had been disconnected at the first alert and hurried away to the boot of a car. Almost as that was being done phones began to ring with a cacophony of madness. Each caller had the same question.

'Is it true?'

'Sit down, Keith.' DS Copeland shut the door carefully and took his time. 'Something's happened – a breach of security. It involves you.'

Tyrell was stunned.

'No, you didn't cause the breakdown, that was a hacker getting into our files. It's been stopped and the appropriate department is tracking them as we speak. Unfortunately, before the intruder could be cut off, they got a copy of a report being sent to the chief constable.'

'I don't understand, sir. I haven't sent any such report.'

'I know. It was a review of your conduct and was, shall we say, very critical indeed.'

Tyrell concentrated on controlling his breathing, trying to steady it and to slow his racing pulse. He was determined to say nothing until he was sure his voice would emerge calm. Before that could happen the door was thrust open and six foot two of muscles in good tailoring stormed in. Frosted curls bounced free of their dressing as the newcomer leaned over Copeland and banged on his desk.

'Rod, this isn't good enough! I'm as sorry for the poor devil as any man but slandering a fine young copper as well as putting at least one current prosecution in jeopardy, it's just not on! All hell's let loose at HQ. The entire press office is running around like a flock of headless chickens and the chief constable's popping blood pressure pills every five minutes. Damn it – we'll all need 'em before this is sorted!'

The DI had stood to attention as soon as Assistant Chief Constable George Hinton had entered. It was only when the ACC drew breath and noticed the movement of

Copeland's eyes he became alerted to the presence of a third person in the room.

'Keith!' The hand held out was large, firm, dry. 'DS Copeland's filled you in?'

'I was in the process, sir,' the super said. 'He hasn't yet seen the report.'

There was pity in Hinton's eyes when he faced Keith Tyrell. 'We'll have to suspend you, pending an enquiry, you know that. Take it as extra leave and spend time with that wife of yours. Why not go and see your father? If you do, give him my regards.'

Tyrell was rigidly erect. 'I gather I've had an accusation levelled against me. If it's possible, I'd like to see a copy of the report?'

Copeland waited for a nod from Hinton before lifting a sheet of paper from his desk. As Keith Tyrell took it he tried to guess Copeland's thoughts from his expression. Sympathy? Regret?

Steeling himself, Tyrell read words that were hammer blows. The prose had been well drafted, its style giving maximum effect. Itemized was every incident, real or imaginary, when Detective Inspector Keith Tyrell had been inefficient, rude, off-hand, or generally insubordinate in a way which insulted the rank and person of Detective Chief Inspector Richard Whittaker.

Lost for words, Tyrell swallowed hard. 'I can see suspension must be automatic, sir. At least the occasions when I'm assumed to be at fault will have been witnessed and can be investigated.'

'Have you a good lawyer you can call on?' Copeland asked.

'Yes, sir.' Tyrell thought of the times he had dragged Jeremy out of trouble. Now it was his turn. 'How many must know about the existence of this report?'

'That's the trouble,' Hinton said. 'It depends when we can lay hands on this damned hacker and get at the equipment.'

'Hacker, sir?' A numbing coldness began to paralyse Tyrell.

'Yes, 'fraid so. Some bloody idiot was slipshod with security.' The ACC waved a hand at Copeland.

A second sheet of paper was handed over and, with growing disbelief, Tyrell read of all the ways in which the aforementioned DI Tyrell had mishandled evidence against Malcolm Henry Foster, prime suspect in the serial killings of four girls in the Forest of Dean.

'If this ever got out –' he began as he looked up at the faces of the two men. In slow motion, horror suffused him. 'The hacker? You don't mean –?'

'Most of that page was posted in a chat room on the Internet. Theoretically, the whole world now knows,' Copeland explained.

'Not only do we have to suspend you because of this, we probably have to let Foster walk. Newspapers have their own code of conduct – more or less – and their lawyers will be working overtime so they can print what they can of this without breaking too many laws but chat rooms on the Internet? How the hell are we supposed to police those?'

Coursing adrenalin had dispelled horror and exploded in anger. 'All that's been done to get Foster to face charges in court!' Tyrell's bitterness echoed around the room. 'Even the CPS would have approved and now this! Has all that hard work been for nothing?'

'We can keep on trying but the CPS will shout loud and clear this makes a fair trial for Foster unlikely. The chances are they won't proceed with the case in the foreseeable future.'

Control was hard, too hard. 'I know I've been expected to take a lot from Whittaker in the past and I know he hates my guts but if he's –'

'Leave it, Keith,' Copeland said and the force in his voice stopped the younger man. The DS looked at Hinton. 'Sir, I think he should be told about DCI Whittaker.'

'Not an option, Rod,' the ACC said and shook his head, clearly uneasy.

'After this, surely it's time?'

'No, the decision's been made and it's not in my remit to change it, so there's an end to it.'

New memories would be indelible. Handing over his warrant card. Walking out of the building escorted by Copeland and unable to talk to anyone. In the station yard they had met ACC Hinton with Whittaker.

'Just taking Richard with me, Rodney. See his car gets driven home for him, will you?'

It had been no consolation to see Whittaker looking badly shaken by the morning's events.

'Keys?' Hinton held out a hand but had to wait for Whittaker, slow and fumbling like an old man, to search his pockets. The ACC tossed the keys to Copeland. 'I'll leave you to see to things here.'

Copeland waited until the ACC's driver had eased the large car out of the station yard and through a seething crowd gathered in the street.

'A few arrived last night because there was a rumour we were holding someone for questioning. News travels fast and it didn't take long to get completely surrounded,' Copeland said. 'I'd better get more troops on the barricades.' He put a hand on Tyrell's shoulder. 'We've a good crew here. Leave it to us.'

Detective Sergeant Meg Sutton was one of Taverner's team. She drove towards Copeland and stopped the car. Her DCI hurried from the back door of the station, a uniformed PC struggling into a heavy raincoat as he followed.

'Reed will be on duty at your gate, Keith,' Copeland said. 'DCI Taverner will be the senior officer with you until the appropriate people get there. Mr Hinton's been on to the chief constable and the Home Office. Everything possible's being done to speed up procedures.'

* * *

Keith sat in his home and was numb. He had offered food, coffee, and Meg Sutton had seen he was still in shock. Tall, fair, reserved, she had taken over in the kitchen and surprised Keith when grilled ham and cheese appeared on toast, sliced tomatoes and chopped chives adding colour and a sense of normality.

DCI Taverner added a small tot of brandy to Keith's coffee. 'Medicinal. You'll need it when the enquiry team gets here.'

'Who'll be sent? CIB?'

Taverner shrugged his shoulders. 'Anyone's guess these days, Home Office initiatives coming out of there thick and fast. I shouldn't worry, if I were you. You've committed no crime. As for the rest – it's based on one man's opinion.'

'What about the evidence on Foster?'

'Oh, come on, man! I've said too much already. Wiser heads than yours or mine decide that.'

An hour later part of that decision arrived at the front door. The senior man of three who walked towards Keith was grey. Hair, eyes, suit, even skin, but it was the grey of steel, chilling and yet resilient.

'Detective Inspector Tyrell, I am Chief Superintendent Morgan.' He introduced his colleagues and explained they were there for a 'chat'.

With DS Sutton, DCI Taverner was despatched seconds after assuring the newcomers no phone calls had been received, DI Tyrell had not used his computer, watched TV or used the radio.

Keith had never been investigated but he knew the procedures that must be followed. Nothing that was happening seemed to fit a known pattern and Keith was unsure whether to be relieved or apprehensive. Coffee was refused but permission asked to look round the house. Keith nodded assent yet was puzzled by the civility. The other two men, a DI and a sergeant, began their search.

Chief Superintendent Morgan smiled, the wintry aspect of him thawing slightly. 'You've not been accused of a crime, so we're here merely to establish a few basics. Your home is very orderly, very organized, so it will make things easier. We'll have to take your computer with us.' He gestured to the machine in the corner of the sitting room. 'Is that your only one?'

'No. I have a laptop – that's already at the station. DS Copeland took charge of it while I was interviewing Foster.'

'Your wife?'

'Jenny has her own laptop, of course. I must warn you her files are subject to privacy rules because of her work.'

'I'm aware of that, Inspector. We'll do only what's necessary. Have you any objection to us taking what we must from your home?'

'No objections. It's essential I'm exonerated as quickly as possible.'

'Worried about your good name, Inspector Tyrell?'

From the tone of Morgan's voice Keith was aware he was being needled into a reaction.

'For anyone, man or woman, a good name's important – a label that attaches itself to what you do, who you are. In the short term, what's vital is the evidence I've helped to establish against Foster. If that's called into question, he walks free. Then there's Frank Kennedy. He'd give a great deal to see my name, good or bad, dragged through the mud. It might get his son acquitted as well as the investigation into his own financial affairs.'

'Two cases concern you, Inspector? You'd better add in every con you've ever helped put behind bars. There'll be queues for appeal when they hear. Evidence against them unsound because of the police officer who collected it? They'll all think Christmas has come early.' Morgan shook his head. 'No, there's more than your reputation riding on this. It'll affect every case you've worked on and every colleague you've ever worked with.'

Keith fought exhaustion. The night before he had had little sleep as he planned questions for Foster. Now this.

'Your feud with DCI Whittaker.'

'It's not my feud,' Keith said, careful to sound calm. 'I've said it before and I'll say it again, DCI Whittaker's good at his job.'

'So, his criticisms of you are justified?'

'I'm not inside the man's mind. How am I supposed to understand how he sees things? All I know is that I've always behaved properly towards him, no matter what . . .'

Morgan waited. 'Go on, Inspector Tyrell. Say what you think.'

A steadying breath helped. 'I think you're trying to drag me into a slanging match. I usually try to stay away from such a situation.'

'Was that what DCI Whittaker wanted? A confrontation? And you constantly refused him? That could be considered provocation on your part, Inspector.'

Fingers curled involuntarily into Keith's palm, the resulting pain steadying him. He knew it was important not to leave it too long before speaking. 'If the DCI believed what he wrote was true, then the report he sent to the chief constable was justified. What's important to me is that all the situations he quoted, as well as his complaints about my methods of collecting evidence, can be checked and double-checked by you and your department. There'll be plenty of witnesses to help you decide the report's accuracy.'

The other men returned to the sitting room and Morgan rose to meet them. With heads bent together they exchanged low-voiced facts, ideas, opinions. Keith saw them agree before they moved to sit near him. Morgan arranged his chair so that he was opposite Keith, the bulkier of his colleagues beside him. It was the sergeant, Keith decided, trying to remember his name. Brinn. DS Brinn. The third was a DI Richards, slighter than his sergeant but both grey men in the making. Richards sat to the side of Keith's chair, slightly behind him so he could study Keith but not be easily faced. It was almost worth a smile. Standard procedure. DI Richards must be the body language expert.

Morgan's expression was a pale mask. He stretched his head back, letting eyelids drop until they were half-closed and drew Keith's attention to him.

'Was DCI Whittaker jealous of you?'

Keith was careful to keep his breathing regular and not take too long in answering. 'I can think of no reason.'

'Come now, Inspector Tyrell. An education in one of our better public schools and then a law degree prestigious enough to let you carve out a lucrative career far away from the stress of policing.' Morgan lifted a hand that was bony yet finely muscled. 'Take your home, for example. No mortgage, which makes you a rarity. I gather you've some fine pieces of silver tucked away and the wines you stock are hardly from bargain bins. After your start in the Met you went up through the ranks like a rocket and came to this county's force with a reputation as a successful investigator, very keen on the truth. Almost in your first weeks you gave evidence on behalf of a man in custody which meant a DI was demoted – a DI close to DCI Whittaker. Financially, you're comfortable and in the fullness of time you stand to inherit Dakers, quite a wealthy estate, I understand, as well as a title to go with it. And you say you can think of no reason why anyone should envy you?'

From the first weeks of cadet training Keith had had to endure harassment which ranged from gentle ribbing to out and out offensiveness. The unseen skin he had grown then became useful again. Morgan's technique was obvious but he was carrying it out well and Keith knew he must be careful.

'Then there's your wife,' Morgan said slowly, licking his lips as he spoke. 'Gorgeous, by all accounts, and a professional. Her salary added to yours must cushion you both from life's little vagaries. Do you think DCI Whittaker thought of the two of you here, in bed, and became – rather frustrated, shall we say?'

Keith almost smiled. In the last year or so it had been Whittaker himself who provided so much practice in staying clear-headed and with a pleasant expression under a barrage of verbal abuse and incitement.

'If anyone fantasizes, sir, that's their problem not mine. By the same token, an individual suffering the agonies of jealousy has a self-induced affliction. I deal with my problems, I leave other people to deal with theirs.'

'You don't think you should reduce the way you flaunt all you have at your disposal?'

'My wife and I live very simply. We work hard and like to spend our free time in our own home. Why should we change the way we live? To do so would be to submit to a form of bullying.'

'Are you saying DCI Whittaker was bullying you?'

'No, sir.'

The interrogation continued without a break, Morgan's questions always incisive but coming from unexpected directions. Richards was still, watching every movement, every twitch even, that Keith made and DS Brinn's gaze was unnerving. Keith was tired, yet determined not to be needled into an involuntary statement. Eventually, he did sense Morgan beginning to slow his inquisition. DI Richards became restless and even DS Brinn began to blink more frequently.

Morgan leaned forward. 'Tyrell, see sense, for heaven's sake. This is your chance to put the record straight. Tell us what really happened.'

The gentleness, sympathy, in DCS Morgan's voice was very tempting. Keith almost succumbed but fought the urge to unburden himself completely. He knew all too well how such outpourings could be interpreted and lifted his chin.

'As far as I'm concerned, sir, the record is straight – and always has been.'

* * *

With Jenny began sanity. Keith held her tightly until the tumult in his mind slowed, silenced.

'Bad day?'

'Mmm.'

'I gather Whittaker finally flipped his lid?'

'Mainly by not using the latest protection program for his laptop. It left a weak spot and a hacker got in. There's a report.'

'I heard. At least you've got some time to yourself. You could even make a start in the garden now the rain's eased.'

Exhaustion held Keith almost as strongly as misery. Jenny fed him and heaped logs on the fire. Coffee was without caffeine and laced with cognac until Keith drowsed on the couch, Jenny beside him. It was peaceful, timeless, in the quiet room until they were disturbed by the ringing of her mobile phone. She took it into the kitchen and he watched logs settle and flare, blue and green in the flames.

Almost as soon as she returned to him, there was another call and Jenny smiled as she talked, then held out the phone to him.

'I rang Brenda from the clinic and gave her this number. It's Brian for you.'

Keith was uneasy. 'I don't want to get you involved!' he said to Brian.

The strong voice of their friend reverberated.

'OK. If that's how you want it.' Keith was too tired to argue. 'Tell me what's happened today.'

He listened, nodding, at times emotion engendered by what he heard almost engulfing him. Full control was back by the time he thanked Brian for all he was doing and Jenny was close enough to hear the big man's reply.

'It's no more'n you'd do for me – or any of us. Take care now – and don't let the bastards get you down!'

'Can't he be disciplined for contacting you?' she asked when the phone was switched off.

'Technically, he was talking to you, not me. Was that

what you planned when you wouldn't let me plug our phone in again?'

'I just wanted us to have some peace and quiet.'

'Who called just before Brian?'

Jenny did not answer immediately, going to kneel in front of the fire and stir the embers with slow movements of the poker. 'Work. No one important,' she added and returned to sit by him.

After the stresses of the day it was healing to sit in warmth and silence, little disturbing them. Jeremy's call was a welcome intrusion.

'Dad told me what happened so I started with the server running the website on which you were first pilloried. Slapped 'em a writ and their pants have become rather brown as a result. Asked a million in damages for that one. Then I had a whisper about one of our revered red-tops down Wapping way. Upped the price for them and promised to increase a writ's demands by half a mill each time an editor annoyed me.'

Keith had had many shocks during the day and this one was the ultimate. 'Jeremy! You can't do that!'

'Why? Because you're a serving police officer? Rubbish! If the first item that appeared in public was a gross libel, then repeating it is even more so.'

'What if you managed to win even one of those cases?'

'You'll be loaded and I'll have a nice little earner.'

'It's not right!'

'And monkeying about with your good name is? Pete's sake, Keith, why not chuck the coppering? Eat your dinners as Dad wanted and come and work with me. Between us we could clean up and you could keep Jenny decently. As things stand I can only get you peanuts by comparison.'

'I can't take money for what's happened.'

'Thought you'd be like that. Get Jenny to help. Decide on a charity and give me the details. I'll have a trust fund up and running in the morning – ready for any contributions.'

'My bosses'll go spare!'

'Sod 'em,' was a leading barrister's opinion. 'They

should have kept Tricky Dicky under restraint when they knew he was unhinged.'

'How did you –? You've been talking to Brian Clarke.'

'Why not? He's a friend of the family. I like him and I trust him.'

'So do I – and I don't want you getting him into hot water on my account.'

'Listen, you idiot. He's his own man and he'll do all he can to get you clear. If the media want to pay heavily for trying to cash in on your misfortunes, then I'll take all the help I can get to burn their greedy little paws for 'em. I assume your phone's out of action because of news-hounds?'

'You've guessed right. We've even got our own police-man on the gate to keep us safe.'

'Should think so too. Never mind, you may find the hordes of the ungodly and unwashed dropping rapidly when it starts circulating that I'll sue editors and owners until their proverbials squeak.'

Keith's father talked to him at length, the older man's support and cheerfulness helping to ease humiliation, a sense of complete failure.

'I warned you this might happen when you decided on the police as a career but you'll get through the next few days and be stronger because of it. It's good Jenny will carry on with her job – the expectation of normality is what brings it about. I'm here if you need me.'

Next day, Keith's mother drove over from Dakers. Small and blonde, she was steel wrapped in natural charm as she persuaded, teased, nagged her son to work in the garden. After lunch, when it rained, they visited Lily.

'You took your time getting here,' she chided her guests with a smile. The women hugged, inspected each other and made their way into the garden, ignoring rain which drizzled annoyingly.

'Come inside,' Keith heard and turned to see Lawrie Grundy at the open door. 'When Lily starts on about her garden, she's best left alone.'

'My mother's the same.' Keith followed Grundy into the house and was handed a very large tot of whisky. 'It's a bit early for me.'

'No, it's not. You must need it after what you went through yesterday. Besides, your mother's driving and you're not on duty.'

'No,' Keith said slowly and twisted the glass, light from the fire broken up into its constituent colours by the angles of precisely cut crystal. 'I'm not on duty.'

'Sit down, boy, and get your chin off your knees. An idiot's made a fool of you. It'll pass.'

'And what'll be left behind?' Keith retorted.

'Get Lily's good whisky down you and relax.'

'How can I? Everybody worked hard – you helped too, and now this. All because of me.'

'Not much sleep last night, I'll be bound. Your mind's been working overtime and all the demons you've ever known are crawling over your skin.'

Keith sipped, savouring smoky malt as it slid along his tongue. Muscles softened and he lay back against the chair's cushioning. Aware of Lawrie Grundy's patience he sighed and surrendered.

'What the hell – I'm suspended. Ask your questions.'

'Easy, boy, I'm not after your secrets. Anyway, I'd guess you've had enough questions thrown at you recently. What's the outfit called that tackles coppers who've misbehaved? Internal Affairs?'

Keith summoned up a grin. 'You've been watching too much American TV.'

'Judging by the change in you since we last met, they were rough on you – whatever name they work under.'

'In the circumstances it had to be done. Let's face it, if the accusations had been true, I'd have arrested me myself.' It was a wry attempt at humour.

The two men sat in companionable silence. They heard Lily and her friend come in from the garden. Water gushed as the women talked, crockery clinked and a kettle whistled, the sound cutting through laughter.

'People talk to me,' Lawrie said at last. 'I've learned

you've made some damned good friends since you were first based at Lydney. It's taken time but respect for you and the way you work is solid. The unpleasantness will soon end and you've the guts to survive it without scarring.'

They were almost his father's words. 'You sound very sure.'

'I am. I may not know you so well but there's not much hidden from me by Foresters. It's common knowledge you did all you could for us. Granted, you did it your way and maybe not ours but you should have been successful.'

Keith's nails beat a tattoo on his glass. 'Somehow, that makes me feel a real failure.'

'Nonsense!' Lawrie reached for the whisky bottle. He was a grey-haired sage in a country-checked shirt and a green-cabled cardigan with leather buttons. 'Tell me, is it likely this chap Foster can walk free?'

'I don't know. His lawyer can insist that any evidence used as a basis for arrest and charging is unreliable. Foster stands a very good chance of being allowed to go home.'

'Free in the Forest? Not a safe place for that son of Satan. Remember, he lives here, knows us and our ways. It'll affect him.'

'Those unseen forces again, Lawrie? Are they going to be organized to destroy him?'

The old man shook his head. 'A sinner brings about his own destruction. All we need do is wait . . .'

'And pray that justice is brought forth?'

'Ah, the Book of Isaiah! You remembered.'

Lawrie Grundy rolled his glass between his palms, watching liquid swirl as he directed. He looked up at Keith, his eyes darkened by bushy grey brows filtering light.

'Be patient, boy.'

Chapter Fourteen

Two days later the debate on how to proceed with the gardening had reached a very healthy level when the front door bell rang. Cecily Tyrell had driven for an hour to breakfast with her son. She was not pleased to be interrupted and rattled crockery as she cleared the table.

'My apologies for arriving like this. I tried to make contact but no joy.'

Lady Tyrell was brought from the kitchen, introduced to Detective Superintendent Copeland and glared at him.

'I do hope you've come to say this appalling mess has been cleared up. My husband and I find it thoroughly unsatisfactory.'

Rod Copeland recognized the steady gaze he was used to in her son but encountered it now sparkling with anger.

'It is indeed, Lady Tyrell. Fortunately the enquiries made so far show every indication Keith will soon be free to resume his duties. We have to follow procedures, as you will understand, but it is important that he, and the evidence he has amassed, can be presented in court with no repercussions. It's in everybody's interests this mess, as you call it, lasts not a moment longer than necessary.'

Keith had heard of Copeland's diplomatic skills. It was interesting to see them in action and Lady Tyrell must have approved. No one ever fooled her and she did become gracious, offering him breakfast.

'Thank you, no,' he said. 'I've come straight here from my home.'

'Then I'll take some tea to that nice constable of yours on gate duty – a charming young man and very efficient. Toast too, I think. It's a cold day.'

'You're very kind, Lady Tyrell.'

'Not at all, Superintendent. Those of lesser rank must always be deserving of our consideration.'

Thoroughly reprimanded, DS Copeland followed Keith into the sitting room, still warm from the previous evening's fire.

'Is there any news, sir?' Keith asked as he gestured the DS to a chair and sat facing him on the edge of another.

'In your case, it is as I told your mother. All your colleagues have been interviewed and files gone through with the proverbial fine-tooth comb. You know these inquisitors – not even a flicker to hint at the outcome – but they do seem prepared to draw their conclusions earlier than I would have expected. It could be due to the urgency over material in the case against Foster as well as the one building against Frank Kennedy. Computer data gathered for the Kennedy son's trial must be deemed admissible if the Serious Fraud Office is to be able to use it to get the father sent down. Having said that, I'm sorry, Keith. It'll still be some time before we can have you back.'

He tried a smile. 'As long as it is "when" and not "if" I can wait.'

'No question of that. Flak from the media is less than we feared. I'd guess your brother's inherited Lady Tyrell's defence mechanism – come out fighting. Will he really go ahead with all the libel cases he's threatened?'

'Jeremy? Yes. We were brought up to keep our word.'

'And a confidence too, I gather. I've a problem to deal with and you're the only one who can help.'

'But if I'm suspended –'

'Don't worry, it's nothing in official records.'

For a split second Keith puzzled over the emphasis Copeland had placed on the word 'official'. 'The baby?'

'Yes. The body – what's left of the poor little devil – has been released for burial. In theory I've no knowledge of any possible next-of-kin. I can ask you to arrange it as it's not technically police business. We're fully stretched, as you know, so I've permission from ACC Hinton for you to handle the matter. It's considered a discreet way of letting you know you're not persona non grata.'

Murren looked the same. Coffee in the Bothy even smelled the same but he decided to risk it.

'Inspector Tyrell! Good to see you back. Have you got business here or can we all breathe again?'

'Just a visit,' Keith said. 'I was surprised to see Matty's cottage being taken apart.'

'Owners were at it day after the funeral. They needed three skips to clear his rubbish before the architect would agree to go in and have a look.'

'Poor old Matty. He and his Sybil were happy there.'

'Poor be damned, he's left thousands! There's a couple of nieces fighting over his cash now he's gone. Wouldn't come near the old man when he was alive and could a done wi' a bit of family. Greedy bitches!'

Keith smiled. 'He'll be remembered, then.'

'Aye – and there's a few'll have mind to you, too. Is it true?'

'The accusations? No. That I'm suspended? Yes. That's why I thought I'd have a wander round today. When I get back to work there'll be a mountain of paperwork waiting.'

'You just be thankful it's not VAT. Those Customs bastards've been going through this place like a dose o' salts. Suspicious or what? Just because Matty and the others drank here and used our Gents as an office.'

'What about the girls?'

'Wendy we've never seen since that night. As for Leanne, she's with Mrs Hackett. Poor devils, they were both in need of company.'

'I'll call and see Mrs Hackett, if she's at home.'

'She will be. Not much really changes in the end.'

His cup drained, Keith waved goodbye to Claire and Des Goldsmith then strolled along Murren's rutted road, avoiding puddles which were in the process of shrinking now the rains had eased. The only person to be seen was Harry Gilbert, taking advantage of a dry day to sweep his garden path. A curtain twitched in Mandy Stone's house. It could have been her hand he saw, or maybe one of her sons staying hidden as he mitched school.

'None of my business,' Keith said to himself as he walked on, accepting that suspension from duty had a few perks to offer.

The smell from Gloria Reilly's house oozed past a closed door and still lingered in his nostrils as he used the knocker on the end house.

'Inspector Tyrell! Come in, do.'

It was good to see Mrs Hackett looking well. She was busy, the rooms not quite so neat.

'Peter's having a nap so we've time for a cuppa. Tea?'

He sat with her in the kitchen where the clothes of a very small boy were draped over a rack by the stove.

'You don't get too tired having Leanne and Peter here?'

'Not at all, it's good for me. Chris, Julie's boyfriend, made me keep her car. I don't drive but he's happy for Leanne to use it for work as long as she sees to me and takes the Miss Averys shopping.'

She chatted on. Leanne worked mornings in an hotel in Blakeney, going back in the evenings to help with dinners and the bar. Peter was the dearest boy and as good as gold, sleeping through anything. Keith already had proof of that but he made no comment, asking instead what had become of others in Murren.

'The young couple with the goats, they got done by the Social. Turns out they were earning on the sly. Both managed to get proper jobs once the giros stopped. Then there's Murren Cottage. The boy's doing well at school, so I'm told, and his mother, Vicky Downing-as-was, she's got a new man, another retired farmer. He comes a few times a week and would probably move in if it wasn't for her mother.' Mrs Hackett shook her head. 'I've known Dorothy for more years than I care to remember but see her smile? Never.' She tutted gently. 'Vicky'll be the same in time.'

'The Misses Avery? In good health?'

She frowned. 'Yes and no – but then with those two you can never tell if anything's wrong.' Mrs Hackett folded and refolded a bib lying on the table. 'They still miss Julie.'

Keith put his hand on hers and she smiled at him through her tears.

'You always understood. That man . . .?'

'Miles Kennedy?'

A nod encouraged him to answer.

'There was some concern with this fuss on the Internet that his lawyers might use it as an excuse to get the case against him dismissed.'

'No!' Mrs Hackett was shocked, fearful.

'Don't worry. He'll answer for what he did.'

The grandmother was relieved. 'You're sure he didn't mean her to die?'

'I think when Julie lost consciousness it was Miles Kennedy's worst nightmare come true. His defence lawyer will probably argue at the trial that even if Kennedy had called for help, Julie would not have lived –'

'Because of the condition she'd inherited from her father?'

'Yes.'

'I never liked the man. Shifty. We were all better off when he went.' It was some sort of epitaph for Idris Parry.

It had taken time but the wander round Murren had made the visit to the Misses Avery appear to be only a matter of courtesy. Everything was as he remembered. There was the same aroma of age and dust, with a hint of lavender polish. Miss Rhoda hurried him into the room they used for special occasions.

'Hester's upstairs changing, she'll be down soon. You have news?'

'Yes.'

There was only time to be offered a chair before Hester was with them, the sense of lavender stronger now.

'Thank you for your letter, Inspector –'

'Please, I've been suspended from duty. At the moment Inspector's only a courtesy.'

'Then you shall have it,' Hester said. 'You've always been kindness itself to us. I assume you're here because all the formalities have been dealt with?'

'They have and I've been asked to arrange interment. Have you any plans of your own?'

The sisters clung together, facing him with tears in their eyes. 'No,' Hester said. 'What do you suggest?'

'Tolland? The vicar there would be most helpful and considerate.'

'No!' Rhoda was horrified, wanting only to protect her sister from further anguish. 'People who know us might see – at the very least ask questions. It's always been a private matter, can't we keep it that way?'

Keith thought quickly. 'There is one person who might help us.' He held up his mobile phone. 'May I try?'

When he returned to the quiet room Keith talked of Father Andrew, made him come alive, until the Averys were assured the baby's last resting place would be peaceful, beautiful, secret.

That evening the front door bell disturbed them as Jenny worked through files and Keith stretched long legs to the fire and listened to a Chopin étude.

'Mickey! You shouldn't be here. I'm supposed to have no contact –'

'Sorry, sir, it's not you we've come to see.'

Rose stepped from his shadow. She was almost hidden by a huge spray of spring flowers. 'We had a whip-round for Mrs Tyrell.'

'She's got you to put up with full time, sir,' Mickey added with a grin.

'Come in, the pair of you. Did PC Reed see you?'

'There's no one there now. All the press boys –'

'And girls,' added Rose, 'they've gone to Lydney. Kellock's been boasting he'll have his client out by tonight.'

'That's why Harry Reed's back at the station. It's a full call-out for uniformed,' Mickey said, 'but there's a blind eye in our direction so Mrs Tyrell could get her flowers.'

'We did have a whip-round for you too, sir,' Rose told him.

'Manny's holding it behind the bar for a party when you get back on duty.' Mickey's grin was infectious, Jenny smiling at the scent of her bouquet and Keith's laughter.

'Anything new – that you're allowed to tell me?'

'Sergeant Willis in a filthy mood? That do for a start? Then the canteen girls say they're fed up cooking so many chips with all the extra bodies in the incident room. Their husbands and boyfriends complain about the smell clinging too long.' Mickey thought hard. 'DS Copeland's spending most of his time with us. The Gestapo's almost had rubber hoses out but they've given up and gone home. Everyone thinks if that lot really meant to carve you up it would have been Kate the Knife in charge and not DCS Morgan.'

It had been a long time since Keith had battled not to smile and the description of DCI Kate Lovatt tested him. Mickey and the others were right. Kate Lovatt headed any team of inquisitors sent in to slice a crooked policeman or woman from a comfortable posting.

'Even the crew from the north have almost finished checking all our files as well as the Gestapo report,' Mickey said. 'Boring really, except when DS Clarke blows his top.'

'Has he done that often?' Keith was anxious for his friend.

'Not really. Only when he's asked some damn fool question. His words, not mine.'

Keith watched as Jenny fed their guests. There was no need to ask of Whittaker. Brian Clarke had rung just before Mickey and Rose had arrived. Tricky Dicky's family had been shunted off somewhere on an extended holiday while

Whittaker was locked away in a clinic north of Cheltenham with a cackle of counsellors.

Jenny had hugged Keith when she heard. 'Once it's part of the enquiry what's happened to Whittaker it scuppers completely the adverse report on you. You're in the clear.'

'Not yet,' he had warned. 'Procedures have to be seen to be followed.'

Her idea of what should be done with procedures had Keith laughing. The Chopin had been an attempt to restore calm and decency.

'The Kennedy dad's in a pickle,' Mickey said, almost curling with glee. 'I heard he tried to cash in on your little problem but DS Copeland gave him what for. Promised to give him "an attempt to pervert the course of justice" to deal with.'

'So, Miles Kennedy does stay where he is and Malcolm Henry Foster really will walk?'

'Looks like it. Mind you, he'll have a job getting out of the station and away.' Mickey saw Keith was puzzled. 'You haven't heard?'

'Heard what?'

'That's why you've lost your reporters. They're all outside the nick, waiting to see what happens if Foster tries to leave. Mind you, even they can't get near the place.'

'Why not?'

'Haven't you been watching the telly?'

Keith and Jenny shook their heads.

'People have come from all over the Forest. They're just standing there. A few carry placards but there's no real protest. It's weird, I can tell you.' Mickey was uneasy, remembering.

'It's the silence,' Rose explained. 'Like being in church when everyone's praying.'

Mickey went on talking, Rose listening admiringly, but Keith and Jenny heard nothing as they realized Lawrie Grundy's prediction was unfolding.

'Can nothing be done?' Keith wanted to know.

Mickey shrugged his shoulders. 'The DS says keep calm

but I think it's why he wasn't unhappy us being here. He wants a few CID spread around the area in case anything pops. If we were in the office when a call came, there's no way we could get out and deal with it.'

'What about uniforms?'

'Being drafted in from all over. DCI Taverner's co-ordinating that. He's getting men and women at Foster's house – and his shops. It's not just us surrounded because we've got Foster. Anything to do with that man's got a ring of protesters.' Mickey frowned. 'Can you call them protesters, even when they make no noise?'

Morning dawned with a clear sky, the air still chill and damp.

Keith was early. He levered his car seat until he reclined, eyes shut, as he absorbed the peace of the quiet road and the lay-by in which he was parked. Too alert for sleep he let his thoughts drift, images parading themselves against closed lids.

Murren. Always Murren. It was only weeks since he first walked along its rutted road and yet he had come to know it and its inhabitants so well. Then there was Whittaker's obsession with the place. The DCI had first concentrated his efforts in Murren after the burglaries became more than a handful of minor crimes. Homes had been robbed right across the Forest yet he had thought only of Murren.

What was it about Whittaker and the country between the Severn and the Wye? Had he, city-bred, seen the Dean Forest as a great amorphous sprawl of greenery and isolated homes? The royal and ancient Forest of Dean was a network of communities which had been forged by hardship and loyalty into a complete unit, its people with a history of power that could defy governments. Was it a sense of a strength he could not harness, under trees that haunted Whittaker like one giant amoeba gorged with chlorophyll? He could have feared it enough to make him focus his efforts on Murren and a collection of families he felt he could control. It had been obvious from the start he despised Foresters generally and, like Foster, he faced the same risks.

Knuckles rapped on the passenger window. Keith pressed a switch, misted glass rolled down and he was bid 'Good morning.'

'Thank you for coming,' he said to Father Andrew. 'Join me while we wait – it's a cool start to the day.'

The cleric, dressed for the occasion, settled himself in the warm car. 'I thought I'd be early and have a word about the ceremony you want. Is everything ready?'

Keith nodded. 'I've been up there this morning.'

'The remains?'

'In the boot.'

'Mm. When the women come the casket should be in the car with us.'

'I agree, but travelling with it on my own I found disturbing for some reason.'

'To you it's a child,' Father Andrew said softly. He saw the grimness around Tyrell's mouth and decided a change of subject was a matter of urgency. 'You've heard the latest news, I expect? Last night's activities will have kept your people busy.'

The anger of a few protesters had seethed past control.

'You mean the shops? Yes, there'll be a lot of clearing up to be done today.'

'And many frightened souls to be comforted.'

Every one of Foster's stores had been attacked by one or two hotheads, the crowds surrounding them silent, motionless. Staff who were working late screamed as they ran from stones, flying glass, flames.

'Was anyone hurt?'

Keith shook his head. 'Not that I've heard.'

The two men watched the driver of a taxi pull into the lay-by and they prepared themselves for a very private little funeral.

In the security of his home Keith savoured whisky, sipped, and had his own private wake. Jenny was at work and the house was empty without her. He switched on one of her CDs, not caring which composer he had chosen, just grateful for the sound reminding him that her spirit was back with him.

The ringing of his new mobile phone had him frowning but he switched on and was polite.

'Tried you earlier. If you had a dog I'd have said you were taking it for a walk.'

'Brian! Good to hear you. What's up?'

'Foster's just been released – not that the crowd outside made it easy for him.'

'Why?'

'They simply blocked his way out, no matter which door we tried to get him through. There was no noise, no fuss, but he was left in no doubt where the good people of the Dean Forest want him – whatever his brief might argue and our top brass agree to.'

'Is he still there?'

'Nope. He had to be smuggled out with a couple of overnighters bound for remand in Gloucester. I suppose you could say it made sense for his only mode of transport to be a prison van.'

'What about Miles Kennedy?'

The Clarke chuckle was deep and full-throated. 'Frank Kennedy was on the move early. He'd had a tip-off Foster would be released and went rushing up to HQ to get his little lad off the hook. I was there when he arrived – some faceless wonder from the Home Office and yet more interviews about you. Kennedy Senior was doing his great "I am" bit when a couple of guys from the Serious Fraud Office just happened to turn up and arrest him!'

'Easier than lifting him in his own home. They'd have all the facilities to hand.'

'Which they used. By the way, one of them sent his regards. Terry Fleming.'

'Regards? Terry? What did he actually say?'

Again the chuckle. 'OK. He told me to get the lazy bugger off his arse and back to work.'

Keith felt laughter bubbling and was grateful. 'That

sounds more like Terry. So, the computer evidence is sound and Miles stays put?'

'He does. Because of the hacker cock-up Foster's out for the time being – but in no doubt about the strength of feeling against him in the Forest. The crowds massed round the nick melted away in no time, once it was realized he'd been sneaked out, but I've heard they've surrounded him in his own house.'

Armchair oblivion was an appealing idea and Keith kicked off his shoes, ready to sprawl in comfort. The door bell made him think again and he was in stockinged feet when he greeted Rod Copeland.

'Sir! Come in.'

It was doubtful if Copeland had slept in the last forty-eight hours. He was grey with exhaustion, moving stiffly and stretching neck muscles as he waited for Keith to shut the front door and lead the way to the sitting room.

'Something wrong, sir?'

'No. I've just come from seeing the chief constable and the ACC. Both the Home Office and the investigators from up north are satisfied you did nothing wrong and the evidence you helped gather is solid. It can't be official until all reports and conclusions are in but it was suggested your suspension is ended – as from start of shift tomorrow.'

A surge of relief almost unmanned him but with a supreme effort Keith released his thanks calmly. 'It was good of you to come in person, sir. I appreciate you taking the time when you must be so busy.'

'You've heard, then? Since you're officially still incommunicado I wonder how that happened? Still, I've more to worry about than your friends sticking by you. You've first-rate people backing you, Keith, and I'm relying on all of you to get Foster battened down as soon as it's humanly possible. Last night's shenanigans were no joke – the man's a damned pest inside a cell or out. The sooner he's tried and put away, the better we'll all sleep. Sleep! If only! Any coffee going?'

It did not take long to get Copeland refreshed, colour suffusing his pale cheeks and alertness returning. 'That's better. You'll be glad to know the hacker's been picked up. A fifteen-year-old boy in Nailsworth. Delights in listening to our radio messages as well as trying to get into our computer system. Wants to join the force, would you believe? God knows what charges'll be brought. At his age he'll probably get some community service and earn a fortune with a dot com business.'

'It's a loose end tied up.'

'That reminds me, it was the funeral today, wasn't it? Everything go well?'

Keith talked of the morning's activities, the dignity of the Avery sisters, the formalities dealt with gently, kindly, by Father Andrew.

'It was good of Sir Guy to let you bury the poor little thing on his land.'

'Yes, it was. He wanted to do all he could and picked the site himself – he even helped me dig the grave last night.'

'Damned decent of him.'

'One odd thing. As I stood and looked round this morning, I realized I could see the mudbank where Julie Parry was washed ashore.'

'Full circle? Let's hope that's an end to it.' Copeland inspected his watch, sighed and heaved himself upright. 'Time to be off. I'll see you in the morning.'

'There is one thing,' Keith began. 'DCI Whittaker?'

Copeland's face tightened. 'Safe – and so're his wife and daughter.' He hesitated, then came to a decision. 'There's a stalker out there and a damned clever one, too. Who? We don't know, nor why, but Mrs Whittaker's been threatened and so have the girls. An attempt was even made to snatch one of them. It's all hush-hush and you've heard nothing from me – understand?'

'Yes, sir.'

'I just thought you had a right to know.'

* * *

When Jenny arrived home she saw the whisky bottle and Keith's glass. 'So that's what you've been up to today?'

He told her of Copeland's visit but nothing of Whittaker.

'Is it really over?'

'The worst of it, yes. Tomorrow morning we start again, trying to give prosecuting counsel all the ammunition he needs to put Foster away for good.'

'Or her!'

'OK, I agree. I don't care who does it as long as Foster never sees the light of day again.' He pulled her to him and rested his chin on the top of her head. 'It's been a rough few weeks for both of us but we've weathered them.'

Jenny was glad she could not look at him. 'Survivors, that's what we are,' she whispered.

'Then we ought to celebrate. Let's go out for dinner.'

'Good idea.' She had heard something in his voice. 'But?'

'Can we drive past Foster's house? I want to see what the set-up is before I start work in the morning.'

The house deep in the Forest stood aloof and isolated.

'Come away from the window!'

'Belt up, Sue,' Foster snapped. 'I want to make sure none of those yobs put a foot inside the gate. If they do I'll have the law on 'em.' Mal Foster might be a free man but he was not in a good mood.

'They're just letting you know how much they disapprove of you killing their girls.'

Her husband froze, then turned his head, gazing at his wife as though he had never seen her before. It was not the pretty blonde girl he had married who faced him down, only the faded, toughened woman she had become.

Sue stared back at him, disgust in every line of her. 'Did you think I didn't twig – that I was too thick?'

'It wasn't me! I was framed! Bloody coppers've always been out to get me – you know that. Just because I live well and drive a car they'd give their eye teeth for and –'

'Not to mention all the girls you've pulled.'

'I tell you, they made up the evidence – filling bags with your bloody dog's hair.'

'You did know the one they called Shelley.'

He was uneasy, determined not to let her see she was needling him. 'Only as a barmaid, nothing more, I swear it.'

'No? She must have thought you'd been seen together enough so she could claim her baby was yours. Still, we know now it couldn't be, don't we?'

Mal refused to meet his wife's accusing eyes.

'Don't we, Mal?' she asked, almost shouting at him. 'She was an idiot, like me. Just like me she didn't know about your little operation, did she? Yet she still thought she could get her hands on our cash.'

'The bitch had no claim on me – and I'd have had the law on her if she'd tried.'

'Haven't you had a sickener of the law? I have, Ronnie Kellock here all hours with his smarmy ways and enough hands for an octopus.' Sue's disgust was apparent, even to her husband.

'Ronnie's good at his job and that's what I pay him for. He got me out, didn't he?'

'And what's to stop you being hauled back in again, whenever it suits? You'll only be off the hook when you've been tried and acquitted – or isn't Ronnie Kellock up to the impossible?'

Mal glared at his wife and was surprised again by the new hardness in her.

Sue caressed Benjy's ears. 'If there's no real evidence against you, you don't need me, do you?'

'No, I don't,' he said, not seeing her lips curl with pleasure as she heard the hesitation in his voice.

'I could be useful, then?'

'Of course. You're a witness.'

'To speak for you and say where you were when girls were going missing and dying.'

'It's only the truth.'

'Is it? I can't be made to testify against you because you're my husband, Mal, not even if I know you've cheated on me and had a secret vasectomy.'

'It was a precaution!'

'So I heard. You didn't want any odd bastard I might foist on you. Nothing about all the ones you've fathered from here to Dublin and back.' Her fury accused him. 'You knew I wanted another child.'

Mal had been staring out at the crowd, their stillness eerie. He had prowled all the windows and from every one had seen the silent watchers, three or four deep in all directions around his home.

He turned back to his wife. 'Tough!'

His coldness stung hot blood to her cheeks. 'You'd do well to remember I can't be forced to give evidence against you but what if I give it willingly? Tell the police you weren't at home the nights your car stayed in the garage? Whenever that happened you sneaked out the back to the car Joey Niblett uses to do your dirty work for you. I didn't know what you were up to then but I've got the dates in my diary in case I ever needed a divorce.'

'You bitch!'

Foster whirled, pulling Sue upright with one hand and slapping her hard with the other. She defended herself as best she could and then sank her teeth into the wrist holding her. With a scream of pain he pulled back.

'That does it!'

Sue followed her husband, running after him up the stairs to their bedroom. Her dressing table was heaved to one side and the curve of carpeting in the bay window was exposed. He reached down and threw back the carpet and its underfelt. Only then did Sue see a steel plate embedded in the floorboards. There was even time to see a keyhole as Mal fumbled in his pocket for a key. The thick slab of metal was a door opening into a cavity filled with envelopes, papers, boxes.

'That's my jewellery! You said you wanted to take it to the bank for safe storage!'

'I never mentioned any bank. Get me Kerry's rucksack – the big blue one.'

Shock had immobilized Sue. Foster was impatient and went to his daughter's room, thankful Kerry and her brother were with Sue's sister in Birmingham. Hurrying back to his cache he saw his wife on her knees beside the safe. She had lifted out a pile of envelopes held together with strong rubber.

'Bearer bonds? How much are they worth?'

'None of your business.' Foster grabbed the bundle, stowing it away in a pocket of the rucksack. Into the main section he pushed packets of notes carefully wrapped in clear plastic. Heavy tubes of Krugerrands were slid down the side. On top went Sue's jewels, emptied from their boxes.

'What are you doing?' she asked, afraid of the answer.

'Even you should have guessed by now. I'm getting out while I can.'

'But where did all this come from?' she wanted to know. 'I do all the books and there's no way –'

'You see to the books I let you handle. I've had a few deals on the side – built up an escape fund.'

'How long?'

He stopped reaching into the safe to grin at her. 'I started when you got pregnant and before we got married. Guess I knew some day all this would come in useful. If we divorced –'

'You had a fortune ready, hidden away from your family.' Sue's loathing showed. 'Everything you've had from me and you were prepared to cheat not just me but your own children.'

'I've only your word they're mine.'

Sue's fear was overridden by blind fury. 'You're impossible! Do you really think I'd have gone on living with you, slaving for you, if you weren't their father?'

'You? You stayed for the money.'

'Yes, and with you making me work all the hours God sent, then cheating us out of every penny you could. What about all the big bills I've scraped to pay when you wouldn't settle tax demands on time? And the VAT? You had the cash all along.'

'Exactly. I had the cash. The house, the businesses, I made sure they were in your name. The generous husband seeing his family had every protection,' he sneered. 'Ronnie Kellock tried to talk me out of that one but, if everything went belly-up . . .' He pointed to the rucksack stuffed with more wealth than she could imagine.

'You'd have gone – God knows where – and I'd have been declared bankrupt and unable to feed the children. Oh, you planned well, Mal Foster, but you didn't think, did you? All I've got to do is call the police, change my statement and they'll have you back in seconds.'

Sue was too wrapped up in her own misery to see the punch coming. By the time she regained consciousness Mal Foster was dressed as a hiker, rucksack hanging from one shoulder.

'I've one more job for you,' he said. 'Get your coat. You're going for a drive. That scum out there won't let me out if they see me but you can get through.'

'What's to stop me taking you straight to the police?'

'Simple. I'll tell them you knew when I'd killed the girls and it was you helped me get rid of the bodies. I could say the last one was your idea. Aiding and abetting before and after the fact. Murder? Think about it. You'll be inside for years and then who'll look after Kerry and Jason? No, lady, you'll help me get clear and you'll keep your mouth shut. Understand? It's your choice. Get me away from here or lose your children.'

Sue held despair in check as she tried to think but she knew what was important. It did not take her long to decide.

'Where're you going?'

'D'you think I'd tell you? No chance! Head towards Coleford. Take side roads to get there and make sure we're not followed. Then pull off the road somewhere quiet.'

*   *   *

In the clearing, Foster's house was the most opulent in a cul-de-sac of impressive homes. It stood apart from its neighbours and in front of the gates was a solid mass of people. At the edge of the crowd Keith saw a familiar face.

'What on earth's going on here?'

Tomorrow Keith would be officially Detective Inspector Tyrell and PC Reed raised a hand in salute.

'It's as you see, sir. They arrived in ones and twos and took up position. No one's talking – not to anybody. They only stand there, shoulder to shoulder so no one can get past. Reporters've had a rough time. Each one got surrounded and just – well – stared at. It's real creepy, I can tell you!'

'Are there enough of you to cope?'

'I'd think so, sir. There's never been any sign of trouble here and DS Copeland's promised reinforcements in the next half-hour.'

They were standing in the open and Jenny lifted her face. 'Rain's on the way,' she said and pulled up the collar of her jacket.

Keith saw she was pale and there was agony in her eyes. 'What is it?'

She held the cloth tightly around her chin. 'I don't know. It's the feeling – as though it's one person standing there. How many are there?' she asked PC Reed.

'Coupla hundred so far, Mrs Tyrell, and we've heard there're more on the move – this sort – not the mindless idiots who smashed up the shops.'

'It's as Mickey said when he saw them surrounding the station,' Keith said slowly.

'Every man, woman and child here is praying?' Jenny shuddered. 'It is. It's one mind.'

'What is it you sense? Hatred?'

She shook her head. 'No. It's colder than that. Implacable. Like the thickest of walls. Keith, I'm scared. They've no intention of letting him go.'

He put an arm around her shoulders and felt her shivering. 'Come on, dinner.'

'Please, Keith. Can we just go home?'

Rain intensified as they hurried to the car, grateful for its sanctuary. As Jenny turned to fasten her seat belt Keith was shocked at the purple smudges under her eyes.

'The sooner I get you home, the better.'

Jenny knew him too well. 'You want to be back there.'

She was right but he saw her need of him. 'Not me! Tomorrow morning? Now that's another matter. Tonight, I'm all yours.'

'No, you won't be. You'll have this on your mind. Lawrie Grundy knew it when he warned you.'

'Leave well alone?'

'That – and what he said about evil.'

'Let the evil one earn his own reward? If he does, my darling, he'll have to do it soaking wet,' Keith said with a laugh as he switched windscreen wipers to full power to deal with a rush of rain. Even then they were no match for a sudden deluge of water.

Rain ceased and all that could be heard was water dripping from branches. Mist hung in swirls and any wind was high above the treetops, a keening in the cold, damp air. The horde of humanity around Foster's home had not moved. Each person, old or young, stood soaked and silent. They had endured a torrent from above, water melding them into a shining black unity, the cold fire at its core undiminished.

A creak, the hum of machinery, had watchers stiffening. All eyes turned to the doors of the double garage at the side of the house. The nearest door rolled upwards revealing the bonnet of a light-coloured Mercedes, its driver already seated. The figure bent forward. There was a flick of ignition and the car's engine became a purr in counterpoint to the whirring of the garage door's mechanism. Slowly, the Mercedes moved forward until the exterior house lights allowed Sue Foster to be seen. Most of her face was obscured by a headscarf and huge dark glasses.

No one in the crowd spoke. There were no orders,

instruction, advice even, yet small movements had every policeman and woman surrounded so closely they could not walk, nor lift their arms. One tried to reach for her baton but the crush of bodies around her was too great.

Mrs Foster drove slowly and the crowd parted a little, allowing her through the gateposts but no further. A murmur, not of words, grew when Malcolm Foster could not be seen. One person pounded on the car's wide boot, then another, and another. At first it was the sound of bare hands, gloved hands, striking metal. Quite when it became rock striking metal not one of the police protectors could say. In the house a dog barked, the noise muffled and ignored as the beating of fists and stones maintained an unholy racket which deafened interminably.

It stopped as suddenly as it had begun. Men and women standing in front of the car to block its way moved aside and Mrs Foster inched through the gap. Slowly, she accelerated until she was free of the crowd, then sped away as if her life depended on it. Behind her, police cars were impeded by sections of the crowd walking in front or behind them, the movements purposeful, almost orchestrated. Minutes passed, then men and women in uniform found themselves able to lift arms, use radios, call for help in an arena that was eerily quiet.

With the car parked in a deserted lane, Sue Foster's fingers shook so much she could barely get the key into the lock. When she did at last turn it, the lid of the dented boot did not rise. She tried pushing it open but her hands slid on wetness until booted feet thumped from inside the cover and she managed to get it open.

Mal Foster was dazed, shaking his head repeatedly as he tried to clear it of noise that echoed and re-echoed around his skull without ceasing. He pushed aside his wife's hands, ignoring what he decided must be a begging whine. He had no time or patience for her and was glad he could hear nothing of the words she screamed at him.

The rucksack was what mattered. He heaved it from the

boot of the car, and threw it on the back seat. Thrusting his wife away from him with relieving violence he drove away.

Behind him Sue Foster was an immobile heap. How long she stayed there she could not imagine but eventually she sat up, then kneeled. From somewhere deep inside herself she gathered energy and stood, leaning against the nearest tree for support.

A long while she rested, until her blood slowed and her breathing steadied. Laying her bruised face against the trunk of the oak she let tears flow, too tired to sob. When it was over she stayed longer, relying on the tree's strength and shelter. Calm once more, Sue realized the rain had stopped and she knew what she must do.

Epilogue

Foster's driving was erratic. His hearing was still a mass of white sound blocking out reason and he suffered dizzy spells which threatened his control of the car. Repeatedly, he shook his head or banged it with a hand, desperate to clear the cacophony ricocheting around inside his skull. The car was warm, the leather upholstery comfortable, and Foster began to relax. He took one road, then another, driving to throw off any pursuers. Always, he headed north.

Foster smiled at the bobble-hatted dare-devil he saw in the mirror. His hearing might have gone but one thing no one could take from him was his sense of direction and he knew this damned Forest better than anyone. If he stuck to the side roads he could evade pursuit and once on the road leading west to Wales and an Irish ferry, he was safe. Foster prided himself on his forethought. He had planned long and he had planned well, buying from a contact a well-used passport. It held his photo and details of a new identity but it had earned its wear in the pocket of an unlucky tourist.

It was some time before he realized he was lost. Cursing, he tried one road, then another, the signposts no help. He was constantly running south, convinced he had been heading in the other direction.

On a narrow lane between close-packed trees he began to be afraid. The roadway dipped suddenly, rising sharply beyond a stone bridge across a stream. There was mud on the road. The car skidded and smacked into solid native stone.

Shouting obscenities, Foster was not able to hear his own curses as he attempted to start the engine and reverse out of trouble. Again and again he turned the key in the ignition, each time feeling vibration but not the gentle rhythm of a running engine. He rested, opening his window to let in cooling air. Lying back in his seat with his eyes closed, Foster breathed deeply, struggling for control.

He thought he heard a sound outside the car and almost cried. Normal hearing was on its way back after all the rabble of bastards had done to deafen him. For a moment he knew relief then an instinct alerted him. Was he hearing sounds made by pursuers?

Getting out of the car he stood in the quiet lane and tried to listen. Nothing. A finger of wind whipped at him and he thought it carried voices, the throb of cars. Frantically, he tried to start his own engine once more but it had died on him.

'I'm not finished!' he screamed at the trees around him.

Doors opened smoothly as he got out of the car and hefted the rucksack on to his back. He slid his arms through the straps, reassured by the heavy weight he carried. Once he was on his way and free he had enough with him to live in luxury wherever he chose to settle. His future was secure and there was only one problem. Which way should he go?

Mist was hanging under the trees. Foster looked up the hill down which he had sped, seeing whiteness whirl slowly, take shape. He blinked, bemused. The mist thickened, bellied close to him and strange, milky faces and bodies silently approached, then faded to be replaced by more.

'Don't be such a bloody fool!' he shouted, unable to hear his own words yet mocked by their echoes.

The other direction was no better. A white haze rolled down the hill, swirling as it came towards him. It reminded him of the body of the last girl as she slid under the water. She would have been fun to know, to seduce, but it had been imperative for his safety she was a stranger to him and he to her.

The stream glistened and beckoned in fitful moonlight, a pathway between trees which surrounded and menaced. Settling his rucksack more comfortably, Foster stepped on to the bank and began to walk upwards, alongside the stream. Above him the wind soughed in branches, high-pitched enough for him to hear it wail. It made him think of a desolate baby and he pulled down the wool of his cap to hide his ears. Weakness was pushed away and he thought only of the freedom ahead, lengthening his stride in a haste to reach safety quickly.

That was his mistake. In recent weeks the stream had flooded so often its edges were slippery. Foster lost his balance and slid into the fast-flowing water, struggling not to become submerged. Kneeling there he berated himself for being an idiot, lifting a hand to grasp a tussock and pull himself upright.

The hand would not move.

Weeds at the edge of the stream had been growing through the winter in deeper water than usual. Stems had become long, toughened, Foster's fall and struggles twisting them into a mesh.

'This is stupid!' he shouted but there was no one to hear.

Trying to stand upright, Foster rocked awkwardly, almost falling again as the weight he carried unbalanced him. He steadied and began to lift a foot clear but it was embedded in mud which sucked at his ankles. Water seeped into his rucksack, adding to its bulk, and he was thrust down by the ungainly mass, into the stream.

Curses scattered in the cold, dank air and Foster battled with fear. He reasoned that with one hand free he could loosen the weeds around the other. Patiently, he twisted a wrist this way and that, realizing too late why the stems were slackening their hold. The water was rising.

Panic soared. He writhed, trying to stand upright, but only succeeded in pulling at the weeds and tightening their grip. Foster grunted like an animal as he shoved hard against the mud with his feet. One foot suddenly came loose and he toppled in an ungainly heap. Opening his mouth to scream he dragged in a huge breath. Miraculously, his hearing became clear, enough that he heard a rushing sound.

The evening's cloudburst had drained from fields on to roads and into waterways. One of these was down a hill between trees and in it lay a man, his hands and feet tangled in the weeds and mud at the edge of the stream.

Foster bellowed for help, the sound of his voice lost in a wind which made the trees dance and mock him. He railed at the green monsters as he screamed his fury and his fear but there was no one to hear him. In the end there was only fear, exploding in pleading, sobbing, bubbling.

Until there was silence.